Flight Behaviour

'There are some beautifully written set pieces . . . The last section has an almost epic quality as Dellarobia, alone on the mountain, moves outside herself and watches in a state of mind akin to ecstasy the apocalyptic fate of the family farm below. It reminds us that humanity seeks destruction as much as we seek stability and happiness.' *Irish Times*

'Enthralling . . . Dellarobia is appealingly complex as a smart, curious, warm-hearted woman desperate to trade her cocoon for wings.' Oprah.com

'Kingsolver has written one of the more thoughtful novels about the scientific, financial and psychological intricacies of climate change. And her ability to put these silent, breathtakingly beautiful butterflies at the center of this calamitous and noisy debate is nothing short of brilliant.' *Washington Post*

'Kingsolver's keen grasp of delicate ecosystems – both social and natural – keeps the story convincing and compelling.' *The New Yorker*

'Dellarobia is a smart, fierce, messy woman, and one can't help rooting for her to find her wings.' *Entertainment Weekly*

'By the end of *Flight Behaviour*, it's clear that Kingsolver's passionate voice and her ability to portray the fragility of the natural world, and why we should care about it, are as strong as ever.' *San Francisco Chronicle*

BARBARA KINGSOLVER

Flight Behaviour

A NOVEL

faber and faber

First published in the US in 2012 by HarperCollins Inc.
First published in the UK in 2012
by Faber and Faber Limited
Bloomsbury House
74–77 Great Russell Street
London WC1B 3DA
This paperback edition first published in 2013

Printed and bound by CPI Group (UK) Ltd, Croydon, CR0 4YY

A CIP record for this book
is available from the British Library

ISBN 978–0–571–29080–2

FSC
www.fsc.org
MIX
Paper from
responsible sources
FSC® C101712

6 8 10 9 7 5

for Virginia Henry Kingsolver
and Wendell Roy Kingsolver

The Measure of a Man

A certain feeling comes from throwing your good life away, and it is one part rapture. Or so it seemed for now, to a woman with flame-colored hair who marched uphill to meet her demise. Innocence was no part of this. She knew her own recklessness and marveled, really, at how one hard little flint of thrill could out-weigh the pillowy, suffocating aftermath of a long disgrace. The shame and loss would infect her children too, that was the worst of it, in a town where everyone knew them. Even the teenage cashiers at the grocery would take an edge with her after this, clicking painted fingernails on the counter while she wrote her check, eyeing the oatmeal and frozen peas of an unhinged family and exchanging looks with the bag boy: *She's that one.* How they admired their own steadfast lives. Right up to the day when hope in all its versions went out of stock, including the crummy discount brands, and the heart had just one instruction left: run. Like a hunted animal, or a racehorse, winning or losing felt exactly alike at this stage, with the same coursing of blood and shortness of breath. She smoked too much, that was another mortification to throw in with the others. But she had cast her lot. Plenty of people took this way out, looking future damage in the eye and naming it something else. Now it was her turn. She could claim the tightness in her chest and call it bliss, rather than the same breathlessness she could be feeling at home right now while toting a heavy laundry basket, behaving like a sensible mother of two.

The children were with her mother-in-law. She'd dropped off those babies this morning on barely sufficient grounds, and it might just kill her to dwell on that now. Their little faces turned up to her like the round hearts of two daisies: *She loves me, loves me not.* All those hopes placed in such a precarious vessel. Realistically, the family could be totaled. That was the word, like a wrecked car wrapped around a telephone pole, no salvageable parts. No husband worth having is going to forgive adultery if it comes to that. And still she felt pulled up this incline by the hand whose touch might bring down all she knew. Maybe she even craved the collapse, with an appetite larger than sense.

At the top of the pasture she leaned against the fence to catch up on oxygen, feeling the slight give of the netted woven wire against her back. No safety net. Unsnapped her purse, counted her cigarettes, discovered she'd have to ration them. This had not been a thinking-ahead kind of day. The suede jacket was wrong, too warm, and what if it rained? She frowned at the November sky. It was the same dull, stippled ceiling that had been up there last week, last month, forever. All summer. Whoever was in charge of weather had put a recall on blue and nailed up this mess of dirty white sky like a lousy drywall job. The pasture pond seemed to reflect more light off its surface than the sky itself had to offer. The sheep huddled close around its shine as if they too had given up on the sun and settled for second best. Little puddles winked all the way down Highway 7 toward Feathertown and out the other side of it, toward Cleary, a long trail of potholes glinting with watery light.

The sheep in the field below, the Turnbow family land, the white frame house she had not slept outside for a single night in ten-plus years of marriage: that was pretty much it. The widescreen version of her life since age seventeen. Not including the brief hospital excursions, childbirth-related. Apparently, today was the day she walked out of the picture. Distinguishing herself from the luckless sheep that stood down there in the mud surrounded by the deep stiletto holes of their footprints, enduring life's bad deals. They'd worn their heavy wool through the muggy summer, and now that winter was almost here, they would be shorn. Life was just one long proposition they never saw coming. Their pasture looked drowned. In the next field over, the orchard painstakingly planted by the neighbors last year was now dying under the rain. From here it all looked fixed and strange, even her house, probably due to the angle. She only looked out those windows, never into them, given the company she kept with people who rolled plastic trucks on the floor. Certainly she never climbed up here to check out the domestic arrangement. The condition of the roof was not encouraging.

Her car was parked in the only spot in the county that wouldn't incite gossip, her own driveway. People knew that station wagon and still tended to think of it as belonging to her mother. She'd rescued this one thing from her mother's death, an unreliable set of wheels adequate for short errands with kids in tow. The price of that was a disquieting sense of Mama still coming along for the ride, her tiny frame wedged between the kids' car seats, reaching across them to ash her cigarette out the open window. But no such thoughts today. This morning after leaving the kids at Hester's she had floored it for the half-mile back home, feeling high and wobbly as a kite. Went back into the house only to brush her teeth, shed her glasses, and put on eyeliner, no other preparations necessary prior to lighting out her own back door to wreck her reputation. The electric pulse of desire buzzed through her body like an alarm clock gone off in the early light, setting in motion all the things in a day that can't be stopped.

She picked her way now through churned-up mud along the fence, lifted the chain fastener on the steel gate, and slipped through. Beyond the fence an ordinary wildness of ironweed and briar thickets began. An old road cut through it, long unused, crisscrossed by wild raspberries bending across in tall arcs. In recent times she'd come up here only once, berry picking with her husband Cub and some of his buddies two summers

4

ago, and it definitely wasn't her idea. She'd been barrel-round pregnant with Cordelia and thinking she might be called on to deliver the child right there in the brambles, that's how she knew which June that was. So Preston would have been four. She remembered him holding her hand for dear life while Cub's hotdog friends scared them half to death about snakes. These raspberry canes were a weird color for a plant, she noticed now, not that she would know nature if it bit her. But bright pink? The color of a frosted lipstick some thirteen-year-old might want to wear. She had probably skipped that phase, heading straight for Immoral Coral and Come-to-Bed Red.

The saplings gave way to a forest. The trees clenched the last of summer's leaves in their fists, and something made her think of Lot's wife in the Bible, who turned back for one last look at home. Poor woman, struck into a pile of salt for such a small disobedience. She did not look back, but headed into the woods on the rutted track her husband's family had always called the High Road. *As if*, she thought. Taking the High Road to damnation; the irony had failed to cross her mind when she devised this plan. The road up the mountain must have been cut for logging, in the old days. The woods had grown back. Cub and his dad drove the all-terrain up this way sometimes to get to the little shack on the ridge they used for turkey hunting. Or they used to do that, once upon a time, when the combined weight of the Turnbow men senior and junior was about sixty pounds less than the present day. Back when they used their feet for something other than framing the view of the television set. The road must have been poorly maintained even then. She recalled their taking the chain saw for clearing windfall.

She and Cub used to come up here by themselves in those days, too, for so-called picnics. But not once since Cordie and Preston were born. It was crazy to suggest the turkey blind on the family property as a place to hook up. *Trysting place*, she thought, words from a storybook. And: *No sense prettying up dirt*, words from a mother-in-law. So where else were they supposed to go? Her own bedroom, strewn with inside-out work shirts and a one-legged Barbie lying there staring while a person tried to get in the mood? Good night. The Wayside Inn out on the highway was a pitiful place to begin with, before you even started deducting the wages of sin. Mike Bush at the counter would greet her by name: *How do, Mrs. Turnbow, now how's them kids?*

The path became confusing suddenly, blocked with branches. The upper part of a fallen tree lay across it, so immense she had to climb through, stepping between sideways limbs with clammy leaves still attached. Would he find his way through this, or would the wall of branches turn him back? Her heart bumped around at the thought of losing this one sweet chance. Once she'd passed through, she considered waiting. But he knew the way. He said he'd hunted from that turkey blind some seasons ago. With his

6

own friends, no one she or Cub knew. Younger, his friends would be.

She smacked her palms together to shuck off the damp grit and viewed the corpse of the fallen monster. The tree was intact, not cut or broken by wind. What a waste. After maybe centuries of survival it had simply let go of the ground, the wide fist of its root mass ripped up and resting naked above a clay gash in the wooded mountainside. Like herself, it just seemed to have come loose from its station in life. After so much rain upon rain this was happening all over the county, she'd seen it in the paper, massive trees keeling over in the night to ravage a family's roofline or flatten the car in the drive. The ground took water until it was nothing but soft sponge, and the trees fell out of it. Near Great Lick a whole hillside of mature timber had plummeted together, making a landslide of splintered trunks, rock and rill. People were shocked, even men like her father-in-law who tended to meet any terrible news with "That's nothing," claiming already to have seen everything in creation. But they'd never seen this, and had come to confessing it. In such strange times, they may have thought God was taking a hand in things and would thus take note of a lie.

The road turned up steeply toward the ridge and petered out to a single track. A mile yet to go, maybe, she was just guessing. She tried to get a move on, imagining that her long, straight red hair swinging behind her might look athletic, but in truth her feet smarted

7

badly and so did her lungs. New boots. There was one more ruin to add to the pile. The boots were genuine calfskin, dark maroon, hand-tooled uppers and glossy pointed toes, so beautiful she'd nearly cried when she found them at Second Time Around while looking for something decent for Preston to wear to kindergarten. The boots were six dollars, in like-new condition, the soles barely scuffed. Someone in the world had such a life, they could take one little walk in expensive new boots and then pitch them out, just because. The boots weren't a perfect fit but they looked good on, so she bought them, her first purchase for herself in over a year, not counting hygiene products. Or cigarettes, which she surely did not count. She'd kept the boots hidden from Cub for no good reason but to keep them precious. Something of her own. In the normal course of family events, every other thing got snatched from her hands: her hairbrush, the TV clicker, the soft middle part of her sandwich, the last Coke she'd waited all afternoon to open. She'd once had a dream of birds pulling the hair from her head in sheaves to make their red nests.

Not that Cub would notice if she wore these boots, and not that she'd had occasion. So why put them on this morning to walk up a muddy hollow in the wettest fall on record? Black leaves clung like dark fish scales to the tooled leather halfway up her calves. This day had played in her head like a movie on round-the-clock reruns, that's why. With an underemployed mind clocking in and out of a scene that smelled of urine and mashed bananas, daydreaming was one thing she had in abundance. The price was right. She thought about the kissing mostly, when she sat down to manufacture a fantasy in earnest, but other details came along, setting and wardrobe. This might be a difference in how men and women devised their fantasies, she thought. Clothes: present or absent. The calfskin boots were a part of it, as were the suede jacket borrowed from her best friend Dovey and the red chenille scarf around her neck, things he would slowly take off of her. She'd pictured it being cold like this, too. Her flyaway thoughts had not blurred out the inconveniences altogether. Her flushed cheeks, his warm hands smoothing the orange hair at her temples, all these were part and parcel. She'd pulled on the boots this morning as if she'd received written instructions.

And now she was in deep, though there had been no hanging offenses as yet. They'd managed to be alone together for about ten seconds at a time behind some barn or metal shed, hiding around the corner from where her car was parked with the kids buckled up inside, arguing at full volume. *If I can still hear them, they're still alive* is not a thought conducive to romance. Yet the anticipation of him prickled her skin. His eyes, like the amber glass of a beer bottle, and his face full of dimpled muscles, the kind of grin that seems to rhyme with *chin*. His way of taking her face in both his hands, dear God. Looking her in the eyes, rubbing the ends of her hair between his thumbs and fingers like he was counting money. These ecstasies brought her to sit on the closet floor and talk stupid with him on the phone, night after night, while her family slept under sweet closed eyelids. As she whispered in the dark, her husband's work shirts on their hangers idly stroked the top of her head, almost the same way Cub himself did when she sat on the floor with the baby while he occupied the whole couch, watching TV. Oblivious to the storms inside her. Cub moved in slow motion. His gentleness was merely the stuff he was made of, like the fiber content of a garment, she knew this. Something a wife should bear without complaint. But it made him seem dumb as a cow and it made her mad. All of it. The way he let his mother boss him around, making him clean his plate and tuck in his shirttails like a two-hundred-pound child. The embarrassment of his name. He could be Burley Junior if he'd claim it, but instead let his parents and the populace of a county call him Cubby as if he were still a boy, while they hailed his father, the elder Burley Turnbow, as "Bear." A cub should grow up, but at twenty-eight years of age, this one stood long-faced and slump-shouldered at the door of the family den, flipping a sheaf of blond bangs out of his eyes. Now he would let himself be shamed by his wife's hardheartedness too, or fail to notice it. Why should he keep on loving her so much?

Her betrayals shocked her. It was like watching some maddened, unstoppable, and slightly cuter version of herself on television, doing things a person could never do with just normal life instead of a script. Putting Cordelia down for early naps while Preston was at kindergarten so she could steal a minute for making intimate bargains with a man who wasn't her husband. The urge to call him was worse than wanting a cigarette, like something screaming in both her ears. More than once she'd driven past where he lived, telling the kids in the back seat that she'd forgotten something and had to go back to the store. She would say it was for ice cream or bullet pops, to shush them, but even a five-year-old could tell it was not the road to the store. Preston had voiced his suspicions from his booster seat, which allowed him a view of little more than the passing trees and telephone lines.

The telephone man, as she called this obsession—his name was too ordinary, you wouldn't wreck your life for a Jimmy—"the telephone man" was barely a man. Twenty-two, he'd said, and that was a stretch. He lived in a mobile home with his mother and spent weekends doing the things that interested males of that age, mixing beer and chain saws, beer and target shooting. There was no excuse for going off the deep end over someone who might or might not legally be buying his own six-packs. She longed for relief from her crazy wanting. She'd had crushes before, but this one felt life-threatening, especially while she was lying in bed next to Cub. She'd tried taking a Valium, one of three or four still rattling in the decade-old prescription bottle they'd given her back when she lost the first baby. But the pill did nothing, probably expired, like everything on the premises. A week ago she'd stabbed a needle into her finger on purpose while mending a hole in Cordie's pajamas, and watched the blood jump out of her skin like a dark red eye staring back. The wound still throbbed. Mortification of the flesh. And none of it stopped her from thinking of him, speed-dialing him, making plans, driving by where he'd told her he would be working, just for the sight of him up the pole in his leather harness. A strange turn of fortune had sent him her way in the first place: a tree that fell on a windless day, bringing down the phone line directly in front of her house. She and Cub didn't have a landline, it wasn't even her problem, but a downed line had to be reconnected. "For the folks that are still hanging on by wires," Jimmy had told her with a wicked grin, and everything that came next was nonsensical, like a torrential downpour in a week of predicted sunshine that floods out the crops and the well-made plans. There is no use blaming the rain and mud, these are only elements. The disaster is the failed expectation.

And now here she went risking everything, pointing her little chin up that hill and walking unarmed into the shoot-out of whatever was to be. Heartbreak, broken family. Broke, period. What she might do for money if Cub left her was anyone's guess. She hadn't been employed or even exactly a regular to human conversation since the Feathertown Diner closed, back when she was pregnant with Preston. Nobody would hire her again as a waitress. They'd side with Cub, and half the town would claim they'd seen it coming, just because they thrived on downfalls of any sort. *Wild in high school, that's how it goes with the pretty ones, early to ripe, early to rot.* They would say the same thing she'd heard her mother-in-law tell Cub: that Dellarobia was a piece of work. As if she were lying in pieces on a table, pins stuck here and there, half assembled from a Simplicity pattern that was flawed at the manufacturer's. Which piece had been left out?

People would likely line up to give opinions about that. The part that thinks ahead, for one. A stay-at-home wife with no skills, throwing sense to the four winds to run after a handsome boy who could not look after her children. Acting like there was no tomorrow. And yet. The way he looked at her suggested he'd be willing to bring her golden apples, or the Mississippi River. The way he closed his fingers in a bracelet around her ankles and wrists, marveling at her smallness, gave her the dimensions of an expensive jewel rather than an inconsequential adult. No one had ever listened to her the way he did. Or looked, touching her hair reverently, trying to name its color: somewhere between a stop sign and sunset, he said. Something between tomatoes and a ladybug. And her skin. He called her "Peach."

No one else had ever called her anything. Only the given name her mother first sounded out for the birth certificate in a doped anesthetic haze, thinking it came from the Bible. Later her mother remembered that was wrong; it wasn't the Bible, she'd heard it at a craft demonstration at the Women's Club. She found a picture in a ladies' magazine and yelled for her daughter to come look. Dellarobia was maybe six at the time and still remembered the picture of the dellarobia wreath, an amalgam of pine cones and acorns glued on a Styrofoam core. "Something pretty, even still," her mother insisted, but the fall from grace seemed to presage coming events. Her performance to date was not what the Savior prescribed. Except marrying young, of course. That was the Lord's way for a girl with big dreams but no concrete plans, especially if a baby should be on the way. The baby that never quite was, that she never got to see, a monster. The preemie nurse said it had strange fine hair all over its body that was red like hers. Preston and Cordelia when they later arrived were both blonds, cut from the Turnbow cloth, but that first one that came in its red pelt of fur was a mean wild thing like her. Roping a pair of dumbstruck teenagers into a shotgun wedding and then taking off with a laugh, leaving them stranded. Leaving them trying five years for another baby, just to fill a hole nobody meant to dig in the first place.

Something in motion caught her eye and yanked her glance upward. How did it happen, that attention could be wrenched like that by some small movement? It was practically nothing, a fleck of orange wobbling above

14

the trees. It crossed overhead and drifted to the left, where the hill dropped steeply from the trail. She made a face, thinking of redheaded ghosts. Making things up was beneath her. She set her eyes on the trail, purposefully not looking up. She was losing the fight against this hill, panting like a sheep. A poplar beside the trail invited her to stop there a minute. She fit its smooth bulk between her shoulder blades and cupped her hands to light the cigarette she'd been craving for half an hour. Inhaled through her nose, counted to ten, then gave in and looked up again. Without her glasses it took some doing to get a bead on the thing, but there it still was, drifting in blank air above the folded terrain: an orange butterfly on a rainy day. Its out-of-place brashness made her think of the wacked-out sequences in children's books: Which of these does not belong? An apple, a banana, a taxicab. A nice farmer, a married mother of two, a sexy telephone man. She watched the flake of bright color waver up the hollow while she finished her cigarette and carefully ground out the butt with her boot. When she walked on, pulling her scarf around her throat, she kept her eyes glued to the ground. This boy had better be worth it: there was a thought. Not the sexiest one in the world, either. Possibly a sign of sense returning.

The last part of the trail was the steepest, as far as she could recall from her high-school frolics up here. Who could forget that ankle-bending climb? Rocky and steep and *dark*. She had entered the section of woods

15

people called the Christmas Tree Farm, fir trees planted long ago in some scheme that never panned out. The air suddenly felt colder. The fir forest had its own spooky weather, as if these looming conifers held an old grudge, peeved at being passed over. What had she been thinking, to name that hunting shack for a meeting place? Romance felt as unreachable now as it did on any average day of toting kids and dredging the floor of doll babies. She could have made things easy on herself and wrecked her life in a motel room like a sensible person, but no. Her legs were tired and her butt ached. She could feel blisters welling on both feet. The boots she'd adored this morning now seemed idiotic, their slick little heels designed for parading your hindquarters in jeans, not real walking. She watched her step, considering what a broken ankle would add to her day. The trail was a cobbled mess of loose rocks, and it ran straight uphill in spots, so badly rutted she had to grab saplings to steady herself.

With relief she arrived on a level stretch of ground carpeted with brown fir needles. But something dark loomed from a branch over the trail. A hornet's nest was her first thought, or a swarm of bees looking for a new home. She'd seen that happen. But the thing was not humming. She approached slowly, hoping to scoot under it, with or without a positive ID. It bristled like a cluster of dead leaves or a down-turned pine cone, but was much bigger than that. Like an armadillo in a tree, she thought, with no notion of how large that would be.

Scaly all over and pointed at the lower end, as if it had gone oozy and might drip. She didn't much care to walk under it. For the second time she wished for the glasses she'd left behind. Vanity was one thing, but out here in the damn wilderness a person needed to see. She squinted up into dark branches backlit by pale sky. The angle made her a little dizzy.

Her heart thumped. These things were all over, dangling like giant bunches of grapes from every tree she could see. *Fungus* was the word that came to mind, and it turned down the corners of her mouth. Trees were getting new diseases now. Cub had mentioned that. The wetter summers and mild winters of recent years were bringing in new pests that apparently ate the forest out of house and home. She pulled her jacket close and hurried underneath the bristly thing, ducking, even though it hung a good ten feet above the trail. She cleared it by five. And even so, shivered and ran her fingers through her hair afterward and felt childish for fearing a tree fungus. The day couldn't decide whether to warm up or not. In the deep evergreen shade it was cold. Fungus brought to mind scrubbing the mildewed shower curtain with Mr. Clean, one of her life's main events. She tried to push that out of her thoughts, concentrating instead on her reward at the end of the climb. She imagined surprising him as he stood by the shack waiting for her, coming up on him from behind, the sight of his backside in jeans. He'd promised to come early if he could, hinting he might even be naked when she arrived. With a big soft quilt and a bottle of Cold Duck. Lord love a duck, she thought. After subsisting for years on the remains of toddler lunches and juice boxes, she'd be drunk in ten minutes. She shivered again and hoped that was a pang of desire, not the chill of a wet day and a dread of tree fungus. Should it be so hard to tell the difference?

The path steered out of the shadow into a bright overlook on the open side of the slope, and here she slammed on her brakes; here something was wrong. Or just strange. The trees above her were draped with more of the brownish clumps, and that was the least of it. The view out across the valley was puzzling and unreal, like a sci-fi movie. From this overlook she could see the whole mountainside that lay opposite, from top to bottom, and the full stand of that forest was thickly loaded with these bristly things. The fir trees in the hazy distance were like nothing she'd ever seen, their branches droopy and bulbous. The trunks and boughs were speckled and scaly like trees covered with corn flakes. She had small children, she'd seen things covered with corn flakes. Nearly all the forest she could see from here, from valley to ridge, looked altered and pale, the beige of dead leaves. These were evergreen trees, they should be dark, and that wasn't foliage. There was movement in it. The branches seemed to writhe. She took a small automatic step backward from the overlook and the worrisome trees, although they stood far away across the thin air of the hollow. She reached into her purse for a cigarette, then stopped.

A small shift between cloud and sun altered the daylight, and the whole landscape intensified, brightening before her eyes. The forest blazed with its own internal flame. "Jesus," she said, not calling for help, she and Jesus weren't that close, but putting her voice in the world because nothing else present made sense. The sun slipped out by another degree, passing its warmth across the land, and the mountain seemed to explode with light. Brightness of a new intensity moved up the valley in a rippling wave, like the disturbed surface of a lake. Every bough glowed with an orange blaze. "Jesus God," she said again. No words came to her that seemed sane. Trees turned to fire, a burning bush. Moses came to mind, and Ezekiel, words from Scripture that occupied a certain space in her brain but no longer carried honest weight, if they ever had. *Burning coals of fire went up and down among the living creatures.*

The flame now appeared to lift from individual treetops in showers of orange sparks, exploding the way a pine log does in a campfire when it's poked. The sparks spiraled upward in swirls like funnel clouds. Twisters of brightness against gray sky. In broad daylight with no comprehension, she watched. From the tops of the funnels the sparks lifted high and sailed out undirected above the dark forest.

A forest fire, if that's what it was, would roar. This consternation swept the mountain in perfect silence. The air above remained cold and clear. No smoke, no crackling howl. She stopped breathing for a second and closed her eyes to listen, but heard nothing. Only a faint patter like rain on leaves. Not fire, she thought, but her eyes when opened could only tell her, *Fire*, *this place is burning*. They said, *Get out of here*. Up or down, she was unsure. She eyed the dark uncertainty of the trail and the uncrossable breach of the valley. It was all the same everywhere, every tree aglow.

She cupped her hands over her face and tried to think. She was miles from her kids. Cordie with her thumb in her mouth, Preston with his long-lashed eyes cast down, soaking up guilt like a sponge even when he'd done no wrong. She knew what their lives would become if something happened to her here. On a mission of sin. Hester would rain shame on them for all time. Or worse, what if they thought their mother had just run away and left them? Nobody knew to look for her here. Her thoughts clotted with the vocabulary of news reports: dental records, next of kin, sifting through the ash.

And Jimmy. She made herself think his name: a person, not just a destination. Jimmy, who might be up there already. And in a single second that worry lifted from her like a flake of ash as she saw for the first time the truth of this day. For her, the end of all previous comfort and safety. And for him, something else entirely, a kind of game. Nothing to change his life. *We'll strike out together*, she'd told herself, and into what, his mother's mobile home? Somehow it had come to pass that this man was her whole world, and she had failed to take his measure. Neither child nor father, he knew how to climb telephone poles, and he knew how to disappear. The minute he breathed trouble, he would slip down the back side of the mountain and go on home. Nothing could be more certain. He had the instincts of the young. He would be back at work before anyone knew he'd called in sick. If she turned up in the news as charred remains, he would keep their story quiet, to protect her family. Or so he'd tell himself. Look what she'd nearly done. She paled at the size her foolishness had attained, how large and crowded and devoid of any structural beams. It could be flattened like a circus tent.

She was on her own here, staring at glowing trees. Fascination curled itself around her fright. This was no forest fire. She was pressed by the quiet elation of escape and knowing better and seeing straight through to the back of herself, in solitude. She couldn't remember when she'd had such room for being. This was not just another fake thing in her life's cheap chain of events, leading up to this day of sneaking around in someone's thrown-away boots. Here that ended. Unearthly beauty had appeared to her, a vision of glory to stop her in the road. For her alone these orange boughs lifted, these long shadows became a brightness rising. It looked like the inside of joy, if a person could see that. A valley of lights, an ethereal wind. It had to mean something.

She could save herself. Herself and her children with their soft cheeks and milky breath who believed in

21

what they had, even if their whole goodness and mercy was a mother distracted out of her mind. It was not too late to undo this mess. Walk down the mountain, pick up those kids. The burning trees were put here to save her. It was the strangest conviction she'd ever known, and still she felt sure of it. She had no use for superstition, had walked unlucky roads until she'd just as soon walk under any ladder as go around it, and considered herself unexceptional. By no means was she important enough for God to conjure signs and wonders on her account. What had set her apart, briefly, was an outsize and hellish obsession. To stop a thing like that would require a burning bush, a fighting of fire with fire.

Her eyes still signaled warning to her brain, like a car alarm gone off somewhere in an empty parking lot. She failed to heed it, understanding for the moment some formula for living that transcended fear and safety. She only wondered how long she could watch the spectacle before turning away. It was a lake of fire, something far more fierce and wondrous than either of those elements alone. The impossible.

The roof of her house when she saw it again still harbored its dark patches of damaged shingles, and there sat her car in the drive where she'd parked it. With her mind aflame and her heels unsteady from what she'd seen, she tried to look at the vinyl-sided ranch house in some born-again way. Whatever had gained purchase on her vision up there felt violent, like a flood, strong enough to buckle the dark roof and square white corners of home and safety. But no, it was all still there. The life she had recently left for dead was still waiting. The sheep remained at their posts, huddled in twos and threes. The neighbors' peach orchard still rotted in place on its perfect grid, exposing another family's bled-out luck. Not a thing on God's green earth had changed, only everything had. Or she was dreaming. She'd come down the mountain in less than half the time it took to climb, and that was long enough for her to doubt the whole of this day: what she'd planned to do, what she had seen, and what she'd left undone. Each of these was enormous. If they added up to nothing, then what? A life measured in half dollars and clipped coupons and culled hopes flattened between uninsulated walls. She'd gone for loss and wreckage as the alternative, but there might be others. A lake of fire had brought her back here to something.

To what? A yard strewn with weathered plastic toys and straggling grass, devoid of topsoil, thanks to her father-in-law's hasty job of bulldozing the pad for the house. One neglected rosebush by the porch, a Mother's Day present from Cub, who'd forgotten roses made her sad. The silver Taurus wagon in the drive, crookedly parked in haste, the keys in the ignition where she always left them, as if anybody around here would drive it away. The faint metal sound like a pipe dropped on its end when she put the car into gear. It could not be more tedious or familiar, any of it. Sadness filled her like water as she turned out onto the highway and clicked on the radio. Kenny Chesney was waiting there to pounce, crooning in his molasses voice that he wanted to know what forever felt like, urging her to gallop away. She clicked Kenny right off. She turned up the drive to her in-laws' place and their old farmhouse came into view with its two uncurtained windows upstairs that made her think of eye sockets in a skull. Hester's flower beds had melted under the summer's endless rain, and so had the garden. They'd finished tomato canning almost before they started. Hester's prized rose beds were reduced to thorny outposts clotted with fists of mildew. It was Hester who loved roses. For Dellarobia their cloying scent and falling-apart flowerheads opened a door straight into the memory of her parents' funerals.

When she got out of the car she noticed one bright spot of color in the whole front yard, a tiny acid-green sock on the stone step where she must have dropped it this morning when she brought the kids. She swiped it up and pocketed it on her way up the steps, abashed to confront the woman she'd been a few hours ago, dying of a sickness. She opened the door without knocking.

Cramped indoor odors met her: dog, carpet, spilled milk. And the sight of her kids, the heart-pounding relief of that, like the aftermath of a car accident narrowly avoided. The two of them sat close together on the living room floor in a tableau of brave abandonment. Preston had his arms around Cordie and his chin nested on her fuzzy head while holding a picture book open in front of her. The collies stretched on either side in alert recline, a pair of protective sphinxes. All eyes flew up to her as she entered, keen for rescue, the grandmother nowhere in sight. Preston's dark, plaintive eyebrows were identical to his father's, aligned across his forehead as if drawn there by a ruler. Cordelia reached both hands toward Dellarobia and burst into tears, her mouth downturned in a bawl so intense it showed her bottom teeth. The TV drone in the kitchen died abruptly, and Hester appeared in the doorway, still in her bathrobe, her long gray hair coiled around pink foam curlers. On her children's behalf Dellarobia gave her an injured look, probably just a slightly less toothy version of Cordie's. It wasn't as if she asked her mother-in-law to watch the kids every day of the week. Not even once a month.

Hester crossed her arms. "The way you run around, I wasn't expecting you back so soon."

"Well. I thank you for keeping an eye on them, Hester."

"I wasn't in there but a minute," she pressed, tilting her head back toward the kitchen.

"Okay, you weren't. It's fine." Dellarobia knew any tone she took with Hester would be the wrong one. These conversations wore her out before they began.

"I was fixing to heat up some chicken fried steak and greens for lunch."

25

For *whose* lunch, Dellarobia wondered. It sounded like one that would require more than baby teeth, not to mention some table knife skills. She said nothing. They both watched Cordelia stand up precariously, red-faced and howling. She was wet, and probably had been all morning. The diaper bulge inside her yellow footie pajamas was like a big round pumpkin. No wonder the child couldn't balance. Dellarobia took a drag on her almost-finished cigarette, trying to decide whether to change Cordie here or just get out of Dodge.

"You shouldn't smoke when you're around them kids," her mother-in-law declared in a gravel voice. A woman who'd probably blown smoke in Cub's little red face the minute he was born.

"Oh, my goodness, I would *never* do that. I only smoke when I'm lying out getting a suntan on the Riviera."

Hester looked stunned, meeting Dellarobia's gaze, eyeing the boots and the chenille scarf. "Look at you. What's got into you?"

Dellarobia wondered if she looked as she felt, like a woman fleeing a fire.

"Preston, honey, say bye-bye to your Mammaw." She clenched the filter of her cigarette lightly between her teeth so she could lift Cordelia to her hip, take Preston's hand, and steer her family toward something better than this.

2

Family Territory

On shearing day the weather turned cool and fine. On the strength of that and nothing more, just a few degrees of temperature, the gray clouds scurried away to parts unknown like a fleet of barn cats. The chore of turning ninety ewes and their uncountable half-grown lambs through the shearing stall became a day's good work instead of the misery expected by all. As far as Dellarobia could remember, no autumn shearing had been so pleasant. After all the months of dampness, the air inside the barn now seemed unnaturally dry. Stray motes of fleece flecked the beams of light streaming from the high windows, and the day smelled mostly of lanolin rather than urine and mud. The shorn fleeces were dry enough to be skirted while still warm off the sheep. Dellarobia stood across from her mother-in-law at the skirting table where they worked with four other women, picking over the white fleece spread out between them. The six of them surrounded the table evenly like numbers on a clock, but with more hands, all reaching inward rather than out.

There was no denying the clear sky was fortuitous. If the sheep had stood in rain and mud all morning waiting to be shorn, some of the wool would have been too fouled for sale. A lot of income turned on a few points of humidity. But good luck was too simple for Hester, who now declared that God had taken a hand in the weather. Dellarobia felt provoked by the self-congratulation. "So you're thinking God made the rain stop last night, just for us?" she asked.

"Know that the Lord God is mighty," replied Hester, who likely could live her whole life as a string of Bible quotes. She looked daunting in a red-checked blouse with pearl snaps and white piping on the yoke. Everyone else wore old work clothes, but Hester nearly always dressed as if she might later be headed out for a square dance. The festivities never materialized.

"Okay, then, he must hate the Cooks." Dellarobia's insolence gave her a rush, like a second beer on an empty stomach. If Hester was suggesting God as a coconspirator in farming gains and losses, she should own up to it. The neighbors' tomato crop had melted to liquid stench on the vine under the summer's nonstop rains, and their orchard grew a gray, fungal caul that was smothering the fruit and trees together.

Valia Estep and her big-haired daughter Crystal both looked at their hands, and so did the two Norwood ladies. They combed the white fleece for burrs and bits of straw as if the world turned on rooting out these imperfections. Neighbors always came on shearing day, starting with ham biscuits and coffee at six a.m. Not the unfortunate Cooks, of course, who had failed to gain Hester's sanction in the five years since they'd moved here. But the Norwoods' farm abutted the Turnbows' on the other side of the ridge, going back several generations, and they were also sheep farmers, so this help would be returned at their own shearing. Valia and Crystal were motivated only by friendship, it seemed, unless there was some vague unmentioned debt. They all attended Hester's church, which Dellarobia viewed as a complicated pyramid scheme of moral debt and credit resting ultimately on the shoulders of the Lord, but rife with middle managers.

"I didn't say word one about those Cook people," Hester said, not letting it go. "Valia, did you hear me say word one about the Cooks?"

"I don't think you did," replied mousy Valia. Dellarobia knew her mother-in-law could command unlimited agreement from these women. Hester's confidence in her own rectitude was frankly unwomanly. She never doubted a thing about herself, not even her wardrobe. Hester owned cowboy boots in many colors, including a round-toed pair in lime green lizard. But at the moment it was the self-interested logic that irked Dellarobia: if Hester and Bear had bad luck, like the winter of terrible chest colds they'd suffered last year, they blamed the repairman who failed to fix the furnace and charged them anyway. But when the Cooks' little boy was diagnosed with cancer the same winter, Hester implied God was a party to the outcome. Dellarobia had let this kind of talk slide for years, showing no more backbone really than Valia or any other toad in Hester's choir.

Until now. "Well, it just seemed like that was your meaning," she said. "That God stopped the rain for us, but not the Cooks. So he must like us better."

"Something's got into you, miss, and it is not good. You'd do well to consult your maker on respecting your elders." Hester spoke down her nose. She lorded her height over others in a way that her tall son did not, even though Cub had a good fifteen inches on Dellarobia. Only Hester could cut her daughter-in-law down to her actual size: a person who bought her sweatshirts in the boys' department, to save money.

"The Cooks are older than me," Dellarobia said quietly. "And I feel for them."

Something had gotten into her, yes. The arguments she'd always swallowed like a daily ration of pebbles had begun coming into her mouth and leaping out like frogs. Her strange turnaround on the mountain had acted on her like some kind of shock therapy. She'd told her best friend Dovey she was seeing someone that day, but not even Dovey knew what she'd been called out to witness. A mighty blaze rising from ordinary forest, she had no name for that. No words to put on a tablet as Moses had when he marched down his mountain. But like Moses she'd come home rattled and impatient with the pettiness of people's everyday affairs. She felt shamed by her made-up passion and the injuries she'd been ready to inflict. Hester wasn't the only one living in fantasyland with righteousness on her side; people just did that, this family and maybe all others. They built their tidy houses of self-importance and special blessing and went inside and slammed the door, unaware the mountain behind them was aflame. Dellarobia felt herself flung from complacency as if from a car crash, walking away from that vale of fire feeling powerful and bereft. It was worse even than years ago when the stillborn baby sent her home with complicated injuries she could not mention. Both then and now, Hester was not one to ask about personal troubles. She seemed unacquainted with that school of thought.

Valia piped up, "Did you all see that one on *Jackass* where they tried water-skiing on a froze lake? The Jeep busted through and sank!" Esteps could be relied on to change the thread of any conversation.

"I can't get over that they let people go on TV for that stuff," said Valia's daughter Crystal, shaking her stockpile of curls. "My boys ought to be famous."

Crystal was a high-school dropout with two kids, no history of a husband, and a well-known drinking problem, but she got to start over with a clean slate when saved by AA and the Mountain Fellowship church. Now she always kept her bottom lip clenched in her teeth, as if she were about an inch away from punching someone's lights out. Salvation had its trade-offs, evidently.

Hester reached back, divided her thin gray ponytail in half, and gave both sides a hard, simultaneous yank to tighten it. This was one of about five thousand personal habits that drove Dellarobia nuts. Why not just get a tighter ponytail band? Her mother-in-law seemed to use hair-yanking as a signal: I'll yank *you*. If Dellarobia meant to live out her natural life in this family, the new policy of speaking her mind was going to be a bite in the butt. It had the effect of setting everyone in a room on edge and looking for the door, herself included. But it didn't feel like a choice. Something had opened in her and she felt herself calamitously tilting in, like that Jeep on the ice. Jimmy was just gone, as others had come and gone before him, she had to admit. She'd never been unfaithful to Cub, not technically, but in her married lifetime she had quit these hard crushes on other men the way people quit smoking, over and over. So the standard joke applied: she should be good at it by now. She'd stopped answering Jimmy's calls, and Jimmy had failed to be persistent. And she still lay awake at night, no longer watching a nearly touchable lover behind her eyelids but now seeing flame in patterns that swirled and rippled. A lake of fire.

Dellarobia inhaled the lanolin-scented air, clearing fire and flood from her head. She was holding up the pace here. It was her job to leave the skirting table every few minutes to fetch a new fleece from the other side of the barn. She bypassed the wooden crate she'd set up as a playpen for Cordie, lightly touching her daughter's fluffy head, and then booked it over to the men's domain. At one door of the brightly lit shearing stall her husband had a grip on both horns of a big white ewe, waiting to deliver it into the hands of the shearer, while their skinny neighbor Peanut Norwood stood at the opposite door ready to escort out the newly shorn. She smiled at the sight of her tall husband in a pink flannel shirt. In many years of laundry days she'd watched that thing fade from burgundy to a plain, loud flamingo, but he still called it his red shirt, and must have seen it so. Cub was not a man to wear pink on purpose.

He motioned her over, giving her a quick one-armed hug that might have been a maneuver to get her out of the shearer's way. There was no making small talk over the racket of nervous bleating, but she stood for a minute getting an eyeful of the shearer, Luther Holly. Not that Luther was eye candy in any ordinary sense. He was a wife-and-grandkids, former-high-school-wrestler type, late fifties or maybe sixty, short and freckled with slightly bowed legs. But when he took up shears, his moves could make a woman think certain thoughts. He took the woolly ewe from Cub and she struggled for five seconds before surrendering with a sheepish sigh as Luther sat her rump down on the shearing mat. He wrapped his left arm arm across her breast in a choke-hold while his right hand pushed the vibrating blade gently from throat to belly in long strokes, as careful as a man shaving his own face. The electric shearing rig looked antique, with its trembling steel cylinder and clipper head hanging from a tall tripod, but in Luther's hands it was an instrument of finesse.

She noticed how each ewe came through the chute to face her duty by first pausing at the entrance, lowering

33

her hindquarters and urinating, giving herself a long moment to size up the scene before walking through that door. Watch and learn, Dellarobia thought, feeling an unaccustomed sympathy for the animals, whose dumb helplessness generally aggrieved her. Today they struck her as cannier than the people. If the forest behind them burned, these sheep would come to terms with their fate in no time flat. Flee or cower, they'd make their best call and fill up their bellies with grass to hedge their bets. In every way more realistic about their circumstances. And the border collies too. They would watch, ears up, forepaws planted, patiently bearing with the mess made by undisciplined humans as the world fell down around them.

Her father-in-law was keeping his distance from Luther's commanding presence, staying near the barn door where he trimmed hooves and conspicuously inspected each shorn animal for razor nicks before sending it out with a slap on the rump. Luther was too skillful to cut up the animals, but she saw Bear make a show of opening the big iodine bottle and swabbing a wound, or the suspicion of one. Bear Turnbow had a talent for attentiveness to minor insults. The collies Roy and Charlie moved in dutiful orbits around the men, perpetually alert to the flow of stock and the men's wishes. At a whistle from Bear, both dogs melted into a black-and-white gush of canine authority, pushing the flock through the maze of stock panels and narrow head gates like sand through an hourglass. Hester wanted them ordered by color, first the whites, then the silver badgerfaces, the brown moorits, and last the black, for ease of sorting the wool. Icelandics came in every shade of a bad mood, Cub liked to say, but Dellarobia liked their patchwork look in a field and the animals' own disregard of color. Brown ewes gave birth to white lambs or the reverse, sometimes even twins of different hues, devoid of scandal. The white ewe Cub brought in now had a big dove-gray lamb tagging along, still trying to nurse at six months of age. The worst hangers-on were the little rams, insatiable boys. Preston had been the same, still begging to nurse when his sister was born, howling to see an impostor baby. She felt permanently caved in from those years she'd spent with one child keening to draw milk out of her and another one fully monopolizing her surface. Effectively deep-mined and strip-mined simultaneously. These little boy lambs would be spared the fight with their successors, as they were scheduled at the slaughterhouse in ten days. Their mothers had to be dried up before the siring rams came in, and the boys couldn't stay in a communal pasture without benefit of castration. So the slaughterhouse had its attractions, all things considered.

Luther nodded at Dellarobia as he kicked a cloud of belly wool from his mat to be discarded, a nod meaning "Howdy Mrs. Turnbow" or "Sweep up!" or both. She grabbed the broom and swept the waste-wool into a rising pile in the corner of the stall. Having removed the unusable portion, Luther flipped over the ewe to shear the rest of her coat all in one piece, from neck to tail and shank to shank, moving himself and his paired opponent through what looked like a series of wrestling moves. That forward-bent posture would make ordinary men weep, but he did this all day, and made it look easy.

A woman's place, however, was not standing in her barn shoes gawking at Luther. Dellarobia gathered up the armload of waste wool and carried it out of Luther's way, dumping it in the big wooden crate she'd set up for Cordie. "Hey baby girl, here you go," she sang, sifting bits of fleece over her daughter like snow. She remembered as a child thinking this was what snow *should* be: soft and lovely, instead of the cold, wet truth. Cordie was thrilled, grasping handfuls of fuzz and tossing them in the air with such force she fell on her bottom, over and over.

Dellarobia hustled back to the shearing stall to get the fleece Luther had finished, which she rolled up like a big bath mat to carry to the skirting table. Before this day's end they would pick over some two hundred fleeces, pulling out bits of straw and the tag ends left from second cuts. The women flew through the work, flinging out each new fleece on the table and falling on it like worried animals grooming their young for fleas. They threw the waste onto the barn floor, a particolored fall accumulating in drifts around their legs. This was the second shearing of the year. Luther also came in the springtime after lambing to relieve the ewes of their coats that had grown felted and filthy over the winter months, so the precious summer fleece would grow in clean. This one, the late fall wool crop, gave the payoff. Once these fleeces were skirted clean, bagged, and stacked in great piles in the front of the barn, Cub and Bear would crate them to be shipped off to the spinning mill.

She knew it would take only minutes for Luther to finish the lamb he'd taken next, ahead of its mother, so she ran back to fetch that soft dove-gray fleece and was careful to keep it separate. The wool from these lambs' first and only shearing was finer and more valuable than regular wool. Hester could get an astounding fifty bucks apiece for virgin fleeces on the Internet, selling to hand spinners, and last year recouped the cost of her new computer in one season. The lambs' flesh was already contracted to a grocery chain and would be consumed by Christmas, but their wool would go on keeping people warm for years.

Dellarobia slid back into her place at the skirting table in time to hear the end of one of the world's unnumbered tales that share the same conclusion: *Can you believe the nerve?* The guilty party was evidently some friend of Crystal's, but the details were hazy. The friend had come to visit and somehow suffered damage from Crystal's kids.

"They're just horsing around like always, right?" Crystal's voice rose to a question mark at the end of every declarative sentence. "Shooting water pistols? So Jazon's trying to get away from his brother? And she's trying to get away from both of them I guess? So that's when Mical slams it. She's all, like, You boys are going to wreck my coat! And then wham, boo-hoo. She was worried about the water on her silk jacket, which she should not have wore to my house, I mean, *hello,* I have *children*?"

Dellarobia was accustomed to Crystal's question-mark oratory and her everlasting train wreck of the past and present tense, but couldn't quite pick up the thread. She looked from Crystal to the two Norwoods, slightly overripe ladies whose dyed-black hair was identically parted down the middle by a stripe of white roots.

"Slammed what?" she asked, when none present offered to pony it up.

"The car door on her hand," Crystal replied tiredly in a descending singsong. She seemed weary of the tale, yet told it with such enthusiasm.

"Oh. Ouch."

"The thing of it is," Crystal maintained, "I am sorry Brenda broke her fingers. But accidents happen. The same could have happened without my kids being there."

"Brenda's asking Crystal to pay her doctor bills, and Crystal don't want to," one of the Norwoods explained in a lowered voice, filling in Dellarobia on the plot as if she were a moviegoer who'd slipped in late.

"You know Brenda, her and her mother does the Sunday school," said the other. One of these Norwoods was married to Peanut and the other was his sister, so how did they look just alike? It was that half-grown-out dye job, a weirdly permanent fixture. Secretly Dellarobia thought of them as the Skunkwoods.

"Let me get this straight, Crystal," she said. "You're thinking if Mical hadn't been there, Brenda would have slammed the door on her own hand?"

"Accidents happen," Crystal repeated with a more strenuous intonation.

"Oh, they do. And many among us have got the kids to prove it."

Hester threw Dellarobia a look, still simmering from the earlier exchange. The ponytail-yank was impending. "You ought to be looking after your own," she said.

Dellarobia was indignant. Her daughter was perfectly content, throwing herself around in the crate of belly wool like a tiny insane person in a padded cell, and Preston was circling nearby making the whooshing noises boys make to imply they are going fast. It was Crystal's pair running wild all over the barn, two freckled, big-for-their-age elementary boys in buzz cuts and tight T-shirts just a little past expired. Jazon and Mical. What kind of mother misspelled her kids' names on purpose? Dellarobia had last seen them jumping off the loft stairs with empty feed bags over their shoulders like superhero capes. Now they were nowhere in sight, not a good sign. Roy, the collie, tended to keep tabs on the kids and now wore a long-nosed look of concern.

"Preston, come here a minute," Dellarobia called. "Where's your buddies?"

He arrived dramatically panting, his straight-cut bangs stuck to his forehead and his little wire glasses askew. "Outside. They wanted to step on poops but Mr. Norwood said they couldn't. Look!" Preston in one vigorous hop turned his back to them, revealing that over his shoulders he wore a full white fleece for a cape.

"You're going to wreck that fleece," said Hester.

He turned back around and said in a cartoon growl, "*I'm Wool Man!*"

"Wow, what superpowers do you have?" Dellarobia asked, but Wool Man was off, orbiting the skirting table and calling out answers on the fly, including being tricky and eating grass. His shenanigans pulled the fleece apart in less than a minute, as Hester predicted, and that was all it took to get the family thrown out of the proceedings. Hester ordered Dellarobia to round up Preston and Cordie and the other two boys and take them in the house for the rest of the day.

She felt bruised, and inclined to argue, but this was Hester's show. Immediately Crystal was demoted into Dellarobia's former position of step-and-fetch, and ran to get the next fleece. No more ogling Luther Holly's biceps until the spring shearing. Dellarobia went to find the kids and tell Cub they'd been banished to the house, in case he should wonder. Her anger collapsed into a familiar bottomless sorrow. It was just the one fleece, and not an especially valuable one. A more forgiving grandmother would have let Preston have it for a day of play, since it clearly made him happy. The woman had no feeling for children's joy. She could take the fun out of ice cream, dirt, fishing with live bait, you name it. Being around Hester tended to invoke an anguish for Cub's childhood that made Dellarobia wish she could scoop him up and get him away from there. Probably that was where all her family troubles began.

At half past five, she lay flat on her in-laws' uncomfortable sofa with Cordie asleep on her chest. The jelly toast Mical had demanded, but not eaten, sat flattened in its plate on the floor where Jazon had stepped on it, and then violently refused to let her take off his sneaker. He'd used his fists. As a personage of third-grade status Jazon was no joke, within striking distance of her own height and weight. Probably one of those kindergarten holdbacks where teachers tried to postpone the inevitable. She'd surrendered to spending some of the afternoon crawling on her knees with a damp dishtowel following that sticky, waffled left footprint over rugs and floors and sofa cushions, imagining Hester's ire if she overlooked one. When Jazon started running and leaping against the wall to see how high he could leave a jelly print, poor little dutiful Preston lost it and started crying, which set off Cordelia too. Dellarobia finally started up a game of Crazy Eights for money—a desperate measure—in which kids were allowed to use shoes for money, and won on purpose so she could gain control of the offending sneaker. She hid it upstairs in a laundry hamper.

Her mind was on temporary leave from the din when her phone caused her to jump, ratcheting its manic jangle from the sofa cushions under her. It must have slid out of her pocket and attempted its own escape. She tried to move Cordie without waking her, but missed the call before she could locate the phone. Dovey. She hit call.

"Help," she moaned. "I'm trapped in that *Twilight Zone* episode where a child has mental power over adults and turns one of them into a three-headed gopher."

"I hate when that happens," Dovey said. "So how does that work, are there three corresponding buttholes?" Dovey and Dellarobia had started life under the surnames Carver and Causey, thrown together in grade school by alphabetical seating. No one had come between them since. "So where are you?" Dovey asked.

"At Hester and Bear's. Hell, in other words, department of child management. Can you come over? I'm seriously losing my mind here."

"Nope. I'm on break, I had to come in to work. Three guys called in sick."

"*Three?* So you have to close, on a Saturday? That

42

stinks." Dovey worked behind the meat counter at Cash Club, a man's world if ever there was one, and was of such slight stature she had to stand on a box to use the grinder. But Dovey held her own. Be sweet and carry a sharp knife, was her motto.

"There's a U-T game today," Dovey said. "I'm sure that's the reason those guys called in, basketball flu. So yes, I'm closing, and we're swamped. That's why I couldn't answer when you texted, like, sixteen times. Jeez, Dellarobia."

"Sorry." She lay down again and eased Cordie back onto her chest, facedown, without disrupting the child's devoted unconsciousness.

"The problem can't possibly be those angels of yours," Dovey said. "It's you."

"Actually it's Crystal Estep's two boys. She and Valia are over here for the shearing, and Hester is using the occasion to put me in my place."

"Oh, God. She stuck you with what's-their-names, Jazzbo and Microphone?"

"Affirmative. I'm in the custody of two small men with plastic AK-47s forcing me into the slave trade."

"Why do they even make toys like that? I ask you."

"Crystal said Jazon and Mical are fixing to be terrorists for Hallowe'en."

"No real stretch there. Okay, look, you have to find your fierce. That's what the instructor says in my kickboxing video. Aim for the groin."

Dellarobia lowered her voice. "To tell you the truth,

43

I'm kind of scared of Crystal's boys. She told us about some friend of hers that came over and the kids broke her fingers in a car door."

"Here's my advice. Run for your life. Maybe put in a really long video first, so you'll get to the state line."

"A video, are you kidding? Jazon and Mical are hating on me here because there's no X-box in Hester world. The only child-oriented thing she's got is this one DVD they're playing over and over, probably for revenge. It's that squeaky-voiced muppet thing with the red matted hair."

"You want to know something? That creature right there is why I have no children. That voice was invented by the drug companies to get all the parents on Xanax."

"My own kids have better taste, I'll give them that much. Listen." She held up the phone. Preston had stuck his fingers in his ears and was walking in a circle shouting the words to "Willoughby Wallaby": *An elephant sat on YOU!*

"Do you hear that? That's my son. He is innocent by reason of insanity. His sister gnawed awhile on a stuffed dog and then she conked out."

"Okay, honey, I suggest you do the same. I have to run, my break's almost over."

"Here I go. This is me, chewing on a stuffed doggie."

"Listen, Dellarobia."

"What."

"Not now, but sometime. Are we going to talk about it?"

"What?"

"You."

"Me and what."

"Whatever happened two Fridays ago. With your telephone guy."

"Nothing happened. I told you that. Over and out."

"But you were like, Category Five obsessed. How's that just over?"

She had told Dovey the outlines of her affair, after the torment rose so high in her throat she felt she would choke. And if Dovey had seen reason to judge, she didn't say so. The better part of friendship might be holding one's tongue over the prospect of self-made wreckage. Dovey had weathered her own run-ins with strange fortune, in several varieties including the man kind, and seemed to understand the appetite for self-destruction. What stumped her now was the return of sensible behavior. Dellarobia could see the perspective. Of the two events, the latter did seem further outside the standard script.

"If I had a reasonable explanation, you would hear it, Dovey. This is all I can tell you: it wasn't my decision. Something happened. I was blind, but now I see."

"Now you're talking crazy. Is this something religious?"

Dellarobia was at pain to answer. In twenty years she'd sheltered nothing from Dovey, but there were no regular words for this. *When you pass through the rivers they will not sweep over you. When you walk through the fire, the flames will not set you ablaze.* That was the book of Isaiah. "It's not religious," she said.

"I *know* you," Dovey said. "And I don't get this."

"Me either."

"Okay, but we're not done."

"Okay, go back to work, bye. I hear the rescue squad."

The shearing crew must have wrapped things up. She could hear them outside the front door, stomping the muck off their barn boots. Dellarobia knew she should look alive so Hester wouldn't call her Lazy Daisy, but the weight of her baby's sweet sleeping body kept her immobile on the couch. The collies rushed in and circled the toy-strewn living room like the sheriff's posse in an old western, surveying the wrecked Indian camp, then retreated upstairs. The tumbling dog feet on the stairs sounded like a waterfall in reverse.

From her horizontal position she watched Bear lean over Luther in an intimidating way, apparently in disagreement over payment due. Surely Bear wouldn't push it too far. Sheep farmers lived in dread of getting crossed off Luther's list for some infraction, such as trying to short the head count when they wrote his check. As the only shearer in the county, Luther's skills probably put him in greater demand than any doctor or drug dealer out there. Dellarobia and Cub had actually changed the date of their hastily planned wedding when it turned out to be the day Luther had put the Turnbows on his calendar for shearing. She'd argued with Hester about it, and still to this day felt humiliated by the priority, but they'd ended up moving the wedding from October to November: first trimester to second. Not that she'd been showing that much yet, but the compromise felt significant. That was over a decade ago, and even then Luther was the last shearer standing. Younger men wanted nothing to do with such hard work, preferring to drive some rig or gaze at a screen.

She glanced around for Cub, but he hadn't come in. Hester had probably left him to sweep up. She and the other ladies were washing up at the kitchen sink, and Crystal was nowhere to be seen, probably off somewhere plotting to have another horrible child and dump that one on Dellarobia too. No word of thanks would be forthcoming, she assumed. She sat up gently and settled Cordie in the sofa cushions, warning Preston to keep the roughhousing away from her. Jazon and Mical were using the edge of a CD to press down cornerwise on Legos and make them pop into the air. She stretched her stiff back, waiting for acknowledgment from someone who had attained the age of reason.

"You're welcome," she announced finally. "I'll go see if my husband needs any help." All four women turned simultaneously to gawk at her, as if her life had become a bad school play. "The kids are hungry," she added. "If y'all are about to feed yourselves, you might think of them while you're at it."

The shadows outside were longer than she'd expected, the long dusk of wintertime. Bear's penned hounds were snuffling and growling low in their throats, maybe catching wind of some raccoon on the ridge they pined to chase down and take apart. The wind banged the doors of the metal building behind the house where Bear had his machine shop, in the middle of what looked like a truck graveyard. Dellarobia had never even entered that shop, knowing it would make her homesick for the long-ago place where her own father built furniture. Even this fleeting thought, the shop doors banging, socked her with a memory of sitting on his shoulders and touching the cannonball tops of bedposts he'd spooled out of wood with his lathes.

She drew a very squashed pack of cigarettes from the back pocket of her jeans and lit up, thinking that if someone had asked her to wait one minute longer for it, she might have taken them out. She was trying hard not to smoke around the kids. Just a couple of sneaks, one of them when she'd gone upstairs to hide Jazon's shoe, and that was it, in over six hours. In truth, Hester's reproach the other day had left its impression. Dellarobia now felt her foggy head clear as she picked her way across the muddy ground and entered the fluffy storm inside the barn, where fluorescent lights blazed and it looked as if it had snowed indoors. She found the broom exactly where she'd left it, beside the leaf rake and boxes of trash bags. If Cub was cleaning up, he was doing it without much in the way of technology. Where was he? When she opened her mouth to speak, she had a weird feeling that squeaky muppet voice would come ratcheting out. And that he would answer in a child's voice. She was not born into this family business, which explained her low-ranking position, but they had no excuse for treating Cub as they did. How could a man amount to much when his parents' expectations peaked at raking up waste wool? Dellarobia doubted she'd have much gumption either, if she'd been raised by a mother like Hester. The woman ran all horses with the same whip. She'd even aimed some hits at the shearer today about second cuts, but he'd ignored her, exactly as he ignored Bear's posturing. Maybe that vibrating metal cylinder next to Luther's skull drowned out the whole family. Dellarobia could use a thing like that.

"Cub?" she called, and heard a faint reply. Animal or husband, she couldn't say. She peered into the paddocks one after another, all empty of sheep. The shearing stall was knee-deep in belly wool, so Crystal must have abandoned her post as cleanup girl after about ten seconds. Lucky her, she could defect without getting court-martialed. Dellarobia called Cub's name repeatedly and heard an answer each time, eventually realizing it was coming from overhead. She climbed the narrow stairs to the hay mow and found him lying on his back across a row of hay bales. This time of year the mow should have been packed like a suitcase, filled side to side and top to bottom, but the cavernous loft was more than half empty. They'd lost the late-summer cutting because three consecutive rainless days were needed for cutting, raking, and baling a hay crop. All

49

the farmers they knew had leaned into the forecasts like gamblers banking on a straight flush: some took the risk, mowed hay that got rained on, and lost. Others waited, and also lost.

"Cub, honey, what's wrong. You dead?"

"About."

"I've seen you further gone than that, and resurrected at the sight of a cold beer."

He sat up straight. "You got one?"

"From your mother's kitchen?"

He flopped back against the hay, taking off his Deere cap and settling it over his face. She sat down opposite him on the lowest row of bales, which were stacked like a wide staircase leading up to the rafters. Not many farms still maintained the equipment to make square bales, instead favoring the huge rolls that were handier to move with a tractor and fork. But these made nice furniture. She dragged one close for a footstool, swung up her short legs and leaned back against a prickly wall of hay, waiting for further signs of life from her husband. Lying on his back, he resembled a mountain: highest in the midsection, tapering out on both ends. He pulled his cap farther down over his face.

"You're just worn out," she offered.

"No, it's more than that."

"What, are you sick?"

"Sick and tired."

"Of what?"

"Farming."

"I hear you." She was conscious of her unfinished cigarette, aware that only a fool or city person would smoke in a hayloft. It could catch fire in a flash. But that would be in some year other than this one, in which the very snapping turtles had dragged themselves from silted ponds and roamed the soggy land looking for higher ground. A little tobacco smoke might help dry out this hay. Cub evidently didn't disagree, for he lay silent awhile. Then spoke from under his cap.

"Dad's fixing to sign a contract with some loggers."

"You mean to cut timber? Where?"

"That hollow up behind our house. All the way to the top, he said."

"What possessed him to do that now? That timber's been standing awhile."

"The taxes went up, and he's got a balloon on his equipment loan. You and I are behind on our house payments. Money's coming in even lower this year than last. He's thinking we'll have to buy hay out of Missouri this winter, after we lost so much of ours."

She looked at the backs of her hands. "Just one month behind, you and me."

She'd been hoping Bear and Hester didn't know about the missed payment, but every nickel gained or lost on that farm went on the same ledger. Bear and Hester knew every detail of their lives, as did their neighbors and eventually the community as a whole, thanks to the news team down at Hair Affair.

"I talked to the man at the bank about our payment,

Cub. It's Ed Cameron, you know who that is. He said it was no big deal, as long as we're caught up by year's end."

"Well, foreclosure on Dad's equipment loan is a big deal."

She felt something in herself drop. "That's not an issue, is it?"

"The word was mentioned."

She wanted to throw something, though not necessarily at Cub. She hated how his parents left them in the dark, even on something so important. Bear earned as much or more on machine repair and metalwork in his shop than from anything that happened in this barn. For years he'd gotten steady contracts making replacement parts for factories and something for the DOT, a bracket for guardrails, was her understanding. Dellarobia kept out of it. Bear seemed to think of these contracts as more valid than regular farm work, maybe because he'd learned welding in the military. He'd borrowed a huge sum to expand his machine shop, a few months before transportation departments everywhere suddenly came up strapped, and people decided they hated government spending. The equipment loan was backed up by a lien on the land.

"So what happens to us, if this farm gets folded in half overnight?"

Cub remained mute and supine on his bed of hay. Cub's only off-farm income was what he made driving a truck that delivered gravel, intermittently, as that company was not seeing a lot of action these days either. Ever since the economy tanked, people had been settling for what they had. Renewing their vows with their bad gravel driveways.

His inert response to this crisis was predictable. In case of fire, take a nap. She tried an easier question. "How'd you happen to come by this information?"

"Listening. He talks more to Peanut Norwood in a day than he does to me in a year."

"Lord, if he's telling the neighbors of his downfall, we must be pretty near the end of the rope. You know your dad."

"Yeah, I do."

"No bad news comes looking for Bear Turnbow that he can't send running."

"I know, I was thinking that. It's worse for the Norwoods, I guess. Peanut wants to log out his side too. They said it works best if they clear-cut the whole deal at once."

"A clear cut. Cub, honey, could you at least sit up and discuss this like a human? You mean where they take out everything down to the slash?"

Cub sat up and gave her a sorry look. He had fleece clinging to his trousers and hay in his hair, a sight to see. "That's where they'll give you the most money. According to Dad, it's easier when they don't have to pick and choose the trees."

She stared at Cub, trying to find holy matrimony in there, pushing her way back through the weeds as she always did. To what she'd seen in him when she was still looking: the narrow face and long chin that gave an impression of leanness, despite his burgeoning middle. The thick lashes and dark, ruler-straight eyebrows like an interrupted pencil line across his forehead, behind the pale forelock that hung in his eyes. The cause of their marriage had been conspicuous at the wedding, but she'd gone a little foggy on the earlier motives. She recalled the nice truck, other plans canceled, an ounce of pity maybe. A boy named Damon who'd kissed her half to death and then left her for dead, on the rebound. And there stood Cub, with his rock-steady faith that she knew more than he did, in any situation outside of automotive repair. His bewildered sexual gratitude, as near a thing to religious awe as a girl of her station could likely inspire. These boyish things had made him lovable. But you could run out of gas on boyish, that was the thing. A message that should be engraved in every woman's wedding band.

"So this is a done deal," she said finally. "Has he talked to the logging people?"

"Whatever's too little to cut up for lumber, he said they can grind into paper."

"Oh, Cub. They'll make it look like a war zone, like the Buchman place. Have you looked at that mountain since they finished logging it out? It's a trash pile. Nothing but mud and splinters."

Cub began pulling white threads of wool from the knees of his jeans, one at a time. The air was so dry they stuck to him, drawn by static electricity. How strange, the humidity dropping like that overnight. She cleared a spot on the floor and carefully ground out her cigarette with the toe of her work boot. "I drive past there every time I go to Food King," she said. "It looks like they blew up bombs all over it. Then all these rains started and the whole mountain is sliding into the road. They have road crews out there blading the muck out of the way. I bet I've seen that six times since July."

Cub's voice flagged in ready defeat. "Well, you won't have to drive past Dad's upper hollow when you go get your groceries." He was already losing interest, ready for a new topic, the same way he went glassy in front of the TV every night and channel-surfed without cease. Some flashy woman in a silk suit would be describing a faux-emerald necklace, and suddenly they're landing the biggest fish in the Amazon. Or Fox News would morph into a late-night comedian making jokes about Christians and southerners. Cub claimed the surfing relaxed him. It made Dellarobia grind her teeth.

"I need to get back to the house," she said. Hester was feeding Preston and Cordie their supper, probably an array of items from the choking-hazard checklist: grapes, peas, hot dogs cut crosswise. There was no point in arguing with Cub, when neither of them had a say in the family plan. She and her husband were like kids in the backseat of a car, bickering over the merits of some unknown destination.

She stood up, but instead of heading for the stairs,

walked on impulse to the end of the loft, where the giant door was propped open to ventilate the hay. A person could just run the length of the haymow and take a flying jump. For the first time in her life she could see perfectly well how a person arrived on that flight path: needing an alternative to the present so badly, the only doorway was a high window. She'd practically done it herself. The next thing to it. The thought of that recklessness terrified her now, making her step back from the haymow door and close her eyes, trying to calm down.

When she opened them she looked down on the sheep milling around in the dusk, surprisingly slim and trim without their wool. Pastor Bobby at Hester's church spoke of Jesus looking down on his flock from on high, and it seemed apt: an all-knowing creator probably would find humans to be exactly the same kind of ignorant little dumb-heads as these sheep. Right now they were butting each other like crazy. Hester said head-butting was a flock's way of figuring out who was boss, so it was normal to some extent, but Dellarobia had noticed that shearing always left them wildly uncertain as to who was who. She had asked about it, but no one in the family could say why. She stood watching now, oddly fascinated. Grumpy ewes lowered their horns to toss off lambs that weren't theirs, the poor little things bunting at the wrong udders, and one old girl in particular was running up against puny year-lings, revisiting arguments long ago settled. Suddenly they were strangers, though they'd been here together all along. In the still evening she heard the dull, repeated thud of heads making contact, horn and skull. They must have some good reason; animals behaved with purpose, it seemed. Unlike people.

And then it dawned on her: scent. They must recognize each other that way. And all their special odors had been removed with the wool. They'd be blind to one another's identities until they worked up a good personal aroma again. Dellarobia felt a glimmer of pride for working out this mystery by herself. Maybe one day she'd inform Hester.

She walked back and sat down across from Cub. "When do you think your folks were planning to clue us in about the foreclosure?"

"I don't know."

"Just one day the phone would ring and they'd be like, 'Hey, pack up the kids, get a new life, we just lost your half of the family deal.' Or that they're moving in with us, or us with them? Cub, I swear, your mother and me under one roof, never again. You'd just as well call nine-one-one right now and get it over with. Because homicide will ensue."

"I know that, hon."

"If he can't make the payment, why wouldn't they just repossess his equipment?"

"Depreciation, I guess. It's not enough. They needed that lien on the farm."

This shocked her. The equipment was so nearly

new. She wondered if anyone totally understood how banks could make the ground shift underfoot and turn real things into empty air, just with a word. "So you think he's really going to do that logging?"

"He said it was as good as done. He's signing a contract."

"Are they from here?" she asked.

"Is who?"

"The logging company. Whoever's in charge."

"Are you kidding me? What man in this county owns anything more than what he squats on to take a crap?"

"Thanks for the visual." She thought of a magazine article that advised keeping your marriage sexy by closing the bathroom door. She couldn't remember whether she'd actually read that article, or just wished someone would write it.

"Naw," Cub said, "a guy came over from Knoxville. And that's not even the main office, the outfit's owned by Warehouser or something. Out west."

"That figures. Come on down. Get the poor man's goods and haul them out of here to make I don't know what. Toilet paper for city people, I guess."

"Well, hon, it's money we need."

"I know. Let's all sing the redneck national anthem: Settle for what you can get."

"I'm sorry you see it that way, but I don't see where we have a lot of choice."

He looked sorry all right. It made her want to punch

something, all that *sorry*. She wished he would get mad. Instead he sat pulling threads of fleece from his jeans in a slow, passive way that made her blood boil. With occasional exceptions in the bedroom, Cub did every single thing in his life in first gear. It could take him forty minutes to empty his freaking pants pockets. In high school Dovey used to call him Flash. She was furious when Dellarobia first went out with him. They'd sworn onto a flight plan, older guys with vocabularies and bank accounts, men from anywhere but here.

Inadmissable thoughts. Dellarobia forced herself now to try being someone else, a wife from Mars with a nicer personality. She'd come down that mountain feeling so sure there was something new here to see. She slowed her breathing and just watched the little threads that clung to his jeans, standing straight out as he pulled them away from the fabric. The night air was crisp for the first time in months, full of promise and static. Spark weather, was how she thought of these fall nights when the air suddenly went so dry her pajamas lit the sheets with little sparks. Why would cool weather make dry air? She'd wondered such things a thousand times, inciting the regular brainless replies: woolly worms predict the weather and the Lord moves in mysterious ways. Good night. She knew she should be patient with those underly endowed with intelligence, but could everyone at once be below average? Most, she suspected, were just sliding by.

She had seen trees aflame on the mountain. For some

reason that knowledge was hers alone. What had she been thinking? The full proposition now flooded her with panic, shutting her into a tight place. "They can't log that mountain," she said.

"Why not?"

"I don't know why not."

A lake of fire, what would Cub make of that? The route to the world's end, a vivid moral suggestion he'd heard all his life and probably believed. The Revelations. Her mind worked differently. Flame and inundation were opposites, they canceled. "The world can surprise you," she said finally. "It could be something special up there."

Cub lifted the plane of his eyebrows. "He's selling trees, Dellarobia."

She balked, knowing his wariness of people who wanted to save trees for trees' sake. An easy want, when they weren't your trees, or your foreclosure. "But what kind of trees?" she pressed. "I mean, are they big or little or red or blue or what? If Bear's signing a logging contract, I think he should walk up there and look at what he's selling. You both should."

Cub stopped picking at his jeans and looked at her as if confronted with a whole new wife. Like those sheep out there, bewildered by the familiar. He took off his cap, ran a hand over his standing-up hair, and replaced it, studying her all the while. For the first moment in a long invisible time, she actually felt she was being seen.

"What for?" he asked, at last.

"What *for*? It's out of the question to walk your own land?"

"Not my land yet."

She had carried the leaf rake up here, and now pictured herself walking to the haymow door and throwing it out, just to hear the satisfying metallic clatter. Cub still drove the same pickup truck they'd dated in, now on its third engine overhaul, with so many miles on it you'd think surely he'd been somewhere. But he hadn't seen a state line, and didn't care. What did it take to move a man who, when he ran out of steam, which he didn't have much to begin with, resembled a mountain?

"If it's not your land, then what are we, sharecroppers?" she asked. "We work this farm, it's almost our entire living, so you might want to claim it. Even if your dad has not passed away as of yet. Why won't you act like one thing in the world is yours?"

"I walked the fences that time when the ram got out."

"Jesus Christ, that was the winter I was pregnant with Preston."

"No need to take the Lord's name in vain."

"I've hardly seen you set your boots outside this barn in five years. That's a fact, Cub. How do you even know what's up there in that hollow? There could be anything. You all are fixing to sell off something, and you don't even know what it is."

"Well, I don't expect there's any gold mines. Just trees. The green ones, I'm a-thinking."

"Trees, okay. But you could go look at them. The logging company could rob you blind. They could tell you the timber is not any count, when it is."

"How do you know what it is?"

"We've been up there, you and me. We've consumed some Ripple in that turkey-hunting shack." She blushed, her fair skin ever ready to give her away. But Cub was so unsuspecting. He would think it was sins of their own she was blushing over.

He smiled. "Maybe we ought to go up there again one of these days, baby."

"Okay, let's do that. We'll have one last look before you go knocking down all the trees with your shock and awe, turning your family's land into frickin' Iraq."

"Ain't no A-rabs on the Turnbow property, Della-robia."

"That's not what I meant. Anyway, for all you know, there could be terrorists camped up there on the ridge. Who'd find them? Nobody around here will get out of their darn pickup trucks. That ridge is probably the safest hiding place in the world."

Cub rolled his eyes, and she felt overwhelmed with futile energy, like a dog chasing its tail. She could see this was going the way of all their arguments, poised to step from the ground of true complaints into the quicksand of trivial nonsense. With full righteous outrage intact. "You and your dad ought to lay eyes on your own property once in a while, is all I'm trying to say."

"Why are you nagging me about this all of a sudden?"

"I don't know. There's just reasons. There could be more treasure than you think in your own backyard."

He shook his head. "What you're saying is what you always say. Work harder, Cub, go faster, Cub."

"Is not."

"Well, what am I supposed to do? The ATV busted an axle last month."

"Busted an axle all by itself, as I understand it. With no help from your drunk friends."

"Nobody was entirely drunk."

Here we go, she thought, into the quicksands of stupid. She stood up. "I'm going in the house. I just thought I'd mention that God gave you feet, to set one down in front of the other, if memory serves me. Seems like you'd go up there and look at what you're selling off before it's gone. It's just good business."

"Good business. Since when did you get your business-lady degree?"

The contempt startled her. That wasn't even Cub, he was just parroting his father in some last-ditch attempt at manhood. She made for the stairs without looking back. "I hear you. Good business, and it's none of mine."

❧

A thicket of reasons led them up the mountain, and Dellarobia's insistence was one strand of it. Bear and

63

Peanut Norwood's mistrust of the logging company, and possibly of each other, comprised the rest. Four men in hard hats had flagged the boundaries of the section proposed for logging and declared that it was up to the Turnbows and Norwoods to see that property lines were respected. The hard-hat men, who were subcontractors for the real decision-makers in California, came from Knoxville in a panel truck that said Money Tree Industries. Suspicion was only natural.

Cub rallied to repair the all-terrain vehicle so they wouldn't have to make the hike on foot. It took four of his buddies and nearly a week of evenings to replace the broken axle. Dovey observed to Dellarobia that there was no end to the amount of effort a man would put into saving himself some work. On a Friday morning the expedition piled onto the ATV with Cub at the wheel, Bear riding shotgun, and Peanut Norwood in the cargo bucket hugging his knees, insufficiently shaped like a bale of hay to fit in there very well. Dellarobia stood at her kitchen window watching the squat vehicle crawl up the steep pasture slope like a broad, flat toad with three men clinging to its back. Her life had become some kind of fairy tale, in which her family members set off one by one to meet their destiny on the High Road. She couldn't have said what she hoped the men would discover up there, but her distraction was acute. Ten minutes after they left, she found herself folding clothes from the dirty-laundry basket while the clean ones sat in the dryer.

Less than an hour passed before the men came back, astounded, to collect their wives as witnesses.

There was no question of everyone riding in the vehicle. They would have to walk. Dellarobia surprised herself by asking to go along, despite the sticky fact of Cordelia eating cereal in her high chair, and Preston needing to be picked up from kindergarten at noon. She asked anyway. Dovey was off work that morning and could come over to mind the kids. Cub made his parents hold their horses while they waited the ten minutes it took for Dovey to get there. Cub was surprisingly resolute on Dellarobia's behalf.

Her heart raced as they mounted the hill, on various accounts. Mostly for the strangeness of reenacting this walk she'd so recently taken with outrageous intent, this time with husband and family in tow. It felt like a reality show, poised to expose and explode her serial failures. The wife who keeps having inappropriate crushes, falling off the marriage wagon, if only in her mind. They navigated the mud at the top of the pasture where the sheep had beaten down the perimeter, cursed with their certainty of greener grass on the other side. Like herself, she thought, when she'd last slipped through this gate. Like a dog in a yard, pacing the edges of her confines to the tune of "Get me out of here." Cub held the gate open for her, and she couldn't meet his eyes.

Beefy, ruddy-faced Bear led the way, the platoon leader. He'd served in the military ages ago and carried certain vestiges: the haircut, the weight lifting, the blood pressure. He'd held on to a muscular build, despite his weight and age, and the natural supremacy that went with a frame of six feet, four inches. Hester bought his trousers from a place called Man of Measure, on rare shopping trips to Knoxville. Cub was nearly as tall but managed to fit into regular Wranglers, size 38–36, which to Dellarobia sounded more like the shape of a TV screen than a man. She assumed it was the tour in Vietnam that accounted for the difference in men like Burley Turnbow Sr. and Jr., so similar in their dimensions and opposite in bearing. Like those boxes that guaranteed they were equally filled, but contents may have settled. She could hear Cub huffing and puffing now as he brought up the rear, saying little. The two older men gave him no chance. Bear and Peanut Norwood were talking a lot but failing to explain anything, mostly contradicting one another's accounts or declaring no explanation was possible. Cub was the first of them to say they thought it was insects.

Hester wheeled on him. "If you're hauling me up this mountain to look at a bug, son, I will slap you nakeder than what you were born with."

Cub pressed on, despite the threat. "It's not regular bugs, Mother. It's something pretty. Wouldn't you say it was, Dad?"

Bear and Norwood, if they could agree on nothing else, both stated that was true, it was awful pretty. Or would be, if there weren't so many they covered up the place.

"You won't believe it," Cub warned. "It's like something taking over the world."

They took the High Road in single file and the men settled down, directing their energy to the climb. A gobbler called from high on the ridge and a female answered, wild turkeys getting down to their family business. Normally one of the men would have wished aloud for his rifle, but today no one did. Dellarobia couldn't remember a sadder-looking November. The trees had lost their leaves early in the unrelenting rain. After a brief fling with coloration they dropped their tresses in clumps like a chemo patient losing her hair. A few maroon bouquets of blackberry leaves still hung on, but the blue asters had gone to white fluff and the world seemed drained. The leafless pear trees in Hester's yard had lately started trying to bloom again, bizarrely, little pimply outbursts of blossom breaking out on the faces of the trees. Summer's heat had never really arrived, nor the cold in its turn, and everything living now seemed to yearn for sun with the anguish of the unloved. The world of sensible seasons had come undone.

At least there was no rain at the moment. Dellarobia was happy to feel warmth on her shoulders through her jacket, and a strength of daylight she'd all but forgotten, even now as they entered deeper woods. The sky was not blue but the cold white of high clouds in a thin reflective sheet. She could have used her prescription sunglasses, if she could remember what junk drawer they were in. But definitely, she was wearing her glasses today. Whatever was up here, she planned to see it clearly. She spied some ribbons of orange flagging tape dangling from the trees, but the men were paying no heed right now to boundaries. Bear kept them moving at a clip. Dellarobia was next to last in the line, behind her mother-in-law and ahead of Cub. She was dying for a rest or a smoke, ideally both, but would drop dead before she'd be the one to ask. She had barely been invited. Peanut Norwood gripped his chest in a promising way, so maybe he'd make them stop. Forget about wiry Hester in her yellow cowboy boots. Onward Christian soldiers. Dellarobia averted her eyes from Hester's skinny bottom in sagging Levi's, and trusted that Cub was finding her own rear view more pleasing. Whenever she complained of being so small, Cub told her she was a sports car: no junk in the trunk, but all you need for speed. Maybe that's how he was keeping his feet moving. Back before marriage, she'd known the power of being physically admired, changing the energy of a room by walking into it. She wondered if that was her problem, missing that. Falling for guys who flattered her. It seemed so shallow and despicable, she hoped that was not the measure of her worth. She peered off through the woods, seeing nothing altered in the last two weeks except for a greater barrenness among the trees. And herself, of course. Nothing had changed except every conscious minute and a strange fire in her dreams.

They rounded a bend in the trail and could see the

whole dark green mountain range laid out above them, stippled with firs along the bumpy spine. Limestone cliffs erupted here and there, gray teeth grinning through the dark trees. Wherever sun fell on them, the tops of the knolls faintly glowed. The color could have been a trick of the light. But wasn't. She turned, risking a glance at Cub's face.

"Is that it?" she asked quietly. "That shine on the trees?"

He nodded. "You knew, didn't you?"

"How would I?"

He said no more. They kept moving. Her guilty mind ran down a hundred alleys, wondering what he implied. He knew she'd been up here? No possibility made sense: mind-reading, sleep-talking, these things happened in movies. She'd told only Dovey, who honestly would endure torture without betraying her. They entered the chilly darkness of the fir forest. Its density was so different from the open sky and widely spaced trunks of the leafless deciduous woods.

"Why in the world did these evergreens get planted up here?" Dellarobia asked. She needed to hear someone talk.

"Bear's daddy wasn't the only one," Hester said. "There was other ones that put them in. Peanut, didn't your daddy plant some?"

Dellarobia had vaguely understood it to be a touchy topic, but now she got it. The family joke, a Christmas tree boondoggle. Probably she should not have asked.

"The extension fellows told him to," Norwood said. "The chestnuts was getting blighty, and they's looking for something new to put in. The Christmas tree market."

"Christmas tree market," Bear spat. "In the nineteen-forties, when a man could cut a weed cedar out of his woodlot for free. They couldn't get two bits for them. It wasn't worth hauling them out."

The old firs stood fifty feet tall now, ghosts of Christmas past. An image landed in her head with those words, the hooded skeleton pointing at gravestones that scared the bejesus out of her in childhood. A library book, Charles Dickens. But that was the Yet to Come ghost, and these were just geriatric trees. Ghosts of bad timing, if anything. She wasn't going to bring it up, but she knew some farmers were planting Christmas trees again, hiring Mexican workers for the winter labor. Presumably the same men who showed up in summers to work tobacco. They used to go home in winter and now stayed year-round, like the geese at Great Lick that somehow quit flying south. She'd seen these men in hard-luck kinds of places like the Cash Rite, which she and Dovey called Ass Bite, a Feather-town storefront where she sometimes had to go for a substantially clipped advance on Cub's paycheck if the bills came in too close together. Christmas tree farms were just proof that every gone thing came back around again, with a worse pay scale.

Conversation ceased while they mounted a steep

section of the rutted trail, then came to the flat section she recognized as the spot where she'd stopped for a smoke. She scanned the ground, knowing Cub would recognize the filter of her brand if he saw it. She felt strung out from nerves and exhaustion. Soon they would round the mountainside and gain the view of the valley, and then what? Several trees along the path bore the bristly things she'd seen before, the fungus, if that's what it was, but the men seemed not to notice. They looked ahead, picking up the pace.

Hester seemed increasingly put out, to be dragged from her routine. She hummed steadily under her breath in a thin, monotonous way. Some hymn. Or a show tune—with Hester there was no telling. Dellarobia could not imagine humming or anything else that required extra oxygen. They were all out of shape except Hester, who stayed miraculously ship-shape on her regimen of Mountain Dew and Camel Lights. Dellarobia counted steps to make the time pass, watching her feet. She noticed little darts in the trail, first one and then more, scattered on the ground like litter. They were the same orange as the flagging tape but made of something brittle that crunched underfoot. Little V-shaped points, like arrows, aimed in every possible direction, as if scattered here for the purpose of sheer confusion. To get people lost in the woods.

They rounded the bend to the overlook and came into the full sight of it. These golden darts filled the whole of the air, swirling like leaves in a massive storm.

Wings. The darts underfoot also were wings. *Butterflies*. How had she failed to see them? She felt stupid, or blind, in a way that went beyond needing glasses. Unreceptive to truth. She'd been willing to take in the run of emotions that stood up the hairs on her neck, the wonder, but had shuttered her eyes and looked without seeing. The density of the butterflies in the air now gave her a sense of being underwater, plunged into a deep pond among bright fishes. They filled the sky. Out across the valley, the air itself glowed golden. Every tree on the far mountainside was covered with trembling flame, and that, of course, was butterflies. She had carried this vision inside herself for so many days in ignorance, like an unacknowledged pregnancy. The fire was alive, and incomprehensibly immense, an unbounded, uncountable congregation of flame-colored insects.

This time they revealed themselves in movement, as creatures in flight. That made the difference. The tree-tops and ravines all appeared in strange relief, exposed by the trick of air as a visible quantity. Air filled with quivering butterfly light. The space between trees glittered, more real and alive than the trees themselves. The scaly forest still bore the same bulbous burden in its branches she'd seen before, even more of it, if possible. The drooping branches seemed bent to the breaking point under their weight. Of *butterflies*. The verity of that took her breath. A million times nothing weighed nothing. Her mind confronted a mathematics she'd always thought to be the domain of teachers and pure invention.

"Great day in the morning," Hester said, looking stricken.

"There you go," Bear said. "Whatever the hell that is, it can't be a damn bit of good for logging."

"I'd say it would gum up their equipment," Norwood agreed. "Or we might run into one of those government deals. Something endangered."

"No sir," said Bear. "I believe there's more of them than we've got people."

The numbers could not be argued. Butterflies rested and crawled even on the path around their feet, giving the impression of twitchy, self-automated dead leaves marching across a forest floor. Dellarobia squatted down and waved her hand over one, expecting it to startle and fly, but it stayed in place, wings closed. Then opened wide to the sudden reveal: *orange*. Four wings, with the symmetry of a bow-tied shoelace. Preston had spent all of a recent morning trying to tie a bow, biting his lower lip in concentration, but here was perfection without effort. He would love to see this. She let it crawl onto her hand and held it close to her eyes. The orange wings were scrolled with neat black lines, like liquid eyeliner, expertly applied. In almost thirty years of walking around on the grass of the world, she couldn't recall having spent two minutes alone with a butterfly.

It flew, and she stood up, meeting the unguarded eyes of both Hester and Bear. They seemed expectant, or even accusing, as if it might be up to Dellarobia to arrange this nonsensical sight into something ordinary and real. She couldn't imagine it. Cub stared at her too, through the moving light, and then startled her by pulling her to him, his arm around her shoulders.

"Mother, Dad, listen here. This is a miracle. She had a vision of this."

Bear scowled. "The hell."

"No, Dad, she did. She foretold of it. After the shearing we were up talking in the barn, and she vowed and declared we had to come up here. That's why I kept on telling you we should. She said there was something big up here in our own backyard."

Dellarobia felt a dread of her secrets. She recalled only her impatience, speaking to Cub in anger that night, telling him anything could be up here. Terrorists or blue trees.

Hester peered into her face as if trying to read in bad light. "Why would he say that? That you foretold of it."

A movement of clouds altered the light, and all across the valley, the butterfly skin of the world transfigured in response, opening all the wings at once to the sun. A lifting brightness swept the landscape, flowing up the mountainside in a wave. Dellarobia opened her mouth and released a soft pant, anticipatory gusts of breath that could have become speech or laughter, or wailing. She couldn't give it shape.

"Here's your vision. I see a meddling wife." Bear shook his head in weary disgust, a gesture that defined

74

him, like the dogtags he still wore after everyone else had given up on his war. A large and mighty man among the trifling, that was Bear's drill. "You all need to get down off your high horses," he said. "We're going to spray these things and go ahead. I've got some DDD saved back in the basement."

"You've got 3-D in your basement?" asked Norwood.

"DDT," Cub told him. "Dad, that stuff has been against the law for more than my whole life. No offense, but it must be something else you've got stored."

"Why do you think I saved it up? I knew it would be hard to get."

"That stuff's bound to go bad on you," Hester argued. "After this many years."

"Woman, how is poison going to go bad? You reckon it'll get *toxic*?" Bear laughed at his own joke. No one else did. Cub normally cowered like a cur under this tone from his father, but was strangely unyielding now.

"There's not enough spray in the world to kill that many bugs, Dad. That might not be the thing to do."

"I guess you've got money to make the equipment loan, then." Bear's eyes were the color of unpainted tin, and exactly that cold. Dellarobia kept her mouth shut. She knew they had received a down payment on the logging, already forwarded in part to the bank and the taxes. Two places, along with the grave, that didn't give back if you changed your mind.

"Listen, Dad. There's a reason for everything."

"That's true, Bear," Hester said. "This could be the Lord's business."

Cub seemed to flinch, turning to Dellarobia. "That's what *she* said. We should come up here and have a look, because it was the Lord's business."

Dellarobia plumbed her brain for what he might have heard her say, but came up empty. Once, in bed, he'd asked what she was smiling at with her eyes closed, and she'd mentioned colors moving around like fire. Only that. Cub now gazed at the sky.

"It's like the tenth wonder of the world," he said. "People would probably pay to see these things."

"That they might," Norwood agreed.

"We should wait till they fly off," Cub declared, as if he'd made such decisions before. "I bet we can get that much grace out of the company, Dad."

Bear exhaled a hiss of doubt. "What if they won't fly off?"

"I don't know." Cub still held onto Dellarobia by the shoulders. "Y'all just need to see the Lord's hand in this and trust in His bidding. Like she said."

This boldness was so unlike him, she wondered if Cub was play-acting, tormenting her as a reprisal. But deceits were beyond her husband's range. He just held her there like a shield in front of his chest. Hester and Bear were scarcely more than an arm's length away, and even that small distance between them filled now with butterflies, like water through a crevice. In every inch of the air they were moving down-mountain along this path, tumbling, a rush of air, a river in flood. She observed something like a diagram of wind resistance around her father-in-law's great bulk, made visible by the butterflies that followed smooth, linear paths over and around him. The people, she and the others here, were human boulders in the butterfly-filled current. They had waded into a river of butterflies and the flood gave no heed, the flood rushed on to the valley, answerable to naught but its own pull. Butterflies crossed her field of vision continuously at close range, black-orange flakes that made her blink, and they merged in a chaotic blur in the distance, and she found it frankly impossible to believe what her eyes revealed to her. Or her ears: the unending rustle, like a taffeta dress.

Hester's eyes dropped from her son's face to Dellarobia's, and what could possibly happen next, she had no idea. For years she'd crouched on a corner of this farm without really treading into Turnbow family territory, and now here she stood, dead on its center. She felt vaguely like a hostage in her husband's grip, as if police megaphones might come out and the bullets would fly. Looking down at her feet made her dizzy, because of butterfly shadows rolling like pebbles along the floor of a fast stream. The illusion of current knocked her off balance. She raised her eyes to the sky instead, and that made the others look up too, irresistibly led, even Bear. Together they saw light streaming through glowing wings. Like embers, she thought, a flood of fire, the warmth they had craved so long. She felt her breathing rupture again into laughter or sobbing in her chest, sharp, vocal exhalations she couldn't contain. The sounds coming out of her veered toward craziness.

The two older men stepped back as if she'd slapped them.

"Lord Almighty, the girl is receiving grace," said Hester, and Dellarobia could not contradict her.

3

Congregational Space

Dellarobia sensed troubled waters at the Café in Christ. Crystal Estep had parked herself at a table front and center, all done up for church, the waterfall of gel-stiffened curls cascading over her shoulders. A regular Niagara of blond highlights was Crystal, sitting alone with her breakfast, gazing at it with such earnest focus, you'd think she was on a first date with that Pepsi and glazed doughnut. People rarely worked up so much innocence without cause, it seemed to Dellarobia. She looked around for the rest of the story and located it near the juice machine, where two tables were occupied by the ex-friend Brenda, of hand-slammed-in-the-car-door fame, and a posse of her mad-looking friends. Dellarobia remembered the injured party was this particular Brenda, one of three sisters who ran the church nursery with their mother. Brenda appeared to be out on disability today, flashing the metal splint on her two middle fingers, basically flipping Crystal the bird in church.

No way was Dellarobia getting involved. The main point of coming to church was to drop off Preston and Cordie in the Sunday school building and take a breather from squabbles over who hit the other one first. Evidently Crystal had already taken Jazon and Mical over there, pawning them off on Brenda's kin. That must have been interesting. Dellarobia downed her scalding coffee in a couple of gulps where she stood, tossed the styrene cup in the trash, and headed down the hall for the sanctuary. The heels of her oxblood boots struck the waxed floor loudly, advertising her traveling whereabouts like a GPS. A disappointed-looking Jesus eyed her from the wall. She'd ruined herself on these boots for sure, by donning them a month ago for the purpose of committing adultery. *Look, look,* her steps called out, *here is a redheaded sinner on the move.* She felt out of control in some new way, unfixable, unless she could fold her life back into its former shape: pre–Turnbow Family Sideshow, premarriage, back to being just one kid trying to blaze her own trail. It was exhausting, to keep being sorry for everything. Sorry she'd had to run out of the café just now. Bereft, actually, over that one. The café had definitely upped her quality time at Mountain Fellowship since it opened in September. The church was a thriving little village of its own, with new kinds of congregational space forever being discussed or under construction. The modular Sunday-school structure had been replaced last year with a red schoolhouse affair, and now with the new wing open, a person could walk around a good deal without technically leaving church. An enclosed walkway connected the sanctuary to the Men's Fellowship room and the sunny, tile-floored Café in Christ, where she could sit and have some alone time with a blueberry muffin, with other congregants who would just as soon get their sermon over closed-circuit. The view of Pastor Ogle's giant pixellated face on the multiple TV screens was perfectly up-close and personal if you didn't need the live experience, which she did not. Church attendance was a condition of her marriage. Cub felt if they laid out on Sundays, his mother would either drop dead or disown him, and he didn't care to find out which. Dellarobia would have been willing to give it a test run. But no, they went.

It did get her out, among people. Whether friend or foe hardly mattered; they ate with their mouths closed and wore shoes without Velcro. She hadn't been much of a player in public after the diner closed six years ago, and she hadn't planned on missing those long days on her feet or the wages that barely covered her gas. But being a stay-at-home mom was the loneliest kind of lonely, in which she was always and never by herself. Days and days, hours and hours within them, and days within weeks, at the end of which she might not ever have gotten completely dressed or read any word longer than *Chex*, any word not ending in *-os*, or formed a sentence or brushed her teeth or left a single footprint outside the house. Just motherhood, with its routine costs of providing a largesse that outstripped her physical dimensions. She'd seen ewes in the pasture whose sixty-pound twins would run underneath together and bunt the udders to release the milk with sharp upward thrusts, jolting the mother's hindquarters off the ground. That was the picture, overdrawn. A gut-twisting life of love, consecrated by the roof and walls that contained her and the air she was given to breathe.

But here was church. An hour in the café, the slake of a tall cup of coffee, and stillness, and wearing shoes, a clean tile floor, time off for good behavior. A reminder that she could belong to something the size of this con-gregation, if they would have her. She was not outside the believer realm entirely. She'd had her phases. Back when her daddy lost everything at once—his furniture-making business, his health, his inner light—she'd prayed for Jesus to bring it all back. When he died, her mother resigned from religion and left Dellarobia working a double shift. By the time her mother got sick, the whole enterprise was tainted with doubt. Cub had persuaded her to give prayer another shot during the years when they were trying and failing to get preg-nant, and finally that one had been answered times two, Preston and Cordie, sufficient for the time being.

So she was what Hester called a 911 Christian: in the event of an emergency, call the Lord. Unlike all those who called on Jesus daily, rain or shine, to discuss their day and feel the love. Once upon a time she'd had her mother for that. Jesus was a more reliable backer, evi-dently, less likely to drink himself unconscious or get liver cancer. No wonder people chose Him as their number-one friend. But if the chemistry wasn't there, what could you do? Dellarobia scrutinized life too hard, she knew that. For a year she'd gone with Cub to Wednesday Bible group and loved the sense of being back in school, but her many questions did not make her the teacher's pet. Right out of the gate, in Genesis, she identified two completely different versions of how it all got started. The verses could be a listen-and-feel kind of thing, like music, she'd suggested, not like the instruction booklet that comes with a darn appliance. A standpoint that won no favors with the permanent discussion leader, Blanchie Bise, cheerleader for taking the Word on faith. For crap's sake, the first rule of *believable* was to get your story straight. Hester let Dellarobia stop coming to Wednesday Bible.

She paused in the doorway of Holy Beacons, the name given the sanctuary, where anyone present might be called out by Pastor Ogle as a beacon. The newly remodeled sanctuary was huge. This church was the biggest show in Feathertown by far. Bobby Ogle pulled people out of bed from far and wide on Sunday mornings, even from the larger town of Cleary, fourteen miles away. Dellarobia studied the backs of all those heads, the females vivid with individualized hues, the males surprisingly uniform. Three hundred people quieting down, readying themselves for what they were about to receive. The nourishment was so real to them. Dellarobia felt a stab of envy, as if everyone here was getting a regular paycheck and only hers bounced. It made no sense. Up on the mountain that first day, she'd had no trouble believing in some large glory tailor-made for herself, but here in this fold she struggled with everlasting doubts as to her status. The sole glory she could hold in mind at the moment was the blueberry muffin she'd planned to buy in the café. She craved it like a cigarette: the sticky, too-big puffiness of that muffin spilling over its fluted paper cup, crumbling all over the table, sweetly filming her throat with whatever it was those things had. Probably something that bunged your arteries like bacon grease in a drain. She weighed her options: that muffin, Crystal, Brenda. No. She located the back of Cub's head towering over his mother's and moved down the center aisle toward them, avoiding eye contact with the sanctuary regulars.

She scooted in next to Cub. He was thrilled, reaching for her hand and threading his big fingers through her little ones. It was mildly painful but authenticating, to have him lay claim to her here in front of Hester and God, in case either of them was looking. That was one thing she could do well, make Cub happy, if only she could apply herself. She took this vow as regularly as she breathed, and reliably it was punctured by some needling idea that she was cut out for something more. Something, someone. She leaned against his shoulder and sighed, wistful for the breakfast that almost was. She could make it through another hour if her stomach wouldn't growl.

She watched Pastor Ogle walk onto the stage, dressed exactly as usual in jeans and an open-collar shirt, nothing out of the ordinary. Yet the congregational atmosphere shifted like weather. Given the drawing in of breath, the speculative waiting, Bobby Ogle could be that famous groundhog that would or wouldn't see his shadow. If she ever had people's attention like that, even for ten seconds, there was no telling what she'd say. Bobby was amazing. And he hadn't even called the faithful to order yet, he was just checking in with the choir director before the opening hymn. She'd seen TV preachers with styled hair and diamond rings that sparked in the studio lighting, and wondered how anyone trusted such showy men with their tithes. Pastor Bobby was the opposite, possessed of the same rumpled appeal Jesus probably had. Maybe in this day and age Jesus would buy his clothes at the outlet stores where the Ogles shopped, and shed the hippie haircut for one like Bobby's, with bangs straight across. He looked like some kid you'd want to invite home for dinner. Though Bobby, unlike Jesus, might empty your fridge. He must weigh 280 at least. He'd played football for the Feathertown Falcons, as Cub did five years later when he got to high school. She happened to know they'd called him Titty Ogle back then, due to his anatomy. Kids are evil. Which of these congregants remembered that now? She'd bet money that some of these churchful people had once laughed at Bobby Ogle in his football uniform with his chest bob-bob-bobbing along the fifty-yard line. But he had made something of himself, gone to seminary school, founded this church with his wife, and raised up a set of twin girls, never allowing bitterness to curdle his spirit. His face told the whole story now, as he listened to the choir director: pure patience. Even though most people found Nate Weaver way too full of himself. Nate seemed dressed for a whole different show, packed into his shiny brown suit like a sausage casing, and his new little goatee did nothing to hide his double chin, if that's what he was thinking. Dellarobia knew these thoughts made her a small person.

Pastor Ogle could look past petty things. He clapped Nate kindly on the shoulder and walked to center stage to stand a moment in the bright stage lights with his head bowed, no notes in hand. No pulpit. Just plain Bobby, standing on the pool of his own shadow. He motioned then for the congregation to stand for the hymn, "What a Friend I Have in Jesus," and all rose. Mr. Weaver pumped his hand to direct the choir in the too-vigorous way that got on Dellarobia's nerves. Hester was hogging the hymnal, making Cub share it on her side, managing to imply even in the Lord's abode that three was a crowd. She looked fanciful as ever today, in a blue dress with a ruffled stand-up collar of the type Loretta Lynn made famous at the Grand Ole Opry. Pastor Ogle had lured Hester over from a harder line of Baptists, and Dellarobia knew some marital compromise was involved. Bear had stopped attending over there. Here he could sit out the service in Men's Fellowship, which had checkers and country music pitched low enough you could still hear the sermon on the closed-circuit if you so desired. Bobby had found the key to modern believers: that many preferred their salvation experience to come with a remote.

Dellarobia thought Men's Fellowship had its appeal, all the more so right now as the audience heaved into verse four of "What a Friend," dragging it like a plow through heavy clay. Certainly in Men's Fellowship no one ever made you sing. She just wished it had a more welcoming vibe for the female of the species. She'd strolled through a time or two to retrieve a Diet Coke out of the machine, and observed that they even allowed smoking. The family always split four ways, Bear going with the men, the kids to the Sunday school, she to the café, and Hester to the sanctuary with Cub in tow, playing her boy like a trout on a line, always reeling him in at the end. Dellarobia had tried to get Cub to go with her to the café, which was mostly younger women, but also some couples, "Christ's love everywhere in equal measure" being the theme of the Ogle ministry. But there was no battling Hester, she was wired to win, just made that way: sinewy, righteous, unbeatable.

Soft, round Bobby was precisely the reverse. He won people over in a different way, using his hands to push and pull his congregants as if kneading dough and making grace rise. Like a humble baker making bread. He was actually a foundling, people said, abandoned at birth, adopted by an elderly minister and his wife who'd since passed away. Dellarobia wondered what that would feel like, to have no inkling of your people. All hers were dead, but at least a known quantity. Bobby dedicated every Mother's Day sermon to the saintly woman who'd taken him in, heeding God's call to embrace the rejected and discarded. Bobby was love personified, to the extent that this was rumored around town to be a no-heller church. Or that in Bobby Ogle's version of heaven everyone would wind up in one place, criminals and Muslims included. Dellarobia could not confirm or deny the accusations; in Bobby's light all things seemed possible. The way he was warming up right now, with everyone singing happiness and love in his general direction, his body seemed to be manufacturing some kind of vitamin from the gaze of the worshippers. Hester's ponytail practically flapped in the breeze of hallelujah.

After the hymn Bobby said quietly, "Would you be seated," no question mark, his hand moving toward the floor as if urging a dog to sit. They sat. Dellarobia kept her eyes open during prayers, a long habit, just a watchful person by nature. She quietly snapped open her purse and made sure her phone was on vibrate, since Dovey liked to text her on Sunday mornings for her own entertainment. There was one waiting now: COME YE FISHERS OF MEN: YOU CATCH, GOD WILL CLEAN. Dovey's fondness for one-liners-in-Christ was bottomless, she collected them off church marquees. Back before texting, she used to pass them over during health or history class on scrims of folded paper. Dovey was Italian Catholic, she and her five brothers with all that darling mess of dark curly hair, and claimed she'd logged enough church hours in childhood to do her for life. Dellarobia fished her glasses out of her purse and put them on, possibly to spite her mother-in-law. "Boys don't make passes at girls wearing glasses," Hester liked to singsong, a joke so tired she could scream. If boys didn't, the woman would not have the grandkids she did at this point in time. People could overlook anything when it suited them, right down to the making of the Lord's baby children.

Bobby wound up the prayer with a reminder to hold the sick and beleaguered in their hearts, and named off congregants who could use that kind of help. The list was impressive. He never used notes. She tried to put the near miss of the muffin out of her mind, but it loomed in the thought bubble over her head, attaining Goodyear-blimp size. Bobby's plaid shirt was from Target; she'd considered that same one, shopping for Cub. No shiny suits for Pastor Ogle, he was not into things of this world. Just love. She caught his mention of upcoming Thanksgiving services before she zoned out again. Her mind was flipping through channels the way Cub did with the TV remote every evening, a form of persistent inattention that made her crazy, yet here she was. The blasted muffin would not leave her brain. They were supposed to go to Hester's for Sunday dinner. She remembered a navy blouse she'd borrowed from Dovey for a funeral back in June. Seeing Eula Ratliff in the choir had caused her to think of that. It was Eula's mother who died. That blouse could easily have hidden in Dellarobia's cramped little closet until someone else died—not that it mattered, her closet and Dovey's were more or less merged by now, they'd worn the same size since eighth grade. The *same* size, meaning they were the size of eighth-graders still. Dovey called that an achievement on Dellarobia's part, after three pregnancies, but to her mind fitting into a size zero did not count for much as an accomplishment. It sounded like nonexistence. She sometimes wondered if subconsciously she'd gone for Cub just for the increase in marital volume.

A couple ducked in late, slid into the pew next to her, and promptly closed their eyes in prayer, leaving Dellarobia free to scrutinize them. The man wore sporty sunglasses pushed on top of his head as if he'd just hopped out of a convertible. But if that was the wife with him, there was no convertible in the story. She'd probably spent two hours getting her hair organized and congealed, the bangs individually shellacked into little spears, all pointing eyeward, which made Dellarobia cringe. She had a thing about eyes. Preston had a habit that killed her, of poking himself along the hairline with his pencil while pondering what to write. Every pointed jab went into her own flesh, her own eyes wincing reflexively. She was tempted to hide his pencils.

The assistant pastor read a Bible passage about the Lord shaking the wilderness and making the oak leaves whirl, presumably to remind everyone it was fall. The man with the sporty sunglasses now seemed to be checking her out on the sly. Dellarobia had gone through her phase of miniskirts in church, egged on by Dovey, who once gave her a creepy antique fox stole with intact head and tail, on a dare that she would wear it here. That was pre-kids. Now she was lucky just to get everything zipped and buttoned, shooting for decency and not for show, a green turtleneck sweater and denim skirt today. But those boots. She ought to throw them in a river.

The choir lit into a rock-and-roll version of "Take My Life and Let It Be," with electric guitars, keyboard, and drums. The congregation was allowed to join in, but on the choir's special numbers the sound system gave them the upper hand and they always sounded great, like hymns on the radio. The pompous Mr. Weaver notwithstanding, the choir looked like they were having a barrel of fun. All except one older fellow who was too earnest, holding his hand to his chest as if asking Jesus to marry him, fearing the wrong answer. The rest looked thrilled, raising their eyebrows and singing an exclamation point at the end of every line: "Take my feet and let them be! Swift and beautiful for thee!" She picked out those who'd been in her graduating class: Wilma Cox in the gigantic checkered top. Tammy Worsham, briefly Squier and now Banning, with her blue eyeshadow and a little more cleavage than necessary for the eyes of the Lord, it could be said.

Quaneesha Williams, the sole African American choir member, who was jiggle-dancing to the music, plainly yearning to bust some bigger moves. Dellarobia was with her, everything here would go down better if you could dance. Some of life's greatest calls were answered not by the head but by the body. Which is what got her into trouble, of course, most lately with the telephone man. Who was she to judge Tammy's husband-collecting and cleavage? Her mood spiraled and crashed like a clipped kite.

Pastor Bobby launched his sermon with a quote from Corinthians: "Take captive every thought to make it obedient to Christ." Well, Dellarobia thought, read my mind, why don't you. She had all but flayed her flesh for months to stop thinking wrongful thoughts, and in the end what it took was a burning bush that turned out to be butterflies. Now she tried often to guide her mind back to the vision of those fiery hills, especially at night, hoping to lie down feeling like a person of some worth.

"Jeremiah seventeen-nine tells us about disobedient thoughts," Bobby said. "'The heart is deceitful above all things and beyond cure.' Now this is hard to admit, because it scares us, but it's true. Every one of us here, and I'm speaking of myself too, we can look something straight in the eye and give it a different name that suits us better." He had wide-set eyes and an entreating way of holding his hands palm-up. It was hard to imagine a lot of domestic drama at his house. But really, who didn't lie to himself? "We might call it ambition," Bobby said. "We might call it a great passion. When the true name of what we're dealing with is greed, or lust. We all have the special talent of believing in a falsehood, and believing it devoutly, when we want it to be true."

"Yes, brother," someone said softly from the darkness.

"That is how our Creator made us. He knows we are thus inclined."

Bobby again was answered with gentle assent. He looked out at his flock with the kindest gaze, like a father having an important talk with his young sons. "The Lord wants us to secure our hearts against things that lure us wrongly. When we're struggling with jealousy, and guilt, and impatience, and hardness of heart, and lust, He wants us to use our rational minds and call these things by their true names. We all want to be in our minds, and not out of them. We need them to behave. How do we do that?"

Dellarobia wondered how many others in this room felt he was reading off their personal résumé. If Bobby had a suggestion, she was all ears.

"There is no use in focusing on a bad thought and trying to chase it away," he said. "Really that just won't work. You'll see nothing in your mind's eye except the one thing you want to shut out. The hunter sees naught but that which he pursues. Do you hear me? You do. There is a different way to go. Philippians counsels us to replace a wrong thought with a good one. 'Brethren, fix your thoughts on what is true. Whatever is pure, whatever is lovely, whatever is gracious, if there is anything worthy of praise, think about these things. And peace will be with you.' "

Dellarobia was impressed with his construction of a persuasive paragraph and use of relevant references. She wondered if he'd taken Honors English in high school, rather than the Jock English they'd set up for football players, which basically required a pulse for a passing grade. She'd bet anything Bobby had taken Honors from Mrs. Lake, as she had, in which case he knew the difference between Homer's Ulysses and the one by James Joyce, and how to get down to business with a metaphor. Principles she had tried and failed to apply in Blanchie's Bible class. But here at least was a form of salvation Dellarobia could appreciate: a once-weekly respite from hearing grown-ups say "Lay down" and "Where at" and "Them things there."

Except that Bobby used *covenant* as a verb, and that really irked her. She'd noticed it before, and he was doing it right now. "Do you see what the Savior is trying to help us do? Can you covenant with me now to appreciate the wisdom of His advice?"

For crying out loud, she thought, how hard was it to say, "Enter into a covenant?" But Mrs. Lake had passed away, maybe the last one to care. The crowd was working up a lather now, calling out, "Yes, Brother Bobby, we do!"

In the café you got to skip the audience participation. She shrank into her green turtleneck. But Pastor Ogle wouldn't embarrass anyone, she knew. He worked the crowd's enthusiasm, encouraging people to share the burden of the hateful things that occupied their minds. No one was going out on a limb. "I have skirmished with evil business," was about as explicit as it went, and "I have trucked with falsehood." She could well imagine the skirmishes under discussion, the porno tapes these men were trying to throw away, the nips of whisky the women wished they didn't crave every afternoon, the minute they got the kids down for a nap. The whole crowd had don't-think-about-it blimps above their heads, which Bobby sweetly ignored.

"You've spoken honestly of the things that have hold of your mind," he said. "But what I want to ask you right now is, What do you love?" He nudged the question again and again, the way Roy and Charlie herded the sheep, gently prodding a wildly disjointed group toward a collective decision to move in a new direction. "What has the good Lord bestowed on your home and family that has brought grace to your life?"

Someone spilled out, "My little grandbaby Haylee!"

A long silence ensued, with many congratulating themselves, no doubt, on being less impulsive than the besotted grandmother. Some ruckus was also going on outside the doors, in the entry hall. Women shouting, barely audible, definitely not congenial.

Bobby covered the awkward moment, congratulating the gushing grandmother and putting her at ease. "Blessed are the little children," he said, "and it's a beautiful thing that you hold your little Haylee first in your heart. I want everyone here to covenant with Sister Rachel and proclaim her a beacon. I want you to tell it."

They told it. "Blessed be, Sister Rachel." The crowd was starting to warm. Dellarobia had rarely paid much attention to the shining of the beacons. But it was touching. An old man with a narrow chest in a big white shirt pulled himself to his feet. "Our daughter Jill has done got over the cancer and her hair grew back pretty. I praise the Lord for Jill's pretty yellow hair."

Dellarobia found herself joining in the blessing of Sister Jill's hair, feeling a startled gratitude she actually feared might lead to tears. There was no knowing what people held dear, it was one surprise after another as they called out the beautiful things: a new porch deck on a trailer home with a view of the sunset. The wedding of a disabled cousin. A pure white calf. Suddenly Cub was on his feet beside her, speaking up. Dellarobia felt unsteadied by his loud voice, almost singing. A beautiful thing like a heavenly host had come on their mountain, he said, and it was butterflies. "You all just can't imagine, it's like a world all to itself. I wish you all would come and partake of it."

"Brother Turnbow, I thank you for that invitation," Bobby said. "Truly I have to say it sounds like a miracle, what you're telling us."

"Praise the Lord," a few agreed, tepidly, in the same way people said, "Have a nice day," when they didn't care if you did. They seemed less convinced than

Bobby that a miracle had transpired on the Turnbow property.

Cub went a little defensive. "You'd have to see it to understand," he said. "My dad and mother can tell you. It's like nothing you ever saw. And she foretold of it, is the thing. My wife here foretold of it." He pulled Dellarobia to her feet, to her profound dismay. "My wife had like a vision or something. She said we all needed to open up our eyes and have a look before we started logging up there. She had this feeling something real major was going to happen on our property."

Dellarobia wasn't sure how public Bear wanted to go with the logging plan, and wondered if he was catching this now in Men's Fellowship, or just reading *Field and Stream*. The outburst was so unexpected, she was losing her footing. Bobby stood perfectly still, studying the family with his wide-set eyes. His gaze settled on Hester. "Sister Turnbow, tell me it's so," he said gently. "That your family has been blessed."

Dellarobia had never seen Hester so subdued. She would not want to disappoint Bobby. "It's true," she said in a soft growl, needing to clear her throat. "My daughter-in-law was the one that told us. I guess she foretold of it."

Dellarobia felt queasy. Cub gripped her around the shoulders hard, as if she might otherwise slide to the floor, which wasn't out of the question. His conviction floored her, and once again she wondered if he could be making a cruel joke to punish her. But these were guilty thoughts, the falsehoods of a poorly directed mind, as Bobby said, luring her from the truth. Cub was as trusting as a child, incapable of cruelty in church or anywhere else. And if that alone did not a marriage make, it still was worth something.

Escalating voices interrupted Cub's moment. Crystal and Brenda, it had to be, having it out in the hallway outside the sanctuary. "Don't you talk to my boys thataway!" one of them cried, and the other shrieked: "I'll slap those kids walleyed if they get up in my face again."

All eyes fixed on Cub, as if his earnest bulk might steady them against the storm outside the door. He stayed determinedly on track, his brow crumpled. "It's got us to thinking where the Lord must be taking a hand in things up there," he said. "We're supposed to be logging that mountain, but we're in a quandary now."

Dellarobia felt the doubtful stares. She'd been sitting it out every week in the café, drinking coffee and making her grocery list, in no way deserving of a miracle. And yet a small shatter of applause broke out, like a handful of gravel on a tin shed. Someone very close to them shouted: "Heaven be praised, Sister Turnbow has seen the wonders!" It was the man who'd come in late, with the sporty sunglasses on his head. And here she thought he'd been checking her out. Grace comes, motion and light from nowhere on that mountain in her darkest hour. She felt the dizziness coming back. It didn't help anything that she'd skipped breakfast. Cub slipped his arms under hers from behind, which may have looked like some unusual form of affection, but it was all that kept her vertical. The last thing she wanted this morning or ever was to be a display model on the floor of a church, but Cub walked her gently to the end of the pew and posted her in the center aisle, like a holy statue.

"Sister Turnbow," Bobby said, "your family has received special grace. Friends, are you with me? Sister Hester, will you covenant with us?"

It seemed like a dare. Hester looked like she'd swallowed a chicken bone. She was accustomed to special favor in all things church, and taking second fiddle to Dellarobia was not on the program. But there would be no slugging it out here. She conceded, "I will."

Pastor Ogle beamed first at Hester, then Dellarobia, as if lifting a big bouquet from the arms of one to the other. Welcome to the fold. He asked all those present to covenant with him in celebrating a beautiful vision of our Lord's abundant garden.

The doors at the back of the sanctuary flew open, admitting Brenda and Crystal in their own raucous packet of atmosphere. Actually it was Crystal versus Brenda's whole family, broken fingers and all. The mother led the pack, trailed by Brenda and the other two daughters, then Crystal, her hellion boys, and a slew of kids from the nursery swarming around the adults like sweat bees.

"I'm sorry for the interruption, Bobby," Brenda's mother said, cocking one hand on her hip, doing a poor job of looking sorry. That family reminded Dellarobia of the Judds, with the mother trying to out-pretty and out-skinny her daughters. Her hairdo was a fright, however. The battle must have come to blows. Pastor Ogle's hands came together as his mouth made a little O.

"I beg your pardon," she repeated, "but me and my daughters need to leave immediately for Brenda's personal safety, and we have got to return these children to their parents." She glanced around and made a defiant little side-to-side move with her head, like the saucy girls in music videos. "I'm sorry. If you all were about done."

The children charged down the aisle with Preston leading, headed for Dellarobia. He grabbed the hem of her sweater and pulled hard, as if he meant to climb her like a tree, and Cordie followed, wailing, with her arms upstretched. Other kids followed like panicked cats, and within seconds were hanging on Dellarobia too. Cub held on hard, keeping her upright. She felt like the pole in that famous statue of soldiers grappling the flag at Iwo Jima.

"Suffer the little children to come unto me," said Pastor Ogle with an appealing little chuckle, recovering his calm. "My friends, I want you to celebrate with all these little ones. I think they must know our sister here has received the grace."

Brenda's mother marched out one hip at a time, exiting with her entourage. The heavy double doors folded closed behind them as if in silent prayer. All eyes circled back from the rear of the sanctuary to the front, wheeling like a great flock of blackbirds flushed up from one place and settling down on another: the spectacle of Sister Turnbow. And it wasn't Hester. The family had a new beacon.

4

Talk of a Town

Hester called the butterflies "King Billies." She seemed to think each one should be addressed as the king himself. "There he goes, King Billy," she would say.

She said it now, in her kitchen. Dellarobia glanced up from her work but from where she sat with her back to the window, she couldn't see it. Instead she watched the butterfly pass in a reflected way as Hester, Crystal, and Valia all faced the morning-lit window and followed the motion with their eyes. Even the collies stood up, ears pricked, alert to the unusual human attention. If someone asked her later, Dellarobia realized, she might think she'd seen that butterfly herself. False witness was so easy to bear.

Seeing King Billy down here around Hester's house was becoming an everyday thing. On Thanksgiving Day, while Cub and the male Turnbow cousins were in the yard reliving their football days, Dellarobia and Preston had sat on the porch steps and counted the passing of eleven butterflies. She suspected they'd been sneaking up the valley to their convention all summer long. Possibly even for years. Everyone could have missed them, given the tendency for all eyes to remain glued to the road ahead and last month's bills. Bear's theory was that the insects had suddenly hatched and crawled out of the trees, which Dellarobia knew was ignorant. If they'd hatched, something had to go up there first and lay an egg. Even miracles were somehow part of a package deal.

"Where'd that name come from, King Billy?" Valia asked. She was fiddling with wet skeins of rainbow-colored wool that hung from an old wooden laundry rack and dripped onto a tarp spread underneath. She poofed and lifted the loops of yarn like a hairdresser working on a punked-out client.

"It's just something I learned from my old mommy," Hester said. "Valia, honey, you need to quit fussing with those skeins or they'll get felted together."

Valia pulled her hands back as if scorched. Hester was poking at her dye pots and didn't notice. She was looking particularly witchy today in her most ruined cowgirl boots and stained apron, with three enormous cauldrons boiling on her old monster of a stove. Witchy with a country-western motif. This was one of Hester's winter projects, dyeing all the yarn that remained unsold when the summer farm market in Feathertown closed for the season. The natural colors did okay, but people reached their limits on gray and brown. Hester's solution was to perk it up with color, and her instinct about that was right, every spring when the booth reopened, the customers were so fed up with winter they'd reach for anything bright. Like zombies stalking a heartbeat.

Dellarobia sat at the table preparing skeins for dyeing, with Cordelia close by in the wooden high chair that had once held her father and maybe her grandfather. This house was stuffed with Turnbow antiques, of the half-their-screws-loose variety. Dellarobia unfailingly checked the legs on that chair before inserting any child of her own, and had furthermore tied Cordie in with a dishtowel because there was no strap. The chair pre-dated the whole notion of child safety. Cordie was eating applesauce and occupying herself obligingly with the toy she called Ammafarm, a red plastic barn with levers that made animals come out and bleat their sounds. A city child would get a sorry education from a toy like this, as the cow, horse, dog, and chicken were approximately equal in size and all uttered the same asthmatic wheeze. None of that bothered Cordelia. "Moooo!" she cried into the face of the petite cow that emerged from its flimsy door.

Dellarobia had asked Hester the same question about the name King Billy. Her mother-in-law had evidently paid some attention to butterflies in her time. She'd mentioned some others by name: swallowtails, tigers, the cabbage eaters. And King Billy, who had lately come to reign over their property.

"I didn't mind when it was just people from church coming up," Hester complained to Valia, "but now everybody and his dog wants the grand tour. After it came out in the paper. It was about thirty of them up here the Friday after Thanksgiving. I want to tell you!

That's not normal, for the day after Thanksgiving."

"No, it isn't," Valia agreed. "People should be at the mall."

"Dog says wow wow wow!" Cordie announced, bobbing her head. Dellarobia had managed to corral her fleecy hair into two wild blond poofs, with a center part so crooked it could get you a DUI, and that was the sum total of grooming the child would presently allow. Dellarobia harbored a secret fondness for that wild streak, something she herself had swallowed down long before her daughter was born, only to see it erupt again in Cordie like a wet-weather spring.

"That article in the paper was good, wasn't it?" Valia said. "I cut it out and saved you an extra copy. Help me remember that, Crystal, it's in my purse."

Crystal, being in Crystal-zone, scowled deeply into her cell phone. She was supposed to be helping with the wool, but had yet to pick up a skein.

Dellarobia knew what Hester had thought of the newspaper article. The reporter was a girl from Cleary, a town fifteen miles down the road where people went to college so they could regard people in Feathertown as hicks. When she'd shown up here in pressed slacks and pointy-toed shoes, Hester had driven her up the mountain in the ATV to see the butterflies, but the reporter only wanted to discuss Dellarobia. Not *actual* Dellarobia, but the one who'd had a vision, who could see the future, who probably peed on dead flowers and made them bloom. Dellarobia had no idea the talk had gone so crazy. She'd barely adjusted to her place in the center of a family controversy before being thrust into the limelight of a church congregation. And now this, the talk of a town. The reporter made Hester come straight back down to Dellarobia's house for a highly unfortunate thirty minutes. The girl had a camera. Dellarobia wore sweatpants and the universal whale-spout hairdo of exhausted mothers. Cordie had skipped her nap and was tromping around the living room with her boots half off, emitting a volcanic eruption of demands, spit, and tears. It was not an environment conducive to journalism. All Dellarobia wanted was to escape the newspaper girl's weird line of questions.

Cub had puffed up like a rooster when the article came out, taking it in to show the guys at the gravel company. He was impressed with all celebrity in equal measure, the type of kid who had cut out pictures of football players, Jesus, and America's Most Wanted to tape on his bedroom wall. He'd confessed to having cried in sixth grade when he learned that superheroes weren't real. Dellarobia was his Wonder Woman. But Hester seemed incensed by the article, which referred to Dellarobia as Our Lady of the Butterflies. Among other complaints, Hester said it made them sound Catholic.

The day darkened outside and thunder rumbled, an unusual sound for the first of December. Rain began to slash at the window, giving the kitchen a closed-in feeling that did not help Dellarobia's prickly impatience.

She put no stock in the sainthood business, but what if this winter was meant to be her one chance at something huge, and she spent the whole thing tying yarn in loops and listening to the Hester channel? She noticed that Cordie had changed the subject of her monologue from "moo" to "poopoo."

"My sentiments exactly," Dellarobia griped quietly, pouting at the armload of skeins Valia was bringing over to plop down on the table between herself and Crystal. The mound of grayish yarn in front of her was already gigantic. She felt like a picky-eating toddler having a spaghetti nightmare. They'd ended this year with more unsold goods than usual, which stood to reason, given the economy. Her job in today's production was to tie each drab skein in a loose figure eight so it wouldn't tangle up in the dye bath, and put it in the sink to soak in Synthrapol while awaiting its makeover. Hester mixed the dye powders based on the weight of goods, and tended the cauldrons. Valia weighed the skeins prior to processing, and Crystal did nothing whatsoever.

"Are we coming to any kind of a stopping place?" Dellarobia asked, wondering if Crystal might get the hint and start helping. "Because I can't stay much longer."

Hester and Valia ignored her. They were discussing the details of the upcoming visit of Pastor Ogle. "Do you think I should move this table out and get a better one in here?" Hester fretted. "Mommy's antique one is up in the attic, we could bring that down. It's smaller, but it's not all scarred up like this one."

The scar she meant was a darkened crescent in the center of the table that now stared at Dellarobia like an eye. During the brief time she and Cub had lived in this house, between their hasty wedding and the rushed completion of their home, Dellarobia had marred the kitchen table with a hot skillet. She'd been seventeen, for Pete's sake. The skillet was burning her hands through the potholders. For these many years that burn mark had remained for Hester what might be called a conversation piece.

"Could you use a tablecloth?" Valia asked. "What are you going to serve him?"

"I thought we'd have coffee and cake. A jam cake, I'm thinking."

Valia nodded thoughtfully, as if foreign policy were on the hook here. "That caramel icing is a dickens to make. But you're right, I bet Bobby would love that. You could use placemats on the table. A centerpiece or something."

"Do you think just coffee and cake will be enough?"

"Alien alert," Dellarobia muttered, finally getting Crystal to glance up from her phone. "Hester just asked your mom for advice."

Crystal's eyebrows arched. "So?"

So, Dellarobia thought, she's had a personality transplant. The idea of Pastor Ogle visiting her home was cranking her into nervous overdrive. It was surprising, actually, that Hester hadn't had him in before. Bobby visited parishioners and their jam cakes with gusto. But the real shock was seeing Hester cowed by the prospect.

"Poopoo!" Cordie shouted again, kicking her legs vigorously to get her mother's attention. She was reaching toward the table with her fingers stretched as wide as they would go, like little starfish.

Dellarobia followed her gaze to a jar of dye powder. "Oh. Purple?" she asked.

"Pupuw," Cordie replied, giving her mother a look of exhausted relief.

"Sorry, baby. Like, *hello*, you're trying to say something here." She kissed her fingertips and reached over to touch the sugarplum nib of her daughter's nose, provoking a blinky grin. Dellarobia picked up another jar. "What's this one?"

"Geen!"

"Hester, did you hear that? Cordelia knows her colors."

Hester appeared unimpressed with her genius grandchild, as only Hester could. Apparently she only had eyes for Bobby Ogle. Dellarobia studied the label on the jar. It had so many warnings, if you read all the way to the end you'd probably want to run for your life. She took a second look at Hester's giant kettles, wondering if they were the same ones they used for the tomato and pickle canning in summer. "You think it's okay for Cordie to be eating applesauce in the presence of"—she studied the tiny print—"tri-phenyl-methane?"

"Cub used to just about drink this stuff whenever we dyed the wool," Hester replied curtly. "And look at him."

No one responded to this. In the awkward moment, Cordie flung her spoon across the table and let loose a string of vowels that made both the dogs look up, wondering if they'd missed something. Dellarobia leaned over to retrieve the spoon. "Maybe we should try doing different colors this time," she proposed. As colorful as Hester was, her dyeing was uninspired. She stuck with the packaged colors, which had alluring names like Amazon and Ruby, but came out plain old green and red. Much like life itself.

"What's wrong with my colors," Hester asked, not really asking.

"We could mix it up a little. I'm sure you could blend these powders together to get in-between colors."

Something between tomatoes and a ladybug, he'd said, touching her hair as if its color alone held exquisite value. Sometimes this still came over her in surprise attacks, the illicit flattery. And all the shame she had to bear, looking back on that, wondering how she'd been taken in. Again. She'd fallen before, never that hard maybe, but that stupidly. Two years ago, the man with sky blue eyes at Rural Incorporated who'd helped her week after week with the Medicaid papers when she was pregnant with Cordie. Before that, the mail carrier, Mike, who sometimes subbed their route. And Cub's old friend Strickland with the biceps and his own tree-trimming business. She knew there was something wrong with her. Some insidious weakness in her heart or resolve that would let her fly off and commit to some big nothing, all of her own making.

Hester and Valia had returned to their earlier topic of the visitors who'd been showing up to look at the butterflies. Hester became herself again, begrudging the presence of a miracle in her vicinity. Bobby's impending visit had let loose the floodgate of his followers, and Bear and Hester seemed to be butting heads over their next move. The miracle was whatever it was, but a logging contract was money in the bank.

Cordie had meanwhile discovered the game of Make Grown-Ups Jump. She threw her spoon on the floor next to Crystal's green Crocs, and watched Crystal's face closely for results. Crystal declined to be distracted from her phone's tiny keyboard, working so desperately to communicate with her two thumbs that the gesture struck Dellarobia as somehow monkeylike. It also struck her that there was no cell signal in this house.

"Crystal, if you can work it into your agenda, could you pick up Cordie's spoon?"

Crystal looked at the floor. "You want me to wash it?"

"Eat a peck of dirt before you die!" chimed Valia, without looking up from her sums. She had to keep track as she weighed the skeins, penciling her numbers in careful columns, and was doing it with what Dellarobia felt to be a desperate air, as if keeping score of some game she was bound to lose. What a mother-and-daughter pair, those two. Valia had no opinions of her own, apologized to her shadow, and did exactly as she was told, all of which signed her on as Hester's BFF. Whereas Crystal lived the whole mistake-parade of her life as the majorette, bowing to the applause, ready to sign autographs. Crystal put the *con* in self-confidence. How could two people get the same set of parts and make such different constructions? But then, there was raising. That had to be taken into account. What could a doormat rear but a pair of boots?

Crystal announced suddenly, "Here's what you ought to do, about all these people coming up? You should charge them."

"See, that's what I told Bear," Hester said. "We both think that."

"What's stopping you, then?" Valia asked.

Hester raised her eyebrows and pointed her chin at Dellarobia, as if her daughter-in-law were a child, oblivious to the codes of adults.

"Hey, don't look at me. Your son's the one that spilled the beans in church, blame him." Dellarobia got up and dumped an armload of tied bundles into the sink. Brethren, fix your thoughts on what is true. Bobby's words came to her out of the blue, and she nearly spoke them aloud. Instead she said, "Let's blame Bobby Ogle, while we're at it. And Jesus, why not Jesus? Credit where credit is due."

"Missy, you are asking for it with talk like that."

"It's Mrs. And you know what? I *never* said it's the Lord's divine hand at work up there. Go ahead and charge people if you want. Why wouldn't you?"

Hester met her eye, and they held a moment in deadlock. The words *born again* rose to Dellarobia's mind, and she contemplated a world where Hester no longer scared her. To turn her back on permanent rebuke, and find other motives for living, wouldn't that be something. Like living as a no-heller, as Bobby was said to be. All recent events considered, Dellarobia didn't mind this part. She turned away, untying the dishtowel that held Cordie in place and using it to scrub the worst of the applesauce from the creases around her chubby wrists. "Sorry to run," Dellarobia said, "but we are out of here. I've got to meet the school bus in front of my house at twelve-seventeen."

"You let Preston ride the bus?" Hester challenged.

"Yep. He wants to ride the big-boy bus. So today I let him. I've got to get over there so he won't wander off down the road. I'm taking Roy with me, okay? That will thrill Preston, to see Roy waiting for his bus."

"Take both the dogs," Hester said.

"No, the kids get too cranked up with both of them." She gave the high chair a lick and a promise with the dishcloth and lifted Cordelia out of it by her armpits, inhaling her sweet-sour baby scent like smelling salts, a bracing relief. With Cordie on her hip, Dellarobia whistled softly and called Roy by name as she left the kitchen, telling Charlie to stay down. To her dismay,

Crystal rose as if she too had been whistled up, announcing she had to go get her boys too. She followed outside and stood by as Dellarobia opened the back door of her station wagon for Roy, then buckled Cordie into her car seat. Dellarobia could feel the rain in little icy pricks on the gap between her sweatshirt and jeans when she leaned into the car.

"You buckle her in, even just to go to your house?" Crystal asked.

"Ninety percent of accidents happen within one mile of home." Dellarobia had no idea if this was true, and honestly might not have bothered with the car seat if she hadn't had the world's laziest mother in attendance. Someone had to set an example.

"It's not a mile to your house. It's like, two hundred feet."

"What's up, Crystal? First and third grade don't let out until afternoon. Don't tell me Jazon and Mical got demoted back to half-day kindergarten."

Crystal rearranged her face, going for wide-eyed and perky. "I just thought we could talk for a few minutes."

"What would you like to talk about?"

"Nothing. Just, stuff."

Dellarobia got in the car and sat with the door open, hands on the steering wheel, waiting. She knew Crystal wanted something; the girl was permanently set on intake mode. Dellarobia went for preemptive. "I am not babysitting your kids."

"I'm not asking!"

"Could I get that in writing?"

The rain was starting to pick up, but Crystal remained planted. People always laughed at rain and said, "You won't melt," but Crystal's body mass was probably 35 percent makeup and hair products. She actually might melt. Dellarobia sighed. "Get in."

Crystal walked around to the passenger's side, flopped in, and conspicuously clicked her seat belt. "Do you really have to be so . . ."

They completed the ninety-second ride to Dellarobia's driveway before Crystal had advanced this line of inquiry. Roy's black-and-white body poured out of the car and swirled in figure eights on the lawn, eager for whatever project he was here to begin.

"Roy, down," Dellarobia said, and he lay flat on the watery lawn before she even had both syllables out. The grass was still faintly green, not yet winter-killed, as they'd had no snow or even a hard frost. Cordie didn't have a proper winter coat, just doubled-up sweatshirts. It wasn't negligence—the kids truly had not needed bundling up yet, the weather had failed to nudge them to Target or the Second Time Around shop for that purpose. The idea of December seemed impossible. A few times when people had asked if she was ready for Christmas, she'd actually drawn a blank: ready for what? And of course felt idiotic afterward. People automatically estimate a mom's IQ at around her children's ages, maybe dividing by the number of kids, rounding up to the nearest pajama size. But the weird weather must have bewildered everyone to some extent. On stepping outdoors she sometimes had to struggle a few seconds trying to place the month of the year, and Cub had said the same. It felt like no season at all. The season of burst and leaky clouds.

Dellarobia set her mind to the worries at hand: Preston's first time on the bus. The driver wouldn't know his stop unless she stood out here by the road. It might even come early. The rain was getting serious, but she couldn't risk going in the house for an umbrella. A five-year-old was too young for the bus. What had she been thinking? Sending him off among strangers was chilling enough, without some distracted bus driver in the mix. She planted herself at the end of the drive between their mailbox and a big old maple, and sent Crystal after the umbrella.

Crystal went in the house and took her sweet time about it. Dellarobia unzipped her hoodie and draped it over Cordie, who was getting soaked. The cattle in the waterlogged pasture across the road raised their heads in brief attention, welcoming her to the sad-sack club. Her phone buzzed, and she fished it from her shoulder bag left-handed with Cordie on her other hip. A text from Dovey: MOSES WAS A BASKET CASE. Dovey swore these adages were genuine, sighted during church drive-bys, usually on her way to work, and maybe that was true. The commercial-type marquees seemed to draw churches into the same competitive cleverness that ruled all advertising. But she suspected a Dovey original here. With her one free thumb she texted back: U R 2.

At length Crystal arrived with the umbrella and they huddled under its greenly lit shelter. It was close quarters in there, given the dimensions of Crystal's hair. Roy sat obediently at Dellarobia's knee but sidled close against her leg as the dampness grew. Cordie, from her hipbone perch, waved at the passing cars and rhythmically kicked her muddy shoes against Dellarobia's thigh. Every pair of jeans she owned was stained with footprints. If she was already a doormat, were her kids then doomed?

A red Chevy pickup slowed almost to a stop, at such close range they could hear the slapping windshield wipers and see the guy inside, checking them out on the drive-by. For heaven's sakes, mothers of children, waiting for a school bus.

"That was Ace Sayers," Crystal said, when the truck had passed. "Somebody told me he had a colonstopy."

"Thank you for sharing."

"So," Crystal said. "I was going to ask you something."

"Imagine my surprise."

"Dell, I swear. Just because everybody at church thinks you're a saint? I'm sorry. But I don't see why I have to kiss your butt."

"Alrighty then, don't. Don't call me Dell, though. I got burned on that one when I started going out with Cub."

"How come?"

She sang it: "*The farmer in the dell!*"

"Oh, right. Ick."

"*Ick* is one way to put it. And not Dellie, either. That would be one of those places where they hand you a sandwich."

Crystal gave her a worried glance. "What is this, the sign-up sheet for hanging out with you?"

"Yes."

They stood in silence while two more vehicles passed, both driven by elderly women, thankfully. Dellarobia wished she were not defensive about her name. In high school when the popular girls all won pert little tags like "Liz" or "Suze," she'd hoped for something snappier too, but that never worked out. Dellarobia she was to be, like the wreath in the magazine. Not a biblical heroine, just a steady buildup of odds and ends.

"Since you brought it up, is that what they're saying at church?" she asked Crystal. "That I'm a saint?"

"I wouldn't know."

She knew Crystal would try to be coy for about ten seconds, then dish the dirt. Three, two, one . . .

"Yeah, some of them are saying that. A whole slew of them, actually. Not the Worshams. The Bannings, the Weavers, and the Worshams? They don't believe it."

"Glad you took a poll."

"No, you know. People just talk. Some of them resents it, you know? That you're in Pastor Ogle's good graces without . . ."

"Without?"

"I guess, not being all that churchy."

"The wild girl that got kicked out of Wednesday discussion group, you mean."

"You did?" Crystal appeared amazed. Her entry into the fold was relatively recent.

"It was a long time ago. I thought 'discuss' meant open your mouth, my mistake. And it was Hester that kicked me out, just so you know. Not Pastor Bobby."

"Did you used to wear some kind of fox thing to church? Tammy said it was like this little shawl that went around your neck and had the head biting the tail."

"A fox stole. Dovey found it somewhere. I can't believe people are still holding that against me. Wouldn't there be, like, a statute of limitations on wardrobe offenses?"

"Okay, but there's other ones, like Sister Cox? She's all, love your neighbor and everything. I think they do believe something happened up on that mountain. Like, you know, a miracle. That's why they're all wanting to come up and see."

"Well, it's something to see. You'd be amazed."

Dellarobia had not been back up the mountain since the day with her in-laws. Hester had taken full charge of the traffic of visitors, which seemed unfair. Suddenly the butterflies belonged to Mountain Fellowship. The church and Hester had their own pet miracle. Not that tour guiding was a career option for Dellarobia, they wouldn't let her show up wearing a toddler as a pendant and a kindergartner for a shin guard. But still, when the groups passed behind her house to get to the High Road, Dellarobia snapped down the blinds, feeling something had been stolen from her, and flaunted.

"Listen," Crystal said. "What I was going to ask you? It's no big thing. I wrote this letter, and I wondered if you would look at it? You're good at spelling and stuff."

From the base of the big maple a squirrel darted out to the shoulder of the road, hesitated, then dashed across in little hops. Roy watched with keen attention, heaving a sigh of self-disciplined anguish.

"A letter, to?"

"To Dear Abby."

Dellarobia hooted, startling both Cordie and the dog. "You want me to proofread your letter to Dear Abby. What's it about?"

"That thing with Brenda. She's the one that thinks I—"

"I know, Brenda with the broken fingers and the whole family that wants to break your face."

"Okay, here's the thing, nobody's heard my side. I found out Brenda's mother was writing to Dear Abby asking her, you know, to settle it once and for all? But she's just going to play up Brenda's side, right? You know she will. I have to write one too."

"Where in the heck does Dear Abby come into this? I mean, jeez, Crystal, some old lady that lives a million miles from here. Who cares what she thinks?"

Crystal gave her a have-your-head-examined look. "Everybody cares what Dear Abby thinks. How do you think she gets in the paper every day?"

Dear Abby had a smart mouth and a kind heart, that's why people read her; the combination was rare. And rarer still, perfect grammar. Dellarobia used to read Abby faithfully, along with the police blotter and national news roundup, until Cub insisted they couldn't afford to renew their subscription to the *Cleary Courier*. She and Cub fought about it. Why pay for the news when you can see it on TV? was his argument. He would never stop channel-surfing long enough for her to get the end of the story, that was hers.

"You know what, Crystal? You go ahead and write your letter, but I think I'll just steer clear. I mean, holy cow, Brenda's mom. You do not want to meet that lady in a dark alley."

"I'm scared for my life, I kid you not," Crystal agreed. "And just so you know, before you look at my letter? I changed some things."

"Changed some of the facts, you're saying."

"No, just small things. Like I didn't mention the drinking, because that's nobody's business now. Clean and sober means starting over. And plus, I said, 'My husband and I,' instead of I'm a single mother."

Dellarobia wondered if this bus would arrive before Christmas. Cordie was writhing like an inchworm, wanting down, but they were too close to the road. And the rain was running in sheets across the asphalt. The ditch had become a creek, leaf-filled and rising. Her tennis shoes were goners. "Let me get this straight. You're fibbing to Dear Abby to get her on your side. And this will help your situation how?"

"Listen, you have no idea how people are. You're married."

"I thought I was suddenly the talk of the town."

"But *married*, okay? I just don't think Abby would give me a fair hearing if she knew my kids were illegitimate. I also told her I've accepted Christ as my personal savior."

"I don't think Abby cares that much. To tell you the truth, I think I saw somewhere she's Jewish."

"You are shitting me!"

At last the bus crested the hill, moving toward them like a golden cruise ship in its broad, square majesty. Dellarobia wanted to jump and wave for joy, rescued from her desert island. The usual parade of impatient drivers followed behind the bus, no doubt cursing their luck at getting trapped in slow-motion hell, stopping every hundred feet or so, with no hope of passing on this curvy road. Dellarobia thought of all the swear words she'd hurled from that position herself, and now as a newly minted mother-of-bus-rider she apologized from her heart to bus drivers everywhere. She wasn't sure if she'd need to flag it down, and was relieved when the amber lights began blinking from side to side. The stop sign swung out like a proud red wing. She waved to the driver, hoping to gain points with this woman who'd been charged with Preston's safety. But she was tugging at the bus window, one of those sliding affairs. It finally came down with a snap.

The driver called out, "Are you her?"

"Preston's mom," she replied, while Crystal simultaneously shouted, "Who?"

"Not you. Her. Is she the one that seen the vision."

"Oh, for crap's sake," said Dellarobia. She hoped that hadn't carried across the road to all those little ears.

"The butterfly lady," the driver persisted. "Are you the one?"

"I'm Preston Turnbow's mother. Have you got Preston on there?"

He popped out the door like the prize from a gumball machine, ablaze in his yellow hooded slicker and a smile so wide his face looked stretched.

"You stay right there, baby," she warned, crossing the road quickly to take his hand and escort him back across.

"Roy!" Preston shouted, running to hug the collie, throwing his arms around the white ruff that ringed Roy's neck. They all headed for shelter, with Crystal hanging on like a tick. Once they reached the dry porch, Dellarobia set Cordie on her own feet and took the umbrella, shaking off the raindrops.

"I want to see it too," Preston said.

"See what?"

"The butterfly thing."

"Not 'Hi Mommy' or how was your day. Just, I want to go see the butterflies."

He looked up at her with such a sorrowful, anxious face, she felt awful. Five and a half years of age, and already he had a worry line between his eyebrows.

"Please?" he said.

She knelt and set down the umbrella so she could put her hands on his shoulders and look him in the eye. "When do you want to go?"

"Now."

"In the rain?"

"Yes."

"It's a long way to walk. A *really* long way to walk."

He grinned. "Mama, duh! We can take the ATV."

"Ah. Your father's son."

Crystal had gone into the house with Cordie and already had the letter out of her purse. Dellarobia peeled off every soaked layer down to her bra, and buttoned on her hooded raincoat, kind of going commando just to save time and a clean shirt. It was getting toward dusk already. She found the ATV keys in the pocket of Cub's red jacket.

"Crystal, let's make a deal," she said. "You stay here with Cordie for an hour, and then I'll look at your letter. My son and I are going to look at butterflies in the rain."

∾

"I'm not very good at driving this thing," she warned. In truth she had never driven it out of the shed, but she was getting the hang. It was more like a riding mower than a car, but faster. She kept one arm clamped tightly around Preston in front of her on the seat, and bounced the two of them around a good bit before managing to slow the thing to a creep on the pasture's bumpy incline.

"It's bumpy when Daddy drives too," Preston offered tactfully. Cub had started taking Preston for rides when he was just tiny, and Dellarobia only allowed them to go in little circles around the yard. Cub was pretty cute, a mother hen himself, fussing with the baby carrier strapped to his barrel chest as he inched the vehicle's fat tires over the ground in fits and starts. It was hard to see the point of taking the child for a ride that went nowhere at zero miles per hour. But he was so proud to have a son.

At the top of the hill she figured out how to take it out of gear and lock the brake before she let Preston jump down and get the gate. She pulled through and he executed the chore of closing the gate with such diligence, all the livestock in the world might have depended on him. She reached inside her raincoat for a dry shirttail to clean Preston's glasses before they proceeded, and was startled to recall she had no shirt on under there. It was like some stunt she and Dovey used to pull, going out naked under their raincoats for kicks. Now her big thrill was just sparing herself the extra laundry. She fished a crumpled tissue from her raincoat pocket and carefully wiped his lenses, then her own, for their viewing pleasure. Ever since the so-called miracle, she'd been wearing her glasses at all times. To heck with boys and passes, she needed to see where all this was going. The High Road was easier to navigate, to her relief. The tires neatly grabbed its ruts, which had been worn by no vehicle other than this one, come to think of it.

"Are you hungry?" she asked. "Because it's kind of chilly. It makes you hungry, when you're wet and cold. We should go back and feed you if you're already starving." Preston was skinny and small for his age, and ran out of fuel easily. Nothing in reserve.

"The ladies feed us lunch at school," he said solemnly, as if reporting on something with which she might be unacquainted, such as prison conditions.

"Well, honey, I know they do. We send in your envelope. But sometimes when you get home you're hungry again." She wondered how soon he would figure out it was a government form, not lunch money, in that envelope. He was one of the free-lunch kids, as Dellarobia herself had been after third grade. A lineage.

Preston made no reply. She hoped he didn't think that she begrudged him his after-school hunger. Once when she was arguing with Cub about the light bill, they realized Preston was walking from room to room, turning off all the lights.

"It's no problem," she told him heartily. "Eating's good. That's how you get big. That's my favorite kind of boy: so hungry he could eat a horse."

He giggled, finally. It took some doing to cajole Preston into behaving like a regular child. She revved the motor a little. "If we see any horses we'll grab you a snack," she said, and he laughed louder.

"I could eat a dog!" he cried. "I could eat *Roy*!"

"Poor Roy, look out," she said. Dellarobia felt unexpectedly free, like a person going out on the town, even though she had technically not left the property.

"There goes King Billy," Preston said.

Her raincoat's hood was shutting out the upper half of her field of vision. "For real, you saw one already?" She slowed to a crawl before she felt comfortable taking her eyes off the track, leaning forward to peer up into the trees. Sure enough, there was his majesty wobbling through the rain. "You've got a good eye. That's what Mammaw Hester says, King Billy."

"What do *we* say?" he asked.

"The same, I guess." She wondered what tales Hester was telling people when they came up here. Dellarobia wished she knew the real names of things to give her observant son. Teachers used to get exasperated with her, the child with the unending questions, and now here was Preston way out ahead of her. She pushed back her hood, as the rain had mostly subsided. The bare trees dripped, but the sky was starting to lighten up. They neared the fir forest and found the air above the path alive with butterflies.

"Let's get off and walk from here," she said, relieved to cut the noisy engine and go on foot. She wanted to watch his upturned face. Despite the wet hair stuck to his forehead and raindrops stippling his wire-framed glasses, Preston was in heaven. "There-goes-King-Billy, there-goes-King-Billy!" he cried again and again, rolling the sentence out in the rapid-fire manner he used for yelling "Five-four-three-two-one-blastoff!" prior to launching flying objects. Soon there were too many kings for each one to get his own announcement, but Preston's mouth still moved silently.

Today there were not so many flying around as before. Not a river of motion, but stragglers adrift. Careening down the trail, they looked a little drunk or crazed, somehow.

"They're probably hungry too," Preston said. "What do they eat?"

"I have no idea," she confessed. He was right, they would surely need to eat, after hunkering in the rain for days without cease. She was embarrassed that her five-year-old was asking questions that had not occurred to her. But she refused to be first in the long line of people who would shrug him off. "We'll have to look that up."

"Look it up where?"

"Google it, I guess."

"Okay," he said.

Googling a butterfly. It sounded comical, like tickling a catfish, but she knew it wouldn't sound that way to Preston. He would clamber up to the computer at Bear and Hester's and punch the keys, finding what he needed in there. Having children was not like people said. Forget training them in your footsteps; the minute they put down the teething ring and found the Internet, you were useless as a source of anything but shoes and a winter coat. But Preston still asked her questions. That touched her, that they were a team. Here in the looming forest he gripped her hand tightly, as if crossing a street, as they approached the trees where the butterflies hung in their droves. Wings littered the ground. "Look up," she said, pointing at the brown clusters drooping from the branches. These trees were completely filled now. Even the tree trunks wore butterfly pelts, all the way up, like the bristling hairy legs of giants. It was a whole butterfly forest, magically draped with dark, pendulous clusters masquerading as witchy tresses or dead foliage. She only knew what they really were because her eyes had learned the secret. Preston's had not. It all waited for him, perfectly still and alive. She watched his dark pupils dart up and around, puzzling this out, looking without yet seeing. *Mine, ours*, her heartbeat thumped, making promises from the inside. This was better than Christmas. She couldn't wait to give him his present: sight.

"What is it?" he asked.

"That's the King Billies too. I know it looks weird, how they're all hanging down. But the whole thing is butterflies."

"Gaaa!" he cried, breaking free of her grip. He ran toward a monstrous bouquet that reached nearly to the ground from above, some thirty feet long, dwarfing a tiny boy. Before she could warn him against it, he reached up to stroke it with his hand, causing it to writhe and awaken. Wings opened and jockeyed within the clump. The lowest piece of the bristly string dropped off, landing with a plop on the ground. In slow motion it exploded, individual butterflies flapping, lifting, dispersing.

Preston looked back at her, expecting a reprimand.

"It's okay. You can check them out. Just be gentle, I guess."

She walked closer so she could see this as her son was seeing it. She hadn't examined the clumps at close range, and even now it was hard to understand how they were constructed. The butterflies didn't seem smashed or stuck to the wings of other butterflies, not like a hundred-car pileup, it was nothing so simple. They seemed to be holding on by their needle-thin front legs to some part of the tree itself, bark or branch or needle, out to the very tips. The tree's basic shape was still visible underneath, the column of trunk and broomlike sweep of the branches, but all enlarged and exaggerated by the hangers-on. Only at the ends of the dangling clusters did butterflies seem to be clinging to the legs of other butterflies. The insecure and the desperate, she thought. No world can be without them.

"Mama, they smell," Preston said.

She inhaled the air, realizing she hadn't had a cigarette for hours, but could not detect any odor. "Good or bad?" she asked. "What do they smell like?"

Very slowly Preston crossed the breach, moving his face through the last few inches between himself and this life form, until his nose touched it. He sniffed, and gave his verdict: "Good. A cross between lightning bugs and dirt."

e

Crystal met them at the back door with her coat already on and her purse slung over her shoulder, ready to light out of there. She had her Dear Abby letter in hand, but had put it back in its envelope.

"Crystal, I'm so sorry, I owe you. I do. We were longer than an hour. You can take my car if you need to go pick up your boys. Where's Cordie?"

"She's down for a nap. I'll just leave your car at Hester's, okay?" Crystal cut her eyes down the hallway and said in a low voice, "There's somebody at the front door."

Dellarobia saw that Roy had posted himself inches from the door, gazing directly as if he could see through the wood. He was not barking but moaning talkatively and waving the white flag of his tail tip in a slow circle. A reliable judge of character, was Roy. No real threat out there, but it needed attention.

"Who is it?"

"I don't know! They've been there, like, fifteen minutes?"

"Just standing there? Man or a woman?"

"It's a little family. A couple and a little girl."

"Good grief, Crystal, it's not an ax murderer if they brought a child with them. Maybe they need help or something. Why didn't you open the door?"

Crystal glanced sidelong at Preston and shielded the side of her mouth with the envelope. "They're foreign," she whispered.

Dellarobia stood momentarily dumbfounded, which Crystal took as her cue to exit via the kitchen door. Preston went to the front hall to stand with Roy, but she knew he wouldn't open the door, drilled as all kids were in stranger-danger. She peered out the windows in the upper part of the door, but saw nothing. She had to stand on tiptoe and look down before she could see them on the porch, the man and woman both about her own height, possibly even shorter. They looked Mexican, or very dark-skinned at any rate, especially the man. Jehovah's Witnesses? Did they travel the world for their cause?

She opened the door immediately. "May I help you?"

It was the little girl between the adults who spoke: "Preston!"

"Hi, Josefina," he said heartily, sounding like the man of the house.

Dellarobia looked from her son to this child and her parents. "Preston, is this a friend of yours?"

"She's in Miss Rose's room too," he said. The two of them hugged in an obedient, ritualistic way, like children at a family reunion, leaving Dellarobia to meet the parents' gaze feeling thoroughly adrift. The man had a large mustache and wore work clothes, a zippered jacket and billed cap. The wife was a bit more dressed up in a summery flowered shift under her blue cardigan. This family hadn't gotten around to the winter coats either, from the looks of it. They both pumped her hand firmly and said their names, Lupe and Reynaldo and a last name she instantly forgot.

"Well, come in," she said. The child said something to the parents, and they cautiously followed, wiping their shoes on the mat and entering the house so tentatively, Dellarobia had some difficulty getting the door closed behind them. She'd halfway unbuttoned her coat before realizing, startled again, she was half naked underneath. The wet clothes she'd stripped off earlier still lay in a puddle in the hallway. These people must think they'd come calling at a pig house.

"I am so sorry to keep you standing out there. We were out. If you all would please sit down in the living room, I'll join you in just one minute. Preston, would you be a real big boy and go to the kitchen and get everybody a glass of water?"

Again the girl spoke to her parents in Spanish, exchanging several sentences this time. Whatever she told them did the trick, as they walked directly to the sofa and sat down. Dellarobia quickly checked on Cordie, who was sleeping, and then scurried to the bedroom to run a brush through her hair and put on something decent. When she returned to the living room, she saw Preston had delivered water in the plastic cups he was allowed to use: Lupe had Shrek, and Reynaldo had SpongeBob SquarePants. They held their drinks formally. Dellarobia noted the wife's plastic summer sandals worn with pantyhose, and felt for her, knowing exactly what it was like to be a season behind on every kind of payment. The man had removed his cap and placed it on the arm of the sofa. His mustache made two curved lines around the sides of his mouth like parentheses, as if everything he might say would be very quiet, and incidental. Josefina was their princess, in flowered bell-bottom stretch pants and a plaid top. She sat between her parents smiling shyly at Roy while her father held out the back of his hand for the dog to sniff, encouraging her to do the same. Roy let himself be rubbed under the chin, then went and lay down in the entrance hall, satisfied that he had secured the perimeter.

"So," Dellarobia said, wondering whether she should offer cookies. She moved a pile of clothes out of the armchair to sit down, and Preston sidled close, sitting on the carpet at her feet. "It's nice to meet one of Preston's friends. He's my oldest, so it's been kind of strange for me, sending him off to kindergarten, where he's got this whole other world I don't know about."

She instantly regretted the "whole other world," which they might take the wrong way, but it was too late, the little girl was already passing it on. They smiled and nodded, seemingly uninsulted. Dellarobia was coming to understand that these parents did not speak a word of English. They must be living in Feathertown if they had a child enrolled in school. But whatever their situation, they were evidently doing it with a kindergartner as their ambassador. Did she go with them to do their shopping and banking? She couldn't imagine. And could not have been more floored by what the child said next.

"My mother and father wants to see the butterflies."

"You're kidding me!"

The girl began to translate, but Dellarobia stopped her. "No, don't say that. Tell me how they know about the butterflies."

"We know about them a lot," Josefina said, this time without consulting her parents. "They are *mariposas monarcas*. They come from Mexico." She pronounced it *Meheecu*, a small, quick slide back to the mother tongue.

"Okay," Dellarobia said, astonished.

"The *monarcas* are from Michoacán, and we are from Michoacán." Josefina flashed a mouthful of white teeth, gaining poise by the minute. She was a little taller than Preston, and seemed much older. They might have had to enroll an older child in kindergarten, to learn the language, Dellarobia supposed. Or maybe she'd just seen twice as much of life as the kids around here. It seemed probable.

"Monarchs," Dellarobia said. "Now see, I've heard that name before." She racked her memory. *Animal Planet*, maybe.

"*Mon*arch-es," the girl repeated, shifting the emphasis around so it was English, or the next thing to it.

"Are you saying they used to be down there, and now they're all coming up here to live?" Dellarobia recognized a familiar ring to those words, which people often said about immigrants themselves, and again she worried about causing accidental offense. But the girl was focused on the butterfly issue.

"No," she said. "They like to live in Michoacán. On the trees. They live in big, big . . ." She drew a wide shape with her hands, struggling for a word, then said, "*Racimos*. Like *uvas*. Sorry, like grapes."

Dellarobia could have dropped her teeth. "Yes, exactly. Like big bunches of grapes hanging from the trees. You've seen that?"

The girl nodded. She said something rapidly to her parents that made them nod vigorously as well.

"My mother, somebody tells her they are coming here like that. Her friend read in the newspaper. We went to another house to ask for seeing the *monarcas*. And that lady sayed us to pay money to see them, so we don't go."

"My mother-in-law, Hester, you mean. A lady with a long gray ponytail?" Dellarobia signaled a line from the back of her head.

Josefina nodded. "Yes."

"She was going to charge you money to see the butterflies? When was this?"

"A long time."

"Around Thanksgiving?"

136

The girl asked her mother a question, who answered with a word that sounded like November. "It was November," Josefina replied.

That witch, thought Dellarobia. Free of charge for churchy locals only. Leave it to Hester to hoard the miracle. "How did you know to come here?"

"Today Preston comes on the bus, and I know you are a nice lady here."

"Well, thank you. You all can go up there and look at the butterflies any day you want to. No charge. That lady you talked to doesn't own them."

The girl translated, and they all smiled. Dellarobia wondered if they meant *now*.

"The only thing is, I've got a baby here napping, so it's not a good time right this minute. We can go later this week, if you want. Could I get a phone number, to call you?" She tore a page from Preston's drawing pad and handed it to the little girl, who handed it to her father with instructions. He removed a pencil from his pocket, wrote a phone number, and handed it back: ten digits, local area code, but the tidy numbers were foreign-looking. He crossed his sevens, like *t*'s.

"So," she said, folding the paper in quarters. "You've already seen this, back where you come from? Where the butterflies all gang up together?"

"In Michoacán my father is a *guía* for the *mariposas monarcas*." The girl was warming up, bouncing just perceptibly on the sofa and speaking a little breathlessly. "He takes the peoples on horses in the forest to see the

137

monarcas, he is explaining the peoples, and counting the *mariposas* and other things for the, for the *científicos*. And my mother makes tamales for the *lot* of peoples."

Dellarobia cupped Preston's head gently in her hand, turning his face upward. "Did you all talk about this at school? The butterflies?"

"Miss Rose said something to Miss Hunt, but not to us," he said. "Josefina asked me if I ever saw the butterflies before, because she did. She said they make the big things all over the trees." He glanced from Josefina to Dellarobia, looking as usual as if he feared he had done something wrong. "That's why I wanted to see them too."

"Shoot! I can't believe this," Dellarobia said, hardly knowing where to start with her questions. "Do you have these butterflies all the time in Mexico? Or do they just show up sometimes?"

"Winter times," the girl said. "In summer days the *monarca* flies around everywhere drinking the flowers, she flies to here to your country. And in winter she all comes home to Angangueo. My town. Every year the same time coming."

"And that's how your parents make their living? From working with the butterflies, and the people coming to see them?"

"They come, they did came . . ." Josefina paused a moment, her eyes fixed on the middle distance while she worked out words in her mind. "The peoples came from every places. Every countries."

"You mean tourists from all over the *world*? Like how many were there, a hundred?" She wondered whether a child so young could possibly know the difference between dozens and hundreds.

"Thousands of peoples. One hundred millions butterflies." That answered that.

"How do you know how many butterflies there are?"

The girl looked a little annoyed. "My father is a *guía*. I help him riding the horses."

"You can ride a horse?" Preston asked in a reverent whisper. He must think she was the second coming of the Powerpuff Girls.

"If you don't mind my asking, why didn't you stay there?" Dellarobia asked.

"No more. It's gone."

Dellarobia leaned forward, hands pressed between her knees, strangely dreading what might come next. Miracle or not, this thing on the mountain was a gift. To herself in particular, she'd dared to imagine. Not once had she considered it might have been stolen from someone else. "Do you mean the butterflies stopped coming?" she asked. "Or just the tourists stopped coming?"

"*Everything* is gone!" the girl cried, in obvious distress. "The water was coming and the mud was coming on everything. . . . *Un diluvio.*" She looked at her parents, asking several questions, which they answered, but she did not say more.

"A flood?" Dellarobia asked gently. She thought of the landslide in Great Lick that had taken out a section of Highway 60 in September. On the news they'd called it a maelstrom, the whole valley filled with boulders and mud and splintered trees. She made a downward tumbling motion with her hands. "A landslide?"

Josefina nodded soberly, her body shrinking into the sofa. *"Corrimiento de tierras."* The mother lifted the girl onto her lap, folding both arms around her protectively. The whole family now looked close to tears.

"I'm sorry," Dellarobia said.

The father spoke quietly in Spanish, and then Josefina said simply, "Everything was gone."

"What was gone?"

"The houses. The school. The peoples."

"You lost your own house?"

"Yes," the girl said. "Everything. The mountain. And the *monarcas* also."

"That must have been so terrible."

"Terrible, yes. Some childrens did die."

Dear God, she thought. *Terrible* was a word with many meanings. The landslide at Great Lick had taken a stretch of highway and nothing else. No school, no lives.

"When was this?" she thought to ask. "What year?"

The girl asked a question, and the mother replied with a word that sounded nearly like February. Josefina repeated, "February."

"Of this past winter? So you *remember* all this? It

140

just happened, what, ten months ago? So you all came here to Feathertown after that, in the spring?"

She nodded. "My cousins and my uncle is working here already a long time."

"Oh, I see. Working the tobacco," Dellarobia said.

"*Tabaco*," both parents repeated. The man pointed to himself and said, "*Tabaco*," and something else. He must have been following the conversation to some extent. Her sense of the family kept shifting. They'd had a home they preferred to this, and jobs, scientific things of some type to assist. Now he was evidently hustling for day labor. She felt abashed for the huge things she didn't know. Mountains collapsing on people. Tonight she and Preston would go over to Hester's and get on the computer together.

She handed back the folded piece of paper and asked, "Would you mind writing down the name of your town for me, where you came from? So I can . . ." What was she going to tell them, that she'd Google it? It sounded ghoulish, like voyeurism. Which, to be honest, was what the daily news amounted to. You could feel more decent watching it when the victims weren't sitting on your sofa.

"So I can learn about your home," she finally said.

The man returned the paper with several words written under the telephone number: Reynaldo Delgado. Angangueo, Michoacán. The last name she'd forgotten, the town that was no more.

They all sat quietly for a long time. Dellarobia had

ridden out prayer meetings aplenty, but had no idea what to say to a family that had lost their world, including the mountain under their feet and the butterflies of the air.

5

National Proportions

The man arrived in a Beetle. His car was in the long train of Monday-morning unfortunates stuck behind the school bus, whom Dellarobia now pitied only half-heartedly as she put Preston on the bus. Gunning their engines, weaving, all these drivers needed to settle down and accept their fate. "Late for work, sucks to be you!" she mouthed cheerfully at the drivers as the bus chuffed its brake-release sound and grumbled away at a snail's pace. She made sure to wave at the square pane of glass that contained Preston's small face like a picture frame.

She was a little mortified, then, when the orange VW pulled out of the line and onto the shoulder directly across from her. Had that guy seen her taunting him? She reached into her coat pocket to touch her phone, which was pointless. She could easily bolt the twenty paces to her front door, in a pinch. She watched an unbelievably tall, thin man get out of the small car, unfolding himself like a contractor's ruler.

"I am looking for the Turnbow farm," he said with a fascinating accent, tilting the words this way and that. Turn-bow, he'd said, as in "Turn around, take a bow." She had the wildest urge to do that.

"I'm Dellarobia Turnbow," she called back, but it came out too fast, a solid unbroken string of syllables that caused the man to laugh.

"Really," he said. "All that?"

"Not even. I didn't give you the middle and the maiden. Catie, Causey."

"Well, then," he said, crossing the road with great long strides to grasp her hand and shake it. "Ovid Byron, a crazy name as well. You might be the first to upstage that."

Creezy neem . . . ope-stage dot—he sounded like a reggae singer. She took note of both names and tilted her neck to stare at the upshot of all that. She was accustomed to men of measure, but this one had a few inches even on the Turnbow men, and it went on from there. Tall, dark, and handsome, but *extra* tall, *extra* dark. Okay, extra all three. He was so many things, this Mr. Byron, that he constituted something of an audience, driving her to invent a performance on the spot.

"You're named for poets. Ovid was that ancient one, right? And Lord Byron." She was casting her net wide here, Honors English was a lot of water under the bridge, but his look said she'd nailed it. "Better than me—I'm named after a wreath made out of nature junk." She made a little curtsy.

"That name again, please?"

"Dellarobia." She ran a hand through her hair, for which the color of his car was a pretty good match: University of Tennessee orange. Maybe he was a UT fan, but she wouldn't ask. He might just like the color, as arbitrarily as she'd been born with that hair. Which had yet to meet a comb that morning. She wore gray plaid pajamas under her coat, and unlaced boots. Meeting the bus each morning was a scramble that left her feeling punch-drunk.

Luckily, this guy seemed unobservant of the pj's. He repeated her name carefully, dividing it in two: Della Robbia. He crinkled his brow in concentration, as if momentarily considering the possibilities. "Also an artist," he declared. "I'm pretty sure of that, an Italian Renaissance painter. Della Robbia. Maybe a sculptor. Of the still life, I'm pretty sure. Nature junk, as you call it."

"Shut the front door! Are you kidding me?"

"No. But I might be entirely wrong." He laughed. "You should look into it, woman. It's your name."

The candor of this stranger took her breath away. *Woman!* And the idea of being named for an artist. A person could be reborn on the strength of that. It pounded in her head while she completed their outlandish conversation and waited for him to retrieve his camera and backpack from his car. She walked him around to the back and pointed out the High Road to the astonishing Ovid Byron, whose accent she finally placed. He sounded just like that crab character who sang "Under the Sea" in *The Little Mermaid*.

The minute he'd hiked out of sight, her impulse was to run to Hester's and get on the computer. She'd never thought to Google her own name. She lit a cigarette instead, and confronted the sight of her back porch with its still life of muddy boots, cardboard boxes, and a miniature Big Wheels bike lying on its side, looking comatose. Cub would be leaving for work in ten minutes, Cordie would want breakfast. Dellarobia exercised the only option generally available to her in times of personal upheaval. She walked to the side of the house where she couldn't be seen out a window, and dialed Dovey.

"Hold your horses, what's his name again?" Dovey asked, after Dellarobia had described nearly every facet of the encounter in a run-on sentence.

"What I'm trying to tell you is, how could a person be so g-d stupid?" Dellarobia said, not quite finished yet with the initial testimony. "Walking around my whole life thinking I'm named after some Martha Stewart thing, and it's an Italian artist."

"So maybe he made it up. It could be a pickup line. Who is this guy?"

Dellarobia was short on details, where that question was concerned. He'd come all the way across the country to see the butterflies. He'd said New Mexico. The state, not Mexico the country. He was American. Someone had forwarded him the *Cleary Courier* article, over the Internet. He'd called the reporter to verify the specifics of what she had seen, and the location. Then flew into Knoxville and rented a car from there. "He's driving a VW Beetle, did I mention? I think he was kind of embarrassed about the car. He said he'd reserved a Prius but instead they gave him the Volkswagen. What kind of company rents out Volkswagens?"

"Wait a sec," Dovey said. "He flew across a whole damn country and drove to your place, to see *butterflies*?"

"That is correct."

"Did he seem, I don't know, insane?"

"How would I know? I spend my life with people that want to eat thumbtacks off the floor."

"How old a person are we discussing here?"

"Older than us, but not *old*. I don't know, forty?"

"What kind of a grown-up takes off on a regular weekday and pays cash money for an airplane ticket, to look at butterflies?"

"You tell me, Dovey. You think I could make this up? I showed him where the road starts and told him to be my guest, go on up. I'm not about to let Hester get hold of him. She'd probably charge him double as a person of color."

"Okay, what color? What's this guy look like?"

"Like, not from around here, right? Six and a half feet tall, skinny as a rail, African American, but not totally. I mean, sort of on the lighter side of that. And the way he talks is unreal. Silky smooth."

"Shoot, girl! That was Barack Obama."

Dellarobia laughed. "Maybe. Traveling undercover."

"But there'd be more Volkswagens in your driveway," Dovey said. "He'd have his Secret Service guys."

"That's true. No Secret Service guys."

Dovey affected a television voice: "In a scandal of national proportions, the president was seen flirting today with a sexy Tennessee woman wearing pajamas outside the home."

National proportions, that part struck her as true somehow. "Who says I'm still in my pajamas?"

"The Tennessee temptress, a married mother of two, denies everything."

"So, guess what else."

"Believe me, I cannot."

"He's coming ba-ack!" Dellarobia sang.

"Well, I should hope so. He's not going to go live on the mountain."

"No, I mean here. To our house." Dellarobia kept an eye on the front porch, but no one was coming or going as yet. "I didn't even ask Cub first. I just invited this guy flat out to come have supper with us."

"You are the bomb. You don't know this guy from Adam, and you, like, *acquire* him."

Dovey's admiration animated her. "I know. It's crazy, right? He told me he's staying at the Wayside, and I guess that put me in rescue mode. That's a scary place, Dovey, you have to admit. Have you been down there lately?"

"You mean, other than when I was looking for some meth or a hooker?"

"Exactly. I mean, the poor guy, traveling all this way, and he winds up *there*. I told him he could not eat the food at that restaurant. It might be fatal."

"So you're cooking for him."

"Oh, jeez. I'll have to figure something out. What should I make?"

"I don't know. That Mexican chicken thing you make with the corn, that's good."

"Well, but what if it turns out he's from Mexico? I think that's a fake recipe."

"*Another* Mexican knocking at your door? I thought you said he was more—"

"Yeah, more black. I think. Kind of. Or, what's Bob Marley?"

"Okay, now you're telling me what, he's got dread-locks?"

"No. Like Bob Marley's cute brother that avoided substance abuse and got an education. Oh, shoot, there's Cub on his way out to work. I've gotta go."

"Are you telling him?"

"You mean Cub? Right now, no. He runs happiest on a short tether. I'll tell him when he gets home from work."

Cub had spotted her from the front door and was motioning for her to come in the house. Dellarobia waved back and pointed at the phone. "It's Dovey," she yelled. "She's got a personal emergency. I'll be there in a jif. Is Cordie in the high chair?"

"Playpen," he said, tucking in his shirttails as he headed for the truck. "They've got gravel deliveries lined up all day. I won't be back any earlier than five."

"I'll personal emergency you," Dovey hissed.

"Sorry."

"You're the one with the international man of mystery coming to supper. Possibly the leader of the free world."

"Yeah, I better get cracking," Dellarobia said. "My house looks like the toxic waste dump of the free world."

"Hey," Dovey said. "You all are just like *Guess Who's Coming to Dinner*!"

"What do you mean?"

"You know, that old movie. Where the white girl brings home her boyfriend and her parents freak out because he turns out to be Sidney Poitier."

"Gosh, that rings a bell. Sidney Poitier." Dellarobia felt deranged, losing familiar names and movie titles. She used to check out movies from the library by the half dozen, along with every book that wasn't nailed down. The library was just little, a storefront in Feathertown with a permanent sheen of dust, now closed, but it used to gather in people of all types. Old guys paging through maritime picture books, housewives checking out romances and household fix-up guides. As a child she loved watching the different kinds of adults, imparting their hints of the many options. Now she moved only among people related by blood or faith, or else, as at the grocery, mute.

Dovey wouldn't give up on her theatrical revelation. "You have to have seen *Guess Who's Coming to Dinner*. They do these, like, Hepburnathons on Turner."

"With opening titles and ending credits, I bet," Dellarobia said. "I vaguely remember those."

"What, you can't stay awake to the end of a movie?"

Dellarobia inhaled, but no words came. Dovey's television, like Dovey's everything, answered only to Dovey. Even as close as they were, how could she really understand a household where information had to be absorbed like shrapnel: movie, sitcom, ultimate wrestling, repeat. Dellarobia turned her face up to the sky, feeling tears, blinking them down. If her unity with Dovey wasn't real, what did she have?

"I don't get out much anymore," she said after a moment.

"Listen, sweet pea, you don't need to. Sounds like the world is beating a path to your door."

&

At ten minutes till six, Dellarobia felt embarrassed by everything in her kitchen. The unbreakable Corelle plates, the cheap unmatched table and chairs, the sheen of snot and applesauce she imagined was still detectable on every surface, despite a day of scrubbing. The washer-dryer combo in the little niche, the laundry piled high behind the flimsy louvered doors. Cub's NASCAR lunch cooler on the counter where he'd flung it down, and the husband himself for that matter, with his too-long hair and slumped posture and his failure even to see that there was anything to be embarrassed about. Sitting at the table reading the sports page of the *Courier*, he looked like a "before" picture. But this was it; she'd married him in haste, and this was all the "after" there appeared to be.

"Where'd that newspaper come from?" she snapped, hearing from herself the same voice she'd used earlier today when she caught Cordie with pennies in her mouth.

Cub didn't look up. "Mom's."

So she couldn't subscribe to the paper, but he could read his mother's. "For goodness' sakes, you could change your shirt, if you're not going to take a shower."

"I done a full day's shift for once, honey. We ought to be praising the Lord."

"Thank you, Jesus, and you smell like it," she said under her breath, actually hating how she felt. She was no better than Hester, treating him like this. She could hardly blame him for reacting to the circumstances she'd just thrown in his face, telling him about the morning's strange encounter and invitation. He'd taken it all in benignly, seeming puzzled but not suspicious, as some men would be if their wives struck up relationships with passing strangers. She'd told Cub this man was older, and that he was black, possibly even a foreigner, thinking this might head off embarrassing surprises. Maybe Cub believed those traits took a man out of the running in some way, so that jealousy wasn't an issue. Should it have been? Dellarobia wanted to weep, for her nervousness. She wished she had seen that movie Dovey told her about. Maybe she'd know how to act. She started to ask Cub to set the table, but thought better of it. At least she could organize things such that Mr. Byron would not get the SpongeBob glass.

If Mr. Byron showed up at all. That question was also starting to rack her nerves, as the man had seemingly vanished. She'd kept an eye out the back window all morning but never did see him come back down through the pasture. She had thought he would stop back in just to say whatever he would say—"Thanks, great butterflies, see you later." By midafternoon she figured he had come and gone, but when she checked out front, the VW still sat there with the big curved smile on its rear end, orange as ever. Something must have happened to him. She could imagine the possibilities: he'd lost the trail, he'd fallen, broken an ankle. He wasn't a country person, anyone could see that.

She towel-dried the macaroni pot and kneeled to put it away, dodging Cordie, who staggered into the kitchen with the green baby blanket over her head. Cub leaned over to scoop her up and squash the happy, squealing bundle of her onto his lap.

"What's in this old bunch of rags?" he asked, jostling her from side to side, eliciting peals of giggles. Half the time Cub didn't seem to recall he'd fathered children, and then there was this, the fact of the matter. They were the apple of his eye. "Honey, have you seen the baby anywhere?" he asked.

"Not for weeks and weeks," Dellarobia replied.

"Do you reckon we ought to throw these old rags in the garbage?" He lifted the green fuzzy bundle over his head, invoking loud hysteria that a stranger might take for anguish, but Dellarobia knew better. Cordie loved disappearing. Which was funny, because not that long ago, Preston could throw that blanket over a toy she was crawling after and Cordie would sit up and howl with despair at its sudden disappearance. She didn't know to look under the blanket, and Preston couldn't resist repeating the experiment, amazed at his sister's conviction that unseen things did not exist. Some time between then and now, Cordie had conquered the biggest truth in the world.

"I ought to go on and feed the kids," Dellarobia said. "I mean, look, it's getting dark. What could a person do outside on a mountain all day?"

Cub set his daughter's bare feet on the linoleum, and off she flew to the living room. "Whatever it was," he said, "I'm sure we'll hear all about it."

"You don't sound thrilled."

"Since when do we grab people off the street into our home to feed them supper?"

Well, here it comes after all, she thought. Leave it to Cub to take a full sixty minutes to realize he was mad. "I guess since we decided to behave like Christians," she said. "Why, what were you planning for tonight, to watch ADHD TV like always?"

Cub loudly exhaled his disgust and went back to his sports page. It wasn't kind, the attention-deficit remark.

Cub had barely followed the thread of high school. But it drove her nuts the way he thumbed the remote and trolled the channels from News to Spike to Comedy to Shopping. What was the use of so many channels? So often, some crazy thing would pique her on the fly-by: a woman swimming alone across an ocean, or a blind couple taking in a multitude of foundling babies. But she would have to snatch the clicker from Cub and sit on it, if she wanted enough time to connect the dots.

She was dying for a smoke, but didn't want to hear what she'd hear from Cub if she stepped out on the porch right now. Instead she checked the oven and yelled for the kids, thinking it best to go ahead and put Cordie in the high chair while she finished setting the table. Preston came obediently when called, shepherding Cordelia into the kitchen and struggling to pick her up, as if he might be able to lift her into the high chair. His desire to be helpful was boundless. Just like Roy and Charlie, she thought. My son has the personality of a border collie. She moved quickly to take Cordie.

"Honey, you can't pick up your sister. She weighs half as much as you do."

"You could get a hernia," Cub offered from behind the newspaper.

She had hoped to feed the kids much earlier and put them in front of the TV while the guest was here. Mr. Byron might not be accustomed to the hullaballoo of the toddler dining experience. But Preston had caught wind of the plan and would have none of it, even when

155

she tried coaxing him with dessert, a no-bake gelatin and cookie thing the kids loved. Preston was no dessert-first man, and he wasn't easy to bribe. If a mysterious stranger had come to town, he was calling dibs.

"I'll be the lookout," he declared now, glancing from the back door to the front, then to his mother. "Which way will he come?"

"I don't know, I guess he's still up the mountain. Cub, do you think we should send out a search party? He's been up there since eight o'clock this morning."

"Lucky for him it's not raining pitchforks," Cub said tersely.

"Not at the moment, for a blessed change," she agreed. Cub folded his newspaper but made no other concession to her sense of this occasion, which would be a disaster if he planned to sulk. She needed his coopera-tion. "He's a visitor in our town," she said quietly, "not just some homeless person off the road. And anyway, what if he was? Be not forgetful to entertain strangers, for thereby some have entertained angels unawares. That's the Bible."

Cub gave her a penitent look. The resemblance between him and Preston sometimes knocked the wind out of her.

"He came all this way to see our special blessing up there," she offered carefully. "I thought maybe I could tell him some things about the butterflies. Since he's interested."

"You could," Cub said. "That's true." She'd been

bending Cub's ear with everything she'd read on Wikipedia about the monarch butterflies. He would probably be happy to take the night off and let someone else take a shift.

A knock at the front door made them all jump. The whole family was wound up tight, even the kids. She would bet money on Cordie setting up a wail, just from the stress. Dellarobia whipped off her apron and scurried to get the door.

"Hello! Welcome to our home!" she said, sounding to herself like a Stepford wife. She led him to the kitchen and introduced him to Cub and the children, then grabbed some potholders and dived for the oven to desist with humiliating herself. She had changed out of her mom clothes into a pink knit tunic and leggings and hoop earrings, and now that felt wrong too. She was overdressed. Mr. Byron asked if he could use their facilities to freshen up.

"You certainly may. Of course! You've been out in the elements all day. Preston, honey, could you show Mr. Byron where it is?" She knelt to peer into the oven. Her original plan was meat loaf, but then she'd panicked: What if he was a vegetarian? It wasn't unheard of, especially among those from other lands. Did sensible homemakers have a plan for the complete-stranger dinner party? She'd decided finally on a macaroni and tuna casserole, a slightly fancy recipe that called for a can of shoestring potatoes and two cans of French-cut green beans. That seemed safe. He surely wasn't French.

Preston leaped from his chair when called upon to help the guest, but then took two sideways steps toward his mother and whispered in her ear: "What's facilities?"

She whispered back, "The bathroom."

Preston nodded and soldiered forth, with the towering stranger behind him. Dellarobia noticed that his hiking boots looked expensive but the rest of his clothes were fairly ordinary—a well-worn jacket, blue corduroy shirt, and jeans. If you could call a thirty-eight-inch inseam ordinary. He would have to cruise the extra-tall shopping lanes, that's for certain. Or his wife would, if applicable. Dellarobia set the casserole on the table and spooned some of the soft, cheesy macaroni into Cordelia's bowl, blowing to cool it. Cordie had a spoon in each hand and was beating the tray of her high chair, eerily like a heavy metal drummer, throwing her fuzzy head to the beat. When Preston returned to the kitchen he gave his sister the once-over and flung his mother a wide-eyed glance: *Please tell me I was never that age.* But at least she wasn't wailing. Cub got the pitcher of sweet tea out of the fridge as she'd asked, and he wasn't wailing either. So far, so good. When the guest returned and everyone was seated, Cub said the blessing: "Father we thank you for this food and fellowship amen." She noticed Mr. Byron didn't close his eyes for the prayer, either. They had that in common.

"So, Mr. Byron, tell us about yourself," Cub said.

The man held up one long, narrow hand like a

traffic cop. "Please! Just Ovid. You will make me feel like an old man." *An old mon.*

"Of course," Dellarobia said, though she knew Cub would not attempt a name that sounded so much like *olive* or *oblong*. She might be loath to try it herself, though she'd been forward with him at the outset. Now she feared the Bob Marley lyrics in her head would burst out of her mouth. *No woo-mon, no cry.* "Except for you, Preston," she added. "You need to call him Mr. Byron."

Preston nodded, his fork poised halfway to his mouth.

"Well, sir," Cub asked, "what do you make of all that, up on our mountain?"

Ovid shook his head very slowly. He took a long drink of his iced tea. "I can hardly begin to tell you what I make of all that, up on your mountain."

"They're monarchs," Dellarobia told him.

Ovid looked at her a little oddly.

"The butterflies," she quickly explained. "Monarch butterflies. You wouldn't believe it, but they are the most amazing of all insects. They gather up like that."

The guest smiled broadly, appearing to understand now. "They do indeed. Gather up like that."

"I mean, not just here, this once. Every winter they come from all over the United States and even Canada I guess, and fly south for the winter, and gang up together in a bunch like that. Just millions. We saw pictures on the Internet, Preston and I. It's the same as what's up there, clusters of butterflies hanging on the trees and practically covering up whole forests. Can you picture it? I mean, of course you can picture it, you just saw them. But can you picture such a little flimsy thing making that long trip?"

"My wife's an expert," Cub said proudly. "She's the one that led us to find them up there in the first place."

Ovid nodded, listening and chewing thoughtfully. "I would like to hear about that," he said. She noticed he had tiny corkscrews of gray in his short-cropped hair, near the temples, and crinkly smile lines at the corners of his eyes.

She shook her head to fend off Cub's compliment, but was nowhere near finished with the subject. "They fly thousands of miles to go south, like birds do. The only insect capable of flying great distances and even over ocean. They can go a hundred miles in a single day. It's unbelievable. They hardly weigh more than a quarter, I bet."

"Not even half that, I would say," Ovid replied.

"Right. But here's the part you will not believe."

"Try me," he said.

"Usually, they go to Mexico." She set down her fork and leaned forward. "Millions of butterflies pile up in this one spot on top of a mountain in Mexico. Always the same one. I mean, why Mexico? What's so special about that one mountain?"

"Good question," Ovid replied.

"Well, I guess a few of them go to California," she

said. "I'm not sure how that part works. But about, I think, ninety-nine percent of them normally wind up in Mexico." The visit from the Mexican family and their disaster darkened her mind, but she was not going to bring that up now. She would like just one beautiful thing to her name, with no downside. She pushed her hair behind her shoulders and beamed at the guest. "Year in and year out, they've been going to the same place I guess forever. Since God made them. And now for whatever reason, instead of going to Mexico it looks like they decided to come here. *Here.*"

"This property's been in my dad's family for close to a hundred years," Cub said, as if that mattered in the slightest. Dellarobia took a bite of her supper, trying to be patient with her husband's view of things. Next he'd be bringing up the logging contract. Who knew, maybe Mr. Byron would be interested in man talk. She couldn't read him very well. She reached over and tried to wipe Cordie's face, but the wild child batted the napkin away, singing "nananana." The artistic temperament of the family. Dellarobia watched her daughter finger-paint with cheese sauce on the tray of her high chair, moving both hands in big circles. Landscape of a planet with two suns, by Cordelia Turnbow.

Everyone had stopped speaking for the moment. In the conversational pause Dellarobia heard muted applause from the living room, the TV no one had thought to turn off. It sounded like some dumb Spike thing, which the kids had no business watching. About once a week she threatened to cut off the cable, but they had a weird package with Bear and Hester that made it essentially free. Also Dellarobia doubted the family could live without it. It was like drugs. These companies mainlined you.

"They eat poison milkweed, too," Preston piped up. "Tell him that, Mama."

"That's right, they eat milkweed, which is toxic I guess. Not the butterflies, they don't have chewing mouthparts, they just go around drinking nectar from flowers. But when they go to lay their eggs, they lay them on a milkweed plant. So when the eggs hatch out as caterpillars, those babies will eat nothing but poison leaves."

Preston added breathlessly, "And when they, when they eat that and grow up, it turns the butterflies poison, too. So nothing will come along and eat them!"

"Poisonous or distasteful to birds," Dellarobia corroborated, quoting from memory.

Ovid crossed his arms over his chest and made a face that said, *Very impressed*, nodding admiringly at Preston. "What a smart young fellow. A little bird tells me"—he circled his finger in the air, then pointed it right at Preston—"that you are a scientist."

"They're also called King Billies," Dellarobia said. "That's what people call them around here. I have no idea why." Was she competing with her five-year-old for this man's approval? She bit her lip.

"King Billy, I have not heard that one," Ovid said.

He turned his chair a little toward Preston and asked in his lilting way, "Now, tell me something. Why do you suppose a butterfly would fly so far to join his companions in the winter?"

Preston put down his fork and closed his eyes, the better to engage every brain cell. Finally he gave it a shot: "He's lonely?"

"A reasonable hypothesis," Ovid replied. "His friends are very dispersed, you know. They fly all about. They cover a large territory. So, coming back to the group gives him a chance to find a wife, right? An extra good wife, from another part of the country, you know? You are too young to be thinking about dat, of course," Ovid winked at Cub. "But one day, when you have a car—" He rolled his eyes and whistled. "Then you will know what I mean."

Dellarobia was taken aback at this turn of the conversation, and prevailed upon herself to keep her mouth shut. She couldn't tell what her husband was thinking as he shoveled in the calories over there. Cub seemed cordial, hungry, slightly out of the loop. His normal self, in other words.

Ovid continued, "Why else do you suppose he might go so far? So far *south*, to be precise. To the sunny land of Mexico?"

"To keep warm!" Preston blurted quickly, like a contestant on a game show.

"So they will not freeze, exactly. Really, Preston, I like your thinking. And now, look at it another way.

What if he is really a creature of warm, sunny places? Like me. I also come from such a place. But life has given me opportunities to wander north, you see, looking for things that interest me a lot. What if the butterfly does this also, but he cannot endure the frosty winter? Then what will our friend do?"

Preston giggled, glancing at his mother. "Buy a coat?"

"If only he could. But he is a butterfly." The man had a winning smile, so wide it showed his eyeteeth along the sides.

"That was a joke," Preston said primly. "He would go back home in the winter. So he wouldn't freeze up."

"Just so." Ovid clapped his hands together, to Preston's pure delight. The man knew how to talk to kids. "So what are we proposing here?" he asked. "Maybe that Mr. Monarch is not really our butterfly at all, here in our gardens. Not flying south in winter. Maybe he is really a Mexican butterfly coming north in summer, just for a visit."

Preston nodded, wide-eyed, actually seeming to follow this line of thinking.

"But a scientist doesn't just make a wild guess, you know. He measures things. He does experiments. How can we discover the truth about Mr. Monarch?"

"Ask somebody?" Preston suggested.

"We ask his family."

"How?" Preston was hooked. A small, four-eyed fish.

"There are ways to do this," Ovid said, leaning back in his chair, crossing his long legs, an ankle on his knee. "People have done it. And do you know what they found? All his relatives are tropical butterflies. In his whole family, which is called the Danaus family, Mr. Monarch is the only one clever enough to seek his fortune in a cold place."

Dellarobia felt numb. Hoodwinked, embarrassed, furious, entranced. "A little bird tells me," she said, pointing at Ovid, "*you* are a scientist."

He spread his hands wide, caught out, smiling so broadly he was a landscape all his own. Like Cordelia's, a world with extra sunshine.

"Well, why in the world?" Dellarobia choked a little, coughing until she recovered. She drank her glass of tea to the bottom. "I just made a jackass of myself, thank you very much."

Cub seemed suddenly to have awakened. He smacked both hands flat on the table, as if getting the joke, and declared, "You're a butterfly-ologist, aren't you?"

"Entomologist, lepidopterist. Biologist is fine. I don't put a lot of stock in titles."

"But"—Dellarobia struggled to frame her question— "you've been to college and studied all this, right? Or, what am I saying, you probably *teach* college."

"I do. Devary University, in New Mexico. I did my graduate studies at Harvard, and *that*"—he gave Preston a knowing look—"is a *very* cold place."

165

"You came all the way here from New Mexico?" Cub asked. "Sheez! That's what, two thousand miles? How long a drive is that?"

"I came by plane. It's a long ride in a small seat, I can tell you that, my friend."

"I've not been on an airplane, nor my wife either one," Cub said, with unbridled awe. Cub himself was an accessory to this voyage; his small place in the world had appeared on the map of the learned man. A dining event of national proportions. Dellarobia felt as if she'd received a blow to the head.

"You came here because you're one of the people who study these monarchs," she said.

"You are exactly right. I spent the day doing a quick census up there."

Quick, she thought, as in nine hours. Had he counted them all? "So, you do what, experiments, or observations? And write up what you find out?"

He nodded. "A dissertation, articles, a couple of books. All on the monarch."

"A *couple* of books," she said to this man, recalling his look when she'd informed him, *They're called monarchs.* So there were worse things than feeding meat loaf to a vegetarian. Like blabbing wiki-facts to the person who probably discovered them in the first place. She was in the same camp with her blithe, cheese-covered daughter here, acting like a toddler with food on her face. Minus the good excuse of actually being one.

Preston, on the other hand, appeared keen to crawl

into the man's lap, and Cub wasn't far behind him. Only Cordie remained aloof, putting the finishing touches on her composition, getting her hair into play. Ovid Byron did not seem insulted by any of it. He was helping himself to seconds on the casserole.

"So," Dellarobia asked, "what kinds of things would you study, on a monarch?"

He finished chewing a mouthful before he spoke. "Things that probably sound very dull. Taxonomy, evolution of migratory behavior, the effect of parasitic tachinid flies, the energetics of flight. Population dynamics, genetic drift. And as of today, the most interesting and alarming question anyone in the field has yet considered, I think. Why a major portion of the monarch population that has overwintered in Mexico since God set it loose there, as you say, would instead aggregate in the southern Appalachians, for the first time in recorded history, on the farm of the family Turnbow."

They all stared, to hear their family name at the end of a sentence like that.

Dellarobia's eye caught the remains of a pink balloon dangling from the fixture over the table, the months-old vestige of a birthday party she had overlooked in today's cleaning binge and many others. Small, limp, and shriveled, it looked like an insulted testicle, and although she obviously didn't have those, she could guess. It pretty well went to her state of mind. You get racked, you keep going, but merciful heavens the hurt.

"Mr. Byron," she said, "why did you let me rattle on

like that through half of supper? When you ought to have been telling *us* about the monarchs?"

He laughed and hung his head, feigning remorse to put her at ease, she could see that. "Forgive me, Dellarobia. It's a selfish habit. I never learn anything from listening to myself."

6

Span of a Continent

Preston gave up hoping for a white Christmas and asked his mother if Santa knew how to drive a boat. That's the kind of December they were having. It fell on them in sheets and gushes, not normal rain anymore but water flung at the windows as if from a bucket. At times it came through the screens, visibility zero, and gusts of air seemed to burst from the ground, swirling the deluge around in clouds of spray. Groundwater was rising everywhere. The front yard became a flat, grassy pool. Dellarobia couldn't let the kids play out there unless they wanted to pull on their rubber boots and splat around on it. She would have considered putting them in their swimsuits, if it were just a hair warmer, so they could run around as they did in summertime under the sprinkler.

But this was winter, the dead of it. Johnny Midgeon on the morning radio show sang "I'm Dreaming of a Wet Christmas," inventing new verses daily, of which Dellarobia had had enough. The rain made her want to bawl. For days without cease it had lashed the window casings and seeped under the kitchen door, puddling on the linoleum. She got tired of mopping and blocked it with rolled-up towels. The times seemed biblical. *Save me, O God, for the waters have come up to my neck*: that line in particular she remembered, from the Psalms, because it sounded dramatic and modern, like something Dovey would say.

Just now Dellarobia was jonesing to step out on the back porch for a very quick smoke, but was thwarted by the pink roll of towel that lay at the bottom of the door like a dank, fat snake. She knew that thing would be cold to the touch, like something dead. She fingered the cigarette pack in her sweatshirt pocket, feeling trapped. Cordie sat on the floor, playing with her toy telephone. Dellarobia was trying hard to raise her kids unfumigated by secondhand smoke. What would Mrs. Noah do? Their house was becoming a boat, her family launched out to sea.

She pulled the door open gently, shoving the pink snake with it, noticing nose prints that covered the storm door up to a height of two feet. They weren't put there by the dogs, either. She left both the inner and outer doors propped open so she could listen for Cordie and slid out to the back porch to light up, inhaling and slowly exhaling a long, silent exclamation mark at what she beheld. The pond was completely blown out. The drainage gully down the center of the pasture had swollen into a persistent, gushing creek. After last night's strong winds, a fresh raft of sticks and small trees had washed down into the pasture and were strewn down the full length of the hill, pinned on their sides like little dams so the runnel broadened and poured over each one in turn. No creek had ever run here, in any year Cub could remember, and now a series of waterfalls climbed the hill like a staircase. Her eye was not used to so much flickering motion back there. It made her fretful. Piles of dark detritus lay in leafy clumps at the edges where the flow had receded, and these, she knew, were not leaves but corpses. The latest round of insect invasion that had swamped her life. Before this year she had hardly looked a butterfly in the face, and now they were star players in her own domestic drama. Which was officially no longer just domestic. She eyed Dr. Byron's camper for signs of life.

The man she'd impulsively invited to supper two weeks ago was now living next to the barn. The arrangement seemed unreal to Dellarobia, like so much else that had arrived out of her initial recklessness. It had been Cub's idea to let him park his RV behind their house, near the old sheep shed, and Cub who had rounded up the all-weather extension cord to hook him up to the electricity in the outbuilding. Dellarobia wouldn't have thought to suggest it. It wasn't her place. Even after all this time on her in-laws' land, she felt connected to security by something far more tenuous than an orange extension cord. All she'd offered at supper that first night with Ovid Byron, besides the casserole, was a warning about the motel. "They call it the Wayside," she joked, "as in, 'fallen by the . . .' " He really shouldn't stay there, when he came back.

Because he was coming back, he'd told them that

very evening. His semester at the college was winding up, and with their permission he would like to bring back a small research team to investigate the question of what the butterflies were doing on their mountain. The "alarming question," as he'd called it. He normally lived in an RV while doing his fieldwork in remote and scattered places, he'd explained, and Cub pointed right out the window. That was where he should park his camper, handy to the scene. That old barn had electricity, and was unused in winter because Hester liked to oversee the siring and lambing from the barn near her house. Dellarobia was amazed; she'd hardly known her husband to take a whiz without first checking in with Bear and Hester, yet he'd thrown out the welcome mat for Ovid Byron, just as she had, within minutes of meeting him. Of course, Cub was inclined to flatten himself before anything or anyone famous. She'd seen him go speechless one time while trying to order fast food when they recognized a NASCAR driver on the premises. So he was helpless to resist Ovid Byron, a very nice man who could probably charm a snake. Educated people had powers.

And the nice man now resided in a white, hump-backed camper attached to the body of a Ford truck, a road-worn affair that looked to have hosted more than a few of his life's events. He had his own little home sweet home in there: stove, refrigerator, the works. He'd driven it from New Mexico with his young helpers, Pete, Mako, and Bonnie by name. They were post graduates or doc-graduates, something, it was too late to ask now because she'd pretended to know what it all meant when they were first introduced. Unfortunately she'd been distracted by the muscle definition in Pete's upper arms, and the fact that dark-eyed, long-waisted Bonnie was much cuter than she had any right to look in cargo pants and a fleece vest. The students were lodging at the Wayside. Dellarobia wondered about the specifics of that arrangement—two guys and a girl— and truly, she regretted the accommodations. But the kids were only staying another week. They were young urban people with advanced degrees. They could fend for themselves.

They spent every daylight hour up the mountain, anyway, except during the most unutterable down-pours. In the evenings they gathered around a sort of dinette table inside the RV, doing what, exactly, she didn't know. She'd seen charts of numbers in stacks, and knew they played penny poker because they'd invited her to join them. Once she did, after Cordie and Preston were in bed. Was a hostess gift necessary, she'd wondered, when invited to a camper home? She brought a jar of dilly beans. They got a little bit rowdy playing cards, while Ovid sat off to the side tapping industriously at his slim computer that opened like a sideways book, tilting its blue glow into his face. Its light made his skin a strange color in the dim camper, and his reading glasses two inscrutable rectangles of light.

She felt guilty about not inviting these people into her house for their after-hours activities, but Ovid wouldn't hear of disrupting her family's life. The deal hinged on it, he said. This was normal life for field scientists, they all had assured her. Ovid seemed proud of his traveling abode. The toilet was in a tiny closet that also became, with the door tightly closed, a shower. The dinette table folded away and the seats pulled together to make a full-size bed. He would need a good-size bed, with that much height, Dellarobia thought. Did he have a wife or family? She was hesitant to ask. If he meant to remain here through the holidays, that didn't bode for much in his family department. But yesterday he'd mentioned he would be going away between Christmas and New Year's, leaving the camper here, and would return in January to stay a good while. She had no idea whether he had people who wanted him home for the holidays, or simply desired to get out of the Turnbow hair at a family-oriented season.

A banging sound, she realized with a start, was coming from inside her own house. Quickly she stubbed out her cigarette in the butt-filled flowerpot and dashed in to find Cordie standing up, gripping her toy telephone's yellow earpiece so the rest of the phone dangled by its cord.

"Was that you banging?" Dellarobia asked.

"Mawmawmaw," Cordie replied.

Dellarobia was stunned to look up and see Hester in her hallway.

"I knocked," Hester declared. "Where were you?"

"Just cleaning, moving some stuff around on the back porch," Dellarobia lied. She took a quick inventory of the things Hester would hold against her this morning: breakfast dishes in the sink, Cordie in just a diaper and shirt. She'd tried to get her dressed, but the child had pelted her all morning with a hail of *no*; she felt like a woman stoned for the sin of motherhood. "All this water is making me stir-crazy," she said. "Come on and sit down, I'll make us some coffee."

"Well, I had some. But all right, I'd have a cup, if you don't care." Hester looked around for a place to hang her dripping raincoat.

"It's not much of a fit day out, is it?" Dellarobia took Hester's coat from her, as if she were a guest.

"Reach down your hand from on high, and deliver me from the mighty waters."

"I was just thinking the same," Dellarobia said, surprised. "Those psalms about the wreck of the world. People think the Psalms are only about nice stuff."

Hester appeared unimpressed with Dellarobia's thoughts on the Psalms. She tried to focus on one thing at a time, hanging up the coat, tidying up the table. Hester was practically a stranger to this house. Everything always happened over at Bear and Hester's: sheep shearing, tomato canning, family discussions, wakes. This two-bedroom ranch house was flimsy and small compared with the rambling farmhouse Cub and his father both grew up in, but dimensions and seating weren't the issue. Bear might condescend to helping his son dismantle and rebuild an engine here, and now Hester of course led her tour groups up the nearby hill. But for practical purposes, the corner of their property occupied by their son's home was a dead zone for Bear and Hester. Eleven years ago they'd built the house with a bank loan, choosing the floor plan and paint colors themselves and making the down payment as a wedding present, when Cub got Dellarobia in trouble, as they put it. Plainly, they'd begrudged the bride price ever since.

"Mawmaw!" Cordelia said again, dropping her phone and bouncing up and down on her bent knees, doing a little dance. Dellarobia was surprised to see Hester invoke happiness in the child, but then realized the radio was blaring "Jingle Bell Rock." She turned off the music, causing Cordie to drop to the floor like a marionette whose strings had been cut.

"I'm sorry, baby, but Mammaw and I need to hear ourselves think."

Cordie sought immediate revenge, picking up the toy telephone and getting down to business with the dial, dragging it with her finger to create a thrilling racket. If any object contained within its depths a horrible noise, this girl would find it.

Dellarobia tried to concentrate on making the coffee. She was rattled by Hester's presence here, which could only mean bad news. Family disagreements were rising over everything to do with the butterflies: charging money for the tours, letting the professor come in. The wildly expanding contentions at church regarding Dellarobia's role in the so-called miracle. A second newspaper article had appeared, with Dellarobia once again the headliner. If Hester and Bear held someone responsible for all this, it wasn't Cub. Could in-laws seek a divorce on their son's behalf? Whatever her mission, Hester was somberly dressed for it, by her standards. Plaid shirt and jeans, big silver belt buckle, old boots. So thoroughly damp, her ponytail was dripping. Did she need a towel?

"I see there's a tree in your den," Hester said, as though remarking that an alpaca had been seen in the bathroom.

"It's looking like Christmas around here, isn't it? Preston and his daddy cut that little cedar out of the fencerow yesterday. We had to move the TV to get it set up in there." Dellarobia was layering on the cheer too intensely, thanks to nerves. But her kids had never had a Christmas tree in their own house, not once. Only the one at Hester's. They did everything over there, including Santa Claus. This year Preston had asked why Santa didn't like their house, and that settled it. She'd made an executive decision.

"We don't have any ornaments, though," she added, hoping Hester might pick up on the hint. Hester had boxes and boxes, so many they could never fit everything on their tree. Weren't grandparents supposed to share such things? Dellarobia had no family left, so the heritage business was one long wild guess where she was concerned. She wished she still had the hand-turned wooden toys of her childhood, things her father made in his shop, a simplicity she only recognized as poverty in retrospect, after he died. She'd been too young at the time to covet the Christmases other kids had, with batteries. She turned on the coffeemaker with an authoritative snap, then realized she'd set the carafe into it full of water, rather than pouring the water into the machine.

"The bottom pasture's full of standing water," Hester said.

Okay, thought Dellarobia, end of the Christmas tree subject. She reorganized and started the coffee again, correctly this time.

"I've got all the breeding ewes down there now," Hester continued, "but I don't like it. It's no good for them."

"Well, the rain can't keep going on this way, can it?"

"They say it could," Hester replied. "That bottomland's good for them usually, the grass down there is good. But not this year."

Cordie's ratcheting phone went on and on. Whoever designed toys, in Dellarobia's opinion, at their earliest convenience, should be smacked. She counted the seconds until the coffee started to pour through. Whatever it was that had brought Hester into this house, it wasn't sheep. "You could put them over here on this field, above us," she offered. "If that's what you want to do. I mean, it's all your land."

"I know it is. But they need to get their CDT shots here soon, and next thing you know they'll start lambing. I like the ewes where I can keep an eye."

"We could keep an eye for you. Preston loves the lambs. I do too, I've always liked that part the best. Seeing the lambs born."

"It's not child's play," Hester said. "You've got to know what you're doing."

Dellarobia made a face, standing at the coffeemaker with her back turned to her mother-in-law. Everything Hester did, she likened to rocket science. But as far as Dellarobia had seen, lambing season mostly involved walking out to the barn each morning to see who'd delivered twins. She said nothing. Hester got up to peer over the half-curtain on the kitchen window, presumably assessing the high pasture for her almighty ewes. Instead she asked bluntly, "Is he in that thing now?"

"Is who in what? I thought we were discussing sheep."

"You know who."

"Dr. Byron? I don't know. He doesn't clear his schedule with me."

The camper's windows had pleated curtains that were yellowed like old newspaper, and usually closed on this side. Hester wouldn't be able to see much. She returned to the table and Dellarobia sat down with two mugs of coffee, sliding one over along with the sugar bowl. She watched Hester shovel in one heaping spoonful after another. Where she deposited those calories was a mystery of the universe. And the sweetness, where did that go?

"He looks foreign," Hester pronounced. "Is he even Christian? He could be anything. And you in here with the children. Bear and I are a hundred percent on the fence about him being here."

Dellarobia put on her poker face. If Hester wanted to play a round, she was ready. "I doubt the man's going to rob us. He's paying us two hundred dollars a month in rent."

"He's paying rent?"

"Long ago decided, Hester. Didn't Cub mention it?" She knew Cub hadn't; he was afraid to bring it up. Dellarobia took a long, scalding swallow of her coffee, making Hester wait. "It was Dr. Byron's idea. He's got a government grant that pays his way when he's doing his research, so we get a certain amount from that. It's called pear diem. That's money that can go toward Bear's loan payment, I guess."

She watched Hester's frown deepen. "He's working for the government?"

"Not straight out. It's a little bit complicated. He works for a college, and this kind of thing is part of his job. I guess the government pays for people to do research."

Hester snorted. "There's a job. Watching butter-flies."

Dellarobia blew across her cup. "As opposed to watching sheep, you mean."

"Sheep put food on the table and clothes on your back."

"Well, I guess God made butterflies for some reason, and He sure put a truckload of them down on us. Maybe we just need to pray about it." Dellarobia felt thrilled by her moxie. She drank her coffee in silence, squelching a grin.

Cordie had begun stalking around the room, saying, "Wow wow wow," still gripping the receiver and dragging the plastic telephone by its cord. Taking her doggie for a walk. Every few seconds she looked back to make sure it was following her. It had no wheels, being a telephone, and made a pitiful pull toy. It kept flipping over onto its rounded side and lolling like a turtle on its back, being dragged by the neck until dead.

Dellarobia was startled when she looked back at Hester to see tears welling in her eyes. "Hester, what's wrong?"

Hester quickly turned her face aside. Possibly she hadn't known she was revealing emotion. When she spoke, her voice was raspy and thick. "I *am* praying about it. And I still don't know what to do."

Dellarobia put out a hand to quiet Cordie, who had now discovered she could lift the phone by its cord and bounce it against the floor like a yo-yo. In the gentlest voice she could muster, she asked, "Do about what?"

Hester's face was the customary knot of anger and disapproval, but the gray eyes seemed to be coming from somewhere else, two pools of expectation.

Dellarobia glimpsed a younger person in there, some-one who could have hoped for things and fallen in love. The girl who wore those clothes to the hoedowns for which they were intended.

"Bear's signed the contract," Hester finally said. "With those Money Tree men. He says he's going ahead with it, rain or shine. King Billies or no King Billies. Now see, I don't know why they couldn't wait a month or two and see what happens. I pray about it every day. The Lord says attend to His glory. You were the first one of us to pay attention."

Dellarobia utterly lost her bearings, sputtering inside herself like a car out of gas. Without the vexation between them, her relationship with Hester had no traction. She stood up from the table, lifting Cordelia onto her hip. She needed a diaper change. Should she leave the room at a time like this? She sat down again, with Cordie on her lap warbling, "Free-too, free-four." Preston had been teaching her to count.

Hester looked at Dellarobia, unguarded. "Cub stood up for you," she said. "First I didn't see the good in that. But see, that was good of him, a good husband. The boy's got a pure heart. But his daddy is not going to let up on him till this is all over."

"So Bear won't budge, on the logging." Dellarobia's own thoughts about the butterflies were so unsettling she'd begun to ration them, like something sweet and scarce. The valley of lights, the boughs of orange flame. She would never be able to tell anyone how it was. That she'd been there first. Already that first day seemed untrue. Hester let her breath out slowly, and Dellarobia could hear a racking tremble in it, as if the woman were bearing up to terrible pain. Sometimes the ewes breathed like that during lambing. A frightening thought. She was still waiting for the birth, whatever monstrous thing her mother-in-law had come to deliver in her kitchen.

"He and Peanut Norwood won't give an inch," Hester said. "I don't think it's just the money. I mean, it is the money. But to be in such a rush over it, not listening to anybody. I think they've put each other up to that. A man-to-man kind of thing."

Dellarobia's mind had pretty well finished beating itself senseless, and now went empty of normal thoughts. For some reason she thought of Honors English, the great themes: man against man, man against himself. Could man ever be *for* anything?

Hester avoided looking at her directly. "I think Cub would stand up to them, if you backed him up."

Dellarobia saw it all then in a flash: Hester weighing the moral choices, swallowing her vast and considerable pride. To do the right thing she needed Dellarobia, mark the date. "Hester," she said, "you look like you could use a cigarette."

Hester's face fell slack with gratitude, like the faces of the women they'd seen on TV last week when their men were finally saved from a mine disaster. Salvation in all forms registered about the same way. With Cordie still on her lap, Dellarobia reached to open the kitchen drawer that hid her ashtray. She slid it across to Hester, along with her own pack of smokes. The wrong brand, but for once Hester might not find fault.

"I need to go change a diaper," Dellarobia said, "I'm sorry. You just make yourself at home, and I'll be back in a minute. I'm going to see if I can put this one down for a little N-A-P before lunch."

Cordie ignored the n-word, busily tapping the yellow head of her telephone receiver against the edge of the table. She frowned in concentration, directing the blows, *tap-tap-tap*. Using it as a hammer, Dellarobia realized. Driving nails, as she'd seen her father do last night when he replaced the weather stripping.

Hester almost smiled. "That child surely has ideas about what to do with a telephone. Everything but talk on it."

Dellarobia studied the toy—bulky body, cord, receiver, dial—and realized it did not resemble any telephone that existed in Cordelia's lifetime. Phones lived in people's pockets, they slid open, they certainly had no dials.

"Why would she talk into it? She doesn't know it's a telephone."

Hester wouldn't get this, of course. In her eyes it was a phone, and that was that. Dellarobia could barely get it herself. She'd seen something so plainly in this toy that was fully invisible to her child, two realities existing side by side. It floored her to be one of the people seeing the world as it used to be. While the kids shoved on.

e‍

When the storm broke, the world was changed. Flat rocks dotted the pasture with their damp shine, scattered on a hillside that looked like a mud finger painting. The receding waters left great silted curves swaggering down the length of the hill, pulled from side to side by a current that followed its incomprehensible rules. *Washed in the blood of the lamb* were words that came to mind when Dellarobia ventured out, though it wasn't blood that had washed this farm but the full contents of the sky, more water than seemed possible from the ceiling of any one county. At the tail end of the storm the electricity had flickered off briefly, so she'd hiked out to the camper to be sure everyone was okay. It felt strange to knock on the tinny door of a camper home, but they'd welcomed her in boisterously, like shipwreck survivors, Ovid and the students all sitting in that dim space around the cramped dinette. They were working with calculators in the glow of a battery-powered lantern. What she'd really noticed were the mounds of wet clothes piled everywhere in that dank little den, from all the days they'd worked in the rain before lightning bolts drove them indoors. Dellarobia tried to imagine loving to do something so much, she would get that miserable doing it. When she'd offered to run a few loads through her washer and dryer, the kids had genuinely cheered, handing over armloads. Mako pulled off his boots and gave her the socks off his feet, which were wet enough to wring out. And later when she returned their laundry, clean and folded, they urged her to sit and chat awhile. This was how she got herself invited to go with them up the mountain. Barring a tornado, they meant to get back to work.

And so they did, on a muddy, after-the-flood kind of morning that brought Noah to mind. Where was their rainbow? As they slogged up the High Road, she was surprised to see how much man-made flotsam had washed down from above, given that no one lived up there: a flat-sided plastic bottle, bright yellow under its ancient patina of dirt. White shreds of plastic grocery bags. A large, rumpled panel of corrugated tin. Old fence posts tangled with barbed wire, from some upland boundary that was surely no longer relevant. Cigarette butts, also traces of some personal past, possibly hers.

Pete hiked in front, talking quietly with Ovid in what seemed to be a foreign language she almost knew: moderated micro-something, ratios, congregation, something-pause. It was the girl, Bonnie, who was most attentive to Dellarobia, hanging back to walk with her and ask about her kids, whether she had grown up here, things on that order. It was a conversation that emptied out pretty quickly, but Dellarobia appreciated the effort. She had never been around people from out of state, and was wildly anxious. Really she'd hardly been around people at all since she quit waiting tables, before Preston was born. As silly as it seemed, she had worried even about what to wear today. Her old, leather-soled farm boots seemed redneck-poor compared with these kids' high-tech boots, which had mesh panels and candy-striped laces and rubber lug soles that looked like astronaut wear. They were like kids on TV shows, whose so-called ordinary families were provisioned by fashion designers and never wore the same thing twice. Farm boots and jeans, however, were what Dellarobia had. She'd noticed that Bonnie usually wore a bandanna on her head, tied in the back under her ponytail, so Dellarobia did the same.

"Do both your kids go to preschool?" Bonnie asked.

"Preston's in kindergarten, half-day, so he gets home at noon. But Cordelia's just eighteen months, so she's a full-time handful. My husband didn't have to go to work today. He's babysitting." Cub hadn't been keen on it, but didn't have other plans, having worked only two full shifts in the last two weeks. Gravel deliveries were the last thing anybody wanted in a downpour. These were facts she did not mention to Bonnie. She wanted to make conversation, but hardly knew how to begin. And she wanted a cigarette so badly her gums ached. People looked down on smokers nowadays, or these people would, she suspected, so she'd decided to go cold turkey for today's adventure. To improve the odds of keeping her vow, she had not brought any cigarettes.

Now, all of fifteen minutes in, she recognized the insanity of the plan and was ready to jump out of her hair. Like the day she'd first hiked up here, in secret. Then, too, she'd felt ready to explode from the combined forces of fear and excitement.

She alone, and no one else in her family, had played penny poker with scientists and done their laundry and gotten invited to see what they were doing here. Hester was dying to know. She'd confessed as much, insofar as Hester ever tipped her hand. She complained that Dr. Byron barely spoke to say hello, when she crossed his path with her tour groups up there, saying little and keeping to his work. Dellarobia thought of the night he'd come to supper, so modest about his expertise they'd nearly missed it. "You kind of have to draw him out. Did you ask him any questions?" she'd asked, knowing Hester wouldn't have, endowed as she was with the glory of knowing it all. The students were also standoffish, in Hester's opinion. Dellarobia would have said the same at first, but could hardly do so now that she'd folded their underwear. That was an icebreaker.

A new creek had insinuated itself on the High Road. For a while they managed to jump the puddles and rivulets, but soon their path was swamped by a brown torrent. A tree had been torn from the ground and pinned sideways, backing up the flow. Pete and Dr. Byron went ahead to find a place where they could safely cross or get around the water. Pete seemed to have seniority over the other two students. And Mako seemed youngest, maybe because of his dense black hair that stood up all over his head like a child's. He had lovely, exotic features, Japanese she would have guessed; California is what he told her. Actually none of the helpers was all that young, probably close to her own age. Pete might even be older. But Cub referred to them as "those kids," and it didn't seem wrong. Because they were childless, she supposed. Free to look at bugs all day.

It was cold out today, she could see her breath. Hunting-jacket weather. She and Mako and Bonnie waited in silence by the washout, staring at the rugged brown roar. Unseen objects under the rushing water made peaks and swales, hinting at the shapes of what lay underneath. She thought of the day she and Cub stood in the flow of butterflies, objects in motion drawing lines around standing bodies. This water was fierce and dark. Clots of foam clung at the banks like dirty dishwater suds. A tattered ribbon of vivid orange flailed in the current, snagged on a twig, and it took her a minute to recognize it as flagging tape from the area meant for logging. That was a shock. From way up there it had traveled to here, this was the path of the flow. Next stop: her house. She'd done some looking on the Internet about the town in Mexico where Preston's little friend and her family lost their home, and logging was a part of it. They had clear-cut the mountainside above the town, and that was said to have caused the mudslide and floods when a hard rain came. The horrifying photos showed houses and the twisted metal of cars all flattened together like sandwiches in the mud. Utility poles snapped like kindling. She'd had to shut off the computer before Preston completely figured out what they were seeing. She told him not to worry, that was a long way from here.

Pete now reappeared and was calling them, showing the way around. The moving water drowned out voices, to a surprising extent. They left the trail and then came back to it higher up the valley, in a place where two separate rivulets came together. Pete pointed out to her how the two different streams merged, one yellowish and silty from the road cut, the other one clear, from the forested side, the dark and light waters running parallel for several yards before they blended. The forest protected against erosion, was Pete's point, but this one felt a little wrecked. Shattered sticks lay all over the drenched leaf carpet. Running water made leaf-banked runnels that scoured the forest floor down to gravel and bedrock. How strange, she thought, to see the forest floor laid bare that way. It gave an impression of the earth as basically just a rock, thinly clothed.

She kept her cold hands in her pockets, and kept up. She was surprised when they left the road and descended into the hollow on a trail she had not known about. Possibly they'd made it themselves. It led directly to the heart of the valley where the fir trees and the butterflies were. She'd seen clumps of dead monarchs along the way, another ingredient of the flotsam washed down by the flood, but here the ground was completely covered with flattened bodies lying every which way, like a strange linoleum pattern. The butterflies never lay open, as she'd seen them at rest or flying, but invariably were dead in the folded position, like praying hands. She hated walking on them, but that's what the others did. They noticed, though, sometimes picking them up and opening them gently like tiny books to read something there. Bonnie showed her how to tell the males, which had darker wing borders than the females and a black dot on each lower wing.

They stopped and unloaded their packs in a serene place where the creek flowed under an old fallen log that was velvety green with moss. All the surrounding trees were filled with hanging clusters of butterflies. Lone individuals dropped from the trees steadily like insect rain, trembling where they landed and taking their time to die. She wondered if this was a butterfly funeral, but you'd not know it from this science crew. They seemed in a fine mood, just getting down to business with their tape measures, plastic sheeting, boxes of waxed-paper envelopes, and smaller instruments she couldn't name. Scales, things for taking measurements. Ovid Byron was a man possessed with purpose, setting his sights on the trees and immediately tramping off into the woods with Pete, pointing and talking as they mounted the incline.

Bonnie and Mako worked together to pull an extremely long nylon tape measure across the forest floor in a white line that followed the curve of the hill, crossing the full length of the area where butterflies filled the trees. Then they painstakingly laid out squares on one side of the tape measure or the other, at regular intervals, for unknown purposes. Their chat when she overheard it was more personal than scientific. They discussed music they'd put on their iPods, names she didn't know, and shared complaints about the place where they ate breakfast, which they called "vile," with its sluggish waitresses and country music. She wondered if it was any different from the Feathertown Diner, where she'd had to wear a tacky polyester apron and the boom box in the kitchen played George Strait and Patty Loveless from opening to closing. What a bewildering verdict: *vile*. Maybe they only meant it at half-strength, in the same way they used "epic" and "heinous" and "stellar." They'd found a Mexican restaurant over in Cleary, deemed "righteous," which was all news to Dellarobia. She sat on the mossy log feeling like a third wheel. These students had all been to Mexico, she'd learned, on a monarch project with Dr. Byron. No older than twenty-five or so, and already Bonnie and Mako had ridden airplanes, moved among foreigners, walked on the ground of other countries. Dellarobia had been nowhere. Virginia Beach, back when her father was alive and had relatives there, but that was it. She couldn't even muster the strength for jealousy, given the size it would have to take. She had no hope even of visiting the Mexican restaurant in

Cleary, righteous or not. Cub wanted nothing to do with foreign food.

She wondered if they knew about the landslide, where Josefina's family had lived. That family had come back to see the butterflies, and sat in her kitchen getting acquainted afterward, a fact she'd withheld from Cub. Lupe and Reynaldo. It was a little awkward, but they were so eager to talk about the butterflies, and knew a lot of facts. That was touching. Lupe did speak some English, once she warmed up. They had two boys, both younger than Josefina, who sat on the floor with Cordelia in awe of her toys. Lupe told Dellarobia she was trying to find work cleaning houses or babysitting, and offered to look after Preston and Cordie if the occasion arose. Dellarobia had laughed, the poor leading the poor. It was a tempting offer, she said, if only she had someplace else to go.

Bonnie startled her out of her funk, calling out, "Hey, can we put you to work?" Dellarobia jumped to attention, reminding herself of Preston. While Mako did something with a handheld GPS, Bonnie gave her a small notebook and explained they were going to spend several hours on their knees counting the insects on the ground. The line made by the tape measure she called a transect, and the plan was to count every butterfly inside the squares they'd laid out along its length, which were called quadrats. They would keep track of the numbers in each square, and the sex ratio, which meant how many males and females. Bonnie asked Dellarobia to identify several butterflies by sex, to be sure she could do it, and Dellarobia was nervous but took her time and made one hundred percent. Her first test in a decade, aced. Bonnie tied yellow flagging along the transect, numbering the squares and assigning ten of them to Dellarobia. Mako and Bonnie would each take twenty.

Many questions occurred to Dellarobia, starting and ending with: Why in the world? If she told her family these people counted dead insects all day, they truly would not believe her. She wondered, were they looking at some kind of a disaster here? These might be dumb questions. All their efforts seemed bent on the simplest of measurements. She kept quiet, watching to see how they went about the task: kneeling, inching forward, noting numbers in two columns for male and female. She also noticed that if one fell from the trees onto their already-counted areas, they did not go back and pick up the tally. She surveyed her assigned corpses in despair, doubting she could count that high without just a wee little hit of nicotine. But she soon grew absorbed, feeling something change in her brain as her eyes shut out everything else in the world but the particulars of monarch butterfly color and gender. And noticing the smell: like dirt and lightning bugs, as Preston had said, and also like the firs themselves, musky-pungent. She hardly paid attention to odors, but this one grew on her. She was ready to agree with her son, the scent was *good*, at least here in its own world. Like dead lightning bugs in a jar, but not nearly that acrid. It was softer, more like rich black soil. Maybe it was the effect of all these deaths. Her lifetime-first miracle was becoming a force of decomposition.

She noticed that Mako and Bonnie took breaks from time to time, sitting back on their heels, closing their eyes or looking up into the trees. Several times he brought dead butterflies over to Bonnie and she measured them with a small silver instrument she kept in her pocket. They also had a hanging scale, a miniature version of a produce scale in the grocery, from which they dangled stacks of butterflies in waxed-paper envelopes. Dellarobia watched their faces as they read the scales and wrote down numbers in a speckled notebook, and felt deeply envious of their absorption in this work, the things they knew. Earlier she'd thought Bonnie and Pete must be a couple, because of the way he gave Bonnie a hand up across the creek, and she later brushed some dirt off the seat of his pants, and even pulled a plastic bag out of Pete's front jeans pocket for him when his hands were full, a gesture that seemed intimate to Dellarobia. But now she observed the same nonchalant physical comfort between Bonnie and Mako when they stood close together, arms touching, while examining something. They reminded her of Preston and his friends absorbed in a game, boys and girls together, their differences undetected or overlooked. Dellarobia wondered how that would feel in adulthood, to be freed from the flirtations and oppressive rules of sex, a dread and thrill she could never seem to escape. Just sometimes, to be with men without being *with* them.

Her heart lurched when a loud crash sounded suddenly from up the valley. Mako laughed and said it was the lumberjacks, meaning Ovid and Pete. Sometimes, he said, they climbed up trees and cut off some butterfly-filled branches, dropping them onto tarps and shaking out all the monarchs to get a count. They'd done this same kind of work last winter in Mexico. They had formulas for estimating branches per tree, trees per acre. "Counting monarchs is, like, madness," Mako told her. "It's like that old joke about the guy counting his herd of cows. Count the legs and divide by four."

It didn't seem like madness to Dellarobia, it seemed pretty methodical. And she knew the butt of that joke would be a farmer, if the person telling it said "cows" instead of "cattle." Why was it so important to count these butterflies? She wished she could ask. Instead she said, "I just found one with a sticker on it. Is that important?"

They both whooped and came running. It was a little white dot stuck on the lower wing of one of her counted dead, something like the stickers her kids got free at the pediatrician's. At first she'd thought it was some scrap of her own unraveling household that had fallen off her clothes. She'd been known to walk around with worse things stuck to her. But no, this dot was something official. Mako pointed out numbers on it she could barely see, a code they would key into a database in Ovid's computer this evening. It would tell them where this butterfly had come from, where it was tagged and by whom.

"But it's dead now," she said, wondering how this information could help the creature in its present state. Bonnie and Mako seemed very excited about the find, putting the tagged butterfly in one of the wax-paper envelopes, and then inside a zip-sealed bag they tucked into a pocket of Bonnie's pack.

"That's the first tag we've found at this site," Bonnie said.

"Really." Dellarobia tried to get her mind around the idea of scientists sending messages in this way across a distance. "Where do you think it came from?"

"That's the big question," Bonnie said. "Could be the next state over, or it could be Ontario. God, Mako, what if it's one of ours?" She and Mako had also done field-work in Canada over the summer, she explained, including tagging butterflies.

Dellarobia was floored to think of these fragile creatures owning the span of a continent, from Canada to Mexico, moving back and forth across the wide face of a land. Each one was so little and sure to die, yet they constituted a force, like an ocean tide. She was relieved Bonnie hadn't suggested the butterflies had come straight here from Mexico. The thought of them running up here after the landslide and flood, displaced along with Josefina's family, was a worrisome possibility she did not want to entertain. It would give her family's mountain an air of doom. If these butterflies were refugees of a horrible misfortune, there could be no beauty in them.

As the day grew warmer they took breaks to stretch their limbs and shed their coats. Mako had to step out of his because the zipper was stuck at the bottom, the kind of thing Preston might do, which was endearing. The butterflies also began squirming around in their colonies, making for a lot of overhead action that Dellarobia found unsettling. Bonnie told her the monarchs couldn't make their own body heat, so they were paralyzed in the cold, unable to move until the sun warmed them to 55 degrees.

"Exactly fifty-five?" Dellarobia asked. "How do you know that?"

Bonnie shrugged. "It's been measured. It's all published. Dr. Byron did a lot of the early work about temperatures inside and outside the clusters. They're most protected in the interior at night, but in sunlight it's best on the outside, so they jockey around all the time for good position."

"Like puppies in a pile," Dellarobia said. Rather than "pigs in a pile," which was the actual expression. She went back to counting and finished her quadrats before the others, because they'd given her fewer of them to do. She went and sat again on the velvety green log, realizing she'd forgotten about smoking for a span of at least five minutes. Maybe eight-point-six minutes. Which made it all the worse, now that she'd remembered. If she'd had matches she would have lit up a twig, just to inhale some smoke. She lay back on the log, trying to put cigarettes out of her mind, staring up into the quivery, shifting, scaly black and orange bouquets. The clumps were massive, like great hanging bears up in the shadows. She thought of deer hunting with Cub years ago, and the way they hung up a carcass to field-butcher it. Wearing the same coat she wore now. A versatile wardrobe, suitable for all manner of dead-animal fun. The sun was trying to come out, winking behind the clouds. Wherever a ray of warm light struck the drooping tresses of butterfly clusters they would light up, butterfly wings opening wide in response, fanning slowly, drinking in warmth. Sometimes for no apparent reason a cluster seemed to break open, with butterflies spilling off it, pouring their motion into the open void. If she tried to follow any single flight through the forest air, it was impossible. They moved around so high in the trees, and there were so many, the eye jumped from one to another.

She was glad when Pete and Dr. Byron returned, even though she'd had no practical reason to miss them. Probably it was just a collie kind of thing, like Roy and Charlie, always relieved when the herd came back together. She helped spread out one of the tarps and they sat on it to eat lunch while discussing the area of the roost, the storm mortality, some things Dellarobia could understand and many she could not. She'd promised not to get in their way, but they went to some trouble now to explain things. The same transect they were sampling and counting today, they had counted a week ago, so comparing the numbers would tell how many butterflies were downed by the storm. This made sense, the matter of keeping track. She was surprised to learn the ones on the ground were not all goners. When the sun came out, a lot of them would bask and shiver to raise their body temperatures, and get going again. If the rain alone caused mortality, that would be different from what they'd seen in Mexico.

Their line of work was not just body counts, Dr. Byron assured her. Ovid. They called him that, and he was their boss, so she could try to do the same. She thought of the evening he'd come to supper and felt embarrassed all over again. But his manner with her was plain and very kind, guiding her into comprehension as he had with Preston that night. He called the butterflies a system, a "complicated system." She was getting used to his accent. "A compli-*keeted* sys-tem, mon," she would say to Dovey later, exaggerating, when she recounted all this. He'd been studying monarchs for twenty years, all over the North American continent. She asked him how long the butterflies lived, and his answer was baffling: generally about six weeks. The ones that lived through winter lasted longer, a few months, by going into something like hibernation. "Diapause," he called it, a pause in the normal schedule of growing up, mating, and reproducing. Somewhere in midlife, the cold or darkness of winter put them all on hold, shutting down their sex drive until future notice.

Like life in an uninsulated house, she thought. Maybe like marriage in general. "And then what?" she asked. It made no sense, a lifespan of a few weeks did not add up to an annual migration of many thousand miles. How did they learn where to go? Dr. Byron explained that no single butterfly ever made the round trip. At winter's end, the now-elderly butterflies in Mexico roused themselves and mated like crazy. The males copulated their brains out, then left it to the pregnant single moms to struggle north across the border into Texas looking for milkweed plants, the sole sustenance that could feed the caterpillars. There they laid their eggs and died without ever seeing their young. Dellarobia was stunned by this tale, which sounded soap-opera tragic, like something on the Oxygen network. She could tell Ovid liked telling it, too. The motherless baby monarchs hatched as caterpillars, grew up, and then flew north to repeat the drill, laying their eggs on milkweed plants and dying. The monarchs they would normally see in these mountains, he said, would be a second spring generation. Their offspring would go north to produce a third. And only those, in the fall, would fly all the way to Mexico.

"Where they've never been," she said.

"Where they have never been," Ovid repeated.

"How can they do that?"

He laughed. "You're looking at one crazy man who has been asking that same question for twenty years."

"Well, yeah, I get it," Dellarobia said. His "complicated system" began to take hold in her mind, a thing she could faintly picture. Not just an orange passage across a continent as she'd imagined it before, not like marbles rolling from one end of a box to the other and back. This was a living flow, like a pulse through veins, with the cells bursting and renewing themselves as they went. The sudden vision filled her with strong emotions that embarrassed her, for fear of breaking into sobs as she had in front of her in-laws that day when the butterflies enveloped her. How was that even normal, to cry over insects?

It wasn't easy for her to stay on the train of the conversation, even if they were running it for her benefit. Pete explained that in recent years their studies had found the range was expanding northward. Meaning the butterfly generations had to push farther into Canada to find happiness, Ovid added helpfully, probably astute to the fact that in her pay grade a range meant a stove. The southern end of things was getting difficult too, he said. The monarchs had to leave the Mexican roost sites earlier every year because of seasonality changes from climatic warming. She wondered whether any of this was proved. Climate change, she knew to be wary of that. He said no one completely understood how they made these migrations. Hundreds of factors came into play. Fire ants, for example, had now come into Texas, where the monarchs were vulnerable. Ants ate the caterpillars. And farm chemicals were killing the milkweed plants, another worry he mentioned. She wondered if she should tell Ovid about the landslide in Mexico. But the students were jumping into the conversation, rendering it less than comprehensible. Biogeography, roosts, host plants, overwintering zones, loss of something-communities, devastation. That one she got, devastation. She held to the vision that moved her, an orange flow of rivulets reaching over a continent, pulsed by its own internal engine.

"They seem sturdy," she said. "Seems like they always find their way."

"They respond to cues," Pete said. "Temperature, solar cues, it's all they can do. It works perfectly until something changes. Like, if they're roused off their wintering grounds to fly north before the milkweeds come up, they show up to an empty cafeteria. Or it's too dry and they desiccate. Every year that we record temperature increases, the roosting populations in Mexico move farther up the mountain slopes to find where it's still cool and moist. But there's only so far you can go before you run out of mountain."

"And then I guess you come to this one," Dellarobia said, presuming this was the answer. "Is that so bad? They're beautiful. We don't get a lot of bonuses around here, let me tell you."

Pete exchanged a look with Bonnie and Mako. Their silence embarrassed her.

"They are beautiful," Ovid said evenly. "Terrible things can have beauty."

"What's the terrible part?"

He shook his head slowly, exactly the same gesture she'd seen that first night when Cub struck up the conversation by asking what he made of their butterfly situation. "Terrible, beautiful, it's not our call," Ovid said. "We are scientists. Our job here is only to describe what exists. But we are also human. We like these butterflies, you know?"

"Of course," Dellarobia said. Good to know, being human was allowed.

"So we're very concerned," he said. "Monarchs have wintered in Mexico since they originated as a species, as nearly as we can tell. We don't know exactly how long that is, but it is many thousands of years. And this year, instead of the norm, something has put them here."

He took a bite of his sandwich, which appeared to be cream cheese on wheat bread, while she chewed on "thousands of years." In her experience, conversations of this nature always ended with the same line: The Lord moves in mysterious ways.

What he said instead knocked the wind out of her. "If you woke up one morning, Dellarobia, and one of your eyes had moved to the side of your head, how would you feel about that?"

"Unh." The repellent image filled her mind for a half second, before she could ward it off. "I'd scream," she said. "I'm scrinchy about eyes, to begin with."

"Well, that is about the sum of it. Your eye might look very pretty over there beside your ear. But what we see here worries us. We are scrinchy, as you say."

All four of them looked at her with such grave expectation, she felt as if her face really might have become rearranged. She couldn't guess if Ovid was pulling her leg. A relocated eyeball. Were they serious? "Well, I guess I'd call the eye doctor," she said. "I despise going. That's about what it would take to get me there."

She ate the lunch she had carried here in a plastic grocery bag because she didn't have a nice little expensive backpack. She didn't have a nice little college education, either. She'd just have to let the smart people figure this one out. She tried to hold on to anger but felt it being swamped by a great sadness that was rising in her like the groundwater in her yard. Why did the one rare, spectacular thing in her life have to be a sickness of nature? These butterflies had been hers. She found them, she'd showed them to her son, in her name they were becoming beloved and important. They seemed to matter, like nothing she'd ever possessed. Already she had made up her mind to throw her one hundred dinky pounds against the heft of her family's men, if it came to that. So how did an outsider just get to come in here and declare the whole event a giant mistake? These people had everything. Education, good looks, boots whose price tag equaled her husband's last paycheck. Now the butterflies were theirs too.

She worked steadily through the afternoon counting insects. She'd had worse jobs in her life. One quadrat she split with Mako, and all the ones still uncounted she did by herself while the rest of the crew did other work. They measured trees by looking at them through a little yellow instrument, and measured wingspans using tweezer things called calipers, and measured what they called wet weights using tiny scales that looked like drug-dealer equipment to Dellarobia, not that she knew. When the light began to wane they headed down-mountain. She was ready to bolt and run toward the sight of her dear children and, more importantly, her cigarettes. But they all walked together, climbing back up through the forest to the High Road and descending it with the sun at their backs. Butterflies that had moved around during the day now flowed toward them up the road, coming home to roost. They'd been out seeking flowers if they could find any here, for nectar, Ovid said. Warm days that got them awake and flying around would deplete their fat reserves. Fat reserves, on a butterfly? Yes. In fact, he said, warm spells might be a bigger danger here than the cold snaps. The butterflies would burn through their fuel much more quickly than in the steady cool of Mexico's high-altitude roost. That was a big problem on this mountain, with no winter flowers for refueling. She tried to picture winter flowers, and came up blank. Poinsettias? *Depauperate* of nectar sources, was what he said. She tried not to take it personally that her mountain was poor in all ways, even flower-wise.

She tried to calm her burgeoning resentments and just float on the tide of butterflies that surrounded them. It was like being inside a video game. Little V shapes of moving orange light kept coming at her, sweeping around. They seemed to magnify the sunlight, igniting the air. She could see how they would need steady cues in their unsteady world. She felt for them. She wanted to like the scientists too, who really did care about the butterflies, probably a far cry more than she did. It was true what Ovid said, they were only taking the measure of things. If the news was bad, that wasn't their fault. They were just people. Kids, for the most part, basically her own generation, with jackets tied around their waists, walking along in a river of butterflies.

Earlier in the day she'd taken a look at Mako's coat with its wrecked zipper, and had considered offering to replace it, but hesitated. Maybe he didn't care one way or the other. She made the offer now.

"*Replace* it? You mean, take out the zipper and put in a new one?" he asked her, apparently unacquainted with the concept of clothing repair. These kids must think their expensive gear grew on trees.

She laughed. "Lay that coat out on a table and use some of those measuring tools you've got to measure the zipper. You can buy one just like it at the Walmart in Cleary, they've got fabric and notions. Bring it to the house tomorrow, if you can get by without your coat for a day, and I'll fix you right up."

"You've got, what, like a sewing machine?" His surprise was genuine.

"Well, *yeah*," she said, "a sewing machine. It's not like an atom-smasher or anything. Just a needle that goes up and down. I used to make just about everything I wore, in high school. Prom dress, the works. It was the alternative to fashion death, in my income bracket."

"But how did you learn to do that?" Bonnie also seemed floored. All these college graduates, mystified by Dellarobia's store of knowledge. She wasn't sure whether to feel proud or mocked.

"It's nothing all that hard, it just takes patience. My mother was a seamstress."

"Really," Mako said. "Like, what would she sew?"

"Her specialty was business suits, if you can imagine. Mostly for women, but some older men still had their suits made to order, when I was little. Before they all went over to buying factory made at half the price."

"In some sweatshop," Bonnie said.

"Or foreign-made at one-tenth the price, right," she agreed. "Mama brought me up to be really picky about double seams and linings, and then set me loose in a world where those things don't even exist."

The students seemed to be digesting this. Maybe they didn't know about seams and linings either. Mako changed the subject, remarking that the washed-out road would hinder her mother's tourism business. It took her a second to realize he meant Hester.

"Oh. That's not my mama. My mother-in-law." She decided not to mention her dead parents, a reliable conversation-stopper.

"Who does she bring up here?" Mako wanted to know. The others were listening too, she could tell, surprisingly curious about these personal things. She was not the only one with questions she was afraid to ask. For the first time all day, it dawned on her that these scientists owned nothing here, and knew it. Her husband's family could kick them out and tear down the trees and the butterflies uncounted, at the snap of a finger. There were two worlds here, behaving as if their own was all that mattered. With such reluctance to converse, one with the other. Practically without a common language.

"Well, it was all church groups to begin with," she said. "This has been a meaningful thing in our church, people appreciate . . ." She hesitated to use churchy words. "The beauty, I guess. It's inspiring for people to see. It helps them respect the earth."

The forest went still under golden evening light that made everything look precious. Even the roar of the water seemed to quiet. "How big is your church?" Bonnie asked, after a bit.

"Over three hundred people," she said, a figure that raised their eyebrows. She wondered what sort of church college students attended, if any. "And it's not just our congregation. First it was just kind of locally famous, but people are starting to come from Cleary and places farther away. Now that it's been in the paper twice." The second time, when a reporter and photographer came, they'd claimed they were there to interview the science team, but it hadn't gone that way.

"Hester keeps the touring pretty well organized. She doesn't like the groups to be more than eight or ten at a time. And if people are, you know, old or something, disabled, or little children, she brings them on the ATV. She charges more for that."

"So no senior discount," Mako observed.

"Nope. My mother-in-law is not one for making allowances. If she were an undertaker, she'd tell her clients to quit whining and walk to the cemetery."

They had a laugh at Hester's expense, and Dellarobia felt a twinge, wondering where her loyalties ought to lie. Certainly she had not planned to fall into any alliance with these students. But she would miss their interesting energy when they were gone. They were all headed home for Christmas, wherever home was, the following week on the twenty-first. The shortest day of the year, according to Johnny Midgeon on the radio, her main educational source. Bonnie and Mako would not be coming back with Ovid after the break, because they were only second-year graduate students and had classes to attend. Ovid taught classes just for the first semester and the rest of the year did his research. He'd recently received something called a genius grant, Bonnie explained, implying this made him a VIP. Dellarobia had heard of stars with their own trailers, but not the type where the toilet and shower did double duty. Pete also might come back, Bonnie said, because he was a postdoc doing research full-time, but he wouldn't stay long because he had to be on campus to run Ovid Byron's lab. Dellarobia thought of mad-scientist labs in the movies, bottles of things boiling over, and despaired at the gulf between her brain and all there was to know. The words "butterfly lab" made no sense.

When they'd dropped back a little way behind the men on the trail, Bonnie also mentioned that Pete was a newlywed. His wife didn't like him gone too long. Dellarobia pointed her chin at the well-muscled shoulders of Pete, and asked, "Would you?"

Bonnie laughed. "I guess not." Dellarobia thought to ask Bonnie if she was also married. She said she wasn't.

If Hester could look past her nose, she would see these kids were not stuck up. Worldly maybe, and heedless of their good fortune, to be sure. But in some ways they seemed young for their age. Dellarobia wished she could do something for them, other than zippers and laundry. And the dilly beans she'd brought them that once, which they'd gone crazy over, practically licking out the jar as if she'd put narcotics in there with the dill and vinegar. She could certainly bring over some more from Hester's, as they'd canned about fifty quarts. How could a person never have heard of dilly beans?

A going-away party, she thought now. Just a little gathering in her living room, Christmas cookies and eggnog. She almost brought it up to Bonnie, but her nerve failed. They were near the end of the trail, the opportunity would pass; she formed the words but found she could not say them. She was embarrassed to invite these people into her house, that was the long and short of it. A man living in a motor vehicle, the others maybe rooming next to a meth lab, but still Dellarobia couldn't bear how they would see her life. Like the country-music diner they called "vile." If these kids didn't know a zipper could be replaced, they had surely not seen the likes of her Corelle plates and stained carpet and pillow-strewn rooms. Her every possession was either unbreakable, or broken.

7

Global Exchange

Every disaster proved useful for someone, it seemed, and flooding was good for the gravel business. Cub was called in to work double shifts through the weekend and into the following week, even missing church, which Hester felt was justifiable for those involved in emergency services. In Cub's case that mostly meant delivering gravel to people whose driveways had relocated onto their downhill neighbors. But it also meant money, which brought no complaints. Dellarobia and Cub would catch up their house payments by year's end, and everything else would go to the equipment loan, including Hester's tour group proceeds. They'd been calling this her "butterfly money," an apt name for such a lightweight source of funds. The impending loan payment was a balloon, and that name was not apt, for something that weighed enough to crush a family. Bear and the Money Tree men struck an agreement to wait a month for things to dry out, two months at the most, before they went ahead with the logging.

Dellarobia had hardly seen Cub since Hester's surprising visit. She intended to mention it, but that afternoon he'd taken the monthly run to the landfill with their trash, and early the next morning she'd hiked up the mountain with Ovid and the students. When she came back, Cub was called in to work to drive gravel to a road washout, the first of many. Now she basically handed him his coffee as he went out the door. This morning she'd wondered where all their mugs had gotten to, and realized they must be rolling around empty on the floor of his truck. His shift ended at four today, and she'd asked Dovey to babysit so Cub could come with her to do some shopping for the kids. Dovey thought they should drive over to Cleary, which had fifty times more stores, at least to window-shop, but Dellarobia couldn't afford to walk into most of those places, and recreational envy was not her idea of fun. Maybe the Walmart on this end of Cleary's outskirts. But they ended up getting a late start, so they would just have to scavenge the subpar storefronts of Feathertown. Cub wasted a full hour putting up a whine. He was tired. A Virginia Tech game was on. Amazing, how men who had no use for college could summon such enthusiasm for college ball. "Why don't you just go with the kids?" he'd asked. "You always do that, put Cordie in the shopping cart and go."

"*Christmas* shopping? As in, Surprise, kids, Santa came?"

She hadn't yet bought one present. A resentment of the Christmas season was fair game, she felt, for people who've lost their parents, have no expendable income, or both. The cedar still stood naked in their living room exuding its prickly scent, as barren of Christmas spirit as the muddy outdoor landscape. She'd asked Cub to mention to Hester they were doing Christmas morning at home this year. And maybe suggest she donate some set decoration for the affair. But she didn't know how that was going, as she hadn't really conversed with her husband in days.

Naturally, given an opportunity at last, she jumped in with both feet and they fell to arguing immediately. It was a rule of marriage: the more desperately you needed alone time with your spouse, the quicker you'd spoil it with a blowout. When they went out to a restaurant without kids for their anniversary a while back, they'd ended up yelling in the car, actually cracking the rear window with a pair of channel locks (hurled in anger but not actually *at* anyone), over why he'd left his greasy channel locks in the car, among other topics. Today's acrimony was less athletic; they were too worn-out now for the major leagues. It was more of an endurance event, dragged through several errands across the four-block span of Feathertown: first the gas station, where she only let him fill the tank halfway so she could buy a carton of cigarettes for a price that nearly brought her to tears, swearing she'd make them last out the month, knowing she would not. Next, the discount hardware where they exchanged the fixture he'd picked up to replace their leaky kitchen faucet, because he'd gotten the wrong kind, as any idiot could plainly see. Now they hauled their dysfunctional date into the dollar store, where they hoped to provision their kids with

215

a memorable holiday for something in the neighborhood of fifty dollars.

"I can't go against my dad on that logging," he said, for the twentieth time.

"You *can*, but you *won't*," she said. Ditto.

"Because I'm not *perfect* like you want me to be." Ditto, ditto. They walked through the glass door and dropped it a few decibels, for decency's sake. "Show me where else you can get that kind of money from," Cub hissed, "and I'll take it to Dad."

The idea of that mountain dragged down, and a certain world with it, was becoming unthinkable to Dellarobia. Her life was unfolding into something larger by the day, like one of those rectangular gas-station maps that open out to the size of a windshield. She was involved in a way, with those scientists. And strangely, also, with Hester. She craved to tell Cub his mother wanted him to stand up against Bear, but she also longed for Cub to be his own man in this fight. A husband who was not just his mother's pawn but also the head of his household: was that too much to ask?

A four-foot-tall Santa figure near the store entrance began to grind his hips and emit a thin electronic rendition of "Joy to the World." It must have had some sensor inside that set the affair in motion when they walked near it. "Okay," she said, "let's focus. Christmas ornaments. Did you ask Hester about letting us have some of her stuff?"

"Here's your Christmas stuff," Cub said, waving at

the aisles. Nobody could argue that one. The store contained enough plastic baubles to cover a hayfield.

"Great," she said. "Family heirlooms made by slave children in China." Her mother used to spit that one out like a curse: slave-children-in-China. Dellarobia was startled by the words she'd channeled, and that drab army of orphans she could still see in her mind's eye. She used to picture them in poorly made caps and jackets, resentful of happy homes everywhere, undercutting her father's handmade furniture business and her mother's work as a seamstress. Eventually those brats even shut down the knitwear factory where her mother had stooped from business suits to underwear, in the last decade of her employable life. In hindsight, Dellarobia could fathom her mother's drinking.

Cub was brewing a bad mood of his own design. He yanked out a shopping cart and began to toss things in: roach and ant killer, Krazy Glue, Clorox, antifreeze, shopping by the same rules he applied to watching TV. Channel-surfing his way through the dollar store. A quest that made her think of the skinny old man they always saw at the landfill, eternally churning the heap with his hoe, seeking some fortune in the dump where fortunes didn't grow. Some called that living.

"Nice Christmas gifts, honey. If everybody on our list is planning suicide."

He rolled his eyes, shook his head. A wife was to be endured. Men learned that from television, she thought.

"Well, why do I always have to be the police? You're over ten dollars already."

"Oka-ay," he said, too loudly. "Since you already blew forty on your tar and nicotine." He trudged off to put the items back, and shortly returned with two T-shirts, Fire Department and Little Pony, in the correct sizes. Six and ten dollars respectively. She took them to consider, rubbing the pathetically thin fabric between her fingers. The side seams of the Little Pony shirt ran right off the edges, already raveling apart.

"Why is girls' stuff more expensive? Look at this. Half the amount of fabric, half the quality, and almost double the price."

He shrugged. "I don't know, because boys wear their clothes out faster?"

"Oh, please. You think anybody's on *our* side?" She tossed the T-shirts onto a shelf, entirely in the wrong place, and she didn't care. Let them hire extra help; people needed the jobs. They turned the cart into the seasonal aisle. "Just ask Hester about the ornaments, okay? She's got dump-truck loads. You could go up in her attic and steal some, she'd never know." Dellarobia thought of the wooden ornaments her father made years ago, which must still exist somewhere. What a complicated life cycle those must have passed through: attic boxes, funeral upheavals, yard sales. Like an insect going through its stages, all aimed in the end toward flying away.

Cub picked up a brassy-looking plastic bell with the

year on it, labeled "Keepsake," and turned it over. "Two dollars," he said. "That's not bad."

"Here's the thing, genius, do the math. You need more than one. You need twenty or something, or the tree looks pathetic."

He put the ornament back. Like a child, she thought. His consumer skills were somewhat more advanced than his daughter's, but not by much. She looked over the bins of tinselly junk and felt despair, trying to find one single thing that wouldn't fall apart before you got it home. Maybe her father was lucky to die young with his pride of craftsmanship intact. What would he make of this world? Realistically, it probably wasn't slave children, but there had to be armies of factory workers making this slapdash stuff, underpaid people cranking out things for underpaid people to buy and use up, living their lives mostly to cancel each other out. A worldwide entrapment of bottom feeders.

"What about all those things you made when you were little, Cub?" she asked. "Those Popsicle-stick stars and stuff she's kept all this time. Wouldn't Hester at least give you those for our tree?"

"Talk about tacky," he said.

"But it's *our* tacky. Isn't that the Christmas deal, pass on the love and all that?"

"The true meaning of Christmas is, Turn it over and look at the price tag."

This struck her as the most insightful thing Cub had said in years, although maybe he just meant it literally.

They began picking through a shelf of shrink-wrapped DVDs labeled "Previously Viewed." She felt degraded, as if shopping for previously chewed meals. Cub held up one labeled "Monster Machines," but she shook her head.

"That's not really what Preston is into now. He likes nature stuff."

Cub smirked and held up another, showing a gigantic python curled around a frantic girl who was showing a lot of leg.

"Read my lips," she said, and then mouthed, "Asshole."

Cub was aware of Preston's new interest, and she suspected he didn't care for it. He wanted his son to be good at sports. Preston's stature, she knew for a fact, was a matter that Cub addressed in his prayers. Heaven forbid he should grow up to be a smart, nearsighted pipsqueak like his mother. There was a TV show Cub liked about geeky young men in an apartment, all geniuses supposedly, always reduced to stammering fools by the hot blond girl next door. Cub laughed and laughed at these boy scientists in their ill-fitting pants and dim social wits. Dellarobia noticed they had a dishwasher, and a pricey-looking leather sofa the size of an Angus steer.

She squinted to read the small print on what seemed to be a documentary about lions. It was hard to tell what you were really getting. And it was $12.50. For a previously viewed video, that was outrageous. Their cart remained empty as they rounded the corner into the toy aisle. Cub picked up a boxing robot game, registered the $20 sticker, and put it back. Then he picked out a large $5 affair that looked to be some combination of automatic weapon and chain saw.

"Every redneck child's dream!" she carped, eliciting a tight, warning look she rarely saw from Cub. She should rein herself in, she knew that. The eruption of loathing came out of nowhere. It scared her. Who was she, anyway? A girl who got knocked up in high school and scurried under the first roof that looked like it might shed water. Now attempting to hang out with a higher-class crowd, getting above her station.

"Ho-ho-ho, you two! Santa's little helpers?"

They looked up to see Blanchie Bise from church. Dellarobia gestured at their empty cart. "Not much help, are we?"

"I saw you were in the papers again, Dellarobia," Blanchie said, tugging at her tightly belted raincoat. Everything she ever wore was sized for a previous Blanchie, before creeping weight gain took its toll. Dellarobia thought of it as the Wardrobe of Denial. Blanchie glanced anxiously from wife to husband, when neither of them responded about the newspaper article. "Well!" she piped. "What do you think of this weather? Should we start building an ark?"

Their argument hung suspended, like a movie on pause. Blanchie got the message and scurried along.

"I'm sorry if we're raising redneck children on a

redneck paycheck," Cub said, in almost a growl. "At least I'm working."

"Oh, and I'm not."

He didn't answer.

"You try running after those kids for a day, then. You'd be flat on your back."

"I babysat them Friday. While you went running after those fancy-pants kids."

"For one day, Cub. Not even a whole day. And you *were* flat on your back."

"I watched them, didn't I?"

"Is that what you call it? They'd emptied out the whole refrigerator onto the kitchen floor when I got back. Preston was trying to put a peanut butter jar in the microwave and Cordie was walking around with a ten-pound load in her pants. You were on the couch watching *1000 Ways to Die*, as I recall."

"When are you going to potty-train her, anyway?"

When am I going to potty-train her, mouthed Dellarobia, to the imaginary audience of her soap opera. Maybe not entirely imaginary. One of the yellow-aproned checkout ladies was pretty much following their every move. "She's not even two yet," Dellarobia hissed. "And what's this about fancy-pants kids? Those students are living at the Wayside."

"Slumming it for a vacation. They'll go home at Christmas and tell their friends all about it."

"I don't know," she said. She was aware that could be true. She felt herself looking at things through their

222

eyes sometimes. A lot of times, in fact. Their days here were like channel-surfing the Hillbilly Network: the potholed roads, the Wayside, the sketchy diner, her tacky house. She herself was a fixture in their reality show, *Redneck Survivor*. It had altered her sense of things, even in this familiar store where she was examining her purchases with some new regard. As if she could go elsewhere.

"You don't know what?" Cub asked.

"I don't know what those kids are going home to. So don't act like you do."

"Whatever. You're the big shot." He rolled his eyes toward the end of the aisle where they'd met Blanchie.

"What, because everybody saw I was in the newspaper? You *bragged* about that, Cub. You were ready to sign autographs at work for having a famous wife."

He pretended to study an array of identical dolls dressed in different gauzy costumes. "I didn't think it would turn into a full-time job," he murmured.

She blew out through her nose, nostrils flared, feeling like a horse. "I didn't even want to talk to them the second time. I told you that. I said they needed to interview Dr. Byron, but he was gone up the mountain. I only talked to them for about fifteen seconds. I just posed for that picture so they'd go away." Also, the first one they'd taken was hideous. She was hoping to expunge it from the record.

Spider-Man socks, $3. Spider-Man underwear three-pack, $5.50. Preston needed both, but did underwear count as a Christmas gift? Cub kept saying he wanted the kids to have a "real Christmas," but she felt off balance, wondering what those words could possibly mean. "Oh, and let me tell you, Cordie was screaming the whole time, with those reporters. Just like the first time. I don't think she cares for publicity."

"Not like her mother."

"Will you quit being stupid!"

A shopper at the end of the aisle looked up. Dellarobia dropped her voice. "You started this, Cub. Announcing it in church. I didn't even say half the stuff in that article, about the butterflies being on holy ground and everything. That's your doing."

"I felt the Spirit, Dellarobia. Something you don't understand, I guess."

His sincerity was untouchable, she knew that. Not just in church, everywhere. He'd even offered Ovid a place for his camper. For whatever else he was or wasn't, Cub bore a plain, untarnished humanity. The fact of that now only cut her anger with more self-hatred. She found herself unable to give in. "*I* was there last Sunday, and you weren't, thank you very much."

She'd had to go it alone with Hester, bearing up under the stares. As a spiritual celebrity she was expected to shine with the Beacons, not slink off for coffee and carbs. The beatitude of Feathertown's miracle had its perks, but some seemed to think Dellarobia was parading herself, and Hester was profiteering. Others weren't keen on the outsiders, Ovid Byron and certain unspoken things he might represent. All this of course was filtered through a couple of screen doors before she heard it, but she could imagine. And she was still trying to figure Hester, whom she'd now seen buckle under three times: first in church under the wide gaze of Pastor Ogle, and again when she got so nervous about his impending visit. And third, when she cried and asked for help in Dellarobia's kitchen. No, four times: up on the mountain when she declared Dellarobia was receiving the spirit. Hester was frightened of something, and she was starting to think it might be God. Church was getting too complicated for comfort.

"So did the spirit move you to agree with your dad?" she asked Cub. "About cutting our mountain down to the stumps?"

"You act like we have a choice. We need the money."

"*He* needs the money. Bear didn't ask us before he took out that equipment loan. Why is this balloon payment our problem?"

"He didn't know he'd lose all his contracts when this economy crap hit the fan."

"Well, but it was his risk."

"And it's his land."

"And we have *nothing*? Whatever gets done on that farm, we help do it. Cub, look at me. Will you just look at me when I'm talking to you?"

He stopped and turned with exaggerated annoyance, looking at her with tired, flat, loveless eyes, as sick of this story as she was. She wanted what could not be.

She wanted him to choose his team. Not mother and son. Man and wife.

"You know I'm right," she said fiercely. "We work that farm, we're raising our children to call it home, and we don't even get a vote? What am I saying? We don't even get any g-d Christmas ornaments! We just beg for your mother and daddy's handouts. Damn it, Cub. When are you going to potty-train *yourself*?"

People were staring. The checkout lady in the red turtleneck looked ready to call someone. Having a marital knock-down-drag-out in public was the trashiest kind of humiliation. The whole tired tangle of her life disgusted her. Suddenly, like the flush in the back of her throat she always felt before a virus came on, she had it back: the bizarre detachment that had pulled her in October and November to run away from her marriage. Riding the crest of that wave that shut out everything but the thrill of forward motion. In this moment, here, she was sane enough to be terrified. That whole almost-affair had been like a dream. In real life there were no clean getaways. In *this* life, she had to line up a sitter just to have a fight.

Cub picked up a sippy cup shaped like a frog, two dollars. She grabbed it from him and tossed it into the cart. So the cashiers wouldn't think they were here to shoplift.

"What did he say, on Sunday?" Cub asked.

"Who?"

"Pastor Ogle. About the mountain."

Cub would go with the prevailing wind, whether it was Bobby Ogle or his mother. He wanted an ally. So did Hester, her ferocity notwithstanding. Everyone wanted to be inside the fold rather than out; maybe life was that simple. "Would that settle it for you," she asked, "if Bobby came out against the logging?"

"I don't know."

"Would it make a difference if Hester did? Or anybody else on the planet, other than me?"

"Everybody on the planet doesn't know about it," Cub said.

"Well, just about. You can't keep a tattoo on your butt a secret in this town. If Bear even wanted to keep it quiet, which he doesn't."

"He's got nothing to be ashamed of. He says it's wrong to break a contract."

"Are we speaking of Bear Turnbow's morals? Oh, just a minute. Let me wave some money in the air and see which way his morals turn."

Cub picked up something called a "whip-around sound wand," just to look at it, but she yanked it from his hand and threw it back at the shelf. A toy whose sole purpose was to drive mothers insane.

Cub was starting to shrink from her temper, the predictable course of things. Whipped, she knew what men called it. All roads in her marriage led to this, the feeling she'd stepped into Cub's life to take over where Hester left off, and that was the most wretched thought of her day. "I'm sorry," she said, handing the wand back to him. He waved it around with no real enthusiasm, and put it back.

"So what does Pastor Ogle think?" Cub asked her again. "About what we should do up there."

"Why should Bobby Ogle decide what we do with our own land?"

Of course she knew why. Why did people ask Dear Abby how to behave, or take Johnny Midgeon's word on which men in D.C. were crooks? It was the same on all sides, the yuppies watched smart-mouthed comedians who mocked people living in double-wides who listened to country music. The very word *Tennessee* made those audiences burst into laughter, she'd heard it. They would never come see what Tennessee was like, any more than she would get a degree in science and figure out the climate things Dr. Byron described. Nobody truly decided for themselves. There was too much information. What they actually did was scope around, decide who was looking out for their clan, and sign on for the memos on a wide array of topics.

Cub had left the toy aisle but returned carrying the ugliest object she'd ever seen in her life. A big planter box shaped like a swan. "Should we get this for Mother?"

She looked it up and down. The shiny orange beak, the cheap molded white plastic that would fall apart in a season. The seam that ran up the neck and down the middle of its hateful, beady-eyed face. "Sure," she said. "Hester will love it."

He vanished again, leaving her to push that blooming swan in her cart for all to see. The close-set eyes made it look like that killer in *Psycho*. A gift that would go on giving, she realized, after Hester filled it with petunias on her porch, and she'd meet that evil gaze every time she pulled in their drive. She felt guilty about despising Hester. Even that was getting complicated. They were allies in some sense, given the new backbiting in the flock. Bobby himself might be on the fence. Last Sunday he'd spoken of a throwaway society and things of this world taking on too much importance, and naturally she thought of Bear and his logging, though she could have been reading into it. He said the Old and New Testaments together had over a thousand passages about respecting God's earth, which seemed pretty direct. But later he blessed all those present in the hope of many things including prosperity, which kind of undermined his point. It made her feel hopeless. Not even Bobby Ogle could read those thousand passages and figure things out on a case-by-case basis. In a world of wars and religious fracas, prosperity might be the sole point of general agreement. Honestly, if you waved a handful of money, whose head *didn't* turn toward it? Only those who'd already paid off their houses, was her guess.

Cub had abandoned her in the toy aisle, still having found nothing that would please Preston. Cordie was easy, she would make wrapping paper a festivity, but Preston was another story. She felt haunted by her son's hopeful gaze and inevitable disenchantment as she looked down the row of married Potato Heads and knock-off Barbies. Her eye landed on a set of green plastic binoculars, shrink-wrapped onto a bright cardboard backing. "Funtastic!" it said. Explore, discover, get close to nature, all for $1.50, carry strap included. Made in China. She held the plastic package sideways up to her eye, trying to peer through, and couldn't even make out the items in her own shopping cart. The quality was exactly what you'd expect for a buck-fifty. It was so tempting to buy a horrible thing you could afford, just because the package said "Explore nature." You could pretend it actually worked, and make your kids shut up and do the same. Child-rearing in the underprivileged lane. She put back the binoculars, feeling so desperate for a cigarette she considered lighting up right there in front of Mrs. Potato Head. She could get in a few good hits before someone made her stop. She knew they wouldn't kick her out of the store. They wanted her damn fifty dollars.

A girl from church, Winnie Vice, entered the toy aisle from the other end with her toddler in the cart. Winnie was a Crystal or Brenda relative, she couldn't remember which. That was another snafu at church: now that Crystal's kids were blackballed from Sunday school, she brought them to the café, so forget about sneaking in there for quiet time—the place was bedlam. Other mothers of the out-of-control were lining up behind Crystal, hanging out together while their young were trained by Jazon and Mical in the art of using the juice machine as a spray gun. The congregation was definitely dividing into pro-Crystal or pro-Brenda factions, and it was hard to guess what might compromise your neutrality. Winnie hadn't seen her, so she could make a clean break if she got out of the toy aisle. Still toyless. Dellarobia grabbed a horribly made plush raccoon that didn't even look like a raccoon, and threw it in her cart because it only cost a dollar. She wanted to punch somebody out. The world made you do this.

Food, here at least was something sensible to buy. She loaded up on two-dollar boxes of mac and cheese, and picked through the cereal looking for those with fewer marshmallow-caliber ingredients. Down the aisle she spied Cub standing near the coffee, and there was Crystal Estep, good night. With her boys nowhere in evidence, Crystal was all smiles, beaming up at Cub's great height, leaning against her cart in a backward tilt that threw her pelvis forward like a kindergartner doing stretching exercises. Crystal spotted Dellarobia, waved at her, and shoved off, leaving Cub to peruse the coffee. Dellarobia steered toward her husband, vowing to try and be sweet, but of course he picked up the can of Folgers. "Put it back, Cub," she said. "Get the store brand."

"I thought we liked the Folgers."

"Six dollars. The store brand is one seventy-five. Which one do we like?"

They arrived together at the Last Chance section at the end of the aisle, ridiculously low-priced items that had gone past their expiration dates. She got a canister of lemonade mix and some fruit cocktail. Who knew canned fruit could expire?

"How's Miss Crystal?" she asked.

"Motormouth, like always," Cub said. "Somebody needs to adjust her idle."

Dellarobia laughed. "That's not nice."

"She says she wants you to look at her letter she's writing to Dear Abby."

"Oh, for crying out loud. Again? You should see that thing, it's like twenty pages long. She ought to apply some of that stick-to-itiveness to getting her GED."

Dellarobia was amazed to see what wound up in the Last Chance section, not just food but also strange hair products and such. Packs of gum. And a packet of condoms! Who in their right mind would buy expired condoms? she wondered. It seemed like the very definition of a bad bargain. Cub naturally went for the hot-fudge-sundae toaster pastries, which she wanted to snatch from his hand and smack against his big belly. But she decided not to add Cub's weight issues into today's fun lineup. If she could pretend ice-cream-flavored break-fast snacks did not cause obesity, he might overlook the less advantageous aspects of lung cancer.

"Hey, buddy! Who's this pretty little lady?" A tall, narrow man in a raincoat and old-fashioned fedora reached across their shopping cart, evil swan and all, to shake Cub's hand. Cub introduced her to Greg, his supervisor at the gravel company.

"So what do you think?" Greg winked at her. "Is it time to start building an ark?"

Ha-ha-ha-ha. Dellarobia was ready for her world to get some new material. Cub chatted with him about how busy they'd been at work. She wondered why the boss would be shopping at the dollar store. Sometimes it seemed nobody at all had any money. But he was *management*, wasn't there maybe a small step up? A two-dollar store? She hung around long enough to seem polite before waggling her fingers good-bye and pushing on. Cub caught up to her in the dog food aisle.

"Mother and Dad feed the dogs," he said.

"Roy spends half his life at our house, in case you didn't notice. When I bummed some Purina off Hester last time, she let me know her feelings. So we need dog food."

Cub studied the offerings and obediently hefted the store brand from the bottom shelf, priced at $4 for the fifteen-pound bag, undoubtedly made of garbage. Rather than the $10 name-brand bag placed at eye level. Cub had retained the lesson from the coffee aisle, she appreciated that, but she felt terrible skimping on Roy. He was a perfect dog, he didn't deserve poverty rations. He should apply for a position in a better household.

"So that's your boss," she said.

"Yep, that's Greg. Large and in charge."

"You could take him," Dellarobia said. "Blindfolded. I'd put money on you."

Cub smiled. "Here's what you need for Christmas." He held up a ceramic mug that read, "Out of My Mind, Back in Five Minutes."

She grinned back. Maybe this fight was over. Maybe they'd even have make-up sex. If they could get out of here without another go-round over the kids and their g-d Real Christmas. She wondered how many divorces could be traced directly to holiday spending. "You know what, hon? We need to face the toy aisle again."

Cub followed her down the end zone and back into the mind-numbing array of unacceptable choices. She picked up a toy ax and jovially pretended to murder Mickey Mouse. Cub's mind was elsewhere. He blew his breath out, looking worried. She put down her weapon. "What? Did Greg say something?"

"No, just . . . I'm thinking about that logging. How are we supposed to decide?"

"I don't know. Look at the facts?"

"What are they?" he asked.

As if she knew. They both stood flummoxed before the T-Rex power squirt guns, sonic blasters, and light-up puffer worm-balls that smelled insidiously toxic.

"Well, for one thing," she said, "when you clear-cut a mountain it can cause a landslide. I'm not crying wolf here, Cub, it's a fact. You can see it happening where they logged over by the Food King, there's a river of mud sliding over the road. And that's exactly what happened in Mexico, where the butterflies were before. They clear-cut the mountain, and a flood brought the whole thing down on top of them. You should see the pictures on the Internet."

She wished she hadn't seen them herself, they haunted her so. There were children involved, a school buried. Her mind would not quit posing horror-movie images against her will, and questions she didn't want asked. Would a village just flatten like a house of cards? Or would the homes lift and float, the way vehicles did, giving a person some time to get out?

"That's Mexico," Cub said. "This is here."

"Yeah. You know what I keep thinking? Our house is *ours*," she said. "It's not much, and I'm the first one to say it. But we've made every payment since we married. The house is the one thing you and I have got."

Her intensity got his attention. "Did you tell *him* about that business in Mexico?"

She knew who he meant. Ovid Byron. "No, I haven't. It's too weird. It's like the butterflies came here, and we might be next. Like they're a sign of something." She was trying to keep the scientists out of her argument for keeping the mountain intact. Their wonder, their global worries, these of all things would not help her case with Cub. Teams had been chosen, and the scientists were not *us*, they were *them*. That's how Cub would see it. Everyone had to play.

"This rain won't keep up," he said. "They're saying

235

it's a hundred-year flood. So it won't happen again for another hundred years."

Dellarobia knew this was wrong, bad luck didn't work that way. A person could have a long losing streak. But she didn't understand that well enough to explain. "It just seems shortsighted," she said. "If we log the mountain, then the trees are gone. But the debt isn't. Does it make sense to turn everything upside down just to make one payment? Like there won't be another one next month, and the month after that?"

"It's just the one balloon. Things will perk up. Dad will get more contracts."

"And meanwhile our house might get buried in mud, that's the deal?"

"Dad says they wouldn't log up there if there was any risk to it."

"The hell they wouldn't. You notice he's not planning to do any logging up above his and Hester's house."

"Well, you try discussing it with Dad," he said. "Would Preston like this?"

She took the flat, shrink-wrapped package he handed her. A dinosaur puzzle. "Not really," she said. "That's kind of for younger kids." Not for the first time, she thought of Mako and Bonnie, wondering if they'd played with toys like these, or if their parents gave them educational things for a head start. If Preston wanted to go to college someday, he was already behind. That, too, went with playing on Cub's team. She looked up from the puzzle.

"Do you know what they're saying about the butterflies being here? Dr. Byron and them? They said it means something's really gone wrong."

"Wrong with what?" Cub asked.

"The whole earth, if you want to know. You wouldn't believe some of the stuff they said, Cub. It's like the End of Days. They need some time to figure out what it all means. Don't you think that's kind of important?"

"Well, if the butterflies fly off somewhere, the doctor and them can go park their camper behind somebody else's barn."

"What if there's no place else for them to fly away to?" she asked.

"There's always someplace else to go," Cub said, in a tone that said he was signing off: Worries like that are not for people like us. We have enough of our own. He wasn't wrong.

"But what if there isn't?" she persisted quietly.

"How about this, for Preston? I had these," Cub said. Tinkertoys, or a plastic version of that, in an enormous boxed kit. It was not your father's Tinkertoys, so to speak. Now they had countless extras, including a little motor to run your creations around on the floor until someone stepped on them and punctured an artery.

She and Cub both inhaled at the price. He put it back.

"So your dad says take the money and run. What do you say?"

"I don't know." Cub blew out his breath, looking at the ceiling. "It would just be nice to have some room. To have a real Christmas for the kids."

It would be. Of course. She wanted the world for Cordie and Preston. But what did that even mean? "What's *real*?" she asked. "Anything in this store? We should just buy them each a box of the most sugary cereal there is, and go home. They're so young, would they really know the difference?"

Cordie might actually go for the sugar-pop Christmas, but Preston wouldn't. Everyone got children so jacked up about Santa Claus. Preston had told his kindergarten teacher that Santa was bringing him a wristwatch, information that Miss Rose passed on to Dellarobia with a conspiratorial grin, as if she'd done the hard part. Now the parents only had to make the thing materialize. This afternoon she'd kept her eye out for a toy one, but what a letdown that would be, a plastic watch from Santa. She could already see her son's brave Christmas-morning face, trying not to be disappointed. The watch he coveted was Mako's, an outsize black thing with tiny yellow buttons, timers and such. Mako had let him play with it. Those students were sweet to Preston, nothing like television geeks, actually the opposite, surprisingly astute about a child's interest and abilities. So now Preston had a killer crush on the whole bunch, dying for their notice. He spent afternoons lurking around the trailer pretending to turn over rocks, working his angles, provoking Dellarobia into a protective defensiveness. He shouldn't throw himself on his sword out there. Why should he even see things he couldn't have?

Cub was studying a large packaged thing that looked like a toy television, with appendages. "You know what he really wants. Super Mario Brothers and Battletron."

"He just hears about those from other kids," Dellarobia argued. "He doesn't really know what they are yet."

"We should get him a Wii."

"So you could play with it," she said, feeling exasperation rise.

"It's educational," Cub maintained.

"If you're interested in your son's education, get him a computer. If you happen to find a wallet full of money. He's getting on the Internet over at Hester's, looking at pictures. He can just about read, did you know that? He knows a bunch of words."

"Great. If he turns out smart like you I'll be outnumbered for good."

She felt blindsided. "Being *smart*, you're going to hold that against me? What kind of message is *that* sending the kids?"

"You tell me. If you want them to have a computer and stuff, we need the logging money. Or"—he spread his hands—"we can keep our trees. And be hicks."

"Right. We cut down the trees and get ourselves buried in mud like a bunch of hillbillies, because we're afraid of raising our kids to be dumb hillbillies. Really you're saying we just do it because *that's who we are*," she said, too loudly. "Who *are* we?"

"Dellarobia, for Christ's sakes, do you have to make everything hard?"

"Hester agrees with me," she said. "Your mother doesn't think it's right to clear-cut the mountain. She told me that, the day she came to the house."

He looked at her, uncomprehending. Dellarobia watched as he rearranged the whole game in his head, and saw his features slacken, defeat rising through to the top. The women who ruled, against him. Of course he would see it that way. They faced each other, a towering, morose man and his small, miserable wife, both near tears. How could two people both lose an argument?

"All I'm asking is just one simple thing," he said. "For the kids to have their Christmas."

People wrecked their worlds for less. She knew that. She'd been so keen on her one great day in the sack, she almost threw away everything, kids included. What a hypocrite, feeling sorry for herself now because she couldn't buy them yuppie-grade toys. She suddenly felt so allergic to Chinese plastic she couldn't breathe. "When you get your one simple thing figured out, let me know," she said. "I'll be out in the parking lot."

Having a seventy-five-cent smoke, she thought bleakly. She headed for the exit lane, but something stopped and held her eye. Of all things, a cloth potholder shaped like a monarch butterfly. Unbelievable. It was hanging in a display of incidental items, jar openers and such, as if it had been passing through and landed there for a moment's rest. The colors made it stand out. She reached on tiptoe to take it down and found that it was surprisingly well made, really like nothing else she'd seen in here. The black stripes were accurately placed, right down to the two black dots on the lower wings. Did they even *have* monarchs in China? She did not know. But somewhere far from here, someone had taken the trouble to get this exactly right. She smoothed it in her hands and pictured a real person, a small woman in a blue paper hairnet seated at a sewing machine. Someone her own size, a mother most likely, working the presser foot up and down to maneuver the careful lines and acute angles of that stitching. Scrolling out a message, whatever it might be. *Get me out of here.*

And what if there was no other place?

She strode to the checkout lane and flipped the potholder on the counter. The yellow-apron lady picked it up for a closer look, observing the quality. "Now that's real pretty," she said, sounding surprised. "That'd make a nice hostess gift."

"Actually it's for my son," Dellarobia said, rounding up four crumpled dollars from her coat pockets. The lady took her money and tilted her head back to look through the close-up part of her glasses, examining the nut-case customer.

Dellarobia shrugged, pointing at the little black dots. "Not that anybody probably cares. But it's a male."

⁓

Thanks to Dovey, she went through with the Christmas party. Dovey was keen to check out this Ovid Byron figure, and scolded Dellarobia for her reticence. "When did you get to be such a wimp?"

"Am I a wimp?" She racked her brain for evidence to the contrary. She thought of herself opening the door that day when Crystal had cowered behind it, hiding from a family of Mexicans averaging less than five feet in height. But common sense did not equal courage, and neither did wearing a fox stole to church. She did recall what it felt like to turn heads every time she walked into a room, as small as she was, empowered somehow with solidity. Confident that she had everything in her that larger people contained, with no wasted space, and a whole lot more in mind. She and Dovey used to drive over to Cleary and hang out in bars pretending to be airline stewardesses or software engineers, whatever they'd cooked up en route. It had still seemed possible they might become these things, which gave credence to their constructions. No matter how outrageous the story, men believed them. Once Dellarobia put on her glasses and claimed to be Jane Goodall's assistant. She and Dovey had seen a show on this lady scientist, and had plenty of chimp facts at hand. The guy who'd been hitting on Dellarobia turned around and asked if she could get him a job. He didn't even pause to wonder what Jane Goodall's executive team would be doing in Cleary.

Today Dovey made her a deal. She would make the grocery run for the party when she got off work at three, while Dellarobia dug around in the junk drawers of her former valor, trying to locate the nerve. Somewhere between outrage and giving up, that was where she found it. She was sick of begging for ornaments to hang on a tree, as part of some year-end conspiracy of alleged joy and goodwill arriving from heaven with no hard currency as backup. Fed up with stories about poor people with good hearts raising their damn cups of kindness. Sick of needing permission to throw a party in her own home, and not asking, because she was too proud to beg favors in this family. That's how the simple folk lived, in her particular Christmas story. It was overdue for a rewrite. After taking half a tablet from her ten-year-old Valium bottle to keep from losing her nerve, she tromped out to the trailer and stuck a note on the door, inviting them all to come over when they got back from their day's work.

The scientists knocked off early that afternoon, a rainy day, big surprise, and came right over to partake in the cheer, leaving their jackets and muddy boots on the back porch. Ovid came in with two wrapped gifts for the kids, which could not be opened before Christmas, he said, rendering them thrilled and manic.

Ovid was wearing his all-star smile that showed his dazzling, slightly lapped eyeteeth. Dellarobia had gone a tad manic herself, baking multiple trays of cookies shaped like stars and bells, which she'd set up for the kids to decorate at the kitchen table. Cordie stood on a chair while Preston knelt on the one beside her, smearing on the icing with the back of a spoon and micromanaging his sister's use of the sprinkles. Preston went immediately into show-off mode in front of the students, announcing he was doing an experiment. He mixed the red and green icing together, yielding a brown-colored product that was not going to be a big seller in any household familiar with diaper changes. Dellarobia just laughed, scraped it out, and started over, no big deal. Powdered sugar was about the cheapest of edible substances. It was one of the mysteries of grocery store economics.

Dovey cranked up Shakira and lured everyone into the living room, dancing around in her slinky silver sweater and a Santa hat bobby-pinned onto her mop of brown curls. The children quickly abandoned the cookies for the living room too, bedazzled to witness a celebration in their home involving adults. Cordie anchored herself to the middle of the floor, bouncing to the music, and loudly sang "Rudolph" over whatever else was playing, hamming for applause. Dellarobia felt young and fearless again watching Dovey snap her fingers and pump her elbows, walking around tipping bourbon into everyone's eggnog. And flirting, Dovey being Dovey. Applying a full-court press to Pete, even though fully apprised of his marital status. They were just having fun, and if someone ended up with the SpongeBob glass, Dellarobia didn't care. She hadn't had a cigarette for hours, and did feel at a certain point as if she might chew up the carpet, but this was over-shadowed by her sense of accomplishment. She'd thrown a party.

They had a Christmas tree, too. She went off-road on that one. She'd scoured the house for cash, shaking out purses and jeans and coat pockets, digging through rubber-band drawers, even running her fingers around all the grubby cupholders in the car. Her search had turned up a thrilling number of small bills, eight ones and a couple of fives, which she pleated into little fans. Not butterflies exactly, she didn't want to go there, but they looked festive. The students got into helping her fold the dollars, and pulled more from their own pock-ets for the cause. Mako knew how to make a bird with a long neck and bill. As a kid he'd helped with a project of folding a thousand of these little birds, which they were led to believe would contribute to world peace. It was that kind of school, he said. The birds looked pretty. When her family saw what Dellarobia was doing here, she would need some world peace. Hester would go through the roof.

Dovey produced a twenty, on loan, and circulated herself. She dropped Pete like a hot potato when she found a partner who could *do* the Mashed Potato. The bump, the pony, the jitterbug, the two-step, holy smokes, Ovid Byron could even moonwalk. They rolled up the rug so he could slide backward across the floor in his wool socks, his head thrown back, eyes closed, smooth as silk. Preston nearly swooned. Mako danced like a robot, and Bonnie just flung her arms around and had a good time. Dovey had brought her iPod and cable, the girl was truly a party in a box, so they went from Michael Jackson to Coldplay to Diamond Rio to Chumbawamba, and that's how things were going when Cub got home from work. Dellarobia heard him drop his lunch cooler and open the fridge before fully registering the commotion. He appeared in the living room doorway.

"Dellarobia, what in the heck?"

"Merry Christmas!" they all yelled.

Dellarobia had fended off Dovey's bourbon, as she had her kids to think about, and the half Valium she'd taken for courage had definitely expired. Yet something made her weak in the knees. She gripped the stepladder carefully and turned around to give Cub a wide smile, showing some teeth. "We're celebrating the true meaning of Christmas."

She was covering the tree with dollars. After they ran out of bills, they bent paper clips into hooks and taped these onto pennies, dimes, and quarters in endless supply. Preston dashed from the tree to Mako and Bonnie to collect the taped coins and hang them on the branches, reaching so high his flannel shirt hiked up,

246

showing his skinny little belly. Preston didn't know about Money Tree industries, and was as hazy as anyone else on the connection between Christmas trees and Baby Jesus, probably too young to grasp the full extent of Dellarobia's insurrection. But maybe not. Between the contagion of his mother's mischief and the showing off, he was acting a little crazed.

She watched Cub study the domestic scene, taking everything in, working up to whatever he was going to make of it. Irony would never be Cub's long suit, but religious blasphemy he could probably pick out of a lineup. He seemed to be getting incensed.

"What the hell kind of priorities are you teaching those kids?" he finally asked.

Preston jumped up and down. "Dad, lookit! We put a twenty on top."

8

Circumference of the Earth

Santa brought Preston the watch he wanted, just like
Mako's. It *was* Mako's. He'd knocked on the kitchen
door the morning he and the other students were leaving town, and handed her the watch as a gift for Preston.
Dellarobia was floored, but Mako insisted. His thanks
for the repaired zipper. He claimed it was not an expensive watch. He had a better one at home, he said, and
showed her some of the functions on this one that no
longer worked. As if she could tell. He wanted it to go
to Preston, who called it the "science watch." Dellarobia
had worried about her son being a pest, but now could
see the flattery angle for Mako, who must not have little
brothers at home pining for his hand-me-downs. She
promised she would tell Preston on Christmas morning
that the watch was from Mako, his hero.

But the day came, and she broke the promise. Preston
tore into the wrapping paper, shouting, "Yesss! I *knew*
it! Santa's real!" Stammering a little, overexcited, he
said he had done an experiment: intentionally, he had
not told his parents what he wanted. It never occurred
to him that a kindergarten teacher might leak information, or that Mako might have guessed. The watch in
his hands was Preston's proof that Santa had read his

mind. Dellarobia found she could not revoke a delusion that made him so happy. "So fantasy won the day," was how she put it to Dovey.

"As usual," Dovey agreed.

"He's so smart, it's scary," Dellarobia said. "What kind of child does experiments to test the existence of Santa Claus? Next he's going to ask me how Santa gets all the way around the world in one night."

Dovey folded the last towel in the laundry basket. "Will you explain to me why people encourage delusional behavior in children, and medicate it in adults? That's so random. It's like this whole shady setup."

"True. At what age do you cross over the line and say, 'Now I'll face reality?' "

"When you get there, send me a postcard," Dovey sang.

Dellarobia thought, but did not say: There's usually a pregnancy test involved. She rarely acknowledged the gulf between her life and Dovey's, but it did exist. She separated the clothes into stacks on her bed and tucked hers and Cub's into the bureau drawers. She and Dovey were spending a morning together in the same spirit that had brought them together since childhood, shoring up one another's psyches against routine wear and tear. Even in the old days they mostly hung out at Dellarobia's house, without all those wild little brothers to contend with. After fifth grade, Dellarobia's household only had the late father and the sad mother, so it was quiet and they could rule.

Now of course it came down to which house had the childproof electric outlets. Dovey lived ten minutes away in a duplex owned by her brother in what passed for suburban Feathertown. This morning she'd helped Dellarobia knock off a pile of year-end tax documents and two loads of laundry, with more to go, plus the deconstruction of the weird Christmas tree, which made the kids whiny. *No, mine, no,* Cordelia shrieked as Dellarobia wrested nickels from her little paws, to discard the hooks. She asked Preston to unfold the dollar bills and flatten them for future use, but he was sentimental about Mako's birds. "We have to keep them for next Christmas!" he wailed as Dellarobia pocketed them one by one, criminally hoping they'd add up to a carton of cigarettes.

"We'll make more next Christmas," she said.

Preston threw himself on the couch. "Mako probably won't even *be* here."

Dovey asked if some law of physics made children apply equal and opposite energy to both ends of the Christmas season. They made no real protest when Dellarobia sent them to their room. Cordie made a nest of toys on the floor and Preston sat on his bed attending to The Watch, pressing its buttons and holding it to his ear, an activity that might engage him into his teenage years, from the looks of it. He was also fond of his gift from Dr. Byron, a calendar with a huge color photo of a different endangered species for every month. Preston could not yet name all the months in order, but had memorized these animals in a day.

Dellarobia fetched the next load of laundry from the dryer and dumped it on the bed in her cluttered bedroom, where she and Dovey could hide, out of the kids' line of sight. She turned on the radio to cover their conversation, keeping it low enough she would still hear a slap fight, should one arise. Cordie was always the instigator. Dellarobia began dismantling the octopus of warm, stuck-together clothing, pulling out socks, while Dovey tried to fold tiny flannel shirts whose seams puckered like lettuce.

"I forgot to tell you, I have a date," Dovey said. "You can do my hair. I brought over this new flatiron I bought. It's got, like, an earth's-core setting."

"You're straightening your hair for some guy? Must be love." Dellarobia yanked on a twist of threads that connected two unmatched socks like an umbilical cord. "Is this Felix? I thought he was just the flavor of the month." Felix was a bartender in Cleary, allegedly hot. Dellarobia had not met him and doubted she would.

"Scam potential," Dovey said. "It's this big bartender-wait-staff blowout, so other guys will be there too. They all worked long shifts last night, so tonight they rage."

New Year's Eve was the occasion of their long shifts the previous night. Dellarobia and Cub had put the kids to bed and split one beer on the couch watching a CMT special while waiting to watch that sparkly ball drop for reasons no one seemed to recall anymore. Cub agreed to stop changing channels for nearly an hour, which for Cub signaled high romance. The girl hosting the CMT show in her teetery high heels was one of those national talent-search winners they couldn't have named, young enough she probably thought having to work on New Year's Eve was awesome. Cub had declared that women who hadn't had children weren't really sexy, they looked like dresses on a hanger waiting to get a body in them. Dellarobia was touched. One thing about Cub, you knew he wasn't faking a compliment. He could also declare your new sunglasses reminded him of a frog, with no offense intended. All that entered his mind's highway went straight onto cruise control. Somewhere between Toby Keith and Kitty Wells they'd both conked out, and a few hours later woke up couch-racked and disoriented, having missed the big event. She dragged herself and Cub to bed feeling achy and sad, hung over without cause. The mood had followed her into this day.

It wasn't that she envied Dovey's social life. Felix was already history, she suspected, certainly no impetus for special preparations. Hair was a long-standing rec-reation between herself and Dovey that allowed them to preen and tuggle each other like beagle pups. "Beauty shop," they used to call this, with increasing irony in high school, but still rising faithfully to the challenge of curling Dellarobia's arrow-straight hair and straighten-ing Dovey's ringlets. Which, in all honesty, struck Dellarobia as part of the same unending march of use-lessness that had occurred to her in the dollar store that day, the factory workers and shoppers canceling each other out. So much human effort went into alteration of nonessential components. Especially for women, it could not be denied.

They flipped a coin for the first turn at bat. Dellarobia won, which meant she sat at the mirrored dresser while Dovey clicked on the hot rollers and went to work. She held the metal clips in her mouth and hummed with the radio, classic country, the stuff they'd loved in high school: Patty Loveless on "Long Stretch of Lonesome," Pam Tillis with "All the Good Ones Are Gone." Dellarobia wondered how her favorite music got declared "classic" while she was still under thirty. The sight of Dovey with the clips in her mouth made her homesick for her mother, who used to spend afternoons with that same mouth-full-of-pins frown, pinning pattern pieces to a bolt of fabric spread over the dining table. The more expensive the fabric, the deeper the quiet and that frown, lest she make a wrong cut and have to swallow the expense. Dellarobia would pull up a chair and read her library book, *A Wrinkle in Time* or *It's Me, Margaret* or *The Name of the Rose*, depending on the year. The oak table had been built by her father, a broad, smooth-grained surface underpinning the family endeavors long after he was gone. She missed that too, the table. Where was it?

Unlike her mother, Dovey had no stamina for silence. After a couple of minutes she spit out the clips and tossed them on the vanity. "So what happened to Ovid, Lord of the Dance. When's he coming back?"

"Next Tuesday." Dellarobia blushed.

Dovey lifted her eyebrows. "What hour and what minute? Have we got butterflies over Mr. Butterfly?"

"Dr. Butterfly to you."

"Excuse me? I got him to moonwalk."

"Because you're a ho. I totally saw him first."

"We can share," Dovey said. "Like we did with Nate Coyle. Remember that?"

"Wow, poor little Nate. Was that sixth?"

"Fifth. I bet he's in counseling to this day." With convincing expertise Dovey used a rat-tailed comb to nick out each long strand of tomato-colored hair, raise it high, and spool it down, a process Dellarobia found entertaining to watch without her glasses. Gradually her head grew enlarged by the corona of rollers. From time to time they heard the thump of Cub's pipe wrench under the house as he made himself useful down there, wrapping the pipes with new insulation tape. The temperature had finally dropped to something close to winter range.

"Hey, here's one for you," Dovey said. "I saw it on the way over here. 'Lukewarm Now, Burn Later!' "

"The thing about you and church, Dovey, is you think everything is about hell."

"Hell yeah!"

Dellarobia found it hard to resist the idea of her parents together in some other sphere, maybe rocking the grandbaby that never got loved in this one. But she had no heart for a system that would punish Dovey and

reward the likes of herself, solely on the basis of attendance. "I don't think I believe in hell," she said. "It's
kind of going out of style, like spanking kids in school.
Pastor Ogle never even mentions it."

"Wait a sec, they canceled hell? Man, will my mom
be pissed off."

"I'm serious, Dovey. Who do you know that's
inspired by the idea of burning flesh? People our age, I
mean."

"Mmm-hm," she said, holding the comb in her teeth
for a two-handed maneuver. "Too campy. Like some
Halloween drive-in movie."

Dellarobia realized this was true, exactly. The last
generation's worst fears became the next one's B-grade
entertainment. "I've heard people say Bobby Ogle is a
no-hell preacher," she said. "Like that's some official
denomination."

Dovey took the comb out of her teeth and pointed it
at the mirror. "You know what? I think Ralph Stanley
is one of them. Now that you mention it. I read this
interview with him in a magazine."

"Wow." Dellarobia could not quite imagine the
magazine that would probe country legends for gossip
about their spiritual lives. But Dovey was a wellspring
of weird facts that turned out to be true.

"So you're saying this famous Bobby Ogle is like a
new-millennium preacher? I pictured him kind of
played out. Way older." Dovey lifted a strand at Dellarobia's nape, making her shudder.

"No. Early thirties, I'd guess. Don't you remember his picture in the hallway, in high school? He was part of the football team that went to state."

"Whoa, that was recent history."

"Well, not anymore it isn't, Dovey. But it was when we were in high school. I guess he just seems more ahead of us in spirit. His parents were old—maybe that's part of it. They were sixty or something when they adopted him."

"He's adopted?"

"Like Moses. A basket case."

Suddenly Cub was at the back door, calling out from the kitchen. "Hon, do you know where my truck keys are at?"

Dellarobia bugged her eyes at the mirror. "No more sex till he quits ending every g-d sentence with a preposition."

Dovey crooned, "Do you know where my truck keys are at, *bitch*?"

"What's funny?" he asked from the bedroom doorway. His face was unreadable, backlit as he was from the bright living room, but Dellarobia could see in his posture the reluctance to enter their zone. Cub was a little afraid of Dovey and herself in tandem, a fact she felt bad about but would never change. Their communal disloyalties were like medicine: bitter and measured, life-prolonging.

"You going over to Bear and Hester's?" she asked. His key ring was on the dresser. She reached to toss them and he caught them out of the air one-handed, *chank*. He was surprisingly coordinated, for someone who moved through the world as if underwater.

"Yeah. I think Mother wants to worm the pregnant ewes today."

"On New Year's Day, how festive." It hadn't been much of a holiday. Cub had spent his days off with Bear repairing the High Road after the floods. He'd brought in two truckloads of gravel on the employee discount. Hester would be able to resume her tour business, and Bear was keen to get the road in shape for the logging trucks, though technically that was the company's job. Bear felt they would make a mess of it.

"She's been after me to help drench them," Cub said. "It's been so warm. I don't know if this cold snap changed her mind, we'll see."

"Okay. See you at supper." She kissed her fingertips and waved them. Cub pointed his finger like a pistol, winked, and was gone.

As habitually as a prayer, Dellarobia wished she were a different wife, for whom Cub's good heart outweighed his bad grammar. Some sickness made her deride his simplicity. Really the infection was everywhere. On television, deriding people was hip. The elderly, the naive—it shocked her sometimes how the rules had changed. A night or two ago they'd seen comedians mocking some old guy in camo coveralls who could have been anybody, a neighbor. Not an actor, this was a real man, standing near his barn someplace

257

with a plug of tobacco in his lip, discussing the weather and his coonhounds. Billy Ray Hatch: she and Cub repeated the name aloud, as though he might be some kin. It was one of the late-night shows that archly twisted comedy with news. Somehow they'd found this fellow and traveled to his home to ask ridiculous questions. After each reply the interviewer nodded in a stagy way, creasing his eyebrows in fake fascination. So the whole world could see Billy Ray Hatch made into a monkey. Cub changed the channel.

"What does that mean, drench the ewes?" Dovey asked, lifting her chin, inspecting herself in the vanity mirror. "I always picture you all running the sheep through a car wash."

"Nowhere near that exciting. It means shooting drugs down their throat with a squirt-gun thing. Leave it to Hester to celebrate a national holiday with deworming meds."

Dovey patted both Dellarobia's shoulders with her hands. "Okay, you're rolled up. Swap." Dellarobia gave up her seat and took up the new flatiron Dovey had brought for a test run. The thing was so hot it scared her a little. It could have set things ablaze while heating up on the dresser. She divided Dovey's massive mane into reasonable paddocks and went to work.

"So," Dovey said, "back to his hotness Dr. Butterfly. He's coming when?"

"Tuesday. And b-t-w, there's probably a Mrs. Butterfly. He wears a ring."

"You never know. Widower, maybe. Or she split, and he's in denial."

"I don't think the man's in mourning. Oh, and Pete's coming back too. Speaking of men with wives."

"How do you know all this?"

"He called, day before yesterday. Ovid." Speaking his name aloud altered Dellarobia's pulse. His voice coming through the phone had connected her with an unexpected longing, as if she'd been on hold for a time, and then there he was. "He and Pete are driving from New Mexico with a van load of equipment. They're setting up some kind of lab out there in the sheep shed, believe it or not."

"Are you kidding? A mad scientist in your creepy old barn. I saw that movie."

A flush of defensiveness surprised Dellarobia, on behalf of the scientists or the barn, she was not sure. "It's not as bad as you'd think out there. They're using the room that used to be the milking parlor back when they had dairy cows here, like, fifty years ago." Ovid had checked out the barn before he left, choosing the milking parlor for its enclosing walls and cement floor that could be hosed down. Bear and Hester had drawn up a three-month lease, for a fee that seemed shocking. The balloon payment on the loan was officially covered. "Pete's just staying a few weeks, and then he'll drive the van back. I guess the vehicle belongs to the college. But the equipment stays awhile."

"Equipment for what?"

She reorganized Dovey's wild mane, trying to separate layers in order to flatten them. The faint odor of scorched hair filled her nostrils, but Dovey seemed unalarmed. "I don't know for what. Analysis, he said. Analys-*ees*," she corrected herself.

"Busy bees, checking out the butter-*flees*."

"Well, I think it's interesting. I know it seems crazy to put so much work into butterflies, or kind of trivial, I guess. But what's not trivial?"

Dovey leaned into the mirror and intoned, "Hair and makeup."

"You spend your days cutting up meat. How's that saving lives?"

"People have to eat to live."

"They buy chuck roasts for Sunday dinner, but they're hungry again on Monday. We raise sheep for sweaters that will wind up wadded up in people's closets because they've got ten other sweaters and that one's the wrong color."

"Your father-in-law makes guardrails. Not trivial. Sorry to bring *that* up."

"He used to, before the interstate ran out of money. And if you think about it, ninety-nine drivers out of a hundred never touch the guardrail. Maybe it's not even one in a million that's affected. So to most people, guardrails are trivial."

"You make a strong case. Let me just go jump off a bridge right now."

"I'm just saying you never know what's important.

He said he's going to need assistants. Ovid." She blushed again, but Dovey gave her a pass, maybe seeing something important was at stake. Dellarobia needed to close herself in a closet and practice saying that name: *Ovidovidovid.* "He's putting an ad in the *Courier* to get volunteers, when school is back in session. But he's hiring, too. He said he'd be training at least one assistant for pay. I feel like he was hinting I should apply for a job."

"Why don't you?"

"Are you kidding? Check my résumé. Experienced at mashing peas and arbitrating tantrums. He'll get somebody from Cleary that's gone to college."

"Don't sell yourself short."

"I *am* short. What do you think I'd sell for?"

"*She's a rocket, she was made to burn,*" Dovey sang alongside Kathy Mattea on the radio with perfect timing, pointing her finger at Dellarobia. "Just make sure you wear that to your job interview." Dellarobia laughed. Her huge black T-shirt had a constellation of holes and a stretched-out neck that slipped off her shoulder. It was one of Cub's, pulled over jeans and tank top as a housework smock. Charlie Daniels Band. It pre-dated their marriage.

"Cub wouldn't want me working," she said. "With the kids and everything. Can you imagine what Hester would say?"

"That right there is why you ought to do it."

"To tell you the truth, Cub and I had a fight about it already. Right after he called."

"What, you told Cub you're going for it?"

"I asked. He said no. It was pretty predictable. 'What will people think? Who will watch the kids?' I told him I could work all that out."

"I don't see why you're not just going for this." Dovey looked her in the eyes, in the mirror. "You *are* a rocket. You go for things, Dellarobia. That is you. When did you ever not?"

Dellarobia shut her eyes. "When there was nothing out there to land on, I guess."

"Now, see," Dovey clucked, "that's a woman thing. Men and kids get to just light out and fly, without even worrying about what comes next."

"No, Dovey, it's an everybody thing. It's just a question of how well you can picture the crash landing."

"Don't picture it, then."

"It's a strategy," Dellarobia conceded. "Works for some."

"I'd help with Preston and Cordie. Any time I could."

"I know you would. And it wouldn't kill Hester to watch them once in a while, either. Or I could even pay somebody. It's good money."

"How good?"

"He said thirteen dollars an hour. Which is more than Cub's making."

"Ouch. There's your trouble."

"It is. But he can't say that to me, you know? Instead he's on a tear about some stranger raising our kids.

'Raising our kids,' he said. News flash, I told him, your son is in school. Strangers are teaching him his ABC's. As opposed to his father, who is teaching him to watch the Dirtcathlon on Spike."

"Your marriage is inspiring."

"I know, for you to stay single. You sure I'm not burning up your hair with this?"

"Positive. Scorch it till next Tuesday if you want, it'll still want to bounce back."

"Me with a job, Dovey. Can you picture it? Maybe I'd learn something."

"Like?"

"I have no idea. Like, how do those butterflies know where they're going? You want to know something? It's not even the same ones that fly south every winter, it's the kids of the kids of the ones that went last winter. They hatch out up north somewhere and it's just *in* them. Their beady little insect brains tell them how to fly all the way to this one mountain in Mexico where their grandparents hooked up. It's like they've all got the same map of the big picture inside, but the craving to travel skips a few generations."

Dovey was examining her nails, disappointingly unamazed. Nothing ever really surprised Dovey, but still. "Think about it," Dellarobia insisted. "How do they find this one place thousands of miles away, where they've never been before?"

"I've never been anywhere," Dovey pointed out, "but I could get to Mexico with the map app in my phone. It's probably about the same size as an insect brain. Heck, my *brain* is probably the size of an insect brain."

"Okay, here's the big question. What if your map thing all of a sudden started sending you to the wrong place? Because that's what's happening here." She pointed her finger to stop Dovey from saying something flippant. "I'm serious. The butterflies can't just go out and get a new brain. Why did they even come here?"

Her friend got the message, and kept quiet.

"I mean, what in the world would make that happen now, when it never did before? Maybe it's something we ought to be worried about."

Dovey reached back and pretended to yank an imaginary ponytail. "Children, get with Jesus, it's the End of Days."

"Dovey," she complained.

"Well, what? You're a downer."

Dellarobia was now making her third pass with the flatiron over Dovey's curls, but they still wanted to spring back. The girl had fortitude, any way you looked at it. Deana Carter came on the radio, singing "Did I Shave My Legs for This?" Once upon a time she and Dovey used to howl this empty-marriage anthem at the top of their lungs, thinking that was funny. The ache in her belly made her want to curl herself into a full-body fist. "Do you know what today is?" she asked.

"National hangover day. Technically we shouldn't be out of bed yet."

"It's the day I had that first baby. That didn't live."

Dovey's face went through several arrangements of surprise. "January first? How could I not know that?"

"You weren't there."

"Well, no, because it's the one month of our lives I was mad at you."

Dellarobia hated the salty burn that sprang to her eyes. This was not planned. She held the hot iron out and up toward the ceiling, like a gun, afraid to aim at anything with blurred vision.

Dovey reached up and held her other hand. "Sweetie, you didn't even tell me for a week or something. You weren't answering your phone. I thought you'd abandoned me for marriage and you guys were out on some monster bender."

"We were at home, asleep. Or whatever you want to call that place. Our one-room marriage at Bear and Hester's house."

Dellarobia turned off the flatiron and set it down, giving up the fight. She glanced toward the door, then opened the vanity drawer that hid her cigarettes and ashtray and scootched Dovey over to sit with her on the one seat. They were both so small they sort of fit, like children squashed on a bench at the grown-ups' table. She lit up, inhaled.

"And it just happened. I woke up with horrible cramps and then we were in the hospital and then it was over. My due date was *May*—I'd been thinking it might even hold off until after graduation. All I could think was, this couldn't be happening yet."

"What did you know?" Dovey said quietly. "You were seventeen."

Dellarobia nodded slowly. "You know what Cub kept saying? It was going to be the first baby of the year. You get your picture in the paper and a year of free diapers or something. Poor Cub. He's always the last one to get it when the joke's on him."

Dovey picked up Dellarobia's left hand again and stroked it, turning the wedding ring around and around on her finger. "I can't believe we never talked about this," she said finally. "I mean not like, how it mattered. You always said it was for the best."

"Nobody talked about it. Cub and I didn't. You don't get to feel sad about a baby that never had a name and doesn't exist." Dellarobia was startled to look up and see tears streaming down her face in the mirror. She couldn't feel herself being sad. The emotions on Dovey's face looked more real to her than her own. Without a word, Dovey got up and stood behind her. She started taking out the rollers, spilling long tendrils that didn't look like anyone's hair.

"Listen," Dovey said after a minute. "I've never said this, either. But I don't get why you stayed."

"Stayed where?"

"The hurry-up wedding, yes, I get that. But when you guys were living upstairs at Bear and Hester's, you

266

hated everything and everybody. After that miscarriage, why not just walk? You two were so not ready to be married."

"Walk where, into hospice with Mama? Do you even remember what things were like at that point?"

Dovey was quiet, her dark eyes round. It was possible she didn't.

"We'd already let the house go. I put our furniture and stuff in storage, but I couldn't keep it paid up." That's where her father's table must have gone. The self-storage place would have auctioned off the contents of unpaid lockers. All that handmade furniture, what a score for someone. Probably some upscale dealer in Knoxville. Those people would know where to go for their treasure hunts.

Dovey leaned down and lifted the cigarette from Dellarobia's hand, took a drag, and shook her head, exhaling smoke in rapid little bursts as she gave it back. Dovey only smoked occasionally to be sociable, and had a knack for making the enterprise look toxic. "You could have moved in with me," she said.

"Oh, right. Your mom didn't even like me staying for supper. You were sharing a room with your baby brother and had that diaper pail in your closet. I remember you having a fit because your prom dress smelled like pee."

Dellarobia got up and opened the bedroom window a crack for ventilation. The pasture fence ran so close to the house on this side, its wire mesh spanned her view like bars on a window. The day outside was hazy and indefinite, a seasonless new year that held no more promise than the old one.

"Here's the thing," she said, sitting down again at the vanity. "Bear and Hester had gotten the bank loan to build this house. That was such a big deal. They'd poured the footers, and it was supposed to be move-in ready by May when the baby came. Cub and I would make the loan payments. That was the plan."

"Well, it wasn't May when you all moved in here. With your two suitcases and your zero furniture."

"No, it took them longer to finish. Baby was early, house was late."

Dovey squinted at the air. "It was Fourth of July weekend, right? Cub and his friends shot off all those fireworks in the yard. What were their names, those two brothers? They were both missing fingers, which did not seem like a good sign."

"Rasp. Jerry and Noel."

"No offense, Dellarobia, but somebody builds you a cozy little box, and you just move in? That's basically one of the concepts they use in pest control."

"No offense, Dovey, but you've always had a home. Rewinding back to sixteen and getting a do-over wasn't an option for me. You kind of need parents for that."

Dellarobia took a long, slow drag on her cigarette, feeling the chemical rush arrive little by little in her blood, her hands and feet, the answer to a longing that seemed larger than her body. "And anyway I'd felt that baby *move*. It would get the hiccups whenever I tried to lie down. Cub was the happiest he'd ever been in his life. We were going to be this little family. There's stuff you can't see from the outside."

Dovey stood very still, holding her in the eye in the mirror.

"We had to use up our savings to buy it a cemetery plot."

At that, Dovey sat down beside her and put her head on her shoulder, close to tears, an uncommon and worrisome sight. If they both fell apart at the same time, some greater collapse might follow. "Here's the thing," Dellarobia said. "He'd be turning *eleven* today. If the child had lived, he'd be that old now. We'd be having a fifth-grader birthday party here. I can't find any possible way to make that real in my head."

Preston suddenly appeared in the mirror behind them, standing in the doorway, startling Dellarobia so badly she nearly dropped her cigarette.

"Mama," he said, "smoking gives you cancer and makes you die."

"Honey, I heard about that too. I ought to quit right now, hadn't I?"

He nodded soberly. Dellarobia made a show of grinding out her unfinished cigarette in the ashtray. She opened the vanity drawer, pulled out her pack of cigarettes, and flung it into the trash basket. It floated like a shipwreck survivor among the wadded tissues and crumpled receipts. Already Dellarobia was plotting its

269

rescue, her mind darting forward to the next time she'd be able to sneak off for a secret hookup with her most enduring passion, nicotine. Who needed hell when you had a demon like this?

"So," Dovey said quietly, after Preston had disappeared again, "how many times have you been through that little routine?"

"I hate myself for it."

"Just don't picture the crash landing in the cancer ward," Dovey said, raising one eyebrow. "Like you say, it's a strategy. Works for some."

"Okay, fine, I'm a jerk, like the rest of them. Lying to Preston, of all people. The congenital Eagle Scout. He deserves a more honest mother than me."

"Who do you think is doing any better? You should see what I do at work—the meat counter is guilty-conscience central. People with 'heart attack' written all over their faces, buying bacon. Or these hateful old ladies commanding me to get them a twenty-pound Thanksgiving turkey, like *that*'s going to bring the kids back home this year. The human person cannot face up to a bad outcome, that's just the deal. We're all Cleopatra, like that Pam Tillis song. Cruising down that river in Egypt. Queens of de-Nile."

The word had weight for Dellarobia, who had been through school-sponsored grief groups after each parent's death. The stillbirth was an unofficial add-on to the second round, in those dim final months of high school she otherwise barely remembered. Denial-anger-bargaining-acceptance, get it over with, was the counselor's advice. "I'm a lot of things," she said, "but not in denial, I don't think."

"Case rests, sugar."

Dellarobia felt disoriented, with all those years inside her that added up to naught. Twenty-eight. She felt so young, especially with Dovey here anchoring her to the girl she'd been at seventeen, and at seven. She and Dovey could make each other over until their hair fell out, but nothing in the core of a person really altered.

"I look like a preteen runaway," Dovey pronounced, startling Dellarobia with her similar frame of mind. But that wasn't it. Dovey's focus was on the flat, flyaway hair. "Who were the little orphan girls in those books we read?"

"The boxcar children."

"Them! I'm a boxcar child."

"You always say that, and you're wrong. You turn out looking like Posh Spice, and I wind up like Scary. Why do we keep doing this?"

"Repetition of the same behavior, expecting different results: that's actually one definition of mental illness." Dovey read a lot of magazines.

"I look like Little Orphan Annie." Dellarobia stood up and shook her curls. Maybe she could get a *Flashdance* thing going, in the off-the-shoulder T-shirt. But there was no question about which of them was the real orphan. Dovey rolled her dark silk floss around like a shampoo commercial, relishing her own existence in any form.

"Or some kind of hooker," Dellarobia persisted, fussing with the curly tendrils around her face. "You have to admit, I look like I have more hair than brains."

"But here's the thing, peach. You don't."

Dellarobia shot her a look. "'Peach.' Where'd that come from?"

Dovey laughed. "This guy that comes into Cash Club calls me that. He's tried to hit on me more times than he's bought ground beef. Cute as the devil, b-t-w."

"How long's this been going on?"

"I don't know, a year? I'm just using him as ammo against the guys I work with. They're always drooling over the ladies that come to the meat counter." She deepened her voice and grunted: "'Hey, I see my future ex-wife out there.'"

Dellarobia did not laugh.

Dovey shrugged. "So this guy's drool bait. My future ex."

"And jailbait, more or less. Am I right, he's real young?"

"Of course," Dovey said.

"A dimple in his chin, right here? Works out, really good pecs and shoulders? A silver gauge in his left ear?"

They read each other's faces in the mirror. "You are totally—"

"I'm not."

"*Him?*"

272

"Him."

"I swear to God, I'm going to take a couple of hams out of that jackass. I mean it. I've got the knives to do it."

"No, Dovey, let him be. He's nothing to me anymore."

Dovey reached up to clasp her wrist and gently pull her down onto the seat next to her. Their side-by-side faces in the mirror were like photos in the twin halves of a locket, some long-gone children in a bargain bin of dead people's jewelry. "This is not turning out to be your day, is it?" Dovey asked.

Dellarobia shrugged.

"Honey, I had no idea."

"How could you have?"

"Shit. Your telephone guy."

"Shit. *Everybody's* telephone guy."

❧

Dellarobia wasted too much of a night and all the next morning on a project of self-loathing. She had been two-timed, and probably worse, by the man with whom she was prepared to cheat on her husband. So she'd been nothing special to him, even as an adulterer. To whom could she possibly complain? She had made her peace with that mistake and taken pains to put it behind her. Yet he still had the power to wreck her.

It never wavered, this bleak helplessness she felt

when confronting her undignified obsessions. Before Jimmy it was the man at Rural Incorporated, when she was pregnant with Cordie, which she'd told herself was not a true flirtation. He had steel gray hair and a gold wedding band, and a confidential kindness that completely unwound her. Those appointments got her from week to week. He always had a lot more time for her and her Medicaid papers than for the other people waiting outside his office, and Dellarobia hadn't minded taking it. She never minded. Cub's old friend Strickland, who lifted weights and ran his own tree-trimming business, kept delivering wood chips for mulching the flower beds she didn't have, and she'd taken that too, letting pile it up for years behind the barn. New Heights, his business was called, emblematic of a can-do spirit she found hard to resist. Cub never knew. She had never let things go that far. Yet she understood the betrayal was real. She envisioned the internal part of a person that buttressed a faithful marriage, some delicate calcified scaffold like a rib cage, and knew hers to be malformed, probably from the beginning.

All of Dellarobia's personal turmoil notwithstanding, the second of January must have been a slow news day. At the stroke of noon, while she was putting out bologna sandwiches for the kids, a TV crew showed up at her door.

She flew to answer the knock, leaving Cordie strapped in the high chair and Preston in charge of making sure she took little bites. Dellarobia was startled to see two strangers on her porch: a beautiful woman in perfect makeup and a man with a bald, pointy head and little horn-rimmed glasses. A huge camera sat on the man's shoulder as if it just lived there, possibly attached somehow to his complicated all-weather coat that had extra pockets and zippers, even on the sleeves. Strangest of all was their vehicle parked in the drive, some sort of Jeep tricked out with oversize tires and a satellite dish.

"Dellarobia, is it?" The pale woman looked her straight in the eye with a shocking force, like a faucet left on. "We're from News Nine—we were hoping for just a few minutes of your time to talk about the phenomenon on your farm."

The *phenomenon*. The man was looking all around the front of the house, as if casing the joint for a break-in.

"I've got small children here that I can't leave unattended." Dellarobia stepped outside, pulling the door closed behind her. No way was she letting these people into her trashed house. It had been a long day already, and it wasn't even noon. Whose idea was it to keep kids home from school a full week and more after Christmas? Preston was having a rocket-science day, using toys as projectiles and sofa cushions as the landing pad. Cordelia did something she called "farmer" with the Cheerios, planting the entire box like seeds in the living room carpet while Dellarobia was in the bathroom less than five minutes. She could see her future in that carpet, the endless vacuuming, the grit on the soles of everyone's feet. Like a beach vacation minus the beach, and the vacation.

"We only need a few minutes of your time," the woman repeated. "I'm Tina Ultner, this is my associate Ron Rains." She shook Dellarobia's hand in her firm grip. Tina Ultner was amazing to look at, a woman with slender everything: face, nose, fingers, wrists. Her hair was the true pale blond that can't be faked, with matching almost white eyebrows and a candlewax complexion. She was only a few inches taller than Dellarobia, but with those looks she could own the world. Her makeup alone was a miracle, eyeliner applied so perfectly, her wide blue eyes resembled exotic flowers.

"Listen, I'm sorry," Dellarobia said, "we're not presentable in here. My kids are eating lunch. I don't know what to tell you."

Tina cocked her head to the side. "How old?"

"Five and almost two."

Tina's face crumpled into a combination of anguish and high-beam smile. "You're kidding me! I have been there, let me tell you. Mine are six and nine, and I never thought we'd see the day. Two boys. What are yours?"

"What are they, good question. This morning I'm thinking monkeys, maybe. So you're telling me there's life after kindergarten and diapers?"

"There is, I promise. It's like principal and interest or something. I don't know why, but at age six they shift from a liability to an asset."

"Perfect," Dellarobia said. "That's when I'll sell them."

Tina laughed, a two-note, descending peal like a door chime, a laugh as tidy as the rest of her. "What I mean is, they start following instructions. You can tell them to go get Daddy, and they'll do it."

Dellarobia grinned sadly. "And that's a plus?"

"Oh, I hear you," Tina said, seeming as if she really might. Was it possible she had done anything as messy as child-rearing with those white-tipped fingernails? Dellarobia was mortified by her baggy T-shirt and naked face in the light of Tina's glow, but Tina seemed not to notice. She appeared ready to abandon her cameraman friend and run off for coffee and gossip. He must not be that interested in children, was Dellarobia's hunch.

"Here's the truth," she confessed to Tina. "If I let you all see my living room right now, I'd have to kill you. And the kids are alone in there, so they're probably scheming to drink the Clorox. I just don't see any way I can help you out."

"Should we come back another time, when you're not tied up?"

Dellarobia shrugged. "After their high school graduations?"

Tina laughed again, the same two-note ripple, and glanced over at the man, sending him some kind of signal. Ron pulled his head to the side in obvious irritation. He had not yet said a word, and now walked away toward their vehicle. Tina waited until he got in the Jeep before she spoke again in a lowered voice.

"Ron's a little intense," she confided. "He'll go ballistic if we don't meet our deadline on this assignment. He's already talked to the neighbors down the road about getting the story from them, but I just can't see going that way. I'm in a bind."

"I'm sorry," Dellarobia said. After only three minutes in the acquaintance of Tina Ultner, it seemed very important not to let her down.

Tina glanced around, appearing to size up the options. "I'll tell you what. Go and do what you need to do with the kids, I'll do damage control out here. But do you think in maybe, about, fifteen minutes we could put the kids in the Jeep and just scoot up there to where the things are, the butterflies, and do the shot? We'll keep everything tight, and the kids won't have to be out of your sight for a single minute. Maybe bring something to keep them occupied in the car?"

Dellarobia studied the Jeep. Ron was in the driver's seat, making a phone call. *You go for things*, Dovey had said.

"Could we get a car seat in that thing? Does it have belts in the back?"

"Absolutely," Tina said.

Dellarobia charged back into the house, feeling jinxed after what she'd said about their drinking the Clorox. And that crack about selling her children— what must Tina Ultner think of her? The kids were fully intact in the kitchen, praise heaven, eating their sandwiches. Dellarobia flew into action, throwing the sofa cushions back together and doing a quick pickup of the living room in case Tina had to come in later to use the bathroom. She stuffed Preston's beloved watch and Cordie's animal-farm toy into the diaper bag, and made quick work of her lipstick and eyeliner. The day was sunny and too warm for a coat, which was good luck, her farm jacket or dorky ten-year-old church coat being the choices. She put on a cream-colored ribbed cardigan the kids had given her for Christmas. Meaning it was picked out by her at Target, wrapped by Cub. And never yet worn, also good luck, so she wouldn't look down and see a big stain somewhere on her front side, as per usual when she went out in public. Jewelry or not, she couldn't decide, so opted for small fake-pearl earrings that seemed classy. Her hair still had some curl left over from yesterday's nonsense with Dovey, so she pulled it back loosely with a baby-blue ribbon, and that was that. Before the kids knew what hit them, they were wedged with their mother into the backseat of the News Nine–mobile, bouncing toward the High Road. Dellarobia didn't find any seat belts, but there was no room for the car seat anyway, she just held Cordie in her lap. They wouldn't be getting up much speed. No actual car had tried out that road yet, save for Cub's pickup with the gravel. But that was the point of all Bear's work, as she understood it. Access to the goods. She leaned forward to direct Ron up through the field toward the gate.

"Preston and Cordelia, I am so glad to meet you both," Tina said, turning completely around in the passenger seat. "What great names!"

"Preston was my dad's name," Dellarobia offered.

"And Cordelia is from *King Lear*. Of course!" Tina reached over the back of the seat to extend her hand to each of the kids. Preston gave the slim fingers a shake, but Cordie just stared, probably mesmerized as Dellarobia was by the manicure. Once again she wondered about Tina's children. Where were they now, while their mother was gallivanting around? She had no idea where these folks had driven from with all their gear. Knoxville? They didn't sound like it. Tina had turned back to Ron and was speaking in a totally different voice, more businesslike.

King Lear, of course! Dellarobia couldn't vouch for having known that, she just liked the sound of Cordelia. Maybe, like her own mother, she had gleaned the name and forgotten the source. She heard Tina ask Ron in a low voice, "Do you think the white will go okay on camera?"

Dellarobia put a hand to her chest, realizing Tina had been scrutinizing her sweater during the introductions. "Should I have worn something else?" she asked.

"No, it's great. Beautiful. Sometimes white goes a little dancey on the camera, is the thing. White, and stripes."

"Actually it's ivory," Dellarobia said. The color of her wedding dress, worn for an audience that was very clear on the difference between off- and white. Maybe Tina wasn't. Dellarobia could have spent all day studying the construction of her coffee-colored trench coat, which had neat parallel lines of white topstitching on the placket and belt and cuffs. Probably designer.

"So, the neighbors," Tina said, again turning backward in the seat to use her let's-be-friends voice. "What's up over there? They don't seem to be on great terms with your family."

Dellarobia was embarrassed about her relationship with her neighbors, or lack thereof. Tina probably knew more about the Cooks now than she did. "Really the bad blood is between them and my in-laws, I've got nothing against them. They've had a run of terrible times. Their little boy came down with cancer, and it got them kind of born-again about using chemicals, so they're into the organic thing. They lost their whole tomato crop. And they put in that peach orchard, which is dying. My father-in-law says when it rains so much you have to spray those kinds of things, or they'll just rot."

"So your father-in-law is not keen on the organic thing." Tina had her left elbow cocked on the back of the seat, her other hand in her lap. Earlier, when they'd gotten in, Dellarobia saw she had a small tape recorder. She wondered if it was running.

"Well, that's kind of typical with farming, people are slow to take up new things. You know, they have to be. When you could lose everything in a season, it's not smart to gamble. I think my in-laws resent the healthy-and-organic business because it makes it sound like what we're doing must be unhealthy and unorganic."

"And your in-laws' view of what's happening up here, with the butterflies. Can you talk about that?"

"I don't know. I mean, their view is their view. You should probably ask them."

Dellarobia was distracted by the renovated road, which she hadn't seen yet. She knew Cub and his father had squared away a lot of downed trees and flood damage, but it was the thick layer of new, whitish gravel that altered everything. They'd turned this little wilderness track into a road, with clean, defined edges against the muddy surroundings. Just a country road like any other, inviting no special expectations, its wildness tamed. Against her will, she thought of Jimmy. And of the person she must have been that day, full of desire, full of herself. Now paved over.

She began seeing the butterflies before Tina did, but soon they couldn't be missed, they were everywhere: the *phenomenon*. At the overlook, the road had been widened into a compact turnaround spot, and Ron stopped the Jeep there, facing out. Tina stared, still belted into her seat. Cordie and Preston also sat up straight and took notice, as they did when a favored program came on television.

"Dat," Cordelia said, pointing through the windshield.

The cavernous valley before them was filled with

golden motion. Cordelia had never seen the butterflies, Dellarobia realized. And Preston just the once, on a rainy day when they weren't flying around. She let Preston get out of the car.

"Stay close, honey, and don't go near the edge where it drops off." She pulled open the door on her side and shifted Cordie to her hip, leaving the diaper bag. "Yes, ma'am, there's the King Billies," she said quietly, "just like at Grandma's." She didn't want Tina to know her kids had not seen this before. It seemed so lazy and housebound or something. It made the butterflies belong to her less. Tina wouldn't understand, the road was new, prior to this week there had been no way to bring a toddler up here.

She watched wonder and light come into her daughter's eyes. Preston stood with the toes of his sneakers at the very edge of the gravel road and his arms outstretched, as if he might take flight. Dellarobia felt the same; the sight of all this never wore out. The trees were covered with butterflies at rest, and the air was filled with life. She inhaled the scent of the trees. Finally a clear winter day, blue dome, dark green firs, and all the space between filled with fluttering gold flakes, like a snow globe. She could see they were finding lift here and there, upwelling over the trees. Millions of monarchs, orange confetti, winked light into their eyes.

"This is your shot," Tina said, out of the car now and suddenly bossing Ron around bluntly, calling into doubt Dellarobia's earlier impression that Tina was afraid of him. She pointed to where he should set up his tripod, and stood Dellarobia on the precipice, so to speak, with the view of the valley and backdrop of butterflies behind her. Tina patted Dellarobia's face with a powderpuff so she wouldn't shine, and explained that they would talk for a while with the camera on Dellarobia, then briefly move it around to shoot Tina as well. Later they would patch it together into one conversation. It didn't matter if Dellarobia said things in the wrong order, or made mistakes. They could cut and paste, Tina said. They would make it all look good.

Dellarobia was flattened with anxiety. The questions Tina asked were mostly personal: Who was she, where did she live, how did she and her family feel about what had happened here? To her shock, even Tina knew the circulating story about a miracle involving Dellarobia and some kind of vision or second sight. Did she want to talk about that? Not especially, was Dellarobia's reply.

"Then say whatever you want. Whatever you think is important," Tina said.

"Well, here's what I think is probably important. Usually these butterflies go to Mexico for the winter. They've never come here before, in something like a million years, and now all of a sudden here they are. As you can see. He said . . . okay, wait. Stop. Can I tell you something?"

"Sure."

"There's a scientist that came here, Dr. Byron. You

need to talk to him, he'll be back in a few days. He knows everything there is to know about these butterflies. Could you come back maybe later this week and talk to him?"

"Maybe, sure. Absolutely. But for right now, let's just be here." Tina gave Dellarobia an indulgent smile. She felt the depths of her own incompetence.

"Okay, sorry. Can I start again?" She stuck her hands in her jeans pockets and tried to calm down. She was supposed to be good with words. Cub always said she could argue the wire off a fence post. She'd done speech and drama in high school.

"As many times as you want. No worries. Just be you." Tina put up her hands and waved them, as if to chase everything away and start all over. "What we want is to be up close and personal with Dellarobia. Tell me about the first time you saw the butterflies. What did that feel like?"

"The first time." She glanced at her kids. Cordie was safely tucked into the Jeep now, playing with her plastic barn, but Preston was inching his way out to the edge of the overlook. "Preston!" she yelled. "Not one more inch, mister! I mean it. Or else you will go sit in the car with your sister." She winced apologetically at Tina, who was still smiling. The patience of a saint. "Sorry," Dellarobia said.

"Nothing to be sorry about. Go ahead."

"What I was going to say before is that these butterflies migrated to the wrong place this year, for the first

285

time ever. I guess in the history of the world. So even though it looks really pretty, it might be a problem. It could actually be terrible."

"And why is that?" Tina asked.

Why was that. Words left her mind. Her hair was slipping out of its tie, the curls around her face moving in the breeze, distracting her, and suddenly she felt completely sure her sweater was buttoned wrong. Or not buttoned at all. This day was crazy. She touched her chest with one hand, checking the button placket. "Hang on a sec, can I just, is my sweater buttoned wrong? I'm sure I look horrible."

Tina cocked her head, a little gesture Dellarobia was starting to recognize. "Do you know what I was thinking just then? Honestly? That this is probably the most gorgeous shot we've set up in I don't know how long. Months. You, that gorgeous hair, the butterflies behind you. It's just about killing me. I'm going to look like a corpse next to you and all that ambery light. You'll die when you see it. How's the light, Ron?"

"Gorgeous," Ron said from behind the camera, startling Dellarobia. Since when was *Ron* on her side? Gorgeous. She wondered if Jimmy would see her on the news, and felt a simmering fury, largely the result of nicotine deprivation and not entirely at Jimmy. But partly at him. Flirting with everything in a skirt. Had he never been serious about her at all? Just because she was older, and married, he'd seen her as a sure thing, sex without risk of attachment. Did he even care that she'd ended it? She hoped the sweater looked as good on her now as it had in the store, the rare dressing-room event. She did not have the vaguest idea what Tina had just asked her. "What was the question?"

"Start wherever you want," Tina said, possibly with a pinch of impatience.

She wished she could just tell the truth. The whole of it. That Bear was about to clear-cut this mountain for cash, and that they really did need the money. Which some people could never understand. Being boxed in. Which is really what brought her up here in the first place, not a man but a desperation. Defective as that impulse may have been, it got her here. She was the first to see.

"This phenomenon is very special to you," Tina said. "The story we're hearing in this town is that you had a vision. So Dellarobia, what happened that day, when you first knew the miracle of the monarchs had come to your farm?"

"I was running away from things. That's the long and the short of it," Dellarobia said. She wanted Jimmy gone, out of her story. Would he see this on television?

"From what?" Tina asked with a softer, concerned voice.

Dellarobia turned her head a little to the side so she could see the butterflies. Just like the first time, it felt like a dream to see that cold fire rising. It was impossible to believe what she saw was real. The end of the world, as good a guess as any. She slowly exhaled. "My life, I guess. I couldn't live it anymore. I wanted out. So I came up here by myself, ready to throw everything away. And I saw this. This stopped me."

"How so?"

"I don't know. I was so focused on my own little life. Just one person. And here was something so much bigger. I had to come back and live a different life."

Tina blinked, casting a glance at Ron.

"Okay, that was, I don't even know what that was," Dellarobia said. A turn down a wrong-way street in crazy town, was what it was. She held up her hand like a cop, shaking her head. "Way too personal. If my family heard that, can you imagine? My kids?"

Thankfully, she saw that Preston had inched his way down the road until he was probably out of earshot. "So, that's off the record, we cut all that and start over, right?"

"Absolutely," said Tina.

❧

Both their phones rang at once, at around ten after nine. Cub had worked late and passed out on the couch watching television, so his phone jangled on and on in his pocket while Dellarobia ran to her purse to get hers. It was Dovey, incoherent. Dovey screaming to turn on the TV.

"It's on," Dellarobia said, her heart lurching. Had she missed some disaster?

"It's you," Dovey kept saying. "Go to CNN."

This was the sort of thing that happened in movies, Dellarobia thought. But movie people could always find the remote control. Dovey kept yelling through the phone while her search grew more frantic. Under the cushions, under Cub, under the couch. The people in movies didn't live with petty criminals who dismantled small electronics for parts and batteries. "Hang on!" she yelled back, abandoning the hunt and going to kneel in front of the television set itself. Sure enough, she found there was no way to control it from the object itself, not even an on-off switch. What sense did that make? A TV set was a modern God! You could only send it your requests from afar.

"What do you mean, it's me?" she asked, trying to calm down.

"That thing you did yesterday! That interview with Barbie. But they're not showing her. It's all you, Della-robia."

Dellarobia stood up, surveyed the room. Cub was still out cold. She could actually hear the murmur of Dovey's television through the phone.

"Oh, my God," Dovey shrieked. "This is crazy. They're saying you tried to kill yourself!"

Shock began to fill Dellarobia with its watery weight, starting from her feet and nearly taking her out at the knees. She shoved at Cub with all her strength to make room for herself on the couch, and kept the phone to her ear while she slid one hand around underneath him, again, unable to call off her hopeless search. Cub's phone had stopped ringing and made the sharp little beep of a new message.

"This is crazy," she said to Dovey. "Say that again. What you just said."

"You were on your way to jump off a cliff or something, and saw the butterflies and changed your mind. It's gone now."

"What's gone?"

"The whole thing. Now they've gone over to . . ." Dovey paused. "I don't know, some war thing in Africa. The whole spot with you only lasted, like, one or two minutes. Maybe more than that. It was almost the top story. They showed you talking, and some other guy I didn't know. One of your neighbors?"

"The Cooks? They talked to the Cooks, next door."

"Maybe him, yeah. He said you all were going to log the mountain and had no concern for the butterflies, and then it said you were the sole . . . something. Sole voice of reason, or something like that, against your family."

"Oh, wonderful," Dellarobia said. She prayed Bear and Hester hadn't seen this. There was a good chance. They didn't watch the news.

"But then this thing about you being suicidal. 'Dellarobia Turnbow has her own reason for believing the butterflies are a special something-or-other. They saved her life.' I can't repeat it exactly. Mind you, I'm here crapping my pants while this is all going on. I'm like, Whoa, that's my best friend! I totally did her hair!"

"Where in the world would they get that, about suicide?"

"Maybe they'll run it again at ten."

"Christ. Maybe I *will* jump off a cliff." She put her head on her knees, genuinely feeling she could pass out. Cub stirred next to her, starting to rouse.

"Here's the thing," Dovey said. "You looked bookoo hot. Can I borrow that sweater?"

The interview did air again, many times in various forms, first as national news and then local. In Cleary it was headline news that a local person had made the news. Reporters called the house repeatedly, and Dellarobia's heart raced every time the phone rang. If she ever saw a camera again, she planned to run for her life. Cub was stupefied by the attention. The local TV channel made it a top story, with nightly updates. The headline banner was always the same still shot of Dellarobia with the butterflies behind her, and a caption: "Battle over Butterflies." These updates made Dellarobia nauseous with anxiety. Waiting for her image to appear onscreen felt like waiting to be slapped. But she couldn't stop herself from watching, either. People at church and the grocery were basically congratulating her nonstop, without regard to anything she'd said, just operating on the guiding principle that being on TV was the peak human experience. It seemed ungracious to tell them it felt like having her skin peeled off, so she held her tongue and let them go on wishing they'd get their turn someday.

Dellarobia referred every interviewer to Bear and Hester. Cub worried that his father was shaping up in this story to be the bad guy, willful destroyer of butterflies, and they deserved a say at this point, but Bear and Hester never turned up on the screen. As crazy as it seemed as a deciding factor, Dellarobia suspected they might not be photogenic enough to be news. Handsome Mr. Cook was interviewed often, sitting on the sofa with his sad wife and their poor little bald son. So was Bobby Ogle, who seemed perfectly at ease with the camera as he spoke of caring for God's Creation. There was even some footage of him preaching at their church on a regular Sunday, which floored Dellarobia. When had news cameras been in there?

The local powers definitely were coming down on the pro-butterfly side. The Cleary news team invited the mayor, Jack Stell, and a heavyset man from the Chamber of Commerce to sit at their big curved desk and discuss tourism opportunity. People all over the world would want to come see the monarchs. The heavyset man used Disneyland as a comparison. Dellarobia felt they should get their act together on some family lodgings other than the Wayside, if that was their game plan. She also felt Ovid Byron should be sitting at that desk. She wished he would get here.

Nobody was asking why the butterflies were here; the big news was just that they *were*.

The Battle of the Butterflies was presumably a conflict between people, although the opposers were something of a ragbag army, hard to pin down. One view was that all the outside attention on the butterflies might disrupt normal life. Dellarobia had heard this sentiment at church and elsewhere, but only oddballs were shown to espouse it on the news: a skinny old man in an undershirt in his trailer home said the crime would go up. Some kids in front of the Feathertown Exxon, who looked like hoodlums, declared they didn't need outsiders in this town. Dellarobia realized these people were being mocked, and remembered with almost an electric shock the old man she'd seen being ridiculed on the late-night program. Billy Ray Hatch. If she'd remembered that painful setup while Tina Ultner was here, she might have slammed the door on her perfectly powdered nose. But she hadn't. Real life and the things inside the TV set belonged to different universes. People on the outside could not imagine they would ever end up as monkeys in that box.

And yet they did, it was unendingly strange. She and Cub watched wide-eyed each night, gasping at each sighting of people or places they knew. They never did see the original interview with Tina, although clips from it appeared repeatedly on the Cleary news, mostly as background like the banner shot. As far as Dellarobia could tell, the suicide angle had been dropped. Initially, in fact, she was sure Dovey had invented it, due to shell shock, but Dovey had not. Clever girl, she figured out how to get the whole clip downloaded on her phone and came over two days after the fact with proof in hand. With Preston away at school and Cub at work, they sat in the kitchen and watched it.

"My life. I guess. I couldn't live it anymore . . . ," said the little Dellarobia on the phone's screen, in a tinny voice that could not be hers. "I came up here by myself, ready to throw everything away. And . . . this stopped me." The voice continued while the screen panned to a wide view of the butterflies covering the trees and filling the air. "Here was something so much bigger. I had to come back and live a different life."

"I swear I never said that."

"It sure looks like you did," said Dovey.

"It sure looks like I did." She could not imagine the carnage if the family saw this. And Hester might, if it was on the computer. Just not Cub, she prayed. For his sake. Dellarobia had almost no memory of the interview itself. She recalled a few false starts, blurting out nonsense that Tina had promised not to use.

"Okay, now check this out," Dovey said, clicking masterfully at the buttons on her very swank phone, like Preston with his watch. "There. This just showed up today."

Dellarobia scowled at the screen, baffled. "The Butterfly Venus," it said. It was Dellarobia, but someone had messed with the image. She appeared to be standing on the open wings of a huge monarch. Little butterflies floated in the air all around her.

"What is this?" Dellarobia asked.

"You're that famous painting, the naked chick standing on the shell." Dovey scrolled over to another image that Dellarobia recognized. The Birth of Venus. Someone had put the two images together and sent it out over the Internet. The similarity was surreal. It couldn't possibly be herself, but it was, her own orange hair blowing loose from its ribbon in back, her left hand in her pocket and her right hand across her chest, posed like the naked Venus girl on the open wings of her shell. Dellarobia couldn't even remember standing like that, touching her chest. She was not exactly naked in the picture, her clothing was faded to a neutral shade, but naked was how she felt. Scared and exposed. This thing looked vaguely pornographic.

"Who can see this?" she asked.

"Everybody can see this," Dovey said. This image that was not real and had never happened was flying around the world.

She remembered then. Why she'd brought her hand up to her chest like that in front of Ron's camera. She was afraid her buttons had fallen open.

9

Continental Ecosystem

"Name?" he asked, not really asking. He answered himself, spelling aloud as he wrote on the form, D-E-L-L-A . . . He paused, his pen poised over the clipboard balanced on his knee. "Is it one word, or two?"

The interview was a formality, Dr. Byron had said. For a government-funded position he had to file certain forms proving he'd gone to the trouble of equal-opportunity hiring. She'd replied that hiring someone like herself should be ample proof he had scraped the bottom of the barrel. She felt nervous when he did not laugh. She had no idea how to behave as an employed person.

"All one word," she told him. They sat facing one another on metal folding chairs. She'd dressed up for this, beige slacks and a black sweater. Dr. Byron wore jeans as always, sitting with his long legs crossed up ankle-over-knee like a grasshopper.

"Ah," he said. "The Italian sculptor is two. My wife confirmed that."

The mention made her blush. A wife there was, then, with whom he had discussed Dellarobia. She imagined them together at a computer viewing the image of her essentially naked, perched on butterfly wings as the Venus. From now on she had to rise each day into a world that had seen her like that. Tellers at the bank, the boys who bagged her groceries, Preston's schoolteachers, present and future. It felt like stepping again and again into scalding water. Blushing had become her skin's normal pastime.

"Do you prefer Mrs. or Ms. or none of the above?"

"Mrs., I guess." She let out a joyless laugh. "Until my husband divorces me for doing this."

He glanced up at her over his reading glasses. "For doing?"

"Taking this job. Don't worry, that was a joke. He won't."

"He has some concerns about you in this lab?"

"It's nothing personal. My family is just, I guess, typical. They feel like a wife working outside the home is a reflection on the husband."

Dr. Byron's look suggested he found this not typical. He didn't know the half of it. People were praying for her family now, on account of that picture on the Internet. Cub's father had told him a woman got such attention only if she asked for it.

"I spoke out of turn," she said. "I'll handle my family."

"Is it a question of safety?" he asked, taking off his skinny glasses and holding them by the earpiece. "Because I can assure you, we will be taking every precaution here, exactly as if we were in a more permanent facility."

Everything, she wanted to scream at him, was a question of safety. All human endeavor bent itself to the same lost cause. Being kept inside a pumpkin shell your whole life was no guarantee against getting flung into space.

"Seriously, don't worry about it," she repeated. Dr. Byron wrote something on his clipboard without comment.

Somewhere in the room behind her Pete was up on a ladder, loudly stapling plastic sheeting to the walls. They were making their laboratory in the sheep barn. Contrary to her expectations, a butterfly lab looked something like a kitchen with outlandishly expensive appliances. For two days she'd been helping them unpack the crates they'd brought from New Mexico, and she knew it was bad manners but couldn't stop herself from asking about the costs of things. They couldn't give her exact answers. The equipment was not necessarily new. Most of it, in fact, seemed to be older than she was, "pre–Reagan administration," they both remarked dolefully, as if that had been some Appomattox Court House with the scientists on the losing side. But when she pressed them for estimates, they blew her mind. A glass box called the Mettler balance, which they handled like a newborn baby, was "maybe a few thousand dollars." So was the drying oven, a drab gray thing about the size of any oven, and the antique-looking round tub called a centrifuge, which weighed so much they left it in its case until Pete could build a heavy table to serve as its throne. The wooden shipping crates, bulky as coffins, would become the foundations of a lab counter, which they called a bench.

When she unscrolled the bubble wrap from a fierce-looking little blender, Ovid had remarked, "Now *that* is a nifty item." In the neighborhood of two grand, he'd said, made in Germany. Its name was Tissuemizer, and its special task was to make a kind of butterfly soup that no one would be eating, as the ingredients were both toxic and flammable. They had ordered a venting hood of the type usually installed over kitchen ranges to eliminate cooking odors, something Dellarobia had never owned. She'd just learned the hard way never to cook anything too fishy. But Dr. Byron needed a range hood, so the appliance department at Sears had been called to come and install one in the Turnbow sheep barn, pronto. They would also be delivering a freezer, the cheapest model available, but even so, a stand-alone freezer. Not a compartment in the top of the fridge, into which ordinary mothers crammed Popsicles and freeze-packs for their kids' bruises. Dellarobia found herself coveting a freezer that was not yet even technically, until delivery, thy neighbor's goods.

The official plan was to keep this lab in operation until the butterflies flew away from their winter roost, which under normal circumstances occurred in March, she was told. Then Ovid would pack up all this equipment and fly away also. She wondered if the freezer might come on the market for a secondhand price at that time, or if he would take it with him. And the nearly new range hood? Would he think to arrange for repair of the hole it left behind? The science crew was going through money in a manner she could scarcely imagine.

"I'm going to ask you to fill in most of this yourself," Dr. Byron said finally, after leafing through several pages on his clipboard. "Date of birth, social security. Employment history, all that sort of thing. It's only this first box, it looks like I am supposed to do that myself."

She wondered how much he knew of her miserable notoriety, the naked-ish picture, the suicide business. Her days swung between fury and humiliation, tethered on nights of permanent anxiety, as she waited for Cub to find out. She envisioned crash landings everywhere. Dr. Byron might be taking her on as a pity case. Or even as some kind of leverage against the family's logging plan. The lease he'd signed for this lab space gave Bear some breathing room, financially, and Dellarobia knew he and Hester were involved in some renegotiations with Money Tree. It was possible they could return the advance money and rescind the contract. They'd been given until March to come to terms. But as long as Bear could wipe out these scientists' reason for being here with a stroke of heavy machinery, she didn't trust him. That might be just the sucker punch that would make him feel big in this town again. And Hester wouldn't hold with that. In Dellarobia's in-law career she had never seen so much light between those two.

"How much science in your background?" Dr. Byron asked.

"Science?" She considered this. "None? Well, biology and stuff. High school."

He looked surprised. "No college?"

"No college. Sorry." She wondered if humiliation ever ran its natural course and peeled off, like sunburn, or just kept blazing. She watched him fill in more lines on his form without comment. He didn't even look up at her. She tried not to flinch with each of Pete's explosive blasts overhead, like repeating rifle shots. Pete was using a construction-grade staple gun to secure giant sheets of plastic over every inch of the walls, for the sake of creating cleanable surfaces. She could see the domestic advantages of plastic sheeting, at least until her kids were grown. Now he was stretching it even across the rough wooden beams of the ceiling.

"Even the ceiling gets covered?" she asked quietly.

Dr. Byron's eyes went upward and then down again, like a man watching a pop-up fly ball. "There's no telling what could fall out of that ceiling," he said. "The number-one enemy of everything is dust."

She'd heard theories in her time regarding the number-one enemy of everything, ranging from Osama bin Laden to premarital sex. The dust theory she liked. Here was a danger she seemed situated to control. Before the men unpacked their crates she had attacked the cement floor with practiced vigor using an industrial mop bucket they'd bought at the Walmart in Cleary, along with the plastic sheeting. And back before they arrived she'd spent a Sunday morning chipping out fossilized manure with a screwdriver and flat-bottomed shovel. She'd like to see some college ho do that.

When Dr. Byron first mentioned this job on the phone, she'd thought he was posing it as a real possibility. Not the long shot it obviously was. She felt embarrassed now, as if caught out on a foray into the kind of false identity hijinks she and Dovey used to pull off in bars, pretending to work for Jane Goodall and the like. Ovid had changed. Gone away was the man who'd moonwalked at her Christmas party, the man with the eyetooth-wide smile. Replaced by a distracted would-be employer grimacing at her poor credentials. She wondered what had happened to darken his mood in the interim. A death in the family, a fight with his wife. Holidays were notorious for family crackups.

Whatever the reason, he'd scarcely noticed she was working her tail off in here already, doing the heavy cleaning, to impress him as a volunteer before asking to upgrade her status. He just stood around looking vexed, listing problems in the making. January had taken a turn, the rain had turned to freezing, his instruments were temperamental. How were they going to heat the lab? He worried about controlling the humidity and temperature fluctuations, the flammable fumes. He was uncertain his chemical reagents could be properly stored here. Something called the NMR he decided to scrap altogether, and would have to send those samples back to New Mexico. There was so much to do, he kept saying. Dellarobia missed the man who'd once come to supper and charmed her clever son. She resented his new list of cares, wondering how they stacked up against, say, a foreclosure notice or a car breakdown you walked home from without any hope of repair. In her experience people had worries or they had tons of money, not both.

"So, no college is a deal-breaker?" she asked. He seemed to have forgotten she was holding her breath here, turning blue. He continued to write for several more seconds. She could not imagine what that was about. He turned a page, looked up.

"Not a deal-breaker, no. Mainly I'm looking for some maturity in this position."

"Maturity," she repeated. "Meaning you're looking to hire an old person?"

He almost smiled. "Responsible, I should have said. When the place is hopping with student volunteers, it can be overwhelming. Sometimes I feel like that old woman in the shoe, you know? How does that one go?"

"So many children she didn't know what to do, yes sir I do know. Who are these kids, and what all will they be doing?"

He swatted a hand at the empty room, his momentary lightness gone. "So much, I can't even tell you. Cardenolide fingerprinting maybe, lipid analysis for sure, that's where we'll start. I can train you to do a lot of the routine work on that."

She felt simultaneous hope and defeat. I can train you to lightbulb candlewax drainpipe. The man was speaking in tongues. "Lipids are food, right? Some kind of fat."

"Fat, yes. We'll see whether these butterflies fattened up prior to overwintering. Usually they travel light during the migration and then pack away a lot of lipid stores just before they roost for the winter. We want to see if they are behaving as a normal migratory population, even though this is not a normal place for migrants to go. I am also concerned about how their physiology is responding to the cold weather. And we still don't have a full habitat assessment. Monitoring the site, recording all the data from our iButtons. It's a whole lot of busy-work."

Was she hired, then? And did he think she had the faintest idea what he was talking about? Her panic must have been obvious. "Don't worry," he said. "I'm not going to throw you to the lions."

"Okay," she said slowly, noting that some other placement was implied.

"We should be getting a lot of help here soon. The college in Cleary will probably send us biology students for internships, and we're tapping other options." He set the clipboard on his knee, interlaced his fingers behind his head, and leaned back, relaxing a little. Those hands, the ultra-long fingers and pale palms, she'd noticed the first time they met. "We'll train these kids and put them on the simple things. Data entry, body counts, doing parasite counts under the scope. But training them all from the ground up, it costs a lot of time, you know? It's time we just don't have."

"So this position would involve supervising college kids?"

"Pete and I will handle the internships. Oh, I should mention, other researchers will be coming through. From Cornell and Florida, maybe Australia." She wondered if he could be joking: How many famous scientists would fit in a milking parlor?

"But I'm talking about the day-to-day, you know?" Dr. Byron went on. "The simple, routine stuff. It means logging a lot of hours. We're looking for some volunteers who can come in after school. High school kids."

Now she did laugh. "You mean doing science on purpose, on their own time? Good luck with that one. Maybe when it comes out as a video game."

He clicked his tongue dismissively. "Volunteerism is a very big part of our effort. Monarch Watch, Journey North, these are national networks of kids mostly, with their teachers, doing class projects. Rearing and tagging butterflies, tracking, and so on. They help us plot arrivals and departures, on the Internet." He tilted his head toward Pete. "Probably half my graduate students got their start as kids doing monarch projects."

"I'm sorry," she said, "but really? These are kids and schoolteachers going outside to study nature stuff?"

"Tell me, Dellarobia. What did you do in science class?"

"In high school? Our science teacher was the basketball coach, if you want to know. Coach Bishop. He hated biology about twenty percent more than the kids did. He'd leave the girls doing study sheets while he took the boys to the gym to shoot hoops."

"How is that possible?"

"How? He'd take a vote, usually. 'Who says we shoot hoops today?' Obviously no girl would vote against it. You'd never get another date in your life."

He seemed doubtful of her story. But it was true, and in Dellarobia's opinion no more far-fetched than the tales he'd told her. Of newborn butterflies, for instance, somehow flying thousands of miles to a place they'd never seen, the land where their forefathers died. Life was just one big fat swarm of kids left to fend for themselves.

Dr. Byron uncrossed his legs and leaned forward, pressing his hands together between his knees and looking at her. For the first time in this interview he seemed totally present. "Is this typical of high schools in this area, what you are describing?"

"Well, I only went to the one." She hesitated, reconsidering how much she ought to disclose. She thought of Dovey mocking her ratty T-shirt: *Be sure to wear that to your interview*. "I had some good teachers," she began again, unconvincingly. "Well, okay, I had one, Mrs. Lake for English. She was about a hundred years old. It's weird, it was like she came from some earlier time when people actually cared. I heard she had a stroke, though. Bless her heart. Probably one too many times hearing some kid conjugate 'bring, brang, brung.' "

Ovid seemed unamused. "What about math?"

"Our high school had Math One and Math Two," she said. "Coach Otis, baseball. Math Two was for the kids who were already solid with multiplication."

His brow wrinkled formidably. "Is this true?"

"Is that, like, massively insufficient?"

"Two years of algebra, geometry, trigonometry, pre-calculus, calculus, and stats." He rattled this off like a ritual prayer in an alien religion. "Nothing there sounds familiar?"

"You ought to try that out on Coach Otis. If you want to see a grown man cry."

Dr. Byron actually seemed agitated. "What are these administrators thinking?" he asked. As if he had a dog in this race, Dellarobia thought. His children, if any, would get started on higher math in some upmarket kindergarten.

"They're not thinking anything much," she told him. "Sports. That's huge, a kid can shine if he's good at football or baseball. Probably get a job later on in the bank or something like that."

"Well, but it's criminal negligence, really. These kids have to grow up and run things. Larger things than a ball field, I mean. What kind of world will they really be able to make?"

"I'd say you're looking at it." She crossed her arms, awaiting Dr. Byron's verdict. Former Feathertown athletes had this town in their hands: the mayor, Jack Stell; Bobby Ogle; Ed Cameron at the bank, with whom she'd pleaded grace on her house loan. In his office that day they'd joked about their semester together in Mrs. Lake's class, which Ed barely passed, and the football squad he led to state semifinals. People liked and trusted such men.

"Look, Dellarobia, I don't want you to take this personally. But I've been wondering about this. I went to that school. Things were not what I expected."

"Feathertown High?" She was startled, unable to picture any intersection between Dr. Ovid Byron and local culture. "When?"

"In December. I wanted to speak with the faculty about getting volunteers in the new semester. It's a great chance for these kids. Exposure to field biology, data analysis, scientific method. If for no other reason, the college résumé. But I got nothing. The counselor asked if we were paying minimum wage."

"Oh, kids in Feathertown wouldn't know college-bound from a hole in the ground. They don't need it for life around here. College is kind of irrelevant."

His eyes went wide, as if she'd mentioned they boiled local children alive. His shock gave her a strange satisfaction she could not have explained. Insider status, maybe. She thought of Billy Ray Hatch, turned into a freak show on TV. Dovey said he was all over the Internet now too, with his *reckon* and *this winter been too mild to suit my coon dogs*. The world's next big laugh of the moment. She'd like to hug that old man around his neck, and punch some cameraman in the kisser.

"Footballers teaching sports in place of science class," Dr. Byron declared, "should not be legal. Are there no state standards or testing?"

"Oh, yes. We flunk those. We are dependable in that regard."

"How can that persist?" He was studying her carefully, for irony she supposed, or some kind of storybook scrappiness. She'd already taken this interview to be a lost cause, but now she resisted. She didn't want to lose on his rules.

"I'll tell you how," she said. "This state has cities on one end of it, and farms on the other. If they ever decided to send somebody out from the money end of things to check on us, they might slap down a fine or something."

"And why do you suppose they don't?"

She laughed. "They're scared they'll get kidnapped by the hillbillies like in that *Deliverance* movie."

"I haven't seen that one."

She leaned forward. "May I ask a personal question? What country did you grow up in?"

He matched her posture, both hands on his knees. "The United States of America. Saint Thomas, Virgin Islands."

"Whoa. America has islands? Besides Hawaii, I mean."

"America has quite a few in fact, in several oceans.

309

Saint Thomas is a protectorate, which is really a glorified colony. We pay taxes, but nobody comes out from the money end of things, as you say, to keep our schools up to date."

She nodded, checking him for irony or scrappiness, she supposed. It made sense of this man, to picture him stalking butterflies on a golden shore and wowing the teachers in some little one-room school. "And here you are anyway," she said, "doctor of all the sciences, Harvard and everything. But see, there's not room at the top for everybody. Most of us have to walk around in our sleep, accepting our underprivileged condition."

"You may be overstating the case," he said, and left it at that. As if she were a child. She had taken things too far, of course. But she felt anger rising, some things still left unsaid. Dr. Byron flipped through what looked like a lot of pages on his clipboard. He had asked to borrow a clock for the lab, and she'd brought out the only one she had, a big wind-up alarm thing shaped like a chicken that Preston had used for learning to tell time. The ridiculous object sat ticking off seconds on a table nearby, measuring out the remainder of her tenure here among the well educated. A machine next to the clock was labeled SARTORIUS, which made her think of *sartorial*, a vocabulary word from long, long ago. *Of or pertaining to the tailor's trade.* What was getting sewn up here?

"I think you can take care of all the rest of this paperwork," he said at last. "I think you will do fine. Our main concern is to get things going quickly, because we have so little time. A matter of weeks. Maybe not even that."

"Thank you. Wow, thanks very much." In other words, he was in a bind, and she would suffice. He stood up and gave her a quick handshake, handing over the clipboard, looking not at all thrilled. He indicated she should sit tight and finish filling out the forms. His impatience made no sense. He was acting like a man who'd been told he had only weeks to live. She wondered if he had spoken to Bear at all about the logging plan.

"Let me just ask," she said cautiously, "what is your main worry, time-wise?"

He clicked his pen, looked at it, put it in his pocket, and then sat down again, looking her directly in the eye. "My main worry, time-wise, is that a winter storm could arrive here tomorrow and kill every butterfly on that mountain."

She was so startled that any possible reply left her head. Even the assault-weapon cadence of Pete's staple gun faltered for a moment, it seemed. How could they put all this effort into such a precarious scenario? That the butterflies could be wiped out, completely apart from the logging she hoped to forestall, was inconceivable.

"The temperature at which a wet monarch will freeze to death," he said very slowly, as in, *Don't make me repeat this*, "is minus four degrees centigrade."

311

"Okay," she said. As in, *I'm listening*.

"That is an inevitable event, for this latitude. The mid-twenties, Fahrenheit. The forest might shield them to some extent, where the canopy is closed. Large trees are protective; the trunks create a thermal environment like big water bottles. That's why you see them covering the trunks. Maybe it's why they ended up in that stand of old conifers for their roosting site when they went off track. These firs are similar to the Mexican oyamels, in terms of chemistry. We have no idea of the cues involved. But to protect them from the kind of winter they will have here, that forest is far from adequate."

"So what normally happens to them, when it goes below freezing?" she asked.

"Normally they are in the Transverse Neovolcanic Belt of Mexico, at a latitude of nineteen degrees north. Where winter as you know it is not an issue."

"So these butterflies would all die off, when it gets bad, and then what? Their eggs would hatch out in the spring?"

"Monarchs don't lay eggs in winter. This is something I think you know."

"You're right, I did know that. Sorry. Technically a tropical guy, just visiting."

"They are obliged to survive the winter in adult form. Even for these individuals with aberrant migratory flight behavior, the reproduction is hardwired. Like ours. If we somehow were tricked into going to live among cattle, we could not give birth to calves or feed them on grass."

"I understand."

"These insects have been led astray, for whatever reason. But breeding and egg-laying are still impossible for them until spring, when the milkweeds emerge."

"So if they die here, they die."

"That's right," he said.

She despised this account, the butterflies led astray. She'd preferred the version of the story in which her mountain attracted its visitors through benevolence, not some hidden treachery. "And the other monarchs . . . ," she began, unsure what she meant to ask. "The ones in Mexico are still doing okay."

"What we're finding in Mexico this year is a catastrophically diminished population in the Neovolcanics. They had unbelievable storms and flooding last spring, which may or may not have something to do with this. We have been waiting all winter for better reports. A lot of people are there now searching the forests for relocated roosts. Higher up the mountain, is what we assumed. But the report is nothing."

She tried to assimilate this news while her brain crashed with thoughts of the Mexican mudslide, the smashed and twisted cars, houses lifted from their moorings, floating downstream. A secret she had thought she was keeping from him.

"The report is nothing," she repeated. "You mean the butterflies aren't there."

"Not in the ordinary numbers. This is not yet public information, so I ask you to keep it private. Not that anyone hereabouts is likely to be very interested."

The insult was unnecessary. She felt accosted. "So what are you saying? That these butterflies here—"

"That this roosting colony is a significant proportion of the entire North American monarch butterfly population."

"Most of the ones that *exist*?"

"Most of the migratory population, yes," he said. "In terms of genetic viability, reproductive viability, what we have here is nearly the whole lot."

Like Job, in the Bible, she thought. All his children gathered in one place for a wedding when a great wind rose and collapsed the roof upon them. All hope and future lost in a day. Of all sad stories, that parable was meant to be the saddest, a loss to make a man fall down on the ash heap and meet his maker or else run to the arms of darkness. She wondered if Ovid Byron knew the story of Job.

"So why does it even matter what you do here?" She looked at the laboratory in a different way. Mission control of a boggling heartbreak. "I'm sorry to ask. But, you know what I'm saying?"

He avoided meeting her eye. "We should be physicians, or some kind of superheroes saving the patient with special powers. That's what people want."

She didn't reply, wondering if he was right about that. Probably it was true. People resisted hearing the details of a problem, even when it was something personal, like their own cancer. What they wanted was the fix.

"We are only scientists," he said. "Maybe foolish ones. Normally it would take years to do what we are trying to accomplish here in a few weeks. We are seeing . . ." He paused. She followed his gaze to the plastic-covered window, a filmy rectangle of light and nothing more. Whatever he saw, it was not there.

"We are seeing a bizarre alteration of a previously stable pattern," he said finally. "A continental ecosystem breaking down. Most likely, this is due to climate change. Really I can tell you I'm sure of that. Climate change has disrupted this system. For the scientific record, we want to get to the bottom of that as best we can, before events of this winter destroy a beautiful species and the chain of evidence we might use for tracking its demise. It's not a happy scenario."

What came to her mind on the spot was one of Cub's shows on Spike TV, *1000 Ways to Die*. People thrived on unhappy scenarios. In this case it was just the one way, freezing to death, and millions of unfortunates. She stilled her mind, trying to embrace this sadness Dr. Byron had asked her to understand.

"One of God's creatures of this world, meeting its End of Days," she said after a quiet minute. Not words of science, she knew that, but it was a truth she could feel. The forest of flame that had lifted her despair, the migratory pulse that had rocked in the arms of a continent for all time: these fell like stones in her heart. This was the bad news he'd received over the holiday. The one thing most beloved to him was dying. Not a death in the family, then, but maybe as serious as that. He'd chased this life for all his years; it had brought him this distance, his complicated system. She had only begun to know it. Now began the steps of grief. It would pass through this world like that baby in its pelt of red fur, while most people paid no attention.

"I'm sorry," she said.

He looked away abruptly from those words, a gesture that gave her to know she might be needed here. Ovid was choking up. She spoke quickly to give him some cover. "I didn't know it was that bad. I want to help out here, I'm glad to."

"Nobody knows it is this bad." He recovered himself almost instantly, willfully, she thought. Rubbing his chin. A man's grief.

"But the news people are all over this thing up here," she said. "Why on earth wouldn't you tell them what's going on?"

He looked at her oddly, studying her without speaking, and she flushed deeply, as if he were seeing her naked. The Butterfly Venus, that's what was all over. "I don't know what you've seen," she said. "But it's out of control. I keep telling them they need to talk to you. I swear, I do. Talk to Dr. Byron, because I'm no expert."

Pete startled her by speaking. "That's why they talk to you. Because you don't really know anything." He'd

316

stopped stapling and was listening in on what she'd thought was a private conversation. She felt ambushed.

She turned around in her chair to scowl at Pete. "Excuse me?"

Pete shrugged. "It's not your fault. They just don't want to talk to a scientist. It would mess with their story."

Dellarobia looked from Pete to Ovid Byron.

"A journalist's job is to collect information," Ovid said to Pete.

"Nope," Pete said. "That's what we do. It's not what they do."

Dellarobia was unready to be pushed out of the conversation just like that. "Then what do you think the news people drive their Jeeps all the way out here for?"

"To shore up the prevailing view of their audience and sponsors."

"Pete takes a dim view of his fellow humans," Ovid said. "He prefers insects."

Dellarobia turned her chair halfway around to face Pete, scraping noisily against the cement floor. "You're saying people only tune in to news they know they're going to agree with?"

"Bingo," said Pete.

"Well, see, I agree with you," she said. "I've thought that too. How often do you tune in to Johnny Midgeon?"

"You're right," Pete said. "I don't want to hear those guys."

"So," she said, "you're the same as everybody."

317

"Well, but it's because I already know what they're going to say."

"That's what everybody thinks. Maybe you do, and maybe you don't."

"The official view of a major demographic," Pete said in an overly tired voice that reminded her weirdly of Crystal, "is that we aren't sure about climate change. It's too confusing. So every environmental impact story has to be made into something else. Sex it up if possible, that's what your news people drove out here for. It's what sells."

"For God's sake, man," Ovid nearly shouted, "the damn globe is catching fire, and the islands are drowning. The evidence is staring them in the face."

Dellarobia's scalp burned with rage and bewilderment. Pete had just accused her of peddling sex, if she wasn't mistaken, and Ovid hadn't noticed because he was on a rant of his own. His voice was thick with the accent of his childhood. *De eye-lands are drowning.* Were they?

Pete picked up his stepladder and hefted it to the opposite side of the room, setting it down hard. End of discussion. He unfurled a length of the clear plastic, dragged it up the ladder, and started shooting the beams again. *Bang, bang.*

She spoke carefully to the room. "I think people are scared to face up to a bad outcome. That's just human. Like not going to the doctor when you've found a lump. If fight or flight is the choice, it's way easier to fly."

318

"Or to sleepwalk," Ovid said. "As you put it."

"I was probably selling my own team short." Defensiveness returned to her in full feather. "Can I tell you one more thing about myself, in this hiring process? I was *going* to college. It's not out of the question for someone here to do that. My teachers said I should. I wanted it so bad my teeth hurt. I know you can't put 'wanted to' on a job application, or we'd all be the president of Walmart or something." She waited for some response, belief or disbelief, which was not forthcoming.

"But I have proof," she added. "I drove over to Knoxville to take the ACT test."

Both men were looking at her. With what kind of interest, she couldn't tell.

"Just me," she said. "I was the only one in my class to try for college, and Mrs. Lake said I had to go take that. I had to start out at four in the morning to get there and figure out those city streets to find the place. All the other kids looked like they'd had a good night's sleep, I'll tell you what. And I'm sure their mamas drove them."

"Really." Ovid seemed impressed by her initiative.

"Yeah, well. A tank of gas wasted. I did okay on the English but math and science, holy Moses. I'd never even heard of most of the stuff they asked. Plus, a baby on the way. That doesn't lend itself."

"Well," he said. "It lends itself to having a child. A recompense of its own kind."

"Do you have children?" she asked.

"I don't. My wife and I are looking forward to that."

She elected not to tell him that first baby only lasted long enough to kick college in the butt and go on its way. He would ask why she didn't try to go to school afterward. People who hadn't been through it would think it was that simple: just get back on the bus, ride to the next stop. He would have no inkling of the great slog of effort that tied up people like her in the day-to-day. Or the quaking misgivings that infected every step forward, after a loss. Even now, dread still struck her down sometimes if she found herself counting on things being fine. Meaning her now-living children and their future, those things. She had so much more to lose now than just herself or her own plans. If Ovid Byron was torn up over butterflies, he should see how it felt to look past a child's baby teeth into this future world he claimed was falling apart. Like poor Job lying on the ash heap wailing, cutting his flesh with a husk. That's where love could take you.

⁓

"Great day in the morning!" cried Dellarobia, even though the expression was probably lost on Lupe, and the kids in the back seat were yelling among themselves. At the sight of the crowd Lupe froze, and reached over from the passenger's side to clench Dellarobia's wrist on the steering wheel.

"Okay, don't worry. I'm not taking you in there."

Dellarobia trusted Lupe's fear, without knowing the specifics. She waited for the release of her forearm, and carefully pulled the car over onto the shoulder. Tall dead grass swept the undercarriage. It hadn't crossed her mind that her new babysitter might have immigration issues. Lupe was watching her kids for five dollars an hour and Dellarobia was making thirteen, so even after Uncle Sam took his bite she would come out ahead, that's what she knew. And she knew that her yard had been empty this morning when she left to go pick up Lupe. Now it looked like the county fairgrounds.

Lupe whirled around and efficiently shushed the children. Her own two boys, wedged in beside Cordie's car seat, seemed to have mute buttons. Cordie whined a few seconds longer but quickly petered out, getting the memo. Dellarobia fished in her purse for her glasses and put them on, frowning through the windshield. The house was still more than a hundred yards away. They had just rounded the bend in Highway 7 where their farm came into view, but even from here she could count more than a dozen cars parked helter-skelter on both sides of the road directly in front of her house. No police vehicles that she could see, and no news-mobiles, but whatever this was, she wasn't going to drive Lupe into the middle of it. She bit her lip, trying to form a plan.

"Okay, here's what we'll do," she said slowly, watching Lupe to assess comprehension. Their efficient translator, Josefina, was at school with Preston, but for over a week now they'd managed the basics of this arrangement each morning until the kindergartners came home on the bus to help sort out the fine print. "See that old house behind us?" She pointed back to it. "Empty. Nobody home. We'll go there."

She backed slowly along the shoulder and then pulled forward into the long driveway of the Craycroft house, which had been for sale so long it was widely taken to be a lost cause. The Craycrofts' son had put them in a nursing home and priced the house insanely above market. Or maybe where he lived, in Nashville, houses sold for that kind of money. Dellarobia's one hope at present was that it hadn't turned into a meth lab in the interim. It looked more than a tad spooky. Some of its uncurtained windowpanes were cracked, and winter-killed weeds stood shoulder high around the foundations. The son could drag his city butt out here and do a little maintenance. She pulled the car all the way to the back where it could not be seen from the road, and cut the engine.

"Okay," she said to Lupe, "you and the kids stay here. You can get out of the car if they want to play. Nobody will see you here. I'm going to walk over there to my house and see what's up."

Lupe nodded formally. "Okay," she said, "shes can play," then said something to the kids that sounded more on the lines of, "Don't move or I'll kill you." Dellarobia felt ludicrous, hiding her child and babysitting entourage in the bushes in order to sneak up on her own home. Yet, here she went.

The intermittent freezing drizzle picked up again as she walked along the edge of Highway 7, avoiding the weedy and muddy ditch. She pulled the hood of her raincoat forward to keep the rain off her glasses, the better to observe the occasional car that whizzed past her and then inevitably slowed to a crawl just down the road, at her house. Their drivers were rubbernecking, no doubt wondering what the fuss was about. You and me both, she thought. She walked the full road frontage of the Cook place, her immediate neighbors, seeing nothing unusual up at their house, and was reassured generally by the absence of ambulances or cop cars. But she was dismayed by the crowd of people who stood close together on her own front lawn, all facing the house as if expecting it to perform. They looked dressed for a camping trip, in boots and backpacks and puffy down parkas. As she drew closer, she saw some white cardboard placards. And heard chanting. A lot of energy directed toward a house where no one was home. Don't shoot till you see the whites of their eyes, she thought, a directive that was never meant for near-sighted people. Not until she'd crossed onto her own property did she realize it was kids. Teenagers or young adults. They looked so slight and fine-boned in the rain.

"Children ask the world of us!" they were shouting again and again, giving Dellarobia to know for certain she had lost her mind. She eased herself into the edge of the fray near the road, where a young couple were getting out of a dented little silver Honda. They both wore brightly colored knit caps with dangling earflaps, like something you'd put on a toddler. The chant died out, and a new one began. A guy standing on her front porch was pumping his arm like Nate Weaver in church, leading chants that the crowd belted out in an exaggerated, rhythmic refrain.

"Stop the logging, stop the lies! Save the monarch butterflies!"

"Oh, crap," Dellarobia said, loudly enough that the knitted-cap couple shot her a glance. She muscled her way among the kids and up the sidewalk to her porch, expecting at any moment to be recognized as the butterfly celebrity here, but no dice. Not in her present guise, with a hooded raincoat covering everything but her water-speckled glasses. A raincoat purchased in the boy's department, no less. The guy on the porch stopped leading the cheer and looked down at her, puzzled. The shouting abruptly died out.

"Would you mind telling me who you are?" she asked him.

The guy had long black sideburns, a style Dellarobia associated with 1970s movies featuring people wearing horrible clothes, though in other respects he looked pretty okay. Skinny jeans, parka, horn-rimmed glasses. He carried a folder under one arm and seemed out of breath, as if he'd been jogging. "How about you tell me who *you* are?" he replied.

"Okay. You're on my porch. I'm the person that lives here with my husband and kids. Now you."

He took a step back, nearly pitching himself backward off the edge of the small porch. Her hunch was correct; he'd taken her for a middle-schooler. He looked her over, reassessing what was under that raincoat, then opened his red folder and flipped madly through some papers. "Burley Turnbow? That couldn't possibly be you, right?"

She waited a beat. "The name I was looking for was yours."

"Oh, sorry. Vern Zakas. I'm president of the environment club at CCC. Nice to meet you." He extended his hand, and she shook it. The community college. It figured.

"Nice to meet you," she said. "What's your business with Burley Turnbow?"

He glanced at the crowd. "Okay. We're protesting cutting down all the trees in the butterfly place. Anywho-dot-com listed this as the residence of Burley Turnbow, the guy that's logging up there, trying to kill all the butterflies."

She pushed back the hood of her raincoat for a better command of the situation, seeing a second flash of surprise as Vern Zakas registered her as an adult female. And the Butterfly Venus, maybe that too, but mortification had its place, and this was not it. "You don't completely have your story straight," she told Vern. "I hate to tell you this, but you've even got the wrong Burley

Turnbow. Believe it or not, there's two. It's the father, Burley Senior, you'd want to speak to. He doesn't live here."

"Oh, Christ, I am so sorry," said Vern. "Somebody messed up." He looked back at his papers as if the fault lay there, the same way people will turn and glare at a sidewalk after they've stumbled over nothing.

"No worries," Dellarobia said. "Look, here's what you want to do. Keep going down this road, that direction, about the length of a football field, and you're going to see their gravel drive on the right. There's a ring of whitewashed stones around the mailbox and this great big planter box shaped like a swan. Really ugly. You can't miss it."

The kids on her lawn stared at her, holding their placards at half-mast in the drizzle. They were a wary-looking bunch, the hoods of their damp parkas zipped close around their faces and their eyes wide, as if standing on a stranger's lawn were way out at the tippy edge of their comfort zone. Their signs were not very impressive. They'd scrawled their demands in such thin marking-pen letters you couldn't even read them from ten feet away. These kids had an anger-deficit problem.

"Yo, people, listen up," she shouted at the crowd. "Thanks for your interest, but you've got the wrong house. You all need to go yell at Bear Turnbow. He lives down that way, less than half a mile. Follow your leader here, Vern. He's got directions."

Vern hoofed it off the porch and headed for his car, beckoning with one arm in the air. The kids folded their placards close to their bodies and filed toward their vehicles, obedient as collies. She saw one sign that said "Resist Authority!"

"Thank you!" several of the kids called out as they left.

"No problem," she said, and went to fetch the family she'd hidden in the weeds.

ℰ

Once Lupe and the kids were safely squared away in her living room, she walked out to the lab. The milking parlor had to be entered through an open section of the barn where Cub had engine parts strewn all over, a fact that embarrassed her not a little. She'd asked him to tidy things up, but men and barns were like a bucket of forks, tidy was no part of the equation. She pulled open the newly fitted laboratory door to find Ovid and Pete hard at work putting butterflies in the oven. She was worried about being late, but Ovid never seemed to take any notice of what time she came in. She took down her lab coat from the peg where she hung it every evening, wondering when it should be washed, and squashed on the rubber goggles that had to fit over her glasses. As distracting as a condom, and just as necessary, she supposed. Ovid really stressed the safety aspect.

On Monday they'd begun a lipid extraction experiment, beginning with one hundred live butterflies carried down the mountain in a cooler. Each was stuffed in its own wax envelope, weighed on the Mettler balance, and dried overnight in the scientific drying oven. So it was no joke, butterflies in the oven. Her tasks so far had been to number the envelopes and record all the weights in a special notebook, pre- and post-oven-drying. From there each brittle butterfly carcass went into its own test tube, tamped down with a little glass rod. She did the carcass crushing, which felt like breaking tiny butterfly bones, and Pete added petroleum ether to each tube. The reagent filled the lab with a faintly automotive smell, like a gas station from across the street, but according to Ovid it was far more flammable than gasoline. They worked under the newly installed oven hood, but even with the vents running, one match could send this place up in a flash and boom they would hear all the way to Cleary. Those were his words. It gave her chills to imagine it. All those children under one roof, next door.

"Sorry I'm late," she said loudly, addressing her excuse not exactly to Dr. Byron but to the room. "I had to do some crowd control outside."

Ovid and Pete were astonished to hear the details of her morning. She was surprised herself as she retold it. At the time it felt like a simple rectification rather than bravery per se, but she'd stood before a crowd of fifty people and told them to go bark up the correct tree. To command this kind of attention was a lifetime first for Dellarobia. Her normal audience was two, with a combined age of six, to what end she could never be sure. Back in school she'd presented things in a classroom, but that hardly counted. She didn't count being on the news either. The audience might be huge, but they weren't there at the time, and her words turned out to be immaterial. This morning, they'd listened.

Pete and Ovid had missed the whole show. The voices hadn't carried back here to the barn. Of course, the windows were covered with plastic sheeting. Dellarobia recalled that this was once proposed by the government as a protection against terrorist attacks. Apparently it had about the same effect as sticking your fingers in your ears.

"Shoot," she said suddenly. "I should have taken names. If those kids are so fired up about the butterflies, we could have signed them up for volunteer work."

"Good idea!" Ovid looked at her brightly through his yellowed goggles, giving her a thumbs-up. His smile went through her like a hit of nicotine.

"Do you know what? I still could. I got the name of their club president. Zack Verkas. No, Vern Zakas."

Dr. Byron nodded approval. She could see that his old generosity was still there, but was sometimes being held captive by despair, like a living thing held underwater. Today he seemed in a fine mood, wearing blue rubber gloves and using the pricey steel-toothed blender. Its fierce high buzz ascended in pitch like an

329

eggbeater as the motor accelerated. The lab was noisy in general, which also could account for their having missed the protest. The shaker bath full of test tubes and warm water made a monotonous shush like a rocking chair. And the spinning centrifuge, if it wasn't perfectly balanced, made a racket like tennis shoes in the dryer. It sat on its own special honeycomb mat so it wouldn't vibrate itself right off the table.

"I'll call that boy this afternoon," she promised, writing his name in tiny letters in a corner of her lab notebook while she still remembered it. "If the environment club wants to save the butterflies, you can give them something to do about it."

"It sounds like you might be on their enemy list now," Pete said. "Do you think you can get this guy to name names?" Pete was extracting the liquid from the test tubes of butterfly-petroleum-ether soup. He ran them through the centrifuge in batches, then carefully drew out each liquid sample with a pipette and squirted it into its own tiny aluminum pie pan. The pipette resembled the device Hester used for decorating cakes, though obviously it was more precise, and required countless disposable plastic tips, one for each sample. They went through a world of little dishes in this lab. Yesterday she had numbered all the aluminum pans, using an empty ballpoint pen to emboss the thin metal. Her handwriting was all over this place already. Today she was supposed to weigh each sample and record the weights in the lab book. The pans were already stacking up, thanks to her tardiness, so she got busy.

"Oh, he'll give me names, he owes me," she told Pete. Some of the tension that had flared between them during the interview had lingered, not as strong as the ether but still in the air. She was not Pete's equal, obviously; she got that. She was trying to learn the boundaries. "He was horrified about protesting at the wrong address. You should have seen them. They just picked up their signs, apologized for the mixup, and headed over to yell at Hester and Bear. They even picked up their trash."

"Kids around here are so polite," Pete said, handing her the little pans one by one. She weighed each one and carried it over to the slide warmer, a long hot-plate affair with a thermometer taped to its side. They'd promised her it did not get hot enough to detonate the place. Needless to say, she passed her workdays now without smoking, having hit on the best ever strategy for quitting: fear of being blown to smithereens.

"It's true," Ovid agreed. "These kids don't sound like the cheeky youngsters we see at Devary."

She turned up the fan on the venting hood and adjusted the little pans evenly on the warm surface, like pancakes covering a griddle. After all the liquid evaporated she would weigh each pan again, and that was the fat content of a butterfly. It made her a little sad to think of all those dead ladies leaving behind their fat as a matter of public record. World's Biggest Losers, for real.

"What are kids at Devary like, Bart Simpson?" she asked.

"Unfortunately less entertaining," Ovid said. "I get e-mails from students informing me of the GPA required to maintain their fraternity status, or what have you, and advising me of how I am to contribute. They cc their parents."

"This girl in my ecology class last year . . . ," Pete said, pausing in his work, tilting his pipette sideways and leaning on the counter to face Dellarobia. She could see he was making an effort and appreciated that. "Okay," he said, "true story. She bragged on Facebook about cheating on the midterm. Another student tipped me off, so I busted her, and she was furious. She filed a complaint saying I'd invaded her privacy."

"Wow," Dellarobia said. "We may not have much around here, but manners we've got. Some of the kids living down this road might steal your lawn mower out of your garage to buy Oxycontin, but they'd leave a note, you know? 'Thank you ma'am. I apologize. Please hold me in your prayers.'"

Ovid and Pete both laughed, but she wasn't kidding. Somewhere along the way between mud pies and sex ed, most kids of her acquaintance lost all courage on their own behalf. Even Preston, inventive as he was, was so serious already about not breaking rules. What would become of him when he had to fight for a place in the world against kids who thought they owned it already? Cordelia might manage; she was born defiant, as Dellarobia once had been. But that had won no favors in the long run either, it seemed. Certainly not with the powers that ruled her life, namely her in-laws.

She wondered whether those environment-club kids would have the nerve for this work. Saving butterflies seemed to kill butterflies like mad. They put them in the freezer alive and drew them out dead. Dr. Byron swore the end was quick and painless. He'd finished Tissuemizing and moved on now to the dissecting microscope, where he was splitting open a batch of females to see what they had going on inside. He wanted to see if they were in what he called diapause, the winter slowdown of normal migrating monarchs. He motioned her over now, pulling out a chair next to his.

"Look at this," he said, waiting while she removed her cumbersome goggles to look in the scope. The goggles left a raccoon ring around her eyes, of which she felt conscious now. "Do you see that?" he asked.

"What am I looking for?"

"Little white pellets. Those are spermatophores, one from each male that mated with her. The little sac is called the bursa, where she stores them."

"I do see," Dellarobia said, determined not to blush. The little lady had been around.

"That's the first one I've found that was mated, in more than two dozen dissections. Nearly all of them are in diapause."

She was close enough to Ovid to smell his aftershave,

333

despite the general ambience of explosive reagents. Since the day she started working in close proximity, the sight of him in his white coat had stirred her unexpectedly. That crisp collar against his dark skin, some kind of wash-and-wear fabric. He was becoming his earlier self. They'd had a crisis, midweek, and he was wonderful about it. The power went off, leaving them in darkness with all those churning machines coasting to a halt, and she'd called in the outage only to learn the problem was her bill. They'd been so stretched after Christmas, so many bills coming in at once, she'd assumed the power company would give them a month's grace. Having forgotten grace was already on the table since November, carved down to the bones. The humiliation of telling Pete and Ovid could have been the worst day of her life, but he was overly kind, insisting it was his mistake, he'd overlooked all the current these machines would be drawing off the same meter as the house. He'd sat next to her with his personal credit card while she went through the power company's phone menu in tears, trying to get through to some real person and explain there was more at stake here than just some family in the dark.

She was unsure now whether he'd dismissed her from the microscope. Ovid was fiddling with rectangular glass slides in a slotted box. "I know Pete needs you back," he said a little absently, pulling out one slide after another and holding it up to the window, closing one eye to peer through. "Our Pete is never satisfied

334

without a lovely assistant at his elbow. But I want to show you just one more thing. Ah. Here." He fitted the slide under the microscope's flat metal elbows, clamping it to the platform. "As soon as we finish the lipids, I am going to put you on O-E counts. This is interesting. Have a look."

She fiddled with the focus, and it jumped up in 3-D: a strange collage of ridged, transparent ovals that overlapped slightly like roof shingles. These were the scales that covered a butterfly's wings, he said, magnified times three hundred. Nestled among the scales she saw smaller, darker shapes like water beetles, and these, he told her, were the parasites. OE for short. He would write down the whole name for her later, it was easier to learn that way. This was a prepared slide he used for teaching, but they would start looking for these parasites on the monarchs. Infestations were associated with butterfly populations that did not succeed in making normal migrations.

"So parasites could be the cause of them coming here instead of Mexico?"

"The cause," he said with a rueful smile, tilting his head, and suddenly there he was, the man who'd sat at her kitchen table. He must be everyone's favorite professor. "Cause," he said, "is not the same as correlation. Do you know what I mean by that?"

She smiled an eager novice's smile. "No."

"Families that take foreign vacations also tend to own more televisions than those that do not. Is that second television causing families to be more adventurous?"

"No, that would be the cash flow."

"Probably, yes. Something else is the cause of both. Cars with flames painted on the hood might get more speeding tickets. Are the flames making the car go fast?"

"No. Certain things just go together."

"And when they do, they are correlated. It is the darling of all human errors to assume, without proper testing, that one is the cause of the other."

"I get that. Like, crows flying over the field will cause it to snow tomorrow. My mother-in-law always says that, and I'm thinking, no way. Maybe it's a storm front or something that makes both things happen, but the crows move first."

"And there you are, Dellarobia. Ahead of half of my college students."

"And all journalists," Pete piped up from across the room.

"Some journalists," Ovid said. "I'm afraid he is right."

"New proof!" Pete shouted. "Facebook use lowers kids' grades! Breast implants boost suicide rates! Smiling increases longevity!"

"Many journalists," Ovid said.

Correlation, cause. She would write the words in the corner of her lab notebook, which was starting to fill with small, encrypted notes to herself.

"Is the parasite sapping the monarch's strength and

preventing a long migration?" Ovid asked. "We don't know. We are seeing a big increase in these parasite infestations. And we have recorded rising average temperatures throughout the range. Is the warmer climate giving the parasite an advantage? It's tempting to say this, but again, we don't know for sure. Not unless we can create experimental conditions that hold everything steady except for temperature. We cannot jump to conclusions. All we can do is measure and count. That is the task of science."

It seemed to Dellarobia that the task of science was a good deal larger than that. Someone had to explain things. If men like Ovid Byron were holding back, the Tina Ultners of this world were going to take their shots.

She stayed a while longer at the microscope slides before she was released again to Pete's elbow to record his sample weights. She was getting better at the Mettler balance and dispatched the pans quickly, sometimes having to wait for Pete to catch up. It thrilled her that Ovid felt she was ready for something more complicated than writing numbers in a book. She thought of Valia weighing skeins of yarn and recording her crabbed columns of numbers in Hester's kitchen, on that long-ago day when they'd dyed the yarn. Two months ago. Impossible. Her world had been the size of a kitchen then. Now she had a life in which she might not see Hester for over a week. Working left her with so little time, her evenings with the kids were a whirlwind of preparation and catch-up. She'd skipped church two Sundays in a row, first for the chance to hose down the milking parlor before Ovid and Pete arrived, and the next week doing more or less the same in her own home, which she'd had no chance to clean. If neither of these qualified in Hester's mind as valid church-excused emergencies, Dellarobia begged to differ.

She wondered how the environment club was making out right now at Bear and Hester's, if they even managed to find their way over there. They'd seemed disoriented, in more ways than one. They should probably be told the logging was on hold for now. And that evidently it was not the worst thing likely to happen to the monarchs. Ovid was keeping track as the temperatures crept to freezing, miserably watching the downward march. After decades of chasing monarchs and their beautiful mysteries, he would now be with them at the end, for reasons he had never in his whole life foreseen. She wished he could explain this to those kids who'd been in her yard. Some deep and terrible trouble had sent the monarchs to the wrong address, like the protesters themselves. The butterflies had no choice but to trust in their world of signs, the sun's angle set against a turn of the seasons, and something inside all that had betrayed them.

And what could any person do to protest the likes of that? Bear Turnbow's business plan was stoppable in theory, but you couldn't stand up and rail against the weather. That was exactly the point of so many stories.

Jack London and Ernest Hemingway, confidence swaggering into the storm: Man against Nature. Of all the possible conflicts, that was the one that was hopeless. Even a slim education had taught her this much: Man loses.

10

Natural State

January made its way like a high-wire walker, placing one foot, then another, on the freezing line. It wavered, rising to forty, dipping to thirty, but never plunged. A small, nervous audience watched. On some nights Dellarobia could not sleep for thoughts of cold air creeping down along the ridgelines. It would fill the forest secretively like a poisonous gas and surround the butterflies in the quarters where they crowded close, riveted to their family trees, lulled into a dormancy from which they would not wake. One crystal clear night it would happen.

No one close to her shared her dread. Dovey wouldn't hear it; her methods of self-preservation were fierce. And Cub was protected in his own way, unable to believe that this outpost of life that had landed in their custody was irreplaceable. She feared Preston would be the opposite, that he would feel the multitude of deaths too deeply, so she didn't tell him everything. He brought home pictures of monkeys and tree frogs cut from magazines at school and taped them to his bedroom wall in elaborate collages, much like those his father had once assembled with pictures of Captain Fantastic and Jesus. With all his might Preston wanted to be a scientist and study animals. But in the lab Dellarobia listened to Ovid and Pete speaking hopelessly about so many things. The elephants in drought-stricken Africa, the polar bears on the melting ice, were "as good as gone," they said with infuriating resignation as they worked through what seemed to be an early autopsy on another doomed creature. *Gone*, as if those elephants on the sun-bleached plain were merely slogging out the last leg of a tired journey. The final stages of grief. Dellarobia felt an entirely new form of panic as she watched her son love nature so expectantly, wondering if he might be racing toward a future like some complicated sand castle that was crumbling under the tide. She didn't know how scientists bore such knowledge. People had to manage terrible truths. As she lay awake she imagined Ovid doing the same in his parallel bed, not so far away across the darkness, joined with her in the vigil against the cold. Because of him, she wasn't alone.

Each morning by daylight she crossed the same distance from her kitchen door to Ovid's camper, pausing there on her way to the lab to record the previous day's high and low temperatures. He used these to estimate the rates at which butterflies were using up their fat reserves when they stayed quiet in the trees, versus warm days when they flew around. Too warm was just as dangerous as too cold, he said. Dellarobia felt like an accessory to the crime as she plotted the numbers each day, but it was one of her tasks. A special thermometer was attached to the camper by means of a metal arm extending from the passenger's side window. She pressed the mechanism's tiny buttons to reveal the day's readings and then zero them out, a small thing to master but it pleased her to do it, like Preston with his watch. Ovid showed her how to make a graph from the two lines of dots, showing the high and low temperatures marching across the month with the survival zone for monarchs pressed narrowly between them.

It was the wavering pencil line on graph paper that first made her think of a high-wire act, and again now she pictured the man in a bowler hat with a white-painted face, expressionless, raising and lowering black-slippered feet in slow motion along his wire. Life in the balance. She couldn't say where she had seen him, but it must have been on television, probably just a glimpse as Cub cruised past on his way to more conventional entertainments. The image was in her mind as she approached the camper. She was not on her way to work this morning, Ovid did not expect her to be in the lab on Saturdays, though he and Pete usually were. Today she'd pulled on her boots and coat in order to help Cub walk the fence line behind their house, at Hester's request. She had decided to move the pregnant ewes over here. Cub had already taken Cordie and Preston over for his mother to babysit while they worked on the fence, but now he sat procrastinating in the kitchen, drinking a third cup of coffee and listening to Johnny Midgeon's morning show while gathering his gumption for a hefty hike in the cold. Dellarobia felt agitated as always with her husband's balky progress. To defuse her impatience, she went outside to take the morning's temperature reading for her notebook, and that was when she saw Ovid Byron naked.

Just a glance. Not his face, it was from armpits to thighs, approximately. She turned away so quickly she nearly fell down in the mud, scarlet with embarrassment, heart pounding. How was she supposed to know he was in there? He was always up at dawn. The camper's pleated curtains with their snap closures stayed permanently closed on the side facing her house. She'd grown used to his durable privacy, never noticing that the other side facing the mountains might be open. Of course he would want that view of the high ridge, which she took for granted. She stumbled toward the house, feeling faint. Feeling vile. A Peeping Tom. Had he seen her? It seemed unlikely. The thought was excruciating. Going to work, ever, seemed undoable if it involved any possibility of looking him in the eye again. His eyes were no part of the snapshot, only the long-waisted torso she could not erase, burned onto her retina. The coffee-colored skin, the surprisingly sculpted abdomen, the shadow line of tightly curled hair like a funnel cloud down the center of his chest, nearly touching down on the dark pubic ground. She wondered how she could have seen so much in a millisecond. She'd turned away before registering anything more than movement and a change of light on the

343

smooth planes she only understood after the fact to be a body. Truly, she hadn't seen what she'd seen. She was sure Cub would see guilt on her face when she entered the back door, scraping her boots, looking at the door-sill.

"Okay, let's get this over with," Cub said, not even looking at her. He rose from the table and pulled the olive-drab dead weight of his farm coat from the back of a chair. She felt unaccountably emptied out. Even this did not matter, then, that she had seen a man so important to her in his nakedness, a biblical act. She felt invisible.

She had failed to record the temperature, obviously. The notebook was still in her hand as they stepped out the kitchen door. She slid it quickly onto the junk table next to a flowerpot jammed with cigarette butts, a still life of her sins, before descending the two steps down from the back porch. What she wouldn't give for a smoke right now. But that was the regular formula, wasn't it? People always gave their lives for a smoke. Cub shivered copiously inside his coat and reset the cap on his head, not one of the countless woolen ones knitted for him by Hester but a baseball cap, a poor choice for such a cold morning. Dellarobia said nothing. She was tired of telling people to put on clothes. If her children and husband couldn't figure out it was winter, the world would still turn.

The temperature must have dropped this morning in the early hours. Frost lay on the ground in patterns, a white powder so dry and fine it flew up in tiny storms of confetti-frost ahead of their boots as they walked. They followed the path of the creek up the left side of the pasture, wordlessly agreeing to climb to the top and work their way across and down. The dusting of frost outlined a zone of temperature differential along both sides of the creek where the water had held in warmth overnight. She thought the words *thermal mass*, picturing the solid pelt of butterflies clinging to the great columnar trunks of the firs, which Ovid had described as giant water bottles. Watercress she had never noticed grew up through the surface of this creek, frozen to blackness in the air above but still green underwater, and also alive in a narrow zone an inch above the surface of the moving creek. She had heard him say the word *thermocline*, and now she could see that too. She had begrudged the clubbish vocabulary at first, but realized now she had crossed some unexpected divide. Words were just words, describing things a person could see. Even if most did not. Maybe they had to know a thing first, to see it.

The vision of Ovid's body, forgotten for a few blessed seconds, returned to agitate her. Men she had seen, in life and in the movies of course, nakedness was everywhere anymore. But not this one. Her boss, the one man whose good opinion she worked hardest to earn. Who scrutinized her routinely from behind the safety of rubber goggles. She envied forgetfulness, and simpler minds than the one she inhabited. She was desperate for Cub to say anything at all, but he was too busy breathing.

"How come Hester finally decided to move the ewes over here?" she asked him.

"I don't know." He added after a beat, "Too wet over there." It would be a conversation of short sentences, then.

"That bottomland is too wet for them now? As in what, hoof rot?"

"Yeah, I guess." He puffed. "And she thinks they'll get wormy."

She was careful of her footing on the slope. The white frost accentuated details of the ground, its ridges and stippled dead grass, the lay of the land. This didn't look good for the butterflies. It felt strange not to know the damage. Someone should go up there.

"You know what?" she said to Cub. "I talked with Hester about that, the day she came over to our house. Before Christmas, that would have been."

"About the ewes? What'd she say?"

"She didn't trust us to keep an eye on them. When the lambs started coming."

"She said that?"

"As good as." Dellarobia panted a little herself with the climb, watching each white breath materialize in the cold air. Her glasses fogged, so she took them off and slipped them in her pocket. Along the top of the pasture bare trees stood upright like bars of a prison, throwing vertical shadows down the length of the hill.

346

All the world enclosed her in black and white. "I told her we could help out when the lambs were born. Preston and I would like it. Hester just kind of pulled up her nose at that."

"But we could," Cub said. "She's got books. You could read up on the lambing."

He'd been reaching up with one arm, maybe to get a book from the shelf. His camper's tiny kitchen cupboards were all crammed full of his books, he'd taken the doors off them. He might have turned toward the window in time to see her scuttling away. Dellarobia struggled for an even conversational keel. "Okay. Borrow me one of those books from Hester," she said. "So I'd know what to do if a lamb came early."

"Boil water," Cub said, and she laughed. Coming from Cub, that was funny. It softened her present distress.

"How were your folks this morning?"

"Mother was fit to be tied. Bobby Ogle's coming over later."

"Really. While she's got the kids?"

"Probably not till after we pick up the kids. But the conniption has begun."

Dellarobia wasn't surprised. It was maybe the minister's third or fourth visit since all this began, and each had launched Hester into a new orbit of anxiety. If spiritual comfort was the goal, things were not going that way. "Why do you think your mother's so nervous around Bobby?"

"Well, you know. He's the pastor."

"Well, yeah. She loves to admire him across a crowded room. But why get so bent out of shape with the one-on-one?"

"I don't know. Dad said she's been vacuuming since the crack of dawn. He was going out to his shop so she wouldn't vacuum him. She had her stuff thrown all over the furniture."

"What do you mean?" Dellarobia envisioned a food fight, but that was her life, not Hester's.

"You know, those lacy things. Covers, I guess."

"Those crochet things she puts on the arms of the sofa, to cover the worn spots?"

"Yeah, all that. She was baking something. It smelled good." He chuckled. "Cordie pooped on the way over. I walked in there with a loaded baby, and Mother about lost it. She said to get upstairs and change that child before she stank up the place. She made me bring the diaper home with me."

"Nice," Dellarobia said. But despite herself, she was moved by the breach in Hester's armor. Someone still had the power to make Hester feel house-poor and embarrassed. Vacuuming up dog hair, throwing slipcovers over a threadbare household, Dellarobia certainly knew the drill.

At the top of the field they found the gate to the High Road standing open. No real surprise there, strangers came through constantly. Hester's tour service was no longer needed, since people just walked or drove

348

themselves to the butterfly site. People with binoculars, butterfly nets, telescopes, expensive-looking cameras, all or none of the above; they were not scientists or news teams now, but mostly tourists. One morning while she and Preston waited for the bus, a young couple wearing bright, matching Spandex pants had walked right past them through the yard, speaking a foreign language. When Dellarobia spoke up, they'd stared at her in stunned surprise, as if they'd been hailed by a ground-hog. People even carried tents up there and camped out, including some polite kids from the Cleary environment club and a trio of young men from California who'd knocked and explained to Dellarobia they were from some international group with a number for a name. Something-dot-org. Dr. Byron was keeping these kids busy with simple tasks, counting and measuring, prob-ably not the nature show they'd come looking for, but they submitted happily to being useful. The three California boys, especially. She'd asked how in the world they found this place, and they showed her a computer program that drew a map directly to her house. All they had to do was type in her address on their little flat screen, and open sesame, there it was. Her address was public knowledge, they said, and so was the photograph taken from the sky, apparently, showing the gray rect-angle of their roof and Cub's truck and her Taurus sit-ting slightly askew in the drive. Not Ovid's trailer. She'd asked about that, and the young men said the satellite photo would have been taken some time back. Before anyone cared, in other words. The Internet had information in storage, waiting at anyone's beck and call. It made her feel helpless to defend herself. That little gray rectangle was all the shelter she had.

These Californians at least had introduced themselves, and she appreciated that, since most did not. All the work Cub and Bear had done to make the High Road passable was probably a mistake. It was being taken as an invitation. And fairly enough, she thought, for that was the way of the world. A road was to be driven upon. The candy in the dish was there to be eaten, money in the bank got spent, people claimed whatever they could get their hands on. Wasn't that more or less automatic? For a human being to do any less seemed impossible. She waited while Cub dragged the fence closed.

"We've got to get a chain and a padlock for this gate," he said.

"I was thinking that. Hester's ewes will wander off into the wild blue yonder if we can't keep this closed." She wondered if the lock would get cut, and knew Cub was thinking the same. He felt all the trespassers were basically the same brand of hoodlum, unwilling to respect private property, but Dellarobia was not so sure. Maybe they thought it was some kind of nature park. The butterflies had now been on the news so many times she'd lost count, which made it seem like anyone's business, just as the Internet gave away their address simply for the asking. Free was free.

She and Cub followed the fence along the top of the pasture, looking closely for breaches in the perimeter. Downed trees lay across the fence in several places, having fallen over from the woods on the other side. As husband and wife they worked together well, exchanging few words as they hefted dead wood from the wire, freeing the fence from the tangle, reattaching wire to post. No livestock had been in this field since early November, before the fall shearing. Dellarobia had a vivid recall of marching up the hill that day and taking her last look back down that hill, like Lot's wife, before heading into a new place. *This* new place was the last thing she'd expected.

Ovid Byron's body in the dimness caught up to her again, and she wished she could scrub her own eyes out. No, not that. But hated how she kept running and her mind still dragged it along, shoving the memory forward, daring her to taste its thrill. It felt acute, like tooth pain, like falling. Not again, this losing her mind to a man. She'd thought surely something had changed, for all the strange fortune those butterflies had brought her. She'd thought she could be free.

A flock of sparrows flushed up from the dead brush with a startling rush of wings. They all disappeared into the woods, save one. This odd loner darted ahead, lighting on one fence post and then the next as Cub and Dellarobia walked along in its direction. "Flying from pillar to post," her mother used to say, when Dellarobia jumped from one infatuation to another in high school. She hadn't thought of those words in years.

Cub stopped to study a long section of fence along a washed-out gully that would have to be restrung. She dug in her pockets for her gloves, found her glasses there, and touched the nub of a pencil, one he'd given her in the lab. If only she had not gone out there this morning. If Cub had been ready for once. She couldn't fathom how tomorrow would go. If she couldn't face him she'd have to quit. The loss hit her like a death.

"Hey, do you want to hear something funny?" Cub asked, and she said yes, she did. She pulled the panel of woven wire toward the post so Cub could nail it. Though she leaned with her whole body, her full weight was barely sufficient.

"When I saw Dad this morning, he told me he caught Peanut trying to get the butterflies to come over on him." Cub paused to finish pounding the topmost U-nail, taking some of the pressure from Dellarobia.

"How do you mean?"

"He's trying to lure them in, I guess. Over the property line onto his land. Dad said he got these humming-bird things, where you put sugar water in them."

She laughed aloud, one small bark, at the idea of Peanut Norwood creeping around with a bird feeder. "Why on earth?" she asked.

"He wants a piece of the action. Dad says there's guys in town talking about making it a Disneyland kind of thing."

"A theme park. That's crazy. Don't they know that's—" She sought some kinder word than *stupid*. "It's useless," she finally said. "The butterflies are all going to die, as soon as the temperature goes down into the teens. This could be it already, they might be dying now."

"Well, but maybe next year."

Dellarobia felt dragged to her knees by the hopelessness of getting from A to B here. It wasn't just Cub; much of the town was in on this nonconversation. "There won't be a next year. It gets too cold, they die, and then it's over. No next generation."

"Tell that to Jack Stell and them," Cub said. "They've got it figured like supply-side economics. The Good Lord supplies the butterflies, and Feathertown gets the economics."

"Really. Just like that, Jesus hands out the butterflies?"

"Why wouldn't our town deserve to get lucky for once?" Cub asked.

Dellarobia recognized the same naive thinking she had heartily shared in the beginning. If anything, she'd been more selfish, wanting the butterflies to be hers alone. She saw them first. She'd been reluctant to surrender her flight of fancy to the scientists' prior claim. "We do deserve it, Cub," she said. "I'm not saying we don't. But luck is just throwing dice. You can't build some kind of industry on just hoping they'll come back. That's what screws people up. Flying blind like that."

They finished pulling the bottom strand, and Cub took the time to yank long, leathery tentacles of invading vines from the wire. Honeysuckle was widely despised for taking over fields and entangling machinery, and it was all over this fence. The leaves had a bruised, purple cast in the cold, but the plant persisted. The sheep wouldn't touch it. Ovid had told her some animals did eat honeysuckle in Japan, where this foreign plant belonged, but they didn't travel with it. No natural predators here, to keep it in check.

"It's not just Dad and them," Cub argued. "The whole state is pushing the natural thing now. For tourists." He clapped his gloved hands together, trying to warm them, and she did the same, the two of them saluting the cold morning with a muffled applause. She knew the "Natural State" campaigns he meant, to which she'd never given a dime's worth of thought before Natural landed in her backyard. Only to find out this so-called phenomenon was unnatural in the extreme. She owed it to Cub to explain this, but hardly knew where to begin. It was like telling a story of childhood damage, backing up to the unhappy parents, then the unhappy grandparents, trying to find the whole truth.

"The trouble with that," she said finally, "with what those guys are saying about the butterflies, is that it's all centered around what they want. They need things to be a certain way, financially, so they think nature will organize itself around what suits them."

354

Cub seemed to consider this. "What else can they do, though?"

"They could talk to Dr. Byron. He's out here twenty-four/seven, looking at all the angles, trying to figure out what's going on." She felt the squeeze of her heart and the race of pulse when she said his name, like a doctor observing a patient. She was surprised to realize she had no intention of running from this, or quitting her job. She had to be part of this story. She would die of him or be cured.

They walked on, she and Cub together studying the fence for need of further mending. From this high part of the pasture they could see in all directions through the barren woodlands. The topography of the farm came clear: the steep, high reach of mountains behind, the narrow drainage of the valley below. It occurred to her how much was obscured in summer by the leaves. With all those reassuring walls of green, a person could not see to the end of anything. Summer was the season of denial.

At the upper east corner of the field they began to make their way down along the property line between their pasture and the Cooks' dead orchard. The skeletal peach trees in their rows leaned into the slope with branches upstretched like begging hands. Casualties of this strange weather. The window in Preston and Cordie's room looked out on these trees, and for a while she'd kept the curtains drawn, it was so depressing. But here they stood anyway. Someone at church had said the Cooks were now in Nashville for the duration of some further treatment, bone marrow or something, probably torturous. That poor child. Poorer still, the parents.

"I was thinking that," Cub said, after a long interval. "What you said about talking to the doctor. Jack Stell and them ought to ask him about the butterflies. But maybe he wouldn't tell them what they want to hear."

"People do manage to cope with bad news," she replied. But it was true, no one in town wanted Dr. Byron's counsel. She'd tried to send newspeople his way, but they didn't bite. The high school teachers hadn't thrown out the welcome mat either. She thought of how Bobby Ogle moved people, persuading them with his demeanor, so loving and forthright. Whatever he said, you wanted it to be right for his sake. Ovid had that same air about him, for the most part he listened and did not judge. It made no sense that people would embrace the one and spurn the other.

"He's not from here, that's the thing," Cub said.

"Just because he's the outsider, he has no say? Should we not read books, then, or listen to anybody outside this county? Where's that going to leave us?"

Cub made no attempt to answer.

"Watching our grass grow, is where." She tried to tame the defensiveness in her tone, knowing this was not Cub's fault. People who'd never known the like of Ovid Byron would naturally mistrust him. They couldn't close out the whole world, maybe, but they could sure find something on their TV or radio to put scientists or foreigners or whatever they thought he was in a bad light. Truly, they were no better than the city people always looking down on southerners, with one Billy Ray Hatch or another forever at their disposal. If people played their channels right, they could be spared from disagreement for the length of their natural lives. Finally she got it. The need for so many channels.

"How do you like that, anyway?" Cub asked.

"Like what?"

"That job. Doing stuff out there in the barn. What do you do?"

She had assumed Cub was incurious and had never tried to explain her days, which were in any case inexplicable. *As soon as we finish the lipids, I am going to put you on OE counts. This is interesting. Have a look.* Never in her life had anyone spoken to her this way, and now someone had, and it made her a different sort of person. Someone she would like to keep on being.

"I see new things," she said simply. "I'm not actually in charge of anything. I'm kind of a glorified secretary."

"You *type*?" Cub asked, and she laughed. She could hardly think when she'd seen anyone use a typewriter, except secretaries on television. Maybe the ladies at the DMV, filling in some form for a driver's license.

"No, I write down numbers in a notebook. I keep track. That's really what Dr. Byron and Pete do, too. They measure different things and write it all down."

"I guess it's in knowing what to measure."

357

"You're right," she said. "That's what it is."

"Same in farming," he said, and she saw he was right about that too, it was astute. Someone on this farm had to check the inner eyelids of the ewes and lambs every week, watching for anemia by degrees as an indication of parasite load. They monitored the hayfield for the right proportion of seedhead to stem. They bred and culled the sheep based on meat yields and staple lengths of the fleece. Hester was the director of operations, and kept the best notes.

"It's more detailed, though," she said. "All this week I counted parasites in the microscope. And helped measure the amount of fat in a butterfly's body. They can measure a thousandth of a gram. A gram is, like, teeny. There's hundreds of them to a pound. In that lab they could weigh your eyelashes and lay them out in order of size."

Cub whistled.

"Not that they actually would," she said. "It's just an example."

"Why do you need to know how fat a butterfly is?" Cub asked.

"It's just knowing all there is to know about an animal. Like sheep, like you said. Little signs tell you a lot. He wants to know what's making the butterflies sick."

"They're sick?"

"They all came here for the winter, and they shouldn't have, because the winter's too cold here. But they came because of things being too warm. Or, I guess we don't know because of what. But he says it's something gone way wrong."

"Now see, I don't hold with that," Cub said. Exactly as she'd expected. Cub would not be disposed to this way of thinking, any more than the people in town or Tina Ultner and her national broadcast audience. All were holding out for the miracle angle. Honestly, it made a better story.

"Suit yourself," she said. They descended the slope, passing near enough to the Cooks' house to see lights on inside and a car in the drive, not the Cooks' farm truck but a white sedan. So someone was looking after the place for them. Dellarobia knew she ought to call the house and ask after the boy. It was so hard. What if he'd passed away?

They paused again to rip the wild, disorganized tangles of vines from the neat rectangles of woven wire. She couldn't even guess how many times they'd done this over the years, ever hopeful they could keep the stuff at bay. It was probably their chief project as a married couple, she thought: tearing honeysuckle out of a fence.

After a while Cub asked, "You're saying butterflies can go wrong in their heads?"

"No, it's not that. Other things go wrong, and they stay the same, so it confuses them. It's like if every Friday you drove to Food King, but then one Friday you did the same as always, followed the same road signs, but instead of Food King you wound up at the auto parts store. You'd know something was messed up. Not with you necessarily, but something out of whack in the whole town."

Cub appeared to take this in.

"So they're here by mistake," she said. "And they can't adjust to it. Dr. Byron said it's like if we got persuaded to come out here for some reason and live among the sheep. We still couldn't eat grass. And we wouldn't have baby sheep, we'd have babies, and they'd be in trouble with the freezing rain and the coyotes." She'd embellished Ovid's example, but felt it was valid.

"What persuaded the butterflies off their track?" Cub asked.

"Well, see, that's what they're wanting to figure out," she said. "And Dr. Byron's not the only one wondering. There's more to it than just these butterflies, a lot of things are messed up. He says it's due to climate change, basically."

"What's that?"

She hesitated. "Global warming."

Cub snorted. He kicked up a cloud of dusty frost. "Al Gore can come toast his buns on this." It was Johnny Midgeon's line on the radio, every time a winter storm came through.

"But what about all the rain we had last year? All those trees falling out of the ground, after they'd stood a hundred years. The weather's turned weird, Cub. Did you ever see a year like we've had?"

They arrived at the bottom of the field and turned

360

along the road, the last lap before reaching the house and barn. A black pickup passed with a German shepherd standing in the bed. Finally Cub said, "They don't call it global weirding."

"I know. But I think that's actually the idea."

Cub shook his head. "Weather is the Lord's business."

She felt an exasperation that she knew would be of no use to this debate. She let it rise and fall inside her, along with wishful thoughts. Every loss she'd ever borne had been declared the Lord's business. A stillborn child, a father dead in his prime.

"So we just take what comes?" she asked. "People used to say the same thing whenever some disease came along and killed all the children. 'It's part of God's plan.' Now we give them vaccinations. Is that defying God?"

Cub made no reply.

"Here's the thing," she said. "Why would we believe Johnny Midgeon about something scientific, and not the scientists?"

"Johnny Midgeon gives the weather report," Cub maintained, and Dellarobia saw her life pass before her eyes, contained in the small enclosure of this logic. All knowledge measured, first and last, by one's allegiance to the teacher.

They made their way along the final stretch, approaching the compound of house and barn and Ovid's trailer, but the sight of home gave her no comfort. Sooner or later he would come out of that camper, they would speak, something would have to happen. Cub getting hurt, she couldn't abide, but damage seemed so inevitable. The sky was lower and darker than when they'd left the house an hour ago, and the air felt colder. On the north-facing slopes the ground was still frosted white. There had been talk of snow. Broad-leaved weeds growing along the ditch stood wilted on their stems like tattered flags of surrender. The short distance to their house was a gulf she dreaded to cross.

Cub made a small coughing sound, a kind of nervous preparation that caused her own throat to narrow like a drain. "We have to talk about something," he said.

Her face felt numb. "Okay, what."

"I don't know how to say it."

"Just say it, Cub."

"I can't."

It would be a kindness to help him, but she could not find words. Their unmatched footsteps made a strange, irregular percussion, their heels cracking the thin ice that rimed the mud along the ditch. Finally Cub said, "It's about Crystal."

Dellarobia felt her mind briefly slip its tracks. "What?"

He inhaled slowly. "Crystal Estep."

"I know who Crystal is, Cub. What about her?"

"She's been coming to the house."

"What do you mean, when?"

"When you're still over there working."

"What, she comes every day?"

"No, it's been four or five times. Always on the days when I was off from work—I don't know how she knows. When I'm there with the kids instead of Lupe. She always starts off saying she wants you to look at that letter again."

"Four or five times in *two weeks*? She can't remember I'm working now from nine to five? Seems like even Crystal Estep could get that one down."

Cub's anguish was visible. He shook his head, looked at the sky.

"Oh, Jesus, Cub. Did you guys—what are you telling me?"

"Nothing. We didn't do anything, Dellarobia. Believe me, she's not . . . She's Crystal. And anyway, with the kids right there, what do you think? I'm a married man."

She remembered Crystal in the dollar store before Christmas, leaning back against her cart, talking to Cub. That weirdly suggestive posture she had dismissed as the body language of habitual desperation. In some crucial way she had branded Crystal as a noncontender. Dellarobia felt dismayed by the abrupt reordering of her world, Cub's place in it, and her own. Absorbed in her own infatuations, so sure of herself as the fast horse in this race, she was last to know the joke was on her. A typical wife, blind as a bat, missing every sign as another woman angled for her husband. She would see Cub as quite the catch, would Crystal. He *was* a catch, ample

363

and uncorrupted. A man whose assets were largely going to waste on the woman who'd landed him by accident.

"I would never cheat on you," Cub said, exhaling spasmodically, close to tears.

"I know you wouldn't, Cub. You're a good man. Better than I deserve."

"Don't say that," he said, running his thumb against the inside corners of both eyes. They had arrived at the gate between pasture and backyard. With effort she avoided looking at the shell-like casing of the trailer hunched between their house and the barn. Everything was close together here, the house and driveway crowded into a corner of the farm that had been carved out of the pasture, back when Bear and Hester built the house. Like the wedding and the house itself, it was a hurry-up kind of fence. They'd used metal T-posts and cheap wire that still looked provisional after these many years, like the afterthought it was. She'd always despised that webbed wire crossing the view from her bedroom window. But it was after all just a fence, whose full perimeter she had walked and repaired. The house stood outside of it, belonging instead to the open road frontage it faced. Cub lifted the gate, and she passed ahead of him into the yard, registering the small metallic knuckling of the chain he latched behind her.

Pete banged loudly at the kitchen door early Monday, startling Dellarobia and the kids, to let her know the work was up on the mountain that day. Dr. Byron was already there, Pete was headed up now, and she was to follow as soon as she was free. He asked her to bring pillowcases. After bafflement over the pillowcases, her first emotion was relief. It would be easier to face him up there than to walk into the lab with the weight of her spy's conscience. Dr. Byron in the woods would be intent on the butterflies and possibly up a tree. Only secondly did she think to worry on the butterflies' behalf. The sky had cleared overnight, and the gust of cold air that rushed in at the door's brief opening lingered unkindly in the kitchen. It must have been worry that sent the men up the mountain at this hour.

The kids were still in their pajamas, eating breakfast. Cordie had a cold that had kept her moody and congested for weeks, mouth-breathing like a bulldog. Dellarobia ached to turn up the heat, but, thinking of the electric bill, did not. Preston would catch the bus at seven forty-five, Cub would be dropping off Cordelia at Lupe's apartment on his way to work, and the house would stand empty all day. How she would get everyone dressed and ready in the next forty minutes was beyond comprehension, but somehow her lunch-packing, coffee-swilling gallop around the kitchen always got the job done.

Pillowcases? Did Pete mean she should bring pillows as well? There was no end to their ingenuity in

365

applying household items to the cause of science, asking her for clothespins or coat hangers or kitchen sponges for their various contraptions. She had revised her notion of them as spendthrifts as she watched them improvise and make do. Even Gatorade had its use in the lab, as fuel for captive butterflies that had to be kept alive for some experiment. But pillows? She held at bay a vision of twisted bedsheets and Ovid Byron's body, though her mind pulled in that direction. She slammed the refrigerator door with her hip. Cordie's hair looked like a golden haystack, but the child was in a rare compliant state, shoveling in breakfast one-handed while keeping a grip on a plaid stuffed bear that dangled from her high chair tray in button-eyed desperation. That was Cordie; from birth she'd kept an eternal hold on something, a toy or blanket or any ponytail that swung into reach. Preston was more self-contained, maybe a boy thing.

Or just a Preston thing. Right now he was ignoring his cereal and poring over his sheep book, one of several Cub had borrowed from Hester to prepare them for possible lambing emergencies after they brought the ewes over. She wished Cub had chosen something more age-appropriate. Preston of course went for the giant veterinary manual filled with every imaginable thing that could go wrong in the barnyard. Poor little guy, he hefted this concrete block of a book from room to room and had asked to take it to school, provoking Cub's twin admonishments that he couldn't read, and that people would call him an egghead. Preston registered both as immaterial. He liked being the teeny guy with the big book. And pictures were abundant. He'd easily found the chapter on lambing. Its many line drawings of unborn twin lambs curled together with twined limbs, nose-to-nose or nose-to-tail, made her think of a sex manual.

Cordelia's attentive eye followed her brother's. "Goggies," she pronounced.

"It's not dogs," Preston corrected. "They're baby lambies."

Dellarobia sat down with a bowl of cottage cheese, her makeshift breakfast, and Preston looked up at her with his eyes full of questions. "Why are they taking a nap in a dog bed?" he asked.

She carefully did not laugh, and told him the oval shape was the womb. The pictures were supposed to show how the lambs looked inside the mother sheep. "They're still in her tummy waiting to be born, like when Cordie was in mine. Remember that?"

He nodded gravely. They both looked at Cordelia, her face spackled with cream of wheat and her runny nose. Probably they were thinking variations of the same question: Who knew *this* was coming?

"Don't forget to eat, big guy. Two more minutes and you've got to run and get dressed. The school bus waits for no man."

He spooned in Cheerios absently while leaning into the text, his interest redoubled by the latest revelation.

His earnest expression and level brow moved Dellarobia to a second sight: Preston would go far. Maybe he'd be a vet, farmers were crying for them around here. Or even the kind of vet that looks after elephants in zoos. For all her worry about his lack of advantages, Preston would be like Ovid Byron. Already he seemed set apart by a devotion to his own pursuits that was brave and unconforming. People were so rarely like that, despite universally stated intentions. Most were like herself and Dovey, the one-time rebel girls with their big plans to fly out of here. Her boldness had been confined to such tiny quarters, it counted for about as much as mouse turds in a cookie jar. Until recently, when the lid blew off, and the whole world could peer in at Dellarobia, and what do you know, she was a mouse. But here sat her lionhearted son. Maybe it wasn't a decision, but something drawn from the soup of birth. A lightning strike.

"Mama, what's this man doing?" he asked, sounding anxious.

"Let me see." She slid the book over, hoping he hadn't come across something that would warp him for life. The drawing baffled her: the man in the picture was holding a lamb by its hindquarters, apparently swinging it through the air. She studied the caption. "Resuscitation," she said. "He's bringing it back to life."

Preston looked at her with frank disbelief, and she corrected herself. "I didn't say that right—if something's dead, you can't bring it back. But if a lamb is not

368

breathing when it's born, this is how you can help get it going."

"By *throwing* it?" he asked incredulously.

She scanned the writing on the page. "He's not throwing it, he's swinging it around in a circle. If the lamb is born with its nose and throat plugged with mucus, this is what you're supposed to do. 'Grasp it firmly by the hind legs and swing it,' is what the book says. The centrifugal force will clear out the nose and lungs."

The text also advised, "Make certain there are no obstructions in your path," but that brought to mind a violent, cartoonlike outcome, so she didn't read that part aloud. She was mindful of how the kids took their cues from her on what to take seriously, even at hectic times like this, the eye of their morning tornado.

Preston asked quietly, "Will we have to do that?"

"Oh, sweetie. No." She eyed the plaid bear that still dangled from Cordie's high-chair tray. How tempted she was to snatch it up by its heels and give it a practice whirl around the kitchen, lightening this mood, giving her children the easy gift of a belly laugh, but the better part of her nature resisted. A life was a life. She'd been orphaned at an age to internalize death as poor material for a joke. And likewise, salvation.

℘

The cold was stupefying. She pulled on her heavy wool cap and mittens as she hoofed it up the hill, wishing for

369

a scarf to pull across her nose. The frigid air prickled inside her nostrils and her eyes felt sticky, as if her tears were freezing up. She'd stuffed four clean pillowcases into a big shoulder bag along with her lunch and other necessities. On the outside chance she'd misunderstood Pete's instructions, those linens could spend a quiet morning hiding out in her purse. She wished she'd taken the time to put on more clothes. She had not checked the temperature at Ovid's camper, did not know when or if she'd bring herself to try that again, but this had to be mid-twenties, if not lower. Or maybe she'd forgotten how to judge the cold, in the course of these mild, dreary months.

At the top of the pasture she was surprised to see a drift of white on the dark tree branches and the shady floor of the woods. Snow had fallen in the night. The sky had cleared and the early light had melted any trace of it from the fields below, if it had stuck there. But up here on the mountain it was winter. The idea of snow on the butterfly trees pulled her toward panic. Snow falling on the butterflies themselves, their brittle wings and tender bodies, was a heartbreak she had failed as yet to imagine. She hit the trail at a hard lope and would have run, if she were a thousand packs of cigarettes younger. Briefly she considered going back to get the ATV, but knew there was no real need. Her presence at this disaster could not alter it, the damage was done.

Snow softened the forest's darkness, dusting ever-green limbs with light and reflecting the bright sky.

Where the trail to the study site branched off from the gravel road, she noted that even this smaller path had become well marked by use. Signs of the visitors and their leavings were everywhere, blackened rocks pulled together for campfires, twinkling bits of broken glass rising through the thin floor of snow. She slowed her pace, to keep breathing, and tried to be observant. Clumps of snow-covered leaves high in the branches caught her eye, squirrel nests, but no living butterflies.

She descended the very steep side trail that led directly into the valley of the roost site, passing near what looked like an encampment fifty feet or so from the trail. Dellarobia had never camped out in her life— the appeal of sleeping in a nylon shroud was beyond her—but plenty of people felt otherwise, obviously, and some of them were living up here. The presence of strangers was no longer especially strange, but she felt an awkward shyness peering into the intimacy of these people's morning lives, hearing the muffled sounds of their zippers and voices. She could smell their coffee. There were six or seven, young men she assumed, but who could say really, hunkered close to their campfire. Wild-haired, like Cordelia on an average day. One of them stood up, trailing a tail of yarn and holding long, crossed needles, and Dellarobia registered that, impossibly, they were knitting. The standing one waved a bandaged-looking paw, slowly and widely as if signaling across some great divide. He, she, or it was dressed in a man's old coat over a cotton dress over jeans tucked into unlaced boots, exactly the kind of outfit Cordie would put together. Dellarobia hesitated before waving back, and then pressed on.

The fir forest when she reached it had its own air as always, dark and still. Within its snow-flocked boughs she began to pick out snow-laced colonnades of butterflies, first a few, then more, as her eyes adjusted to their wintry aspect. She stopped to pull off her mittens briefly and kneel down to touch the brittle skeins of veined wings heaped in the path at her feet, many more casualties than she'd ever seen before. Insect bodies lay in heaps directly under the colonies, pitifully wasted it seemed, like mounds of withered tomatoes fallen from the vines in a failed harvest. She stood up with both hands drawn to her chest and looked at the trees, trying to assess what remained. The forest still looked filled with the immense dark fingers of these clusters, lit from above, laced with orange at their edges where the sun reached through. If their numbers were diminished, she couldn't guess how badly, as their numbers had seemed infinite to her all along. The simplest conclusion was that they survived. Part of the world was still in place.

The little glade at the valley's bottom was becoming familiar to her, like a room in a house, the study site. She paused among the trees at its edge to let her heart stop pounding. Day by day she was getting her lungs back, since she'd quit smoking. Since stepping into the flammable atmosphere of Ovid Byron. He was there, on the opposite side of the glen. He and Pete stood together looking into the treetops, with their backs to her. She was surprised to see four field helpers already here too, moving solemnly around the clearing. Vern Zakas was one of them, breaking sticks across his knee to feed a small campfire. She'd recruited these kids, whom Ovid put straight to work. Last week they'd made a low table from a sheet of plywood siding Cub scavenged for them, propping its four corners on big rocks, and the ground around the table already looked trampled. This morning the field balance was set up there, flanked by half-open equipment packs spilling their contents. Waxy rectangles of glassine envelopes splayed across the table like cards after an abandoned poker game. She wondered if men could even see the messes they made, or if they had differently structured eyes, as Ovid had told her cats and dogs and insects did. She should get over there and organize things. The boys seemed subdued, their ordinary conviviality suspended, presumably for the urgency of this day. She felt oddly territorial. They'd gotten here before she did.

She saw Pete's back arch peculiarly, and it took her a second to interpret the odd posture. He was drawing back an arrow across a bow. It flew almost straight up into the treetops, then fell back at its stilted angle, bouncing and coming to rest in the limbs fifteen feet above their heads. Dellarobia knew there was a bow-hunting season for deer but could think of no tree-dwelling creature they might want to shoot. She watched for a long while, disinclined to show herself. Vern and the others watched too, she noticed, each time Pete let an arrow fly. He was retrieving it by means of some sort of filament she couldn't see. Fishing line, maybe. Every pass of the arrow through branches disturbed the roosting colony, sometimes causing small clumps of butterflies to drop to the ground, but this was evidently not the goal. She gathered he was trying to pass a line over the top of a tall fir tree. On the fifth try she witnessed, the arrow cleared and a whooping cheer rang out as if he'd made a touchdown. Boys.

She took the opportunity of their distraction to enter the group without direct salutation from the boss. Her anxiety since Saturday had condensed around the moment when she would meet his eyes and learn in a flash if he knew he'd been seen, yes or no. Nakedness again, of a kind. Avoiding that moment now felt crucial. She walked directly to Vern, who had begun trying to unloop the long nylon tape measure and was openly relieved to see her. Dr. Byron wanted them to census the butterflies on the ground, he told her, and they were clueless. She could well imagine how that had gone, Ovid confidently pummeling them with a flurry of unretainable instructions and walking off. Luckily she knew this one—it was the first task she'd done up here, with Bonnie and Mako. She aimed Vern north to walk the length of the site, stretching the tape as he went, and laid out one-meter squares along the transect. Pete came over to greet her.

"Did you remember the pillowcases?" His face suggested doubt, so she was thrilled to unzip her shoulder bag and draw them out one at a time like a magician's scarves. The number, four, seemed to please him too. Pete directed the helpers to scoop all the butterflies from four of their square-meter quadrats into pillowcases after they'd counted them. "Dead or alive," he told Vern. "One quadrat per pillowcase, doesn't matter which ones you choose, and we'll take them back to the lab."

The boys went to work on their assigned plots, accepting the strange assignment without question. She recalled her own first days spent here with a tight lid on her normal curiosity, afraid of betraying her expansive ignorance. These kids were even more earnest than she'd been, judging by the way they pressed their knees into the soggy black leaf mold, all of them mindless of their jeans, which would never recover. Except Roger, who wore shorts in all weathers. Roger and Carlos were two of the three Californians who'd introduced themselves to Dellarobia when they arrived. They'd camped up here ever since, increasingly unkempt but uncomplaining. The third one had gone home. Pete called them "the Three-Fifty guys" instead of using their names, and she wondered if that was meant to be disparaging. She and Pete seemed allied, now that other people had come onto his turf, and it fascinated her, the rules of the club. She was a little seduced by the chance to be an insider, and invented the code name Sideburn

Vern for Pete's amusement. But she felt bad about it after Vern turned out to be such an eager worker. And she really liked the California boys, who were unfailingly sweet and respectful, unlike a lot of the tourists who tramped through here, demanding water and directions from Dellarobia as if she were a hired hand. If they conversed with her at all, their syllables would sometimes broaden as if she might need help with English.

She ran to catch up with Pete. "What's the deal with the bow and arrow?" she asked him. "I could report you for shooting butterflies out of season."

He smiled. "We're stringing up the eye-buttons."

"Eyes?"

"*I*, the letter. Little *i*, big *B*." He opened an equipment pack and extracted a ziplock full of dime-size silver discs, like watch batteries but thicker. iButtons were tiny computerized devices that recorded temperatures over the course of time. A Velcro attachment was used to anchor each button inside a short length of PVC pipe to shelter it from rain and sun, and these would get fastened to the fishing line he'd shot over the tree. They would run them up the flagpole, so to speak, at intervals of every five meters from earth to treetops. "They save data in real time," he explained, "like the black box in your car engine." He also told her, though she didn't ask, the buttons cost ten dollars each.

If her station wagon had a black box, it was news to Dellarobia, but she got the gist and went to work alongside Pete, proving adept at rigging up the housings and attaching them to the filament that would hoist them. She remembered the résumé she'd given Dovey prior to landing this job: experienced at mashing peas and arbitrating tantrums. She could now add: owns pillowcases, good at Velcro. They would leave the iButtons up the tree for forty-eight hours and then bring them back to the lab. "Weren't you here when we did this the first time, back before Christmas?" Pete asked.

"No. I only came up with you guys just the once. We did body counts."

"That's right," Pete said, contorting his mouth sideways as he tightened a knot with his straight, white teeth. Braces, she thought. Someone paid good money for those, he ought not to use them as pliers. "The temperature varies, all the way up," he told her. "Especially in these evergreen forests. You'd be surprised. There's a ton of temperature data recorded on the Mexican overwintering sites by Brower et al. We want to see how the thermal characteristics of the Feathertown site compare to normal roosting sites."

She pictured these words, the Feathertown Site, appearing someday in a science book. Not the Cleary Site, or the Turnbow Site. She wondered if she was disappointed not to have her own name memorialized. That's what it would be, a memorial, the place where a species met its demise. It was crazy, all this hard work, to that end.

"So we bring the buttons back to the lab, and then what?"

"There's a reading device that plugs into the computer. It takes a while to download all the data and then plot it," he warned. "Get ready for a tedious day."

"As opposed to this one," she said, pausing to breathe on her frozen fingers.

"As opposed to this one."

She found she could not make herself say Ovid's name. "Is he worried?" she asked finally. "Is this really terrible for the butterflies?"

"It could be worse." Pete seemed to be making a point of showing no emotion. "It was definitely low twenties last night, so the microclimate of these firs is protecting them up to a point. Like they do in Mexico. I guess he wants a temperature profile of the roost through this cold stretch to see what they can actually survive."

"Where did he go?" she asked.

"He had the camera. I think he's doing a photo census."

She remembered a detail Pete had forgotten: to record the serial number of each button before sending it up the tree. He did seem a bit rattled, so maybe things were worse than he was willing to say. She asked about the plan for the pillowcases.

"Oh, right," Pete said. "Those can't lie around up here all day, somebody needs to take them down to the lab this afternoon. What you do," he said, giving her to know who *somebody* would be, "is you shake the butterflies to the bottom and pin the pillowcases up on a clothesline or something. Open-side up. You can rig up a line in the lab. And then you just watch them."

"You watch pillowcases full of dead butterflies?"

"They're not all dead. There's a bunch of sleepers in there, you'll see. When they warm up they start crawling up the inside of the pillowcase. At the end of the day you count the living and the dead, and do the math. You get a proportion. Multiply that figure times all the bodies we counted on the ground, and that's your mortality estimate."

She thought this through, stepwise. "Could I hang them up in my house?"

"Sure. It's probably warmer than the lab," he said, which was true, but she was thinking of Preston when he came home from school. He would sit on the edge of a chair and watch those pillowcases for all he was worth. He'd race to tell her each time another sleeper struggled from its stupor to begin the slow climb, pressed between soft walls of fabric. She and Preston would cheer for the stragglers, because at the end of the day, it was something they could do. Count the living and the dead, and do the math.

❧

Dellarobia forgot about eating her lunch until well past noon. Pete had left her rigging up more lines for buttons while he shot more arrows. Sometimes he crouched on his heels at the plywood table and entered sequences of mystery data into Ovid's small computer. Ovid himself remained at large. The sun gained its legs in the forest throughout the morning, warming the air by imperceptible degrees until she realized her fingers had thawed and she no longer needed some of her outer layers. Around the time she shed her coat the temperature touched some threshold that set off an extravagant spectacle of butterflies twitching open and even launching. The air got crowded with little celebratory bursts of action, like rice at a wedding. She stopped tying fishing line through bracelets of pipe and lifted her gaze. Pete looked up from his keyboard, the boys stopped counting bodies and rose unsteadily from the ground like soggy-kneed zombies. As a congregation they lifted their eyes in thanks. There was no whooping or back-slapping, as when Pete's arrow bested the tree. The difference was understood.

She felt lightheaded, then, and remembered hunger in its full measure. She grabbed her shoulder bag and headed for the big mossy log that was still the study site's best furniture. Carlos and Roger were there, black knees and all, their coats flung on the ground, shirtsleeves rolled to the elbows, standing on the log bridge with their crossed arms in front of their chests, playing some game of trying to bump one another off. Carlos was the taller, with gingery hair, despite the Mexican-sounding name. Roger's two-week beard and perpetual baggy shorts made her think of Snow White's dwarves.

"Hey, Dellarobia," they both called as she approached. They seemed to relish pronouncing her name, in a manner she'd seldom experienced. Maybe in California people took the unconventional in stride. Automatically she assessed the distance the boys could fall, maybe a sprained ankle's worth, and the cellophane skins of their former lunches spread over the log. A mother, regardless of job title. She resisted the urge to clean up and seated herself a safe distance from their roughhousing. The peanut butter sandwich in her purse had burrowed to the bottom, and she had to unload a pile of things to unearth it, setting them beside her on the log: four disposable diapers, socks, a box of Bug's Life Band-Aids, and an ice-cube tray for which she had no good explanation.

Ovid Byron materialized and took a seat on the other side of her little pile. Her face flooded scarlet as she hastily squirreled away the weird collection and unwrapped her sandwich. "Morning," he said cheerfully, heedless of the exact time, or her trauma. He seemed to have no special feeling about seeing her. "How are you holding up?"

"Fine." The answer, then, was no, he wasn't aware. Heaven help her. She could stay on this log and in this world. She studied her PBJ, the strata of brown and florid purple between white cushions of bread. Or maybe he knew, and didn't mind. Was that possible? He must have seen that image of her on the Internet, essentially naked, and had certainly never mentioned it. Cautiously she glanced at his sandwich, something bulbous and store-wrapped, probably picked up by Pete in town. Ovid's enthusiasm suggested it was the first food he'd seen on a long, cold day. He had been up here since dawn.

"Have you got enough to eat there?" she could not help asking.

"It will have to be," he said. She risked a glance at his face, and he disarmed her with a look of frank gratitude that made her falter. For what? She had nothing to offer. She'd been so flustered this morning, she hadn't even brought a thermos of coffee.

"You know what I could do," she said, winging it utterly. "I could make a pot of soup this afternoon and bring it up here to feed everybody. Pete wants me to take those pillowcases of butterflies to the lab. If you all mean to be up here till dark, you'll need more than a sandwich to go on."

"It's so funny you mention that. I was just thinking of my wife's noodle soup."

This, she found, was not what she wanted to hear. "Is she a good cook?"

He smiled, rubbing his chin with the back of his hand. "She is a terrible cook."

Dellarobia was unconscionably cheered by this news. "Well, I make a pretty decent chicken noodle soup. I could probably get it up here in a couple of hours."

"I think that would make you the queen of our

tribe," he said. "Especially the Three-Fifty boys. I don't think they've had a proper feed in a couple of weeks." Roger and Carlos had finished playing Robin Hood without incident, cleared their trash, and sauntered back to the body count. Practically whistling while they worked.

"Why does Pete call them that?"

"It's their organization. Three-fifty-dot-org."

"But what does that mean?"

"Parts per million," he said in a muffled way, between bites. "Honestly, I'm a little worried about those two. They exist on political commitment and gorp."

She thought: Gorp? But asked, "Parts per million?"

"Three hundred fifty parts per million," he replied. "The number of carbon molecules the atmosphere can hold, and still maintain the ordinary thermal balance. It's an important figure. I suppose they want to draw attention."

Roger came back to retrieve his coat from where he'd left it on the ground, offering a quick little wave. The coat was patched copiously with duct tape. If he gets cold enough, Dellarobia thought, maybe he'll tape up those bare legs as well. She wondered if she should offer to find him some trousers at Second Time Around.

"It's a greenhouse gas, carbon," Ovid added. "It traps the heat of the sun. That number has been going up. Right before our eyes, as they say."

"You're telling me somebody counts the atoms?"

"It's not very difficult. With the right equipment."

Her heart was still thumping like a drum, as it had all morning whenever she saw or thought of seeing him. But his talk steadied her, and his vulnerability. He had practically swallowed his sandwich whole. She set hers aside and dug in her purse for something presentable in the way of an emergency food supply. "So the carbon goes up, when we burn oil and stuff." She was working to hold her thoughts in place.

He nodded. "Up, up, up."

She found what she was looking for, a single-serving cup of diced peaches, and handed it to him. "So what goes out of whack, when it hits three-fifty?"

"The thermal stability of the planet." He studied the little plastic cup for a moment before grasping and pulling off the foil seal. She watched him down it like a glass of water, and tried to think of any other edibles she might be carrying on her person.

"What are we up to so far?"

He swallowed a few times before speaking. "About three-ninety."

"What? We went *past*? Why hasn't everything blown up?"

He studied the empty cup in his hand. "Some would say it has. Hurricanes reaching a hundred miles inland, wind speeds we've never seen. Deserts on fire. In New Mexico we are seeing the inferno. Texas is worse. Australia is unimaginably worse—a lot of the continent is in permanent drought. Farms abandoned forever."

She pictured orchards like the Cooks' dying on the other side of the world, for the opposite reason. Rain being sent to the wrong places, in the wrong amounts. "Why wouldn't they just irrigate the farms?" she asked.

"Because of firestorms."

"Oh."

"Walls of flame, Dellarobia. Traversing the land like freight trains, fed by dead trees and desiccated soil. In Victoria hundreds of people burned to death in one month, so many their prime minister called it hell on earth. This has not happened before. There is not an evacuation plan."

She remembered telling Dovey that hell had gone out of fashion. They sat in silence. Through the trees she saw Carlos stand up from his crouch and do some kind of a yoga pose, folding his arms together over his head to stretch his muscles. They never complained, those two boys. "Is the number still going up?" she asked.

"Everything that has brought us here continues without pause," Ovid said.

She thought of Cub kicking at the frost. "So will winter just *end*, then?"

"I suppose it might, but it wouldn't be our worry anymore. It will only take a few degrees of change, global average, to knock our kind out of the running."

She stared, her first completely direct look at him since the accidental sighting. "What do you mean, out of the running?"

"Living systems are sensitive to very small changes, Dellarobia. Think of a child's temperature elevated by two degrees. Would you call it normal?"

"A hundred, that's low-grade fever," she said. "Aches and chills." Dellarobia disliked the thermometer she kept in her makeup drawer, the treacherously slim glass pipe and its regime of wakeful nights, the croups and earaches. Her children's cheeks hot to the touch, their racked sobs that wrenched her will for living.

"And if the temperature keeps going up?" he asked.

"More? At a hundred and three I'd head for the emergency room. That's four and a half degrees. More than that, don't make me think about."

"Interesting," he said. "I just read a UN climate report of many hundred pages, and its prognosis for a febrile biosphere matches the one you just gave me in a sentence. Degree for degree."

She felt very unsettled by the fever talk. Just the smell of rubbing alcohol weakened her knees.

"It keeps me awake nights, that report," he said, shadowing her thoughts. "A four-degree rise in the world's average temperature might be unavoidable at this point. So we are headed for the ER, as you put it. The accumulation plays out for a very long time, even if we stop burning carbon."

"If you stop something, it stops," she said, sounding a little too fine.

"We used to think so. But there are unstoppable pro- cesses. Like the loss of polar ice. White ice reflects the

386

heat of the sun directly back to space. But when it melts, the dark land and water underneath hold on to the heat. The frozen ground melts. And that releases more carbon into the air. These feedback loops keep surprising us."

How could this be true, she thought, if no one was talking about it? People with influence. Important people made such a big deal over infinitely smaller losses.

"So it's not a question of having Floridian winters in Tennessee," he said. "That is not even under discussion."

"Is there some part of this I can actually see?"

"You don't believe in things you can't see?" he asked.

She thought of Blanchie Bise and Bible class. The flood of Noah, Jesus. She did try. "It's never been my long suit," she confessed.

"Your children's adulthood?"

That nearly floored her of course. Or creeked her. Since that's what was below this log, if she'd swooned off of it. How dare he belt her with that one?

"A trend is intangible, but real," he said calmly. "A photo cannot prove a child is growing, but several of them show change over time. Align them, and you can reliably predict what is coming. You never see it all at once. An attention span is required."

It occurred to her that she didn't have a single photo of her kids from the last six months or more. Maybe Dovey did, in her phone. She should be sure to get some before Preston's baby teeth fell out.

"I can break it down for you," he said. "Water, you can see that. Warm air holds more water. Think of condensation on a windshield. Multiply that times all the square meters above you, and it's a hell of a lot of water. It evaporates too quickly from the hot places, and floods the wet ones. Every kind of weather is intensified by warming."

"So flood and fire, basically. Like the Prophecy."

"I don't know about that. What does the Bible say about the ice albedo effect?"

He was mocking her, probably. "I don't think the Prophecy applies in real-world terms," she said. "People assume it's out there, I guess. The lake of fire and everything. But they figure it's still a long way off. Way past the end of T-ball season. After the kids' graduation, after the wedding."

She stopped, before Cordelia and Preston came into this picture. The afternoon was already waning, its softer light filling the sky like a liquid seeping between the trees. Ovid's attention to her felt like a promise, and she wanted to trust it, only that, not the particular words. To leap, and forget the crash landing. She finished her sandwich while he talked. He told her that forests absorb carbon from the sky, but not when they are dying of drought or burning. That oceans also buffer the atmosphere, but not when their carbon levels make them too acidic for life. The oceans, he said, were losing their fish.

"And coral reefs. Have you ever seen a coral reef?"

She wished she could just touch his hand and stop this. She noticed the crow's feet around his eyes, his exhaustion. It must have been true about this keeping him awake. "I've seen the beach," she said. "I guess that's not the same."

"One day I will tell you about the reefs. It's all I wanted to do as a boy, swim in the reef and make my little studies. My mother said I would turn into a fish."

She couldn't see these things at all, stricken forests or killing tides. What she saw was the boy inside a man who was losing everything. She felt the way she did when her children howled over outcomes she couldn't change. Helpless. Everything goes. "They say it's just cycles," she said after a while. "That it goes through this every so often."

He let out a little hiss between his teeth, which scared her. "All right. In the Pleistocene most of this continent was under ice, and the rest was arctic desert. At other times the ice caps melted and this very place was under the ocean. So yes, cycles. With millions of years between events, my friend. Not decades."

She did not like *my friend*. She did not hazard a comment. But he prodded. "Dellarobia, what do you see?"

"We've never had rain like we did last year. I'll grant you."

"I'm asking literally. What do you see?"

She looked at the trees, the forest floor. "A million dead butterflies," she said. "Sorry as hell they ever landed here."

A live monarch dropped through the air and landed on a clump of grass near Ovid's boots. She watched it crawl slowly to the top of the drooping seed head, clinging upside-down beneath the arc. It folded its wings together, closing up shop for the night, waiting for a better day tomorrow.

"Humans are in love with the idea of our persisting," he said. "We fetishize it, really. Our retirement funds, our genealogies. Our so-called ideas for the ages."

"I really hate this. What you're saying. Just so you know."

"Sorry. I am a doctor of natural systems. And this looks terminal to me."

In the branches over their heads, small bursts of butterflies exploded into the sun like soundless fireworks. The beauty was irresistible. "I just can't see it being all that bad," she said. "I'd say most people wouldn't."

He nodded slowly. "Do you know, scientists had a devil of a time convincing people that birds flew south in winter? The Europeans used to believe they burrowed into muddy riverbanks to hibernate. They would see the swallows gathering along the rivers in autumn, and then disappearing. Africa was an abstraction to these people. The notion of birds flying there, for unknown reasons, they found laughable."

"Well," she said. "I guess seeing is believing,"

"Refusing to look at the evidence, this is also popular."

"It's not that we're all just lazy-minded. Maybe you

think so." She struggled to articulate her defense. On first sight, she'd taken these butterflies for fire and magic. Monarchs were nowhere in her mind. Probably he wouldn't believe that. "People can only see things they already recognize," she said. "They'll see it if they know it."

"They use inference systems," he said.

"Okay. That."

"And how do they see the end of the world?" Ovid asked. "In real-world terms, as you put it."

She considered this for a long time. "They know it's impossible."

He nodded, surprised. "Golly. I think you are right."

She took the plastic cup from his hands and wrapped it in the cellophane that had held her sandwich. She could feel where her fingertips had brushed his. "I don't know how a person could even get through the day, knowing what you know," she said.

"So. What gets Dellarobia through her day?"

Flying from pillar to post, she thought. Strange words. "Meeting the bus on time," she answered. "Getting the kids to eat supper, getting teeth brushed. No cavities the next time. Little hopes, you know? There's just not room at our house for the end of the world. Sorry to be a doubting Thomas."

"Well, you're hardly the first," he said. "People always want the full predicament revealed and proven in sixty seconds or less. You may have noticed I avoid cameras."

"You did well, though," she insisted. "Explaining it to me. I'm not saying I *don't* believe you, I'm saying I *can't*."

"You underestimate yourself. You have a talent for this endeavor, Dellarobia. I see how you take to it. But choose your path carefully. For scientists, reality is not optional."

"Are we at least allowed to hope the butterflies will make it through this winter?"

He leaned forward, peering up at the sky. "That is not a little hope," he said.

She thought of other times, other dire news. Pregnancies, wanted or not. It was never real at first. She recalled the day of her mother's diagnosis, holding her bone-thin arm, its yielding skin, walking her out of the doctor's office onto the crumbling, shaded parking lot. Little humps of moss that swelled along a scar in the asphalt like drops of green blood. All these vivid external details suggesting nothing had changed. They'd decided to go to the grocery with no more mention, that day, of the end of the world.

Suddenly she felt an acute craving for the Diet Coke she knew to be in her purse. She dug it out with little trouble, cracked it open, and offered Ovid the first sip, but he held up a hand and shuddered as if she'd offered a bite of dirt. "My wife drinks those diet things," he said. "Aspartame, or whatever it is. It tastes like soap to me."

She threw back a slug of the fizzy, tepid liquid,

noting that it did as a matter of fact taste a little soapy. But caffeinated. She pictured an obese wife chugging diet sodas and burning toast in the kitchen. "What's your wife's name?"

"Juliet," he said.

Give me a break, she thought. "So, Pete says I need to hang up those pillowcases indoors, to give the sleepers a chance to wake up. I count the ones that crawl up the sides, and keep track of numbers, and then what? Do I bring them back up here?"

He clapped his hands together, smiling. "No. This is good, you will like this. We give the sleepers one last chance to sink or swim. It can be a lot—maybe two-thirds of these bodies on the ground are actually alive. But you have to give them every chance."

She thought of Preston's veterinary book, with its surprising advice on lamb resuscitation. "What do we do, butterfly CPR?"

"We pitch them into the air one at a time. It's sink or fly, really. Last winter in Mexico we launched them from the balcony of our hotel over a courtyard where people were dining. Everyone was cheering for the flyers." His smile grew, remembering that happier place. Dellarobia wished she had been there with him, or anywhere at all, even if it meant flinging herself to the void. To be given the same chance.

"I will come back down to the lab while we still have enough light," he said. "To help with that. I don't suppose you have any balconies at your house."

393

She raised one eyebrow. "Not hardly. Do you?"

She should let him speak of his home and his wife, if that's what he wanted. His Juliet. She did ask. But he merely said, "No balconies."

So that's how it would be. She would go home to make soup that was better than Juliet's, and return here as queen of this tribe. At dusk she and Ovid would climb together to the barn loft. They would stand in the open door of the haymow and take these butterflies in hand, one at a time, and toss them into the air. Some would crash. And some would fly.

11

Community Dynamics

Dellarobia's phone buzzed. A text from Dovey, one of her church sightings: GET RIGHT OR GET LEFT. Dellarobia texted back: LTS GO.

She was nowhere near ready to go, still in her bathrobe and ratty yellow slippers. But Dovey was one of those people who traveled in a medium-size pod of tardiness on which others came to rely. Dellarobia poured herself a second cup of coffee and pulled out a kitchen chair to put her feet up. In a lifetime of hearing people celebrate weekends, she finally saw what all the fuss was about. By no means did her workload cease on Saturday, but it did shift gears. If her kids wanted to pull everything out of the laundry basket to make a bird's nest and sit in it, fine. Dellarobia could even sit in there with them and incubate, if she so desired. Household chores no longer called her name exclusively. She had an income. She'd never before understood how much her life in this little house had felt to her like confinement in a sinking vehicle after driving off a bridge. Scooping at the toys and dirty dishes rising from every surface was a natural response to inundation. To open a hatch and swim away felt miraculous. Working outside the home took her about fifty yards

395

from her kitchen, which was far enough. She couldn't see the dishes in the sink.

A steady ruckus rose from the living room, where Cordie sang at the top of her lungs, *"Lo mio lo mio,"* something she'd learned from Lupe's little boys. It meant "mine" in Spanish, Preston had explained, astonishing Dellarobia with her first sense of being an outsider to her children's lives. Preston was now making vocal crashing noises, each followed by howls of make-believe pain from Cub. She scooted her chair forward to peek through the doorway. Cub lay on his back on a blanket outstretched on the living room floor, with Preston beside him arranging an armada of vehicles: Matchbox cars, a red plush fire engine, a plastic tractor.

"What in the Sam Hill are you all doing?" she called out.

"It's a parking lot," Preston replied. "I'm running over Daddy with everything."

"Poor Daddy. Does your victim need a refill?"

Cub lifted his coffee cup. She carried in the coffeepot and kneeled on a corner of the blanket to fill his mug. "Should we call this a blood transfusion?"

"Nah," Preston said. "He's just smooshed."

A far cry from veterinary medicine, she thought. But Cub was good about letting the whole boy out for a run, where Dellarobia would have reined him in. Cub was not always in the mood, but when the kids did get him down on the floor he gave himself over wholly, letting them direct their play, however silly or tedious or grotesque.

"Lo mio lo mio!" Cordie's voice bounced with her fast little steps as she came running from her bedroom carrying a board book, which she pretended to stuff into Cub's mouth. Cub made chomping sounds, *gnowm gnowm*, and Cordie shouted gleefully, "Dat's hay!" She dropped the book and ran to fetch another bale.

"I'm not just smooshed," Cub informed Dellarobia. "I am also a cow."

"Husbands with secret lives. I'm calling Oprah."

Through the front window blinds she saw Dovey's vintage Mustang slide into the driveway. Her double honk set the kids to shouting, "Dovey's here!" Dellarobia ran to get dressed. The kids were ready an hour ago, far keener to meet a blue convertible than any school bus, all keyed up for a wild ride with Aunt Dovey. Dellarobia heard the clamor as they tackled her at the door, begging to ride with the top down.

"Brrr, no way! It's freaking February the second, you guys," Dovey said. "Hey Cub, what happened to you?"

"Same old same old," he said. "Vehicular homicide."

Cub planned to help Hester move the pregnant ewes today while Dellarobia took the kids shopping with Dovey. They were headed for Cleary to check out a huge new secondhand warehouse. Dellarobia's usual haunt was the Second Time Around, a store so tiny it was actually in the owner's house, but Dovey disliked it on the grounds you were sure to run into people you knew, or their stuff. Admittedly, Dellarobia often saw items she recognized, including suits made by her mother, and once, in full sequined glory, the very magenta prom dress worn by the girl for whom her old boyfriend Damon had dumped her. This was years after Damon had married the girl, and in fact also divorced her, yet there hung the dress, glistening like a stab wound. Cleary seemed a long way to go for bargains, but she had to concede, exchanges could get intimate in Feathertown.

Dovey looked jaunty in a suede newsboy cap and maroon turtleneck, well put together as usual. *Duggy and Stoked*, they used to declare this, as if they were their own cable show: two girls dressed and ready for action. A worldlier, female version of *Wayne's World*, in which all things came off as planned. Dovey's convertible, on the other hand, always seemed provisional to Dellarobia, especially with the top closed, flapping as if something important was about to come loose. It had no shoulder harnesses in the backseat, only lap belts, so the kids' car seats fit in a sigoggling way that was probably unsafe. The kids of course adored this.

"Hey, look!" Preston shouted. "A smooshed groundhog, like I did to Daddy." Dellarobia was amazed he could see roadkill from the backseat. The animal was as flat as a drive-through hamburger.

"And here it is Groundhog Day," Dovey said genially. "Sorry, Mr. Hog, not much shadow there. I never can remember, does his shadow cause there to be more winter, or less?"

Dellarobia considered and dismissed both cause and correlation. "Neither," she said. "It's just something people made up to get themselves through the homestretch."

"Right." Dovey had an endearing habit of nodding once, curtly, an assent of bobbing curls. "There's going to be exactly six more weeks of winter no matter what. Because it is freaking February the second."

Six weeks. The butterflies would have survived to fly away by then, or they would have died. His large hope, her job, the whole deal soon departed. Sometimes everything hit her, as in *everything*, the approach of flood and famine, but mostly she could not see a day past the middle of March. Dellarobia gripped the door handle as Dovey took the curves a little fast. This road was fifteen miles of hateful, winding around the mountain from Feathertown's outer pastures through intermittent woods and hamlets of mobile homes. She was surprised when they passed the infamous Wayside, meaning they'd already crossed the county line. Cleary was not that far away, but Dellarobia couldn't say when she'd been there last. It had the college and a lot of restaurants and bars, and might as well have been located in another state, as far as her married self was concerned. Obviously Dovey thought of it as no distance at all. She had roaming capabilities.

"Okay. I am so moving out of that stupid duplex," Dovey announced.

Dovey had been so moving out of the duplex for nine of the last ten years, while her brother drove her crazy with his never-ending remodel. He was the ambitious one, Tommy. He'd bought that house on Main as a fixer-upper when barely out of high school and extorted an obscene amount of rent from his siblings in the decade since, capitalizing on their desire to leave home at an early age. The parents were all for it; they'd cosigned Tommy's loan. Dellarobia didn't really get it—the boys were still crammed in and bunked up together, two of them sharing a bedroom to this very day, as men in their twenties. Dovey at least had a whole side of the duplex to herself, but still. The walls were thin. They knew more about each other's lives than adult siblings should.

"How's Felix?" Dellarobia asked.

Dovey sighed casually. "I need to get Felix over with." Dovey did love life the way Cub watched television. "Shoot," she added, "I need to text him. His wallet's been in my kitchen for two days." She reached for her purse, but Dellarobia snatched it away.

"No, ma'am, not with my kids in your car. 'Honk if you love Jesus, text while driving if you want to meet up.'"

Dovey actually claimed to have seen that one on a sign, and probably regretted having conveyed it. She rolled her eyes. "So what's new in the Land o' Science?"

I have a talent for the endeavor, she thought. His words. Dellarobia was concealing nothing specific, but

400

felt a capacious welling of things she couldn't talk about. The sensation was physical. "Pete left yesterday. He packed up a bunch of frozen butterfly samples and took off driving back to New Mexico."

"Back to the missus he goes," Dovey sang. "And what about the good doctor? He seems to be kept on a longer leash."

"There is a wife, Juliet. She exists. She's a bad cook."

"So bad he has to live in a different time zone?"

"I guess people have their reasons," Dellarobia said. "But I don't see it. Why be married and live apart?"

Dovey shrugged. "Do I look like Ask Miss Marriage?"

She hadn't yet told Dovey about Cub's confession. With the kids always around, she hadn't had a chance to get into the Crystal Estep saga, nor any real zest for the telling. She felt embarrassed, both for herself and for Cub. And anyway, nothing had happened.

Dellarobia was surprised by their hasty arrival. They pulled into the parking lot of the strip mall and zoomed into the perfect space, courtesy of Dovey's muscular engine and belligerent driving, right near the sliding front doors. The Try It Again Warehouse was big-box-size and a tad dilapidated, with piles of recently dropped-off items spilling like dunes over the pavement in front of the plate-glass windows. A green toilet sat primly upright between boxes of wadded coats and plastic toys. "What is this place," Dellarobia asked, "some charity, like the Salvation Army?"

"No, it's somebody's business they started up. The

ads say they'll come clean out your attic or whatever. I'd say they make their money on volume."

Dellarobia found it odd that people would donate their discards to a private enterprise instead of a charity. Passers-by must see the stuff piled up here and automatically eject their own castoffs, a townie equivalent to the wildcat landfills that grew alongside country roads. Some universal junk-attraction principle.

Dovey was not a secondhand shopper by nature as Dellarobia was, but she'd heard this place had racks of worn-once designer dresses. Appearances did not suggest that Vera Wang was on the premises. Inside the dusty storefront they met a boggling display of items that were all going for twenty-five cents. Salt shakers, unmatched but decent flatware, a cheese grater, a set of cast iron skillets of the type Dellarobia had never been able to afford. She set a dollar's worth of high-quality cookware into an empty cart and lifted Cordie into the fold-down seat. The twenty-five-cent shelves went on and on. Dellarobia was stupefied by the bargains.

"Why isn't everybody we know here?"

"Mama, you could put Daddy's picture in this," Preston suggested, holding up an overlarge canary yellow picture frame.

"You are so right," she said. Preston moved on to a tape recorder. Dellarobia examined a big meat platter with a treelike gravy gutter built into it, exactly like one her mother used at Thanksgiving and other big-deal family meals, occasions that had always left Dellarobia feeling their family was insufficiently large. Why hadn't her parents had more children? As a child she'd never thought to ask, and now she would never know. So much knowledge died with a person.

Cordelia was determined to climb out of the cart, which she called the "buggy." Where did she learn that? Dellarobia lifted her out of the wire seat, kicking, sending one blue plastic clog flying, which Preston ran to fetch and put back on his Cinderella sister. She accepted the compromise of standing up in the cart. "Buggy mama buggy mama," she chanted, grabbing both sides and rocking, her pale hair a wild waggling halo. Her unassailable wardrobe choice today was her favorite striped summer dress, with corduroy pants underneath and sweaters over it. Dellarobia thought of those ragtag campers with the knitting needles she'd seen up on the mountain. She could see Cordie running off to join that tribe.

Dovey moved out of twenty-five-cent range to nab a pair of silver high-heeled sandals. She and Dellarobia gravitated toward a long rack of wedding dresses, mostly in majestic plus sizes, just to run their hands over those expanses of satin and organza with their pearl-encrusted bodices. So much whiteness, perfectly seamed. "They're all in such great condition," Dovey said reverently.

"Duh. This is not a garment that gets a lot of wear."

"Oh, yeah," Dovey laughed. "Hey, is there a maternity bride section?"

"Ha ha. Actually there should be."

Cordelia started up a weird double-time stomping routine in the buggy, like something from an exercise class. The child seemed energized by commerce. As they cruised between close-set racks of women's clothing, she chirped continually, "Like dis, Mama?" Dellarobia wasn't looking for herself, but noticed the vintage jackets with interfaced collars and lined sleeves. So much quality going for nothing, like those cast-iron skillets. The older merchandise here was better made than literally everything in the dollar store. She tried on a fitted corduroy blazer, forest green, circa Angie Dickinson. It made her feel like a higher-quality person. She decided to wear it around the store. Her daughter set herself to pulling down every flowered, sequined, or otherwise gaudy blouse from the racks, tilting each one cornerwise off its hanger and asking, "Dis cute?"

"She has her own sense of style," Dovey observed. "You've got to give her that."

Dellarobia did give her that, but wondered why. Preston was indifferent to fashion. He had drifted downstream, floating out the mouth of the clothing aisle into an estuary of household appliances where he was trying everything out: pushing all the buttons on the blender, popping the toaster, ironing with the iron—something he must have seen at Lupe's house, not hers. All other appliances here were greatly outnumbered by the irons, a whole battalion of them lined up like pointy-headed soldiers at attention. She was getting the gist of this place: long on items that people were ready to part with.

Dovey had paused to commune with her phone, probably remembering to text Felix about his wallet and while she was at it, check the weather in Daytona Beach or something. Dellarobia knew little about Internet devices, except that her son's hunger for information was already pulling in that direction. Since the day of her first paycheck and *last* last smoke she'd paid up the mortgage and opened a bank account in her own name. Cub knew about the former, not the latter. He didn't even know exactly what she earned. Dellarobia handled the finances.

She followed Preston around the corner into a world of housewares, somewhat randomly assembled, shockingly cheap. The linen section had uniform pricing: blankets, bedspreads, and curtains all two dollars each; sheets one dollar. She couldn't believe her eyes. New sheets, even of the worst quality, cost a fortune. She found twin sheets for Preston's bed and a set for their double plus two crib sheets, six bucks total, and stuffed these finds around Cordelia, who was not taking kindly to being hemmed in. Briefly Dellarobia confronted the thought of Cordie outgrowing her crib, the kids getting too old to share intimate space. Everyone in their little house was going along with the story they could afford: that no one would grow, nothing would change.

Dovey wheeled her cart up to join them. "Whoah.

You're buying used sheets? You don't know who's slept in those."

"As opposed to the sheets at your house. Where I do know."

"Good point," Dovey said. "Nothing a little Clorox won't cure."

An elderly woman pawed through sheets while the little boy at her side yanked down slick bedspreads from a pile, inciting waterfalls of polyester. The woman crooned in a steady voice without ever looking up: "You're a stinker, Mammaw is going to give you to the froggies. Mammaw is going to throw you in the garbage can." Dellarobia pushed Cordie out of earshot, not that she was above such thoughts, but still. They should be the accent pieces of a parenting style, not wall-to-wall carpet. At the far end of bedspreads, a leather-skinned man was unfolding comforters to assess their heft. He picked out two extra bulkies and wheeled toward the checkout with nothing else in his cart. Homeless. So free enterprise was standing in for the charities on both ends here.

"Look at this," Dellarobia said, amazed to find handmade quilts and afghans tucked between ratty blankets, all in the same two-dollar category. She spread out a crocheted afghan in hues of blue and purple. "So much work went into this, and now it's lying here begging. Why would somebody give this away?"

"Mammaw died," Dovey proposed, "and the kids are trying to forget her."

Dellarobia put the afghan in her cart to save its dignity. Dovey arranged a pair of crocheted watermelon slices over her shirt like a bikini, but tossed them back as Preston approached. He was carrying a pillow that looked like a pig wearing a tutu.

"I thought Cordie might like this," he said. Cordie reached for the ballerina pig and let out a howl that earned some attention from nearby shoppers.

"Tell you what, Preston. Let's get her out and you two can poke around together. But stay right with her, okay?" Dellarobia knew he would. Cordie threw her arms around the pig and ran after her brother. Dovey perused a shelf of exercise tapes: *Atlas Abs*, *Bun Buster*. The floor beyond was crowded with exercise equipment in like-new condition, cast aside in haste. This place was a museum of people's second thoughts. Dellarobia clucked her tongue. "New year's resolutions didn't last a month."

"Christmas presents," Dovey agreed. "All those husbands and wives dreaming of a slim, sexy version of the old ball and chain."

Cordie and Preston were about thirty feet away, trying out what he was calling the "exercise things." Dellarobia heard him say, "Mama won't get that for you, we can't afford it." She kept the kids in her radar as she and Dovey ambled past a row of Venetian blinds and bathroom items. The categories were mysterious.

"Here you go." Dovey brandished a rolling pin engraved with the words "Husband Tamer."

"Now see, they should sell that as a package with the exercise equipment. To help keep the old ball and chain on the bike. Like an extended warranty."

They exited the aisle and encountered a sobering wall of crutches hanging on a huge pegboard. Wooden crutches, aluminum walkers, items the previous owners were definitely glad to get out of the house. Some were barely used, souvenirs of some kid's brief hiatus from school sports, while others had a deep gloss of wear on the hand grips, and rubber tips as worn as the oldest of shoe leather. Whoever gave those up had moved into some other mode of transport. By wheelchair or by pall-bearer.

At the end of another aisle, a couple of college-age kids were removing everything from a shelf, presumably because they wanted to buy the shelf. They wore shorts and flip-flops, and the girl had a tattoo that resembled barbed wire encircling her ankle. Dellarobia imagined their lives, setting up some little apartment. Unmarried.

"What's with these kids running around half naked in winter?" Dovey asked.

The maternal tone surprised Dellarobia. "Maybe winter's not that big a deal for them," she suggested. "They probably don't have to be outside their cars or buildings that much." She found herself fascinated by this young pair. A store employee materialized and began to argue with them, putting items back on the shelf with exaggerated fatigue as he shook his head.

Evidently this was routine. College kids were all over the clothing racks too. She'd watched a girl with an expensive haircut and highlights try on the same green blazer Dellarobia was now wearing around the store. Maybe that's why she'd kept it on, competition. That girl had a fat, sparkly diamond on her necklace and probably a daddy paying her tuition. She didn't need to be here.

Preston appeared, with Cordie in tow, making his way down the aisle carrying a box with a handle that was much too heavy for him. A slide projector, she could see from the picture on the box. One of those carousel things they used in ancient history.

"I thought Dr. Byron could use this," Preston said.

"You know what? Maybe he could. Let's leave it here, but I'll ask him." She checked the tag. "Ten dollars is a good price. You can tell him about it Monday."

Preston lit up. Dellarobia let him come to the study site sometimes after school, finding simple things for him to do that made him insanely happy. Dr. Byron didn't seem to mind, even when Preston hung around him with too much vigor, throwing his arms around Dr. Byron's legs by way of greeting. Attaching like a barnacle, Ovid called it. "Here is my friend, Barnacle Bill!" And the cautious response, "No, Barnacle Preston." The sight of them together filled Dellarobia with complicated emotions she had to ignore.

Past the crutches was a giant rack of purses: fake leopard, red sequins, gold lamé. So many, you'd think the world contained nothing but females and their money. Cordie dropped the pillow and went for an extra-large fake alligator bag. She took off after Preston at her fast little trot, grabbing bottom-shelf items and stuffing them in the purse. A shoplifter-in-training. When they were gone, Dovey asked, "So who else is in love with Dr. Butterfly, besides Preston Turnbow and his mother?"

"He's my boss, Dovey."

"He's your boss, *and* you blush every time his name is spoken."

She made no answer. They arrived in the toy and child-equipment area, which was hopping with unsupervised children. She watched Preston and Cordie move down a long line of child-safety seats on the floor, carefully sitting in each and every one.

"What level of seriousness are we discussing here," Dovey prodded, "on a scale of one to ten? Eight being that hottie friend of Cub's that used to bring you wood chips, nine being that kid that lured you up there to quote-unquote end your life. I'm not even counting the geezer at Rural Incorporated."

A federal assistance representative, a tree trimmer, a lineman who was frankly a child: all her life, men had been lining up, it seemed, to ask nothing of her whatsoever. Her mother's social security number, baby where'd you get those eyes, the hard questions had topped out right around there. Until now. None of those men ever saw the person inside. Or the one she might become.

Dovey had hit on the subject she couldn't discuss. "Zero point zero," Dellarobia said. "He has a wife."

"And gripes about her cooking."

"Not really. To tell you the truth, he never talks about her at all."

"No heat in the kitchen, then."

"I don't know. I just know he's not very happy."

Dovey cocked an eyebrow. "*And there'll be* happiness," she sang, "*for every girl and boy*." Clint Black, slightly revised.

Dellarobia watched Preston tug a pair of water wings onto his sister's arms over her sweater. "You need these so you won't fall in the water and drown," he advised. Cordie flapped her inflated wings and ran from him in loopy circles like some kind of moth. Then abruptly stopped and climbed aboard a rocking horse.

Dellarobia said, "I don't want to play this game."

Dovey pushed her cart away without a word, steering around a fake tiger rug with sad-looking eyes. Dellarobia stayed where she was, in Playland, fighting back inexplicable tears as she walked through what seemed like acres of bike helmets and strollers and child safety seats. Every ambulatory child in the store was here flinging toys around, tentatively cavorting with strangers. Older kids were patently bossing the younger ones, shouting, "You're going to break that!" Or the universal affront, "That's for babies." She browsed a shelf of one-dollar toys, pausing on an alphabet-learning

411

contraption called Little Smarty. It had dials that turned to match letters to pictures, the kind of thing Preston could play with all day long. But the name put her off. Obviously it was manufactured in a different era. What modern parent wanted her kids to be Little Smarties? The word was a rebuke: smart-mouth, smarty-pants. Don't get smart with me.

A grandmother-toddler team joined her at the toy shelf, the kid leaning out of his stroller in all directions to grab anything he could. Every child on the premises was being conveyed by a Mammaw, it seemed. This one idly handed her grandson a plastic baseball bat, which he turned around and choked up on like a pro, swinging at nearby shoppers. Dellarobia scooted away and found Dovey with Cordie on her hip checking out a throng of baby dolls gathered under a sign: SMALL BABIES 50¢, ALL OTHERS $1. The petite devalued as usual, Dellarobia thought with rancor. Poor Preston, if he didn't start catching up to his classmates soon, she might join Cub in his prayers for their son's growth spurt. "Have it, have it?" Cordelia chanted as Dovey picked up dollies and made them talk. The selection was overwhelming. Few looked like actual babies, and some were weirdly sexy, with factory-installed eye shadow and big pouty lips. Cordie grabbed the homeliest of the lot and shoved it head-down in her alligator bag.

"Baby!" she declared when she saw her mother, offering it up for approval. The thing had a potato-like head, created by someone who'd stuffed a nylon stocking and sculpted the eyes, mouth, and cheekbones with a needle and thread.

"Sorry," Dovey said, "I'm buying your daughter the March of Dimes child."

"Look at all those tiny stitches. Can you imagine?"

Dovey gave the doll a second look before setting Cordie down. "Hester could probably make things like that. She does all those crafty woolly things."

"If only she were grandchild-inclined." Dellarobia pictured her own mother hand-stitching a doll. The grandma Cordie would never meet, like the fish that got away.

Immediately behind them, a twenty-foot-long wooden crate of fifty-cent sweaters was attracting attention. Shoppers surrounded it on all sides like livestock at a trough, churning the contents. Winter had dawned on the neighborhood.

"Oh, man, look at this!" Dellarobia extracted a huge Crayola-orange sweater.

"Yikes," Dovey said. "You put that on Cub, y'all will look like a solar system."

Dellarobia laughed. "It's not for anybody to wear. There are these girls up on the mountain that are knitting monarch butterflies out of old sweaters."

"Excuse me?"

"They pull sweaters apart to get the yarn. Recycled. That's their big thing." Dellarobia tried to assemble words to describe the ragamuffin girls who were

413

camping out near the study site. "They're from England," she said. That was a starting point.

"And they crossed the ocean blue to come here and pull sweaters apart?"

"Well, yeah, they're crazy, number one. I guess they don't have kids or anything. They saw us on the news and came to do a sit-in against the logging, and now it's a sit-in about global warming. They sit up there all day and knit little monarch butterflies out of recycled orange yarn. They hang them all over the trees. It looks kind of real."

Dovey looked skeptical.

"It's on the Internet," Dellarobia maintained. "They told me they have this campaign of asking people to send in their orange sweaters, to help save the butterflies. For these girls to rip up, and knit with. They're getting boxes and boxes of sweaters, that much I can tell you. Anything with 'butterflies' in the address comes to our house."

"This I have got to see." Dovey had her phone out. "What do I search?"

Dellarobia thought for a moment. "Knit the Earth," she said. "Or Women Knit the Earth. Something like that."

Dovey's eyes grew large. "Holy cow," she said, standing by the sweater bin, peering into the World Wide Web. "This is happening on your property? It's like, *huge*. They've got over a thousand Likes on Facebook."

"So that's a lot?" As usual Dellarobia felt out of the

loop. She had squirreled $110 into her account thus far, her computer fund, but dreaded asking Dovey about prices. She probably wouldn't get in the ballpark before her job ended next month.

"W-O-M-Y-N," Dovey added. "That's who's knitting the Earth."

"Well, they're from England," Dellarobia said. "Maybe spelling is not their long suit. These girls are kind of rough. But they're good knitters, you should see their little monarch butterflies. Are there photos?"

Dovey nodded slowly, stroking the face of her phone. "There are." After a minute she put it away. "What else are you not telling me?"

"Find some more orange sweaters, and I'll tell you." Together they combed the bin and fished out nine altogether, in various shades of hideous. The knitter-women had hit on a jackpot scheme. Nobody really wanted to keep their orange sweaters anyway.

Dellarobia wasn't hiding anything. She'd only gotten the story on the knitters this week when the boxes arrived. The rest was all science, monitoring and sampling, nothing Dovey wanted to hear. "Hester thinks God is keeping the winter mild to protect the butterflies," she said. "There's a faction at church that thinks that too. The butterflies knew God was looking after things here, and that's why they came to Feathertown."

"Your mother-in-law is a hot mess," Dovey said.

Dellarobia could not dispute the diagnosis. "I'm actually kind of worried about her. It's a trap, you

415

know? If she's got God in charge of all this, and then something bad happens to us, she'll have to admit God knew what He was doing. Mainly it's a big fat incentive to ignore bad news." Such as global warming, a subject whose very mention now made Cub angry, as if there were some betrayal involved.

Dovey picked up an umbrella with mouse ears that had fallen into the aisle. "I saw where somebody's putting up money to move the whole kit and caboodle."

"Move what, the butterflies?" This was news to Dellarobia.

"Yep," Dovey said. "To Florida or something. They would capture them some way and move them. This guy owns a trailer rig."

"Wow. I never even thought about that. Where'd you hear this?"

"Topix," Dovey replied. "It's this site where people can post local news. It mostly ends up being trash talk, though."

"Oh, well, I bet there's plenty about me on there." She checked out an eight-dollar bike, too big for Preston now but perfect for next Christmas. But where could she hide it? Where would they all be in a year's time? The consideration made her feel a little light-headed, almost the same swoony feeling she'd had that day sitting on the log, when Ovid mentioned her children's adulthood. Why should it feel so risky to count concretely on a future?

"So is there?" she pressed. "Gossip about me?"

Dovey waggled her head from side to side. "Don't be so sure you're the center of the universe. Why is Hester so wrapped up in the whole butterfly thing?"

"I don't know. She and Bear are butting heads. I guess Hester sees the monarchs as . . ." Dellarobia couldn't finish the sentence. Maybe some form of redemption for a family she saw as having gone to the dogs: lazy son, troublemaking daughter-in-law, inexplicably uninteresting grandkids, a husband sitting out church in Men's Fellowship pretending it's a honkytonk, minus the beer. Certainly Hester wasn't jumping on the financial opportunity. She'd nailed a coffee can to the pasture gatepost with a sign suggesting a five-dollar entry fee, which the sightseers managed to overlook. No one in the family had time to monitor the onslaught of visitors. The tree huggers, as Cub called them.

Dovey laughed aloud, and Dellarobia turned to see the kids marching toward her toting suitcases from a matched set, both the same red plaid. Preston had the medium-size, Cordie the little overnight bag. Their smiles matched too, both oversize.

"Thinking of going somewhere?" she asked.

"Africa," announced Preston.

"Affica!" screamed his sister.

"Okay. Watch out for lions."

They giggled and ran to catch their plane. Africa, the unimaginable place where migrating birds went, while people thought they were burrowing into the riverbank.

"There's probably a Mama-bear suitcase with that set," Dovey suggested.

"Wouldn't that be something, just to blow out of town," Dellarobia said, feeling heavy. Dovey had avoided her question. "It's probably the same stuff I hear at church. The gossip you're seeing on Facebook or whatever. That I'm getting above my station."

"They're jealous," Dovey conceded. "That is the long and short of it."

"What do I have, that anybody wants? Dovey, look, *me*. Competing with homeless dudes for bargains on used bedding. Jealous of what?"

Dovey shrugged. "You're world-famous."

"And that has gotten me what? Money? Any say over anything?"

"You got a job," Dovey offered.

She wheeled on her friend. "Is that the story? That I got the job because I'm some kind of Internet soft-porn queen? I had nothing to do with that picture. Do people think I just slept my way up?"

"Whoa, nellie. Defensive much?" Dovey said. "And b-t-dubs, you're still wearing that blazer you put on half an hour ago. You might not want a shoplifting charge on your wall of fame."

Dellarobia took off the blazer and threw it into a wooden bin full of inflated balls. "You *know* why I have that job. I invited a stranger to supper, like a decent person. That is the one and only reason Ovid Byron is friends with us."

"I remember," Dovey said, uneasily. "I hear you."

"You were impressed. That's what you said on the phone that day." There had been some jokes about a Tennessee temptress, but it wasn't like that. Be not forgetful to entertain strangers, for thereby some have entertained angels unawares.

They turned down an aisle of uniforms and scrubs, arranged by color: pink, green, yellow, birthday party colors. To be worn by medical personnel while attending the mortally injured. "Why does everybody want to be famous," Dellarobia asked, "and at the same time they want to hear the ugliest trash about famous people?"

"I guess they hate what they haven't got."

"Everybody wants to be rich, too, but there's still some kind of team spirit. You should hear Bear on his rant against raising taxes on the millionaires. He says they worked for every penny, and that's what he went in the military to protect."

"Wow. He was a gunner in 'Nam to protect CEO salaries?"

"I guess."

"Well, yeah," Dovey said. "That's America. We watch shows about rich people's houses and their designer dresses and we drool. It's patriotic."

"Not me. I think I hate rich people."

"Yeah, but you're an equal-opportunity hard-ass. You hate everybody."

"I do not," Dellarobia exclaimed, surprised. "Am I that bad?"

Dovey reconsidered. "*Hate* is a strong word. You don't let people get away with much. Except me. Somehow I got a lifetime pass."

"I keep thinking if I go to church I'll learn to be sweet. Bobby Ogle is so good. And Cub is sweet. My kids are, basically. So what's my problem?"

"Diabolical possession," Dovey suggested. "Just a hunch."

Dellarobia picked up a bathroom set, soap dish and toothbrush holder, brand-new, still in the box. Two dollars. It probably started life in the dollar store, for sixteen. Why didn't everyone just come straight here? "Seriously," she said, "is it hateful if you don't agree with your home team about every single thing? Because I can agree on maybe nine out of ten. But then I start to wander out of the box on one subject, like this environment thing, and *man*. You'd think I was flipping everybody the bird."

"Now, see, that's why everybody wants Internet friends. You can find people just exactly like you. Screw your neighbors and your family, too messy." Dovey's phone buzzed, and she laughed, ignoring it. "The trouble is, once you filter out everybody that doesn't agree with you, all that's left is maybe this one retired surfer guy living in Idaho."

The entire back wall of the warehouse was packed with books, in shelves that went all the way to the ceiling where no one could possibly get at them. A pear-shaped man with half-glasses and dyed black hair in a ponytail stood in the aisle reading a hefty hardback. Preston had found the children's books. He shot his mother a pleading look.

"One Book, One Buck," she read aloud from the sign. "We can take home a couple, but looking's free." Preston began pulling books off the shelf like a manic consumer in some sort of stopwatch-driven shopping spree. He and Cordie made a fortress of books and happily dug in.

"My, my," Dovey said. "You've got yourself a couple of little bookworms."

Little smarties, Dellarobia thought. "I hate that the library closed."

Dovey gave her an odd look. "The one in Cleary is open. Not that I've ever darkened the door. But people say it's good. I guess with the college here."

Dellarobia wondered why Cleary had felt off-limits all these years. Enemy territory, as Cub and her in-laws would have it. The presence of the college made them prickly, as if the whole town were given over to the mischief of the privileged. In the 1990s there was supposedly an event where some boys got drunk and rode horses naked on Main Street. And the football rivalry, of course. Cleary High unfailingly beat Feathertown at homecoming. These complaints made her feel foolish and exposed, as if she'd been playing house in a structure whose walls had all blown away.

"Do you know what?" Dovey asked abruptly. "I've had it with Facebook. We should invent Buttbook. It's

421

more honest. You'd have Buttbook Enemies. You would Butt people to inform them you did not wish to be their friends."

"You could do worse," Dellarobia proposed. "You could Poop them."

At the end of the books was a display of luggage large and small, solid and plaid. This is where the kids had found the suitcases, and had put them back, too, nestled against a Mama-bear version, just as Dovey supposed. Most of them looked new. Dellarobia felt bleary again, looking at this unused luggage: the golden anniversary cruise that detoured into the ICU, the honeymoon called off for financial reasons. Every object in this place gave off the howl of someone's canceled hopes.

Dovey seemed deaf to the chorus. "Remember when we were going to be airline stewardesses?" she asked. "But they don't actually go anywhere, do they? Fly around all day and end up in the same place, bringing snacks to grumpy people, who needs it?"

Dellarobia thought that sounded exactly like her life.

Preston came galloping toward them with a book, breathless. He opened it to a particular page and asked what it said. "Where's your sister?" Dellarobia asked.

"Don't worry, she's with our books," he replied.

"You can't just leave her." She looked up the way to make sure she could still see Cordie. The place was teeming with unattended children. Preston's book was an encyclopedia of animals. The objects of his curiosity were a Mollymawk and a Goony Bird, Denizens of the Lonely Seas. Preston accepted this information as if he'd suspected it all along, and turned to another page. "Tasmanian Devil," she read. "He mates in March and April." The book had a quaint look about it. She paged back to a section titled: Why Nature Is Important to Your Child. "Herbert Hoover was an outstanding geologist," she read aloud. "How come scientists don't run for president anymore?"

"Can I have it, *please*?" Preston begged.

"It's kind of old-timey," Dellarobia warned. She looked for a date: 1952.

"But it's *animals*," Preston argued. "They stay the same!"

"The price is right," Dovey advised.

"Okay, it's yours." Dellarobia wished her son could aspire to more than a bargain-basement science book. Obviously, that's why most people didn't shop here. They didn't want to think of themselves as people who shopped here. But Preston looked thrilled as he ran off to rescue his sister. Down at the end of the books, the pear-shaped man was still reading, halfway through that big book with intent to finish. Maybe he came here daily.

She and Dovey pushed down an aisle of pet items. Birdcages hunkered like skeletons alongside quiescent hamster wheels. Old, crusty aquariums lined a shelf, bricks of emptiness in a wall. The ghosts of all these dead creatures in their former homes made her think of

423

the invisible baby that built her own house. The baby she and Cub had never discussed. That Preston and Cordie might never know about.

"I hate this," she said to Dovey. "Pet cemetery."

"Oh, no," Dovey said. "Those pets just grew up and went away to college."

"So how come we didn't do that?"

They came to a halt by a wig stand, wigless: a white Styrofoam bulb the size of a head, notable only for the face drawn on it with colored markers. The portrait was inexpert but extremely detailed, down to the eyelashes and lip liner and well-placed freckles, obviously the handiwork of a young girl. One who had needed a wig. Dellarobia said the word people never wanted to hear: "Cancer."

She and Dovey stood in silent company with the young artist who no longer needed the wig. For better or for worse. Nothing stays the same, life is defined by a state of flux; that was basic biology. Or so Dellarobia had been told, perhaps too late for it really to sink in. She was an ordinary person. Loss was the enemy.

A gentle tap on her forearm made her jump. "Jeez, Preston!" She put her hand on her chest. "You snuck up on me."

He looked up at her through his smudged glasses, penitent, hopeful, sure of his next move. All things Preston. He held up the same book, this time open to a horrific close-up. "Magnified face of the common housefly," she read aloud.

"Cool!" Preston paged ahead. "What are these?"

"Ants," she read. "Flying."

"Ants fly?" Dovey and Preston asked at the same time.

"The Marriage Flight," she read aloud, and skimmed ahead to summarize. "At certain times of the year the nest has winged individuals, both males and perfect females." She glanced at Preston. "That's a quote," she told him, "perfect females. For some unknown reason, one day all the other ants will turn on the winged ones, attacking them mercilessly and driving them out of the colony. They test out their wings for the first time on the so-called marriage flight." She looked up at Preston again. "It's an old book. I think nowadays they'd say mating."

He nodded gravely.

"After mating, the female tears off her wings and crawls in a hole to start her own colony. After rearing a small nucleus of workers, she becomes an egg-laying machine."

Dovey shuddered. "Sheesh. And they all live happily ever after."

"How do they tear off their own wings?" Preston asked.

"I don't know, sweetie. But we're taking the book home, so we'll find out."

"We're getting this one too? It's not the same book I showed you before."

"Let me see that." The spine was marked Volume

425

16. "Uh-oh," Dellarobia said. "There's a whole series of these, Preston. It's an encyclopedia."

"I *know*, Mama, it has *all* the animals," he said. Considerately leaving off the *duh*.

"I don't think we can buy all sixteen." She weighed the options, but sixteen dollars was a lot, for something this outdated. If they could hold out for a computer.

Preston looked at the volume with a longing that made her miserable. How much would she deny him for the sake of something that might not materialize? But he came to grips, as always. "I'll get the ants, and the Goony Bird," he pronounced. "Cordie wants the baby elephant one, and lizards. Two each, okay?"

Dellarobia took a deep breath. "Honey, I don't think they'll let us break up the set." This made no sense to Preston, so she tried again. "It's all sold as one thing. Like, they wouldn't let you buy the lid of the teapot, and not the teapot."

"Well, if it's all one thing, then it costs one dollar," he reasoned.

Dovey looked at Dellarobia, eyebrows raised.

"Technically you're right," Dellarobia said. "It has to be one or the other. I could ask. But I don't think the store people will see it our way." Her mood sank at the thought of haggling and pleading. For someone's thrown-out books.

"He's the master persuader," Dovey said. "Let him go ask."

Dellarobia watched fear overtake her son as he

426

understood this proposition. His razor-straight eyebrows lifted as his eyes met hers, hoping for a bailout.

"Here's the thing, Preston. If I ask, they'll say no. I'm nobody here, they won't do me any favors. But you're this awesome kid that wants his own encyclopedia, right? You totally have a shot." She backed up her cart to look down the length of an aisle to the checkout registers. There were two cashiers, a heavyset kid with tattoos covering his arms, and an older lady with a ponytail. "Come here," she said. She stood behind him with her wrists crossed over his chest. "Which one, you think?"

He picked the tattoo kid, no surprise there. In Preston's world, grandma types were not automatically on your side. Dellarobia told him to gather up as much of the set as he could carry, and go make his argument. She and Dovey watched him make the long walk down the towering book aisle, like a prison inmate going to meet his justice.

"Quiet on the ward," she said to Dovey.

"Gulp," Dovey replied.

She had noticed her son's wrists sprouting like wheat stems out of his sleeves, and now also noted the visible expanse of sock above his shoes. A growth spurt, finally. Perfect timing, she could upsize his wardrobe on the cheap here if she could drag him out of his books. Somberly he gathered an armload of the yellow volumes, ignoring his sister, who was stuffing books in the alligator purse and dumping them out. Preston waited an eternity at the second register behind a woman buying a floor lamp, who seemed to have an issue with it. The tattoo kid at the register seemed attentive to her monologue. A good sign, it went to character. Dovey and Dellarobia stood mute with apprehension. From the distance, they couldn't hear, but watched as Preston articulated his claim. The kid took one of the books from Preston, looking it over carefully.

"At the college where Pete and Dr. Byron teach," Dellarobia said quietly, "the students send them e-mails to demand what grades they want. Can you imagine?"

When the cashier gave his verdict, they saw Preston's whole body react, the pump of his fist, the faintly audible hiss of joy, *yesss!* He turned and looked back across the long jumble of castoffs toward his mother, meeting her eyes with a cocksure expression wholly unlike anything she knew of her son. She felt pierced by loss. He would go so far. Maybe she had the same stuff inside, the same map of the big picture, but the goods had passed through her to lodge in her son and awaken him. Already he had the means and the will for the journey.

e~

A strange fog rolled over February. Hester called it an omen, but in a winter so persistently deviant as this one, most people were sick of weather talk and greeted the latest act without a salute. For Dellarobia its downside just now was that it reduced morning visibility nearly

428

to zero. Clouds lay low on the mountain, erasing its peaks, making the rugged landscape look like flatland. With binoculars she scanned the yellowish roost trees in the valley where the fog's veil dimmed all the forest colors to a uniform dun like an old photograph. She sat in a lawn chair, not ten feet from the spot where she'd first laid eyes on the monarchs. The place was unrecognizable now, thanks to the graveled turnaround Bear put here and the traffic flow his engineering had helped facilitate. She wasn't here to count sightseers, but this morning had seen six. This was the end of the road, as far as vehicles were concerned. Some tourists parked and hoofed it down the path toward the study site for a better view. Others stayed in their cars, taking their gander from here and then heading back home.

Dr. Byron had told her the fog was no mystery, but a predictable part of a warm front. He could even make physics safe for consumption, in small, digestible bites. Warm air held more water; that made sense to her. The sudden crispness of autumn days, the static sparkling in her rayon pajamas on frigid nights, this was air with the water squeezed out. A glass of iced tea dripping in summertime was hot air, wet as a sponge, meeting its match. These things she could see.

A maroon SUV bumped up the rise into the turnaround and parked at an angle. She watched a couple get out, a trim middle-aged woman and super-skinny husband in cross-trainers. "Look, they're here today," he said in a loud whisper, and they stood at the edge of the precipice holding hands, thrilled with their luck. As if the butterflies might have been elsewhere. None of the visitors had spoken to her today, addressing their questions, if any, to a man in khaki who was passing out leaflets to the intermittent visitors, asking them to take some kind of pledge. He wasn't one of the Californians like Carlos and Roger. Those boys had gone home, taking their wrecked clothes and good cheer. This man was from another organization in a city she didn't recognize, and he was no kid, either. He had white hair and a snap-brimmed hat and slightly crossed eyes behind thick glasses. He was here in no official capacity, despite all the khaki. It was his retirement project to travel from place to place distributing the pledge, which Dellarobia had yet to read. He'd actually talked her ear off this morning with rambling tales of people he'd met and unfriendly encounters with officers of the law and with wildlife, always winding up with the baffling declaration, "And that's all she wrote!" Who was *she*? This man, Leighton Akins by name, somehow came out ahead as the hero of all his own stories, Dellarobia noticed. A sure sign he was not from the South. Hereabouts, if a man told a story in which he was not the butt of the joke, or worse yet, that contained no jokes at all, his audience would shuffle off at the first appreciable pause. Without that choice, Dellarobia listened awhile, then tuned him out, and finally told Mr. Akins in the politest way possible that she was working as a biologist here and had to concentrate.

She was supposed to watch the roosting colonies and track their flight behavior. The butterflies were showing some signs of restless movement, actually leaving the roost trees in significant numbers. It did take concentration to watch for the small explosions of flyers, then locate individuals with the binoculars and follow the wobbling specks that vanished through gray air. The weighty binoculars made her anxious, probably three or four months' utility bills right there, highly breakable. But Ovid had hung them around her neck as if it were no high occasion. Costume jewelry, not diamonds.

He wanted to know which direction the flyers were headed, in what numbers, and whether they returned in the afternoon. They might be seeking water or nectar sources. After surviving all other onslaughts in this alien place, it could be the warmth rather than the cold that killed them. The sunny, warmer days that brought them out of dormancy to fly around, as they'd seen, would tax the butterflies in a way that the cool, steady clime of the Mexican mountains did not. They might burn through their fat reserves and starve. Ovid had asked if anything could possibly be flowering here in late February, a question she'd passed on to Hester. Hepatica and skunk cabbage and harbinger of spring and maybe cutleaf toothwort, was her astonishing answer. Could any of these be nectar sources for an insect? Hester didn't know, but surprised Dellarobia by offering to help her find some flowers. The hypothesis could be tested with live monarchs in the lab.

The sightseeing couple took a barrage of photos with a camera whose very shutter clicks sounded expensive. After chatting cordially with Leighton about his pledge, they set off down the steep trail for a close-up view of the butterflies, as she'd known they would. For her own entertainment she was predicting hikers vs. turn-arounds on the basis of body mass and shoe type. She was batting a thousand except for two teenage girls who defied all expectations, charging down the mountain in stiletto boots.

The SUV couple didn't stay very long. They returned and drove off in short order, possibly daunted by the fog. Almost immediately Dellarobia heard the approach of another vehicle that didn't sound like a car. A motor-cycle, maybe, though what kind of crazy person would try this steep, gravelly track on a motorcycle? She heard it slipping and keeling, its engine revving. And then by way of answer she saw Dimmit Slaughter. She'd gone to high school with Dimmit. He kicked the stand and dismounted his machine, helmetless, his T-shirt stretched to within an inch of its life across his broad belly, where the letters distorted outward like horror movie credits. He hitched his jeans and whistled at the view. Or at something. She tried not to stare at his mid-section, but it did draw the eye, ballooning under the yellow shirt he'd tucked into his belt, sub-belly, in the most unflattering way imaginable. As men so often did. How they toted such physiques around so proudly was a mystery to Dellarobia. Women spent whole lifetimes trying to camouflage figure flaws that were basically undetectable to the human eye.

"Well, well, Miss Dell," he said. "I heard you were hanging around up here. Where's the Farmer?"

"Not hanging around up here," she replied. Leighton Akins started to approach with his pledge pamphlet, but reconsidered.

"And are we having fun yet?" Dimmit asked.

"I'm working."

He looked her up and down in her chair. Probably he'd looked at her the same way on some nasty little screen, that Internet portrait of her as the almost-nude on the half shell. "Nice," Dimmit said. "If you can get it."

"What is, work? You ought to try it out some time. For a change of pace."

"Who pays you for that, the government?"

"Who pays your disability, Dimmit? Santa Claus?" She'd heard about a back injury, a fall out a window. But not while working. "I get paid out of a grant," she told him. "From the National Science Foundation."

He picked up a brittle monarch from the muddy ditch at the edge of the gravel and brought it over, flipping it with his thumb onto her notebook. "Here you go, science foundation. Why don't you perform a dialysis on that to see what it died of?"

Mr. Akins seemed alarmed, but Dellarobia had no fear of Dimmit. He and Cub moved in some of the same circles. She might not be much liked in town these days, but if Dimmit misbehaved, he could find himself disliked a good deal more. "I see you've gained some substance in the world," she observed. "Since I saw you last."

He cupped the sphere of his belly in both hands, and winked. "Baby, that's the fuel tank for my love machine."

She rolled her eyes sideways. She wouldn't mind having Dimmit's self-confidence, but would not take that body as part of the deal. Like waking up pregnant every morning till death do you part.

The fog had congealed into a low, thick cloud cover, and she'd seen no butterfly action for an hour. A thermos of coffee she'd left at the study site was calling her name. But Dimmit had now approached Mr. Akins, they were blocking the path, so she waited until their encounter was complete. It didn't take long. Mr. Akins explained he was asking people to sign on to a lifestyle pledge to reduce their impact on the planet. Dimmit nodded serenely, took the flyer, folded it into a paper airplane, and sailed it high across the foggy valley. Then he kicked his Harley into gear and tore off, throwing gravel.

"That's just Dimmit," she apologized to Mr. Akins, leaning her folding chair against a tree. "I've known him my whole life. Sometimes you shouldn't even try."

"I *always* try," Mr. Akins said brightly. His snow-white bangs were cut straight across and he had a gap between his front teeth. "That's why I come to places like this, instead of Portland or San Francisco. You people here need to get on board, the same as everyone else. If not more so."

She didn't know what to say about that, so she headed down the path in her leather-soled farm boots. You people here. If not more so. She felt heat rise from the collar of her shirt. She remembered Dovey's declaration that she hated everyone, which was not true, but beginning to seem that way. Leighton Akins and his snappy L.L. Beans. Apparently all those tourists ignored her because she and the Dimmits of this world were *you people*. She descended into the fog-shrouded forest, a little disoriented by the whiteness that lay on the air. In the mixed, barren forest surrounding the fir grove, craggy old pines stood out in relief. A solitary woodpecker laughed. The path crossed a streambed whose banks were deeply encrusted with monarch bodies washed down from the center of the roosting site, dumped here like litter.

At a distance she saw the lanky frame of Ovid Byron walking downhill, charting his own course between the butterfly-clad trunks. She picked up her pace to catch up to where he would meet the trail, stumbling a little over a tree root. She wondered if he would mind that she'd left her post. "Hey," she called, getting his attention. "I got to thinking about hot coffee, when that sun went in."

He waited for her with his arms crossed, standing behind all the gleaming teeth in his smile. "Great minds have similar thoughts."

435

"I have something amazing to tell you," she said when she caught up. "Oh, is it okay if Preston comes up after school tomorrow? That's not the amazing thing."

His smile notched up, like flipping the headlights to brights. "Preston *is*, actually. I have to admit, Dellarobia, I envy you. A child like that."

"Thank you."

"Yes, it is fine. I have a little project for him I have been thinking about."

Her heart tumbled, and she held her tongue, lacking faith in it. Why did he not have his own children? What argument, what divide, what kind of wife. She fell into step behind him on the trail, watching her footing, thinking the words *head over heels*.

"The amazing thing," she said, "is this man has volunteered his truck to transport the butterflies to Florida. Some nature park, I guess, where he's got family ties." She hesitated, recognizing a level of absurdity. "I just thought I'd mention it. I called and talked to the guy last night. He really cares, you know? About the monarchs surviving."

"Surviving," Ovid put back. Even from behind, she saw the absent enthusiasm.

"It's a bad idea. Sorry." A cold drop of rain hit the back of her left hand.

"Very generous, though. This man, who is he?"

"A long-haul trucker, Mr. Baird is his name. He lives in Feathertown. He really means well. But okay, dumb idea."

"In Feathertown," Ovid said. "It's really quite touching, the good intentions, you know?" He stopped in the path to look up through the canopy as more drops fell.

"Is this rain picking up?" she asked.

He nodded, aiming his finger like a pistol down through the trees toward the blue tarp shelter at the study site, and they made a break for it through the sudden shower. Ovid covered the ground in a deerlike way with his long strides, dodging fallen branches. She reached the shelter behind him and shivered, pulling her sweatshirt hood close around her face and tucking her hands in her sleeves.

"Why is it a bad idea?" she asked.

The rain was loud on the plastic tarp. He seemed to be waiting his turn to speak. Ovid and Pete had strung up this shelter one rainy day using a taut rope stretched between two trees to form a ridge, with ropes through metal grommets in the tarp's four corners pulling it outward, also tied to trees. Dellarobia had marveled to watch them construct a simple, perfect roof that seemed to levitate over the plywood table and single folding chair. Here they now stood, she and Ovid together, in their little house without walls.

"An animal is the sum of its behaviors," he said finally. "Its community dynamics. Not just the physical body."

"What makes a monarch a monarch is what it does, you're saying."

He stood looking out at the forest, arms crossed. Not exactly facing her, but not turned away. "Interactions with other monarchs, habitat, the migration, everything. The population functions as a whole being. You could look at it that way."

She did, often. This butterfly forest was a great, quiet, breathing beast. Monarchs covered the trunks like orange fish scales. Sometimes the wings all moved slowly in unison. Once while she and Ovid were working in the middle of all that, he had asked her what was the use of saving a world that had no soul left in it. Continents without butterflies, seas without coral reefs, he meant. What if all human effort amounted basically to saving a place for ourselves to park? He had confessed these were not scientific thoughts.

The rain softened its percussion on the roof, a little. Light passing through the tarp bathed them both in a faint cerulean glow. The study site was completely deserted. She wondered if he also felt the concentrated atmosphere of their aloneness.

"But do they *have* to move? Could the whole being just stay in one place?"

"The problem is genetics," he said. "You are who you are, because of a history of genetic combinations. So are they. The monarchs rely on a particular alternation between inbreeding and outbreeding."

Dellarobia corrected her impression of the moment. Ovid was not alone with her here. It was not going to be that scene in the movie. He was in church: with these

438

ideas, the companionship of creatures. Every day she rose and rose to the occasion of this man.

"Tell me what that means," she said. "The alternation."

"For most of a year the genetic exchanges are relatively local. Summer generations breed in smaller groups as they move north. Some might fly only a few miles from where they are born before mating and dying. But then, in winter, the whole population comes together in one place. The gene pool is thoroughly blended."

"I get that. Okay. Like mostly swapping your goods at the secondhand store in town, and then once a year doing the international-trade thing at the dollar store."

Ovid laughed. "You are *good*. I wish I could put you in front of my students."

She tried not to smile too hard. Her thermos of coffee was on the table, hidden among the plastic boxes and someone's raincoat. She shuffled through other junk to find their two stained mugs that stayed on-site as permanent fixtures. She tossed out the grainy dregs of yesterday's coffee and held the cups outside the shelter to collect a little rain, then wiped them with her shirttail. She unscrewed the thermos and filled both mugs. Housekeeping in the invisible house. She and Ovid liked their coffee black, they had that in common.

He took the mug, nodding his thanks, and sat on an upended section of log they used as furniture. "We don't know of anything else like it on earth," he said. "This system of local and universal genetics makes a kind of super-insect. The population can fluctuate five-fold in a year. It's an insurance policy against environmental surprises."

Environmental surprise within known limits, he would mean. He grew broody as he drank his coffee, looking out through the rain. He'd left her the lawn chair, but she stayed on her feet. Long clusters of butterflies began to drip. Hangers-on at the bottoms of their strings twisted slowly in an imperceptible wind, like the caricature of a hanged man. A chunk of a cluster near the shelter dropped suddenly onto the ground, severed from the great beast. Grounded butterflies could not hope to lift themselves in a rain like this. She watched this fresh legion of the extinguished, taking their time to die.

"Nobody else came to the site today?" she asked.

He shook his head.

"I've left a couple of messages with Vern, but he doesn't call back. It seems like we're losing our volunteers. Maybe they're having exams."

Ovid said, "Not everyone has the stomach to watch an extinction."

She noticed the fabric over their heads had begun to droop in spots where the rain pooled. The roof of their invisible house, collapsing. What wouldn't, under all this? She was slowly submitting to his sense of weather as everything. Not just the moving-picture view out a window. Real, in a way that the window and house were not.

A scattering of butterflies in the fallen mass twitched open and closed, while getting pounded, showing their vivid orange a few last times. *Rage, rage against the dying of the light.* That was the end of a poem, brought to her by the one bright spot in her education, Mrs. Lake, now dead. Dellarobia suddenly found she could scarcely bear this day at all. She stepped out in the rain to pick up one of the pitiful survivors and bring it under their roof. She held it close to her face. A female. And lady-like, with its slender velvet abdomen, its black eyes huge and dolorous. The proboscis curled and uncurled like a spring. She could feel the hooked tips of the threadlike legs where they gripped her finger. She held it out and the wings opened wide, a small signal.

"So you're one of the people that can," she said. "Watch an extinction."

He did not quite break his communion with the day, his vigil, whatever it was, but asked, "If someone you loved was dying, what would you do?"

She refused that sentence its entrance. Preston and Cordie, no. Not another runaway loss. The Cooks she could think of, barely. Their boy. You do the bone marrow transplants, whatever it takes. She had examined Ovid's sadness by degrees, but now it hit her fully, the nature of his loss. "You do everything you can," she said. "And then, I guess, everything you can't. You keep doing, so your heart won't stop."

The butterfly on her hand twitched again, and she held it sideways to the light. On the gloss of the wings

441

she could see every scratch, like the marred lenses of an old pair of glasses. "If they could just breed and lay eggs," she said. "A few. I'm not saying truck them all to Florida. But just to get them through this one winter?"

He glanced up at her. "It's not my call, Dellarobia."

She considered this. To whom did a species belong? She wondered if that kind of law was even on the books. She sat down in the lawn chair, and saw he was getting restless, eyeing a stack of field notes on the table. "I am not a zookeeper," he said. "I'm not here to save monarchs. I'm trying to read what they are writing on our wall."

Dellarobia felt stung. "If you're not, who is?" She could think of some answers: the knitting women, the boys with duct-taped clothes. People Cub and her in-laws thought to be outside the pale of normal adulthood.

"That is a concern of conscience," he said. "Not of biology. Science doesn't tell us what we should do. It only tells us what *is*."

"That must be why people don't like it," she said, surprised at her tartness.

Ovid, too, seemed startled. "They don't like science?"

"I'm sorry. I'm probably speaking out of turn here. You've explained to me how big this is. The climate thing. That it's taking out stuff we're counting on. But other people say just forget it. My husband, guys on the radio. They say it's not proven."

"What we're discussing is clear and present, Dellarobia. Scientists agree on that. These men on the radio, I assume, are nonscientists. Why would people buy snake oil when they want medicine?"

"That's what I'm trying to tell you. You guys aren't popular. Maybe your medicine's too bitter. Or you're not selling to us. Maybe you're writing us off, thinking we won't get it. You should start with kindergartners and work your way up."

"It's too late for that. Believe me."

"Don't say that, 'too late.' I hate that. I've got my kids to think about."

Ovid nodded slowly. "We were not always unpopular. Scientists."

"Herbert Hoover was one! I read that." Preston's encyclopedias had already made it to show-and-tell. Flying Ants were making the rounds.

Ovid seemed the smallest bit amused. "I meant more recently than Herbert Hoover. Fifteen years ago people knew about global warming, at least in a general way, you know? In surveys, they would all answer, Yes, it exists, it's a problem. Conservatives or liberals, exactly the same. Now there is a divide."

"Well, yeah. People sort themselves out. Like kids in a family, you know. They have to stake out their different territories. The teacher's pet or the rascal."

"You think so, it's a territory divide? We have sorted ourselves as the calm, educated science believers and the scrappy, hotheaded climate deniers?"

Dellarobia definitely felt he was stacking one side of the deck with the sensible cards. Where did wild-haired

443

girls knitting butterflies in the woods fit into that scheme?

"I'd say the teams get picked, and then the beliefs get handed around," she said. "Team camo, we get the right to bear arms and John Deere and the canning jars and tough love and taking care of our own. The other side wears I don't know what, something expensive. They get recycling and population control and lattes and as many second chances as anybody wants. Students e-mailing to tell you they deserve their A's."

Ovid looked stupefied. "What, you're saying this is some kind of contest between the peasant class and the gentry?"

She returned his look. "I definitely don't think I said that."

"Something like it. One of your teams has all the skills for breaking the frontier. And the other seems to be nursing a restive society that grows in the wake of the plow."

"Huh," she said.

"But would you not agree, the frontiers of this world are already broken?"

"I guess. Maybe. Well, no. It depends."

"Really?"

"Well, yeah. If it's true what you're saying. That this whole crapload is going to blow. Then what, we start over?"

Ovid said nothing. She knew she'd crossed a line of disrespect, putting it that way. This was like church to

444

him, or children. The thing that kept him awake at night. "Sorry," she said. "I'm just saying. The environment got assigned to the other team. Worries like that are not for people like us. So says my husband."

His brow wrinkled gravely. "Drought and floods are not worries for farmers?"

"You think any of this is based on *information*? Come on, who really chooses?"

"Information is all we have." Ovid stared at her, somehow managing to look as naked as she'd ever seen him. Which was very. "Everyone chooses," he said. "A person can face up to a difficult truth, or run away from it."

She shook her head. "My husband is not a coward. I've seen him stick his whole arm into the baling machine to untangle the twine while it's running. Trying to save a hay crop with rain coming in. I mean, if we're talking guts. He and my in-laws face down hard luck six days a week, and on Sundays they go pray for the truly beleaguered."

He seemed to take this in, even though he probably didn't know as many men as she did who'd lost an arm to a baling machine. "These positions get assigned to people," she said. "If you've been called the bad girl all your life, you figure you're already paying the price, you should go on and use the tickets. If I'm the redneck in the pickup, fine, let me just go burn up some gas."

Ovid seemed perplexed. Maybe he knew more about butterflies than people.

"I hate to say it, but people are not keen on a person like me coming up here to work with a person like you. Pete sure wasn't, at first. He got over it. But not everybody does." She'd finally had a look at the gossip site Dovey mentioned, and it scalded her. By many accounts Dr. Byron was a foreign meddler in local affairs. By some, Dellarobia was carrying his child.

"Was there some difficulty with Pete?"

"Pete's great. Bonnie and Mako, they all were. For some reason you all decided to let me in. But trust me, if you'd first run into me as your waitress down at the diner, you would not have included me in the conversation about your roosting populations and your overwintering zones. People shut out the other side. It cuts both ways."

She could imagine herself in an apron bringing them coffee at one of the grease-embalmed booths at the Feathertown Diner, rest in peace. Ovid actually might have asked her opinion, even there. *I never learn anything from listening to myself*, he'd said that first night. The moment for her to shut up would be right now.

"Humans are hardwired for social community," he said. "There's no question, we evolved with it. Reading the cues and staying inside the group, these are number-one survival skills in our species. But I like to think academics are the referees. That we can talk to every side."

"Could, maybe. But you're not. You're always telling me you're not even supposed to *care*, you just measure and count." Okay, she thought. *Now* shutting up.

446

"It's a point," he said. "If we tangle too much in the public debate, our peers will criticize our language as imprecise, or too certain. Too theatrical. Even simple words like 'theory' and 'proof' have different meanings outside of science. Having a popular audience can get us pegged as second-rank scholars."

Dellarobia was surprised to hear it. If people behaved sensibly anywhere, surely it would be in an institute of higher learning. Although "second-rank scholar" was not an exact equivalent to "whoring with the enemy."

"Is that why you don't talk to reporters? Because, honestly, you're good."

He exhaled such a long breath, she wondered if he might collapse. "It's a hazardous road. For ecologists especially, my field. Ecology is the study of biological communities. How populations interact. It does not mean recycling aluminum cans. It's an experimental and theoretical science, like physics. But if we try to make our science relevant to outsiders, right away they look for a picket sign."

"I could see that," she said.

"If I hear one more milksop discussing the environment and calling it 'the ecology,' honestly, Dellarobia. I might break a Mettler balance on his head."

"Wow."

"In my field, we can be touchy about this," he said.

No kidding, she thought.

The cloudburst was winding down. The rain would move on, sweeping its chill up the valley. Ovid stood up

447

from his log and smacked the tarp with the flat of his hand, discharging the puddle that had collected there. He drained his coffee cup and set it with finality on the plywood table. "I think we can safely return to our posts," he said. "I should get down to the lab. I want to dissect some of these females under the scope to see if they might be coming out of diapause. What did you see this morning?"

"Some flying around," she said. "A lot, early on when the sun was almost out. Mostly they were headed down the valley to the west."

He shoved his hands into his raincoat pockets. "If the rain stays away, it would be good if you could keep watching this afternoon. I'm curious to know if they're coming back to the roost. Probably these are short forays for water or nectar, rather than the start of a spring dispersal. But we really don't know."

He picked up the red-and-white cooler they used for transporting live butterflies and stepped outside the shelter, squatting on his heels to pick through the fallen pile. He was choosing among the already doomed to get specimens for his afternoon's dissections. At least they would give their bodies for science. Dellarobia knelt beside him to help. They would need to pack up the equipment. This front was supposed to bring a lot more rain and possible high winds. "When they do that, the spring dispersal," she said, "if we get that far, where will they go from here?"

"Where will they go from here," he repeated. He

said nothing else for such a long time, she stopped waiting for an answer. She picked up stiff, brittle bodies, one after another, and flicked them away. Most of these were already too dead.

Finally Ovid said, "Into a whole new earth. Different from the one that has always supported them. In the manner to which we have all grown accustomed."

She found a live female, still pliable, faintly flapping, and dropped it into the open cooler. These little six-pack-size coolers were also used to carry organs from a deceased donor to the hospital where someone waited for a transplant, maybe with an empty chest, the old heart already cut out. She'd seen that on television. It seemed such a dire responsibility for just an ordinary cooler.

"This is not a good thing, Dellarobia," he added. "A whole new earth."

"I know," she said. A world where you could count on nothing you'd ever known or trusted, that was no place you wanted to be. Insofar as any person could understand that, she believed she did.

She was unprepared to meet Leighton Akins at the top of the trail, still occupying the small gravel territory she would like to have had to herself. He was sitting in her lawn chair, no less. He had made a sort of tent over himself and the chair with a plastic poncho and seemed to have entered a dreamy state. He jumped when she hailed him.

"I was just about to go," he said, surrendering her chair. "I ran out of my flyers. The paper airplane, that was all she wrote. But I had to wait out that rain."

"Shoot," she said. "I wanted to see one of those."

"I have *one*," he said. "But I need to keep it. To make more copies. Is there a copy shop in the little town here? Because I've looked, and I see *nada*."

"Did you happen to see the bank?" She settled into her chair, grudgingly grateful he'd kept it dry. The sky was beginning to lighten, and she saw movement in the lower valley. She scanned a stretch of empty fog. These binoculars took some skill.

"The bank?"

"Yeah. They've got a copy machine they'll let you use. Everybody does."

"The bank. Who would have thought." Mr. Akins just stood there. She wondered what he went home to at night, if anything. Probably the Wayside.

"So it's a pledge?" she asked, keeping her binoculars trained on the mist of the valley, hunting out the bobbing specks. Finally she caught it, one butterfly. Three butterflies. "So what are we people here supposed to sign on to?"

In her periphery she saw him digging in his backpack. "I could read it to you," he offered. "It's a list of things you promise to do to lower your carbon footprint. That means to use less fossil fuel. To relieve the damage of carbon emissions to the planet."

"I know what it means," she said.

"O-kay. Sustainability Pledge," he read. "The first category is Food and Drink. You want me to read down the list?"

"I could just look at it."

He gave her a clouded look, clutching that paper like a last will and testament. Was he thinking she might pull a Dimmit on him and launch it? "Okay, fine," she said. "Hit me. I'm supposed to be keeping my eyes on the prize here." She had five butterflies in her sights now, moving together in no solid direction. She thought of the flying ants in Preston's book. If Preston came tomorrow, they would remember to ask Dr. Byron about the mysterious reference to "perfect females."

"Number one. Bring your own Tupperware to a restaurant for leftovers, as often as possible."

"I've not eaten at a restaurant in over two years."

"Jesus. Are you serious? May I ask why?"

She was tempted to glare, but didn't want to lose the butterflies in her sights. Cub had been known to get fast food while he was on deliveries. She'd find the evidence on the floor of his truck, and he'd swear it wouldn't happen again, like a man caught fooling around. He knew it was not in their budget. Cub was not the subject of this discussion.

"Okay, number two," Mr. Akins said. "Try bringing your own mug for tea or coffee. Does not apply, I guess.

Carry your own cutlery, use no plastic utensils, ditto ditto. Okay, here's one. Carry your own Nalgene bottle instead of buying bottled water."

"Our well water is good. We wouldn't pay for store-bought."

"Okay," he said. "Try to reduce the intake of red meat in your diet."

"Are you crazy? I'm trying to *increase* our intake of red meat."

"Why is that?"

"Because mac and cheese only gets you so far, is why. We have lamb, we produce that on our farm. But I don't have a freezer. I have to get it from my in-laws."

Mr. Akins went quiet. His dark eyes swam like tadpoles behind his glasses.

"Is that it?" she asked.

"No. There are five other categories."

"Let's hear them."

"We don't have to."

"No really. You came all this way. To get us on board."

"Okay," he said, sounding a little nervous. "Skipping ahead to Everyday Necessities. Try your best to buy reused. Use Craigslist."

"What is that?" she asked, although she had a pretty good idea.

"Craigslist," he said. "On the Internet."

"I don't have a computer."

Mr. Akins moved quickly to cover his bases. "Or find your local reuse stores."

"*Find* them," she said.

"Plan your errand route so you drive less!" Now he sounded belligerent.

"Who wouldn't do that? With what gas costs?"

He went quiet again.

"What are the other categories?" she asked.

"Home-office-household-travel-financial. We don't have to go on."

She put down the binoculars and looked at him. She'd lost track of the butterflies anyway. "Let's hear financial."

Mr. Akins read in a rushed monotone: "Switch some of your stocks and mutual funds to socially responsible investments, skip, skip. Okay, Home-slash-Office. Make sure old computers get recycled. Turn your monitor off when not in use. I think we've got a lot of not applicable here." He gave her a fearful look. "Household?"

"Good one," she said. "I have a household."

"Switch your light bulbs to CFLs. Upgrade to energy-efficient appliances."

She needed to talk to Ovid again about the electric bill, because February's had come in. Electricity, on or off, being the household question of note. "Sorry," she said. "If it involves buying something, check me in the bad-girl column."

"But the savings are worth the cost."

"I'm sure."

"Okay. Set your thermostat two degrees cooler in winter and higher in summer."

"Than what?" she asked.

"Than where it is at present."

"Technically that's impossible. You'd just keep moving it down forever."

Leighton evidently took this for a refusal, and leaped in for the kill. "Well, there's only one planet! We all have to share."

She nodded slowly, exercising what she felt was laudable restraint.

"Almost done," he said. "Transportation. Ride your bike or use public transportation. Buy a low-emission vehicle. Sorry, no buying anything, you said. Properly inflate your tires and maintain your car."

"My husband's truck is on its third engine. Is that properly maintaining?"

"I would say so, definitely."

She had a feeling Leighton Akins would not find the bank. He and his low-emission vehicle would just head on out of here. She and Dimmit Slaughter would claim their place among his tales of adversity.

"Okay, this is the last one," he said. "Fly less."

"Fly *less*," she repeated.

He looked at his paper as if receiving orders from some higher authority. "That's all she wrote. Fly less."

12

Kinship Systems

The pregnant ewes looked like woolly barrels on table legs. They had scattered for their morning graze, facing this way and that all over the muddy field, but froze in an identical aspect of attention when the women entered the pasture. Every head faced them, each triangular face framed by its V of splayed horns. A thin horizontal cloud drifted from each set of nostrils in the cold morning light, trails of ruminant breathing. All those present waited for a cue to the next move, including the collie at Hester's side and Dellarobia herself. She'd volunteered to help vaccinate the ewes this Saturday, with little idea of how it would go. Hester gave the grain bucket a loud shake, and that was the answer to all questions; the sheep began slowly to move. Hester whistled Charlie out in a wide arc to the right and the collie raced uphill in a smooth gallop, gleaming joy in black and white. The old boy still had it. Charlie was thirteen, in this family longer than Dellarobia herself. The sheep responded to the dog's pressure, gathering in.

"Charlie, look back," Hester called, and he altered his course, aiming for the back fence. A trio of white yearlings had perched atop a rock pile but gave up their game at the dog's approach and leaped down. Higher up the hill, though, four of the reddish brown ewes Hester called moorits stood their ground, camouflaged against the mud. Charlie dropped to a wolfish crouch and inched toward them, one white forepaw at a time, until these four also conceded to join the flock. The multicolored flow converged, moorit, white, black, and badgerfaced silvers all loping together downhill in their lumbering gait, rolling fore-and-aft like an unsynchronized troop of rocking horses.

They were pastured here for the higher ground, but after the past week of torrents any former notion of high ground was called into doubt. Dellarobia's spattered house loomed drearily, as did the old barn that contained the lab and now also sheep when they needed shelter. The ewes paid no mind to the mud, only to their pregnancy-tuned hunger. Their hooves threw clots of muck high in the air as Hester led them into the barn, holding her bucket of sweet feed up out of their reach, a ponytailed pied piper in cowboy boots. She had induced Bear and Cub to repair the waist-high walls subdividing two large stalls inside the barn's front gallery, enclosures well separated from the lab in the old milking parlor at the back. Still, Dellarobia sometimes heard the rustle and bleating of the ewes through the plastic-sheeted wall, especially on long rainy days when they all gathered restlessly under roof. Hester now wanted Cub to build lambing jugs, where new mothers with tiny lambs could be isolated safely from weather and trampling hooves. Lambing would begin in late March. One month hence.

The enriched warmth of the barn struck all Dellarobia's senses at once as they entered. The presence of animals had changed this barn, a long-dead place smelling of dust and fuel oil transformed into an environment rich with the scents of sweet feed and manure. She stepped over shiny mounds of sheep droppings nested on the barn's hay-covered floor. They looked like whole boxes of raisins dumped out in piles on a carpet, a sight she had seen, thanks to Cordelia. Hester let Charlie do most of the work, pressing the animals forward when asked, otherwise holding back with faultless restraint. Charlie was Roy's sire, the older of the two collies. The kids loved Roy because he could be drawn into their romping and tussling, but Charlie was old-school, above all that.

The ewes pushed urgently into the larger stall, crowding to get to the feeding shelf where Hester poured out a ten-foot line of grain. These cunning Icelandics worked hard to find forage even in the dead of winter, stripping bark from fence posts and dead leaves from trees. She and Cub also threw out some hay every morning, bales purchased out of Oklahoma for a harrowing price because this farm's meager hay crop had molded, along with all other hay within a hundred miles. Their cattle-raising neighbors were losing a fortune on hay this winter, with little choice but to start selling off calves for nothing. Dellarobia knew it had been Hester's decision many years ago, over Bear's objections, to switch over from cattle to this self-reliant breed, and finally the men were seeing the wisdom in it. These ewes only got extra minerals and a grain ration because they were near lambing, and plainly today they wanted that something extra, a craving Dellarobia knew from her own pregnancies. The winter she'd carried Preston she'd been possessed of such strange hungers she sometimes felt like chewing on wet laundry.

The sheep murmured and belched and shoved, arranging themselves by an order of dominance that Hester told her ran in family lines. Bossy brownies, she called the four moorits who'd been last to come in, now first at the trough. Hester pointed out the mother and three daughters, all from different years, who were now the leaders. The others knew to get out of their way. Hester sifted through the big metal toolbox she used for carrying supplies, picking out the necessary needles and vials for the booster shots they would give today. Dellarobia liked being with the sheep in close quarters. She was fascinated by the color lines and horn configurations and the odd tuft of wool on the top of each head, the sole body part that was never shorn. When she walked among these girls they parted slowly like heavy water and looked up at her with an outlandish composure, their amber eyes eerily divided by dark horizontal pupils.

Hester ordered Charlie to stay by the barn door, and Dellarobia to close all the sheep into one stall while she drew off a bottle of vaccine into her auto-repeat syringe. Administered this late in pregnancy, the vaccine would cross the womb and protect the newborn lambs from all the dire things that waited in the new world to greet them. Dellarobia's lack of fondness for needles was average, but she'd argued for keeping the ewes here with the insistence that she could handle problems, so she knew it was time to show her mettle, if mettle she had. They'd already gone over the emergency kit Hester had organized for her in a plastic pail, and hung it on a nail on one of the barn's upright timbers. Dellarobia was unnerved by Hester's hasty accounting of iodine and towels and arm-length plastic gloves, things that might be needed for pulling a stuck lamb. Hester's trust astonished her. Every night Preston and Dellarobia read from the manual about nourishing pregnant ewes, working their way up to milk fever and breech twins, the many things that could go wrong. Preston seemed steadied by the mass of information. But his mother's imagination was poised to grab each new mention of danger and fly off with it, to worry and pick apart, like a crow on carrion.

Hester handed over a bright orange grease crayon the size of sidewalk chalk, with which Dellarobia was to mark each ewe after it was immunized. Hester handled the syringe, squeezing its V-shaped grip to land each shot through wool into skin behind the shoulder. The sheep hardly reacted to the needle, seeming more offended by Dellarobia's swipe at their hindquarters as she marked them off. The bright, waxy orange streak across rough wool reminded her of crayon accidents on her living room carpet. Sometimes she missed on the first try and had to pursue one anonymous fuzzy rump as it swam among so many like it. Soon she and Hester both were wading through the woolly mass of orange-streaked bodies, chasing after the unmarked.

They stepped outside the barn when Hester needed to refill the syringe and have a smoke. Dellarobia quickly shook her head when Hester offered the pack. She studied the orange electrical cord looped neatly on a hook, and the perfect rectangle of very dead grass where the trailer usually sat. He'd been leaving on the weekends. He'd mentioned a place called Sweet Briar where he met other scientists. She felt the trailer's absence as if she too had been unplugged and unmoored, deprived of her charge.

"You ought to start keeping a close watch on them in the middle of March," Hester said suddenly, pinching out her cigarette and taking the syringe from its holster. "Sometimes one will surprise you and bring her lambs early."

"How close?" Dellarobia asked. "Should I sleep out here in the barn?"

Hester kept her eye on the glass vial as she drew in the fluid. She wore a red bandanna on her hair and an old denim coat that looked stiff as cardboard. "You could. Your other job's winding down right then, you said. So you'll start you a new one."

"Minus the thirteen dollars an hour," Dellarobia said quietly.

Hester glanced up, a brief flash of surprise, then looked back to her business. So Cub hadn't told her. That Dellarobia was tops in the family, wage-wise.

Over the next hour the sharp chill receded and the stall filled steadily with orange-striped backs. Hester asked her to get some of them out of the way so she could see what she was doing. Dellarobia opened the stall door and guarded it like a valve, shoving in or scuttling out ewes as needed, grabbing horns low near the skull, as she'd seen Hester do. Most of these girls outweighed Dellarobia, but she managed to sort out a few dozen of the moderately willing. They waited in a nervous clump near the stall door, still inside the open barn. Charlie remained at his post in the bright open square of its doorway, his tranquil gaze fixed, his body immobile, like a bronze statue of all dog virtues.

"That'll do, Charlie," Dellarobia called, again in imitation of Hester. She felt an odd thrill of power as Charlie came to her side and the ewes moved like magnets on an opposing pole, skirting the opposite side of the barn to flee out the doorway as Charlie left it. Move the dog, move the sheep, a ton of body weight at her command. She hoped Hester would not catch her childish flush of pride.

Only the flock's shyest members now remained, nervous, flighty girls that Hester had to grab left-handed by a horn while she swung the syringe with her right.

461

Rebelliousness ran in families too, Hester told her. Everything ran in the genes, to be culled or preserved at will. "It's no good to complain about your flock," she advised. "A flock is nothing but the put-together of all your past choices." She told Dellarobia she never kept polled ewes, born without horn buds, preferring the convenience of sheep with handles. Likewise she culled lambs with short-stapled fleeces or puny dispositions. A big white ewe with a freckled nose, Hanky by name, was one of the last holdouts against today's vaccination program, and Hester declared her a misjudgment. There are always a few, she said, that you wish had gone in the deep freeze.

"Why don't I hold her and you jab her," Hester said, abruptly handing Dellarobia the blue-handled syringe while she struggled with the thrashing animal. Hester gripped one of its horns in each hand and used her hip to pin Hanky against the barn wall. "Now," she grunted, not a question, and Dellarobia moved without thought, aiming up on the shoulder, following the point-squeeze motion she'd watched in infinite repetition. She felt the needle sink, then stepped back as the big ewe struggled free and leaped away, landing hard but scrambling to her feet. Her eyes rolled hard, showing the whites.

"You didn't make too bad a job of that," Hester said.

Dellarobia replayed the event as if watching it from the outside: herself in a green windbreaker, red hair swinging as she leaned down to deliver the injection. *I see how you take to this.* She did this all the time now.

Imagined how he would see her while she stood at the stove cooking supper. While she read to the kids, putting them to bed. For no good reason, it made these routine parts of her life seem consequential.

She asked Hester, "How'd you learn to do all this vet stuff?"

"Well, you know. Dr. Gates won't come till death's at your door, and Dr. Worsh won't come even then. They both charge sixty dollars to step out of the truck. I'd say I got tired of paying sixty dollars to hear that I had a dead sheep."

Hanky milled with a few others near the hay manger, eyeing her options. One of which might be to leap over the waist-high wall of the stall. "There ought to be more vets in this county," Dellarobia said. "As much livestock as people have. That's crazy."

"I'd say it is," Hester agreed. "Steady work for the asking. Worsh and Gates are old men. Kids ought to be lining up to take their place."

"Oops." Dellarobia pulled out the grease crayon she'd stuck in her pocket while sorting out the takeaways. "We forgot to mark Hanky."

Hester laughed. "Think we'll forget and chase down that she-devil twice?"

ᘓ

They finished by midmorning and turned out the ewes to settle down again in their muddy country. Dellarobia

463

could see now how they assembled along family lines. A hole had broken in the clouds overhead, a ragged blue scrap ringed with cold white that made her want to bellow her small relief. This last week of rain had stacked up more layers of crazy on folks who had lost whole harvests and the better part of their minds to a year of drizzle. Water torture, they were calling it on the radio. This morning she'd heard about a man in Henshaw who walked outside and unloaded his Smith & Wesson into his old horse, claiming he'd seen a vision of it drowning in mud. The vision was familiar to most by now. Dellarobia had never known to be thankful for so simple a thing as a dry, white snow.

She and Hester passed through the upper pasture gate with its empty donation bucket nailed to the post. If someone could find the time to watch this gate, it would help. Maybe pass out leaflets, like Leighton Akins. Dellarobia considered what she would put on her questionnaire: *How 'bout this weather? Do you know the difference between correlation and causation? Do you have thoughts of shooting your horse?*

"Do you ever find yourself just thinking about the *sun?*" she asked aloud. It was not a Hester kind of question, so she didn't expect an answer. Her mother-in-law had agreed to help her look for nectar flowers that might be blooming the last week of February. Both struck Dellarobia as long shots: winter flowers, and Hester's cooperation. But she'd promised, and now here they were on the High Road, with no idea how to talk to one another. After a minute Hester paused on the gravel, turning this way and that.

"*Yes*," she finally answered emphatically.

"About the sun?" Dellarobia asked.

"Yes," Hester confirmed, now striking downhill away from the traveled road. To Dellarobia's surprise they were on a path, faint and steep and not at all well maintained but definitely a path. She'd never noticed it, in all her days up here.

"They say this might be permanent," Dellarobia said, and then corrected herself. "Scientists say that. The weather will just get all wild instead of settling down."

Hester walked ahead of her in the path and made no response. The tail of her red kerchief bobbed with every step.

"Some places it's gone dry," Dellarobia plowed on. "Where they had to abandon farms, I guess, for the drought. Like Texas. One big fire sale. I don't know what's worse, to burn up or drown."

"Burn up," Hester said decisively. "That'd be worse."

"But look at all the crops here that molded on the vine. And us, having to buy hay for our sheep. You have to wonder, you know. Who's going to feed who?"

"What do they say is doing it?" Hester asked.

Dellarobia considered possible answers. There was no easy way to talk about the known world unraveling into fire and flood. She came up with a reliable word. "Pollution," she said. "You pollute the sky long enough, and it turns bad on you."

465

"Stands to reason," Hester said.

"Where are we headed?"

"There's a bottom over south that gets more sun, where Cub and I used to go hunt chicken of the woods when he was little. I've seen the harbinger flowers out there. Not at the same time, though. Chicken of the woods is in fall time."

"What is that, chicken of the woods?"

"It's a mushroom you eat. It's good. Like chicken."

Dellarobia recalled Hester collecting bark and such for her dyes, years ago, before everyone's tastes ran to the bright, fake colors. But she couldn't picture the young mother taking her boy on scavenger hunts. "Where'd you learn all this woodsy stuff?"

"My old mommy," was all she said, an answer Dellarobia had heard before. She knew little of Hester's family. They were poor, they'd died off. One brother and a slew of cousins remained over in Henshaw, but Hester had cleaved to Bear's family and left her own behind, it seemed. The sky grew a notch brighter. They passed through a stand of walnut trees with branches angled like elbows, still hanging on to last year's walnuts. Like skeletons fixing to play ball, she thought. The steep ground was eroded everywhere from the rains. Leaf-lined troughs ran down the mountain, parting the soil between banks of detritus they'd carried along the forest floor. Among the clumps of leaves were dead monarchs, not so thick as at the study site.

Dellarobia was startled to see a woman approaching

466

them through the trees. Two women, carrying arm-loads of sticks. "Hallo!" they called.

She knew who they were, or what, though she had not met these two in particular. The young one had on men's coveralls with sweatpants sticking out the bottom and two layers of sweaters at least. The elder wore a more normal coat, but her hair hung in two white braids, not a style you saw every day in the senior set. Both sported stiff woolen hats that stood gnomishly on their heads. Dellarobia stepped forward to shake hands, but instead clapped both in a friendly way on their coat sleeves, since their hands were full. "I'm Dellarobia Turnbow," she said. "This is Hester Turnbow, my mother-in-law."

"Brilliant!" said the younger one, shuffling her bundle of sticks into one arm, pumping Dellarobia's hand and Hester's. "This is my mum too! Myrtle, and I'm Nelda. We came over here for firewood, hope that's okay. Our little valley has got picked over."

Both women wore neat fingerless gloves, probably of their own making, but what hooked Dellarobia was the accent. "Li-ul valley, picked o-vah." She could listen to this girl all day, like a radio station. "You all must be freezing," she said. "All this rain."

Nelda laughed in a burst. "Drenched!" she cried. "We're drowned rats! And now it's gone a bit parky, hasn't it?"

Dellarobia didn't know the answer to that. She wondered what Hester made of these women who claimed to be knitting the earth together, one unraveled sweater at a time. Maybe they weren't all from England anymore. They seemed to be multiplying up here. She'd discussed the basics of their arrangement with Hester when they'd asked for permission to camp, and had set up a post-office box for the orange sweaters, which were coming in now by the bushel. There were cash donations, too. The women paid for their P.O. box and a modest weekly fee for camping.

"Hester knits," Dellarobia offered. "You should see some of the sweaters she's made for my husband. She does all those cables and things."

"What do you think of our little fellows, then?" Myrtle set down her firewood and dug in her colorful shoulder bag that was knitted in concentric diamonds of red, yellow, and green. At length she extracted a complicated little mess of orange and black yarn on wooden needles like oversize toothpicks. "Well, here," she added, pulling out a whole knitted butterfly, actual size. "Here's the final product. He's a bit better looking."

Hester turned over the work in her hands. Dellarobia noticed that both Nelda and Myrtle wore old leather shoes, not the high-tech boots that outdoorsy folks seemed to favor. Every single thing secondhand. That must be the point, she realized, feeling slow on the uptake: their fashion statement was to wear nothing they'd bought new. They were second-time-arounders. Not unlike her family, only prouder of it.

"You use double points and carry the second color across," Hester observed.

"Yes!" both women answered, with identical enthusiasm. Dellarobia had seen these knitted butterflies by the hundreds hung up in the trees, but hadn't taken note of the effort involved. It was made all of a piece, wings and body, the black veins knitted right in. She thought of Mako's story of folding all those paper birds in grade school for world peace. The impulse to keep the hands moving, feeding tiny answers to vast demands. Like spooning peas into a child who would still be hungry for decades. It wasn't wrong.

"You use black yarn too," she said. "I never saw mention of black sweaters."

"We've got loads," Nelda said.

"Too much of the black, never enough orange," Myrtle agreed. Dellarobia noted they were not a perfect physical match: Nelda plump and rosy-cheeked, her mother fine-boned. The resemblance blazed in their wide brown eyes and the way they nodded, the gnomy caps bobbing. Mother-daughter adventurers. She felt a pang of longing, as she often did in church. Everybody had a mother and a God; those were standard-issue.

Hester handed the object back. "I don't see how it works," she said.

"People are chuffed to bits on it!" Nelda said. "You should see the messages we get. Look at this." She pulled a phone from her bag and touched its screen with her fingerless-gloved hand, reading aloud, " 'Go

469

knitters, stop global madness, we love you.' That's from Australia, it came this morning. Here's another, 'Go ladies, green and clean, from Betty in Staten Island.' There's loads. You want to see?" She scrolled down and showed them countless messages in blue type, along with some of the same pictures Dovey had found, of the masses of knitted butterflies hanging in trees. The forest-dwelling women appeared in the photos too, arms around each other, flashing peace signs, citizens of their own cheerful universe despite their full awareness of its unraveling. The fact of the phone itself struck Dellarobia, though. There had to be someone at home to pay that bill. Fathers or husbands.

Hester still seemed perplexed. "I don't see how you'd get them on," she said.

"On what?" Myrtle asked.

"On the King Billies," Hester said.

In the small hush, Dellarobia felt a wave of protectiveness. Fierce, sturdy Hester should not be mocked. She could have made the same mistake herself. "They're for show," she explained gently. "Like little stuffed animals. They're not to keep the butterflies warm."

Hester's eyes found Dellarobia's and lit briefly there.

"Icons," Nelda chimed in. "Or symbols, yeah? So people all over the world will know about the monarchs' plight."

Hester's features shifted. "You all are getting as drowned out as the butterflies. I ought to knit some little hippie girls so they'll know about your plight."

"You should!" sang Nelda, and she and Myrtle laughed the same bright laugh, another likeness. No one was offended. It broadened Dellarobia's unspecified hopes, like a hole in the clouds. "Cheers, then," Nelda said after a moment's pause, picking up her bundle of sticks, and the two sets of women walked their separate ways.

Dellarobia carried a canvas bag containing empty cottage-cheese cartons and a hand trowel. Something in there was making a hollow little rattle with every step. If she found flowers, she was to dig some up and bring them to the lab to test their potential as butterfly resources. She remembered Ovid calling this place "poor in winter flowers," one long-ago day. She'd taken offense, at the time. As if one mountain had to have everything. What a mindset.

"Do you ever think what will happen when all this goes away?" she asked Hester.

"You mean the people or the butterflies or what?"

Dellarobia wasn't sure what she'd meant, beyond the impossible idea of returning to her previous self. The person who'd lit out one day to shed an existence that felt about the size of one of those plastic eggs that pantyhose came in. From that day on, week by week, the size of her life had doubled out. The question was how to refold all that back into one package, size zero. "The butterflies might die," she said finally. "That's out of our hands. But maybe they wouldn't. I'm saying, what if?"

It struck her now that probably it would happen, the folding back in. She was no longer world-famous or a national event. As of late, she wasn't even all that town-famous. People forgot so quickly, or moved on. Her influence, if any, was now limited to the family domain. Her marriage. That was about the size of it. She could easily end up back where all this started, launching her heart on some risky solo flight after a man.

"Is Bear going back to those logging men, at the end of March?" she asked.

"That's about to get settled," Hester said.

"How do you mean?"

"We're having a prayer meeting on it. With Pastor Ogle, after the service."

"Tomorrow?"

"No. Tomorrow is dinner on the ground. Sunday next."

Dinner on the ground meant a potluck meal after church, not necessarily on blankets outdoors if the weather was bad. The fellowship hall had tables. "Who's *we*?"

"Anybody in the family that wants to come. You and Cub come on."

"Bear's agreed to this?"

Hester didn't answer directly. "Our place has been raised up by this," she said.

"You could do a lot, if they came back. You know Lupe, that keeps my kids?"

No answer came. Rattle, rattle, went the cartons in

472

Dellarobia's bag. Hester knew very well who Lupe was. Dellarobia persisted. "She and her husband used to do this kind of business in Mexico. They say it's better to keep people back from the roost site and take them up on horses. Make a little program for people, and they'll behave."

Hester seemed to take this in. "That'd be something to ask Rick Baker at the insurance. Horses. I expect he'd say no to that."

"Well, you'd have to get some kind of a rider. You would charge an admission. There could be enough in it to hire some people. There's even a thing where you can get money to leave your woods standing."

"Says who?"

Dellarobia didn't answer that. Who else? "It's some business deal. Companies wanting to junk up the air will pay you to keep standing trees, to clean it back out."

"Pie in the sky," Hester said. "Sounds like."

"Well, it is that," Dellarobia said, smiling. She liked bowling over Hester. "It pertains to the sky."

They were stopped by a fallen tree that lay at a slant across the trail. Hester left Dellarobia on the trail and walked twenty paces to the tree's lower end and sat down on it, facing back the way they'd come. "I've got to take a breather," Hester said, holding up her pack of Camel Lights like a flash card. "You quit, didn't you?"

"Lead us not into temptation," Dellarobia said, covering her eyes.

473

Hester lit up and blew smoke at the sky. "I knew you would."

"Would quit? How do you figure? *I* didn't know I would."

"That's just you. You make up your mind on something, and it's done." A little wind scuttled across the forest floor and rattled the beige leaves that clung to the slim trees all around them. Hester added, "Not like some in your house. That has about one idea in a year, and gets so worn out from it he has to go lie down."

Dellarobia almost smiled, but didn't. The man had no defenders. "Why do you always treat Cub that way?"

"Like what?"

"Like a child."

"Because he's my child. Why do you?"

The downed trunk angled across the trail at chest height to Dellarobia. She folded her arms and leaned in, as if bellying up to some rodeo. Hester was out of her line of sight, off to the left in her own little cloud. "Cub has his good points," she told Hester. "But a wife sees a man for what he is. You're the mother, that's different. You're supposed to be blind to his faults."

"Can you not see your kids for what they are?"

She considered this. Cordelia was reckless, cheerful, physically striking in a way that would get noticed, self-centered in a way that might persist. Preston was thrillingly quick to understand facts, a little dweeby about people. In time he might grow secretive. "I can," she conceded. "They're human. I know that. But I'd lay down my life for my kids, Hester. I would."

"So you would," she said. "So I would."

How dare she, Dellarobia thought. Pretending she'd die for anyone. She would probably light a fire with her own kin if she got too cold. Certainly she had no use for her grandchildren.

Hester spoke again from her little grove of trees. "A child doesn't have to walk on water for you. But a husband does."

"What's that supposed to mean?"

"Children are born so small. But yet you love them that way, all dumb and helpless, so you keep on. With a husband you don't get that chance. Him you've got to look up to."

"I'm five-foot-nothing, Hester. I look up to everybody."

"No, you don't. Not Cub. You never did."

Dellarobia felt socked. The vision that ambushed her was of Crystal in the dollar store that day. How she'd looked, talking to Cub. Craving, yes, but also admiring, cherishing. By any measure, looking up. How much more of a man Cub would be if he'd married some sweet, average-minded girl who thought Cub Turnbow hung the moon. Dellarobia felt loss as wide as a river. For what she'd taken from him.

"You two were no match," Hester said. "I told Bear that from day one. You wait, I told him. That smart gal will not stick around."

"But I did!" Dellarobia marched through the thicket

475

of little trees to face down Hester where she sat. "Am I not standing here?"

"Yes!" Hester said back. "But it wasn't something to count on."

"What in the *hell*. Sorry for the language, Hester. I'm just a little shocked." Dellarobia stomped back to the trail, crunching through the leaves, canvas bag rattling. She threw the bag on the ground. There was nothing breakable in there anyway. She wished there had been. She was in the mood to break something into a hundred pieces.

"So I wasn't good enough for your son. Is that what you're saying?"

"You know it isn't." Hester's voice had grown quiet. She spoke straight out through the upright trunks of the bare grove as if having a prison visit with God.

"Well, why, in the name of . . . Well, *Jesus*, Hester. You never saw fit to mention this before? Like after we lost that baby? We could have called it quits right there after six weeks of marriage and gone our ways. If you thought I was so unsuitable."

"Wasn't my place."

Dellarobia said nothing to that. They'd just tried to do the right thing. For the sake of Cub's parents as much as anyone. The breeze made a large and continuous shushing sound in the leafless forest, under the low winter sky.

"But I never made up a feather bed for you either," Hester said. "If you noticed."

476

"Oh, I noticed." Dellarobia took off her gloves, fished a tissue out of her pocket, and blew her nose. She contemplated walking over there to snatch Hester's cigarettes and smoke the whole pack.

"If you were going, you were going, I figured. Taking those babies with you."

"Preston and Cordie?" Dellarobia turned to stare. Could any of this be true? That Hester expected to lose them, all this time? The woman had practically pronounced the marriage vows herself, she and Bear, and thrown together that house before the ink was dry. Built, though not paid for. "You built us a house," she said.

"It's what we owed our son."

"And you think I've had one foot out the door. All along."

"Have you not?"

"No!" Dellarobia drew the vowel out into two syllables as in, No, *stupid*. She made herself breathe slowly, feeling numb. It was an earthquake, an upheaval of buried surfaces in which nothing was added or taken away. Her family was still her family, an alliance of people at odds, surviving like any other by turning the everyday blind eye. But someone had seen the whole thing.

❧

After they had their words, they could only keep walking. The trail climbed to the rocky spine of a ridge that divided the butterfly valley with its dank, looming firs from the broader south-facing hollow above Bear and Hester's house. The lay of the land was plain from up there, the patchwork of brown farmlands below and the blue-gray wall of mountains that contained all. The sky opened by degrees, and it grew nearly too warm for brisk walking inside layers of winter wool. As they descended the south-facing incline, Dellarobia saw a glint of sun reflected off the steep tin roof of Bear and Hester's farmhouse far below. They passed through more groves of these little trees that held on to their leaves for no good reason she could guess, except to rattle like worn-out lungs with any faint movement of air. The woods possessed but one color, brown, to all appearances dead. Yet each trunk rose up in its way distinct. Shaggy bark and smooth, all reaching for the sky, come what may. Hester could have said what they were. She was a fount of strange woodland names like boneset and virgin's bower, for which no person of their acquaintance seemed to have any use. That must be lonely, Dellarobia thought, to have answers whose questions had all died of natural causes. The trees were skinnier here and the woods more open, though still as varied as any standing congregation of human beings. She knew this valley had been cleared of its timber in Cub's youth. So this had all grown up during her own time on earth. The thought amazed her.

In the clearing she spied a flower and let out a small *oh*. Hester must have seen it too, the sole speck of white in the winter-killed monotony, just a handful of little fringed blossoms no taller than a shoe. Dellarobia knelt down to get close, the myopic's everlasting impulse, and saw each blossom was a whole cluster of petaled flowers. Black specks danced on filaments held above the flowers' gullets. There were no green leaves, only the floral bunches on naked pink stems poking straight up through matted dead leaves. That looked eerie, like some posy handed over from the other side, from death.

"That's them," Hester said. "I thought there'd be more."

"Well, there might be." Dellarobia was not about to dig this one up if it was the sole delegate. She remained on her knees, connected through her thigh muscles to all the hours she'd spent in that posture as if in prayer or surrender, counting dead butterflies. She feared taking her eyes off this one live thing. It could disappear.

"Mommy called them harbingers. Some of them says salt-and-pepper flower."

Dellarobia found it hard to imagine the people who knew, much less disagreed about, the name of a Cheerio-size flower that bloomed in the dead of February. What would possess them to come out here and find it?

"I see more," Hester said. Dellarobia removed her pink wool scarf and laid it in a ring around the first one so as not to lose it, but Hester was right, there were more. Salted across the dun floor of the woods she counted three, four, a dozen small bouquets. Once her eyes knew how to see them, they became abundant. She took the trowel from her bag and dug into the dank forest floor, which was wet and gravelly just under the top inch of matted leaves. While she chipped at the inhospitable garden, the air stirred and in plain sight the experiment ran ahead of itself. Monarchs were already here, this source discovered. She saw two bright drifters coasting tentatively in the woods, and near Hester's boots, the duller orange of folded wings at rest on a flower cluster. Nectaring, that was the verb. King Billy nectaring on the harbinger.

❧

Beyond all half-answers and evasions one question had persisted, since forever, and it was *why*. In Dellarobia's childhood it plagued and compelled her, one word, like one silver dollar on the floor of a wishing well, begging to be plucked up but strategically untouchable. Unsatisfactory answers crowded the waters around it, she could measure her life in those: because you are too young, because it was his time, because it isn't done, because I didn't raise you to behave that way, because it's too late, because the baby came early, because life is like that, just *because*. Because God moves, it goes without saying, in mysterious ways.

Why the butterflies, why now. Why *here*?

Ovid had three theories. Not at first. In the beginning he resisted, wielding nonanswers with the best of them: untestable hypotheses, too many variables. Herbicides, for example. Their sole larval food is milk-weed, a plant whose last name is "weed." Pesticides too, spraying on the increase, as warming temperatures bring in the West Nile mosquito. New weather patterns affect everything in the migratory pathways. Both the fire and the flood. But at length he consented to certainty about these few things: It has become much too warm at the Mexican roost sites. With climate change the whole forest moves up those mountain slopes, a slow-motion slipping uphill, a thing she could imagine. The trees have their requirements. With arboreal stoicism they edge toward the peaks, and from there they cannot levitate.

But that explains *why not there*. That is not *why here*.

His second line of thinking was the OE parasites he'd shown her under the microscope. They stunt wingspan and lifespan. Monarchs highly infected with this parasite cannot fly very far. The annual trip to Mexico seems to weed out the most burdened, keeping the population healthy. But west of the Rockies is a different group, an outsider's club of monarchs that are very infected, and do not fly to Mexico but seek their winter shelter in scattered groves of trees along the California coast. Maybe they portend what is coming. Warmer temperatures correlate with rising infection rates. If the parasite reached a critical level in eastern populations, natural selection might favor short migrations and dispersed winter roosting everywhere, not just in California. The hypothesis is immense, with its multiple bonds of cause and effect, some of them testable. To this end she cut small squares of cellophane tape, pressed them against the abdomens of one hundred live monarchs, and under the scope, counted the dark parasite spores nestled among the ridged, translucent scales. It took hours of acute ocular focus, a headache beyond all known proportions, and an appointment with the eye doctor for new glasses (overdue). Counting the microscopic dots on every centimeter-square of tape was not unlike counting butterflies on squares of forest floor, except that the numbers kept rising. Measuring and counting are the tasks of science. Not guessing, and not wishing. The potential answers are infinite, and no preference among them is allowed: there will be no just-because, or unjust-because.

She understood. But still, it's *why not there*. Not *why here*.

His third theory concerned devastation in the "spring range," which is what he called a funnel-shaped area on the map, fundamentally Texas. Monarchs that eke out winter in the Mexican Neovolcanics awaken from their torpor to an unruly sexual madness. Males are hormonally driven to assail anything—a quaking leaf, other males—eventually enclosing within their embrace the host of congregated females, and afterward they are spent, fulfilled. Their mates flee with gorged ovaries toward a nonnegotiable deadline, the deposit of perfectly timed egg on the first unfurling leaf of a Texan milkweed, moving inside the consecrated clock of a ticking earth. This, he said, tapping the map on the glass screen of his computer, is all our eggs in one basket. The spring range. Steady through the ages, now its rhythms abruptly faltered, ransacked by drought and unquenchable fires. By fire ants marching north, consuming 100 percent of the monarch caterpillars they chance to meet. Suppose a genetic mishap sent a handful of fall migrants just to the northern edge of this realm of fire ant and firestorm. This far south in the autumn, and no farther, he said, drawing one long finger from the Texas panhandle to the Carolinas, a scattering of migrants overwintering here, where they would not be forced to come back across that desert. A Bible Belt latitude, favorable for its mildness, but a mountainous place high enough to cool an insect pulse to dormancy for the winter wait. Suppose there is only one such place. And that they had been coming here for years, in small numbers, cloaked by this forest, mostly unsurviving. Until precipitous natural selection against the Mexican migrants destroyed most of the population, shedding favor on these pioneers. Their gene, suddenly, the inheritance of a species.

The explanation was far from complete. A population was only as valid as its habitat. Winter nectar sources remained problematic, when repeated warm spells broke their dormancy, and so did the spring milkweed emergence. There are always more questions. Science as a process is never complete. It is not a foot

483

race, with a finish line. He warned her about this, as a standard point of contention. People will always be waiting at a particular finish line: journalists with their cameras, impatient crowds eager to call the race, astounded to see the scientists approach, pass the mark, and keep running. It's a common misunderstanding, he said. They conclude there was no race. As long as we won't commit to knowing everything, the presumption is we know nothing.

And even while he warned her of these caveats, Dellarobia felt a settling down of her lifelong plague of impatience. He did not claim that God moves in mysterious ways. Instead he seemed to believe, as she did, though they never could have discussed it, that everything else is in motion while God does not move at all. God sits still, perfectly at rest, the silver dollar at the bottom of the well, the question.

On the way to the study site a pine cone war broke out among the kindergartners. The boys took it more to heart, predictably, although the instigator was a big, rough girl in a decrepit parka whose fake fur hood was matted like old shag carpet. She shimmied up a pine trunk and fired away, ignoring Miss Rose's escalating threats about getting sent right straight home with what she called a pink note. Dellarobia had a whole new impression of Miss Rose and what she was up against, in general. This girl, Comorah, exemplified a category of children whose parents, if applicable, would not be impressed by a pink note. She came down when she was good and ready, with gummy black stains all over her clothes and hands that Dellarobia knew would not give in to soap and water. She'd had her own tangles with pine sap up here. Preston seemed both thunderstruck and distressed by Comorah, needing to tell her the munitions were cones, not "pine combs." Undaunted by her indifference, he sidled up to her with this information again and again, just the way Roy would carry around his old tooth-punctured Frisbee to drop at your feet while you did yard work, all afternoon if need be.

Dellarobia held herself a little apart from her son, curious to observe this ecosystem he regularly navigated without her. She saw that he was reserved but not shy, that other kids ran to him with their special finds such as beetles, and that he stuck close to the willowy, confident Josefina. She was his partner or protector— Dellarobia couldn't quite read it. For all she knew, they might be the only two free-lunch kids, though she doubted it. Some of these youngsters appeared to be well-heeled—she'd actually spotted a cell phone—and others, like Comorah, were turned out in gear that had seen many generations of hand-me-down. But Josefina and Preston seemed to represent some subtle divide of maturity, like the automatic segregation of seniors from sophomores at a dance. Dellarobia recalled their spontaneous hug, that first day Josefina's family showed up on their porch. In retrospect she saw in it some element of rescue.

Dellarobia felt an unaccustomed remove from all the children in terms of nose-wiping and pink-note threats, which were handled by the proficient Miss Rose and two helpers she'd wrangled for the day. Some of the kids knew she was Preston's mother, but for this field trip she had acquired an aura of special esteem; she was *in charge*, a teacher-superior kind of personage evidently on par with the principal or Dora the Explorer. Obviously the class had been prepped. Dellarobia had no prior experience in this realm and was struck by their goggle-eyed regard and physical deference. They did not tug unremittingly on her limbs, whine to be carried, or put her outer garments to use as a nose rag. This was quite something, being in charge.

They began their field trip in the lab, where Ovid understandably had safety concerns. His compromise was to allow eight kids at a time just inside the door for a quick lecture while they waited to be shuttled in groups to the top of the High Road. One of the teacher-helpers drove a van. The livestock that shared real estate here with science became an unexpected challenge. Sheep, especially while undertaking their bodily functions, proved vastly more interesting to some than the lab lecture. Ovid was a good sport. "That is biology too," he said serenely, during a particularly worthy expulsion of methane. Instantly the boys were on his side.

This outing had been all Dellarobia's idea. She and Ovid had had several well-tempered disagreements about ordinary people mistrusting scientists, and this seemed such a natural starting place, he had to consent. He wasn't crazy about the interruption, but warmed to the occasion, as he was still the gentle teacher who'd pointed at Preston their first night at supper and declared him a scientist. A moment, Dellarobia now believed, that changed Preston's life. You never knew which split second might be the zigzag bolt dividing all that went before from everything that comes next. Ovid was patient with their questions about scientists (Do they like to blow up stuff? Could you make a human being?), steering them onto the general butterfly topic. They responded well to any mention of poison. *Aposematic coloration* was a bright orange butterfly or a wildly striped caterpillar, the bold fellow whose hugely magnified photo was tacked to the wall of the lab. These colors are a stop sign, Ovid explained, warning other creatures not to eat him, or they might very well throw up. Or even die! Dellarobia was touched to see him dressed as she'd never seen him before, in a dress shirt and tie for the kindergartners. Like a slightly more hip Mister Rogers.

From the lab they proceeded to the roost site in a slow-moving swarm, like bees moving with consensus but no strict arrangements from one hive to another. Dr. Byron promised to join them up there to answer more questions at lunchtime, by which Dellarobia hoped he meant in thirty minutes or less. Meanwhile she was to take the reins. The walk from the van to the study site was eventful. In addition to the pine cone war, which devolved to a beetle-throwing contest, there were some warriors down with scraped arms, a good deal more pine sap, and one winter coat utterly, magically gone missing. Lunch boxes fell open everywhere. Three girls felt they saw a bear or a deer, which occasioned some sustained shrieking. None of it threw Miss Rose, their young teacher whose perfectly streaked, flipped hairdo, cool furry boots, and earnest composure conveyed a touching respect for the endeavor of kindergarten. Like Ovid's tie. Dellarobia felt underdressed, prepared for a regular science day. A small boy in a puffy white jacket like the Michelin Man walked very close to her, constantly picking up the caps of acorns from the trail and handing them over for safekeeping. He was amazingly good at finding them. She probably pocketed thirty in the distance of a hundred yards. He called them "egg corns." Emboldened by his presence, several girls walked in a little assemblage just behind Dellarobia with an air of the chosen. Their know-it-all leader announced the names of shrubs growing alongside the trail, universally wrong: cabbage, water sprout, hash plant. Where did she get *that*?

A few children noticed the butterflies as they approached the roost, craning their necks to declaim their astonishment, gathering the whole audience into gasping goshes and wows. Dellarobia heard a few soft curses, probably channeled directly from parents or TV. Butterfly trees, encapsulated branches, prickling trunks: she tried to see it as new, through their eyes. Trees covered with corn flakes. She wished it were one of the magical days when the butterflies swirled like autumn leaves, but being here at all was something for these kids, who seemed unacquainted on principle with the outdoors. Only four had been up here before, two besides Preston and Josefina, though all claimed to have seen it on TV. Today was cold; there was no movement in the trees, and winter had taken its toll. This roost had held upward of fifteen million monarchs, by Ovid's early estimates, but had suffered about a 60 percent loss, much of that in the last few weeks. Even now they dropped, the pattering sound of little deaths almost continuous. So close to the end, they were literally failing to hang on.

In the little clearing of the study site, the kids settled in a half circle on their sit-upons, which were doubled squares of waterproof fabric stitched together with yarn in anticipation of this very occasion. They had tie-strings and were meant to be worn around the waist like a backward apron, but that didn't work out, so Miss Rose carried them from the van to be distributed, each to its maker, and at long last sat upon. When asked to give Mrs. Turnbow their full attention, the children's settling down looked like popcorn in a hot-air popper, but in time the eyes turned up, ready for the zigzag bolt. Dellarobia was nervous, as new to this as any of them, but did her best to tell the story. That the striped cater-pillar is also the orange butterfly, not different but the same, just as a baby that becomes a grown-up is still one person, though they look very different. That the forest of butterflies is really all one thing too, the monarch. She explained how the caterpillar eats only one plant, the milkweed, so that is also part of the one big thing. And she told how they fly. Carrying a secret map inside their little bodies, for the longest time content to hang out with their friends, until one day the something inside wakes up and away they go. A thousand miles, which is like light years to a butterfly, to a place they've never been. Probably they never even knew they could do that.

At some point Ovid arrived. She sensed some change in the children's attention and blushed scarlet to realize he'd been behind her, listening. She was finished any-way. Ovid, tall and stunning in his tie and genuine over-coat, not his ordinary field gear, clapped his hands slowly and sincerely for Dellarobia, inciting Miss Rose and the children to do the same. He said he didn't have much to add, except to mention what was not so good about see-ing these butterflies here. Their ordinary home in Mexico was changing, trees getting cut down and cli-mate zones warming up, much too quickly for their lik-ing. He asked the kids if they ever had a big change at home they didn't like. Every hand went up. Dellarobia envisioned tales of broken transformers or foster care agencies—kids this age could hardly differentiate levels of grief—but Ovid kept to the subject of the wider world and its damage. Animals losing their homes, because of people being a bit careless.

"Making pollution," Dellarobia added, thinking a neutral word might head off trouble, but Miss Rose was all over this. They'd discussed it in class.

"And what are some of the things we can do to help out?" Miss Rose prompted.

"Shut off the lights when we're done," one boy said.

"Pick up our beer cans," said another.

Miss Rose laughed. "Whose beer cans?"

"Our dads'," another replied, eliciting general agreement.

They were shy about asking questions, but then got over it. They wanted to know what could kill a butterfly. Dellarobia knew some answers, but Ovid could list many more, including cars! He said scientists in Illinois discovered that cars smashed half a million monarchs there in just one summer. The kids rallied to the word "smashed," yet there was a collective "Awww" for the roadkill monarchs. A boy put up his hand, pulled it down, then put it up again, and finally asked, "Are you the president?"

Ovid laughed heartily. "No, I am not," he said. "What makes you think I might be the president? Is it because my skin is dark?"

The little boy appeared forthright. "Because you're wearing a tie."

Ovid looked startled. "A lot of men wear a tie when

491

they go to work," he said. "Maybe your dad does that?"

"No," said the boy, and Dellarobia could see Ovid taking this in: no on the tie, or no on the going to work, maybe no dad, period. She felt this was a productive meeting of minds. The kids wanted to know a great deal more about Dr. Byron: if he lived in the lab, and if those were his sheep. Preston waited patiently for his turn and asked, a little out of step with the crowd, whether the butterflies were like flying ants that go out and start new colonies. Ovid said that was different, the ants had to stay together almost always because of their kinship system. He said insects have many different ways of being families, and they could discuss it more at lunchtime, which he proposed was now.

It was a good call, given the extent of eruption already under way among the lunch boxes. Dellarobia was surprised at how quickly the kids fell back into their former social groupings: the Chosen, the Beetle Throwers, the Shriekers. One troupe of permanently smitten girls tracked Miss Rose like bridesmaids. The Michelin Man–coat boy sought solitude as if long accustomed to it, finding acorn caps as he went. And, Dellarobia noted, her son left Josefina flat for the chance to talk shop with Dr. Byron. She'd have the loyalty chat with Preston, later. She moved quickly to fill the gap. "I know the best lunch spot," she offered, and Josefina gratefully took her hand. The true best spot, the big mossy log across the creek, was already taken, so they headed to the uphill edge of the clearing and sat on a smooth spot at the base of a fir colossus.

Dellarobia felt buoyant. Everything had gone better than planned. Ovid needed to do this; he was obviously good at public relations but harbored a blind spot, an inexplicable breach in his confidence. A breach she had filled. The word that rose in her thoughts was *partnership*, and it thrilled and sent her reeling as such thoughts did, in a life spent flying from pillar to post. He was sitting down there on the log with Preston, *he* had the best seat in the house, he who occupied her thoughts while at work and at rest and probably when she slept. He sat with his lunch on his lap and seven kids lined up like ducks in a row, but it was Preston who had his ear. She could see the two of them chatting it up about insects and the different kinds of families. She looked in her purse for the tuna fish sandwich she'd barely had time to slap together this morning, while Josefina extracted from her little paper bag a fully cooked meal in several parts: the sandwich-equivalent rolled inside tortillas like long, yellow cigars, the sauce in a paper cup covered with cellophane, the brown beans in another. A large reused sour cream carton held crisp, triangular chips.

"Wow, you've got the gold-star mom," Dellarobia said, realizing that might be an obscure way to put it for a newcomer to the language. But Josefina thanked her, seeming to get it. Her English had improved noticeably. Lupe said the time the kids spent together helped. Dellarobia watched Josefina lay out her complicated lunch without self-consciousness on a cloth napkin, and wondered what it would feel like to be in *that* kind of a family. Or any kind, other than the one whose walls contained her. Whatever incentive she might have for flying away, there it was, family, her own full measure, surrounded by a cheap wire fence built in one afternoon a long time ago. Her Turnbow dynasty. Where she'd never belonged in the first place, according to Hester. What kind of ties were those, what did they bind? She could so easily belong to someone else.

Josefina ate her meal with a fork, but after a moment paused to push her dark hair back over her shoulders and look straight up. Dellarobia was moved by the sight of her throat, the vulnerable little bulb of her Adam's apple, rising from her zipped corduroy coat, and this child's unaccountable poise in the midst of a life that had been wrecked. A house borne away on shifting ground, a world away. Dellarobia looked up too, taking in the dizzying view of the butterfly tower anchored behind their backs. Butterflies prickled all the way up the trunk in perfect alignment, like a weathervane collection. Butterflies drooped heavily from the branches. "What do you call the bunches?" Dellarobia asked.

"Racimos."

She repeated the word, trying to remember this time. She'd asked before. It seemed better than *cluster* or *colonnade* or any other word Ovid used. More specific. "Does this remind you of home, being up here?" she asked. "I mean home in Mexico?"

Josefina nodded. "In Mexico people say they are children."

"The caterpillars are the children, though. These are the grown-ups."

Josefina shook her head quickly, like an erasure, starting over. "Not *children*. Something that comes out of children when they die."

Dellarobia thought this sounded like a horror movie. But she could see it mattered to Josefina, who had put down her fork. "I can't remember the word," she said. "When a baby dies, the thing that goes out." She placed both hands on her chest, thumbs linked, and lifted them fluttering like a pair of wings. "It flies away from the body."

Suddenly Dellarobia understood. "The soul."

"The *soul*," Josefina repeated.

"They believe a monarch is the soul of a baby that's died?"

The child nodded thoughtfully, and for a long time they both gazed up into the cathedral of suspended lives. After a while Josefina said, "So many."

❧

Cub was cutting firewood at Bear and Hester's and called to say he was staying for supper, but Dellarobia declined to bring the kids over and join them. Hester's confession in the woods had left her with a new and strange detachment ringing in her ears. Not exactly unwelcome, but unbound; there was a difference. She felt invisible and light. It was Friday night. She would fix something she and the kids favored like soup and fish sticks, and they'd watch some program from beginning to end. Assuming they arrived in one piece. Dovey was picking them up from Lupe's and coming over too. The phone beeped on the table, and it was that bad girl, texting: GOT EM, ON OUR WAY.

Dellarobia shot back: TXT WHILE DRIVING IF . . .

:) was the prompt reply.

Dovey wasn't the fish-stick type but would eat gravel to get away from her duplex, where her landlord brother was tearing out tile for no apparent reason. Dovey was *seriously* moving out, she said, like the boy who cried wolf, his cries ignored by all. She would stay put as long as Dellarobia's place served her so well as a halfway house. Just as Cordie and Preston provided her the option of halfway motherhood.

Dellarobia was surprised to hear them pull up in the driveway so soon. Roy went to the front door and signaled an alert: ears up, tail down. Dellarobia went to look out the little upper windows in the door and was startled to see the white News Nine Jeep in her driveway. Tina Ultner in a belted white coat was out of the car, head down, the corn-silk hair pulsing with each fast step as she came up the walk. Dellarobia dropped to the floor to sit face to face with Roy, her back pressed against the doorjamb. There was not time to run and hide in the bedroom. She heard the hollow tick of a woman's heels on the porch steps, and felt the shift of light as Tina moved in close to the door's glass panes. Roy looked at Dellarobia and cocked his head to one side, the collie question mark. She held up a finger and Roy stood fast. The house took on the feel of a bomb shelter.

Rap rap, came the little knock. *Rap rap*, again. Then silence.

Roy glanced from the door to Dellarobia. He licked his lips and yawned, dog signs of nervousness. The tidy knock revived.

Dellarobia remembered she'd pocketed her phone after Dovey's text, praise be. She put it on vibrate before keying carefully: DON'T COME TO THE HOUSE.

The reply from Dovey was immediate: ???

GO AWAY. XPLAIN LATER

WE R HERE. BEHIND JEEP. WTF?

Tina rang the doorbell. Roy yawned again, but didn't move.

I M HIDING. GO!

A minute passed. Roy did an anxious little skitter, stepping back and forward, dancing at the edge of self-restraint. Dellarobia stared at the screen until the reply appeared. PRESTON HAS TO P. ME TOO. CORDIE ALREADY DID.

DO U HAVE DIAPERS?

FOR ALL US???

Dellarobia's mind went blank. The knocking had stopped. Another text came from Dovey. OMG. SHE SEES US.

Then, ten seconds later: DON'T WORRY I'LL HANDLE. COMING IN.

Dellarobia knew not to bet the farm on Dovey's don't-worry-I'll-handle plans. This one failed faster than most. She heard Dovey explaining with fair conviction that Dellarobia wasn't home while Preston opened the door, plunging Dellarobia and Roy unexpectedly into the scene, at eye level with a pair of gorgeous gray suede boots. Dellarobia took them in, then turned her eyes upward into the nostrils of Tina Ultner.

"Dellarobia, *hi*," Tina said, waiting for Dellarobia to find her feet before extending the cool little hand. The whole effect of Tina rushed her like a hit of some numbing drug. The pale eyebrows and huge, direct eyes, the otherworldly complexion. Her coat was winter white, the color she'd frowned on when Dellarobia wore it that first time. Both kids rushed into the house, followed by Dovey, then Roy, leaving Dellarobia on the porch with Tina.

"I'm not doing this," she said. "Not again."

"Listen," Tina said, "this is a really special thing we do. Hear me out. It's called our 'in-depth' segment. Very few stories get this kind of coverage, just the absolute viewer favorites. When there's a ton of interest, what we'll do is we go back and follow up on a story six weeks later, to see how things turned out."

"Six weeks?" Dellarobia said, thinking several questions at once. Did Tina even have a clue how her camera trickery had upended Dellarobia's life? Had it been six weeks, and had anything turned out? This was in-depth? She remembered Ovid's complaint about the media's short attention span. The living room blinds waggled sideways and Dovey stepped into view in the front window, behind Tina's back. Dovey held up crossed index fingers as if to ward off a vampire.

"Is that Ron in the car?" Dellarobia asked. The figure in the Jeep looked slighter and blonder than Ron, with more hair.

"It's not Ron," Tina said, with some diffidence. "That's Everett."

"Okay, get Everett. Get whatever you need and come with me." Dellarobia strode down the steps and around to the back of the house, leaving it to Tina to get her game on. She did not want to knock on the metal door of the camper, which felt too intimate, so was relieved to see lights on in the lab. She led Tina through the mucky barn, in those boots. If Tina was horrified by her surroundings she was good at pretending other-wise, looking around with the calculating eye Dellarobia remembered, as if storing away all these sights for later. They paused outside the lab door to wait for Everett, and Dellarobia threw down some background info on Dr. Ovid Byron. She spelled the name so Tina could type it into her phone device. Tina stood frowning at the little screen, intermittently tapping it in frenzied bursts with her manicured fingertips. "You're kidding me," she finally said. "You've got this man here? In a *barn*?"

The diminutive cameraman Everett arrived in haste, organizing and shoving black cables into his coat pockets as he came, disheveled in every aspect except for his hair, which looked shellacked. He gratified Dellarobia with a grimace of frank horror at the barn floor. Dellarobia rapped on the plastic-covered door, and they entered as a group to find Ovid sitting down, writing notes. To accommodate his reading glasses, he had pushed up his safety goggles on his forehead like a skin diver briefly out of water. His look of vulnerable surprise demoralized Dellarobia utterly. He stood up to meet Tina's forthright handshake and quickly shed the goggles and glasses, revealing a small, surprising vanity that fueled Dellarobia's anguish. Astonished, she watched Tina drop her former mom-to-mom allegiance as if it had never been, aiming the force of her charm in a brand-new direction. This lab was so great, unbelievable, she'd wanted to be a science major in college but the math, oh man! After the introductions Tina said they had to go up on the mountain to repeat the shot with the butterflies flying in the background. That was customary for these spots, to help key in the viewer visually to the earlier story. Ovid told her the follow-up in this case was that most of the butterflies were dead. Also it was too cold for them to be flying, and too late in the day. Tina clicked her tongue. They'd planned to get here earlier, but she'd had a breaking spot on a homicide.

She drummed her white-tipped nails on the

plywood lab table, looking all around. "You know what?" she finally pronounced. "It's fine. We still have all that great footage from the first interview. We'll just cut the butterflies into this one when we do the edit."

Ovid eyed her, looking piqued. Make the butterflies undead?

Tina set herself to the project of framing what she called a doable shot in the lab. She loved the caterpillar poster on the wall, colorful. She liked Ovid in his lab coat, but not all the mess. The pile of aluminum pans from the last lipid analysis had to go. Tina directed the cleanup with a slightly pained expression, as if confronting grime, though really it was just clutter: glass reagent bottles, blue wire test tube racks, rectangular plastic containers stacked up like blocks, computer printouts. And this was *clean*. Dellarobia always tidied up on Fridays. Ovid was first reluctant and then unnerved by all the shuffling. When Everett approached the Tissuemizer, Ovid barked at him not to touch it. Tina laughed sweetly at this to make it a joke. Dellarobia suddenly had full recall of that little two-note laugh, and its many uses.

Ovid said, "I think you had better go ahead and take your shot."

Tina and Everett exchanged a consequential glance, and she moved in to clip a little mike to Ovid's lapel and slip its attending box device into a pocket of his lab coat. Dellarobia saw his eyes roll upward as Tina fussed with him, just exactly as Preston's did when Dellarobia knotted his tie for church. Gone was the friendly confidence of the scientist meeting the kindergartners. Tina powdered her nose and cheekbones, then snapped her compact closed and nodded at Everett. She switched on her lubricated news voice. "Dr. Ovid Byron, you've been studying the monarch butterfly for more than twenty years. Have you ever encountered a sight like this?"

"No," he replied. He looked desperate for escape.

Tina waited. Like a store mannequin, Dellarobia thought, with the waxy complexion and flower-stem posture. She'd been too struck, when she herself was in the headlights, to notice that the woman was far from perfect. The bones in her face looked stony under the colorless skin, too prominent. She looked unhealthy.

Tina began again. "Dr. Byron, you're one of the world's leading experts on the monarch butterfly, so we're looking to you for answers about this beautiful phenomenon. I understand these butterflies often flock together in Mexico for the winter. So tell me, in a nutshell, what brings them here?"

Ovid actually laughed. "In a nutshell?"

Tina gave a stern little nod, signaling him to go on.

"That won't fit in a nutshell."

Dellarobia saw the door budge. Dovey appeared, scooting quickly inside with the kids. Dellarobia sidled over to lift Cordie onto her hip for safekeeping, and they all stayed near the door. Tina marched to the table to dispatch a blue-handled pair of scissors and a roll of tape from the background of her shot, and yanked at the crumpled plastic dust sheath that covered the microscope. Ovid spoke miserably. "It's not a movie set."

Tina eyed him, and he spread his hands. "This is what science looks like."

"Fine," she replied. She returned to her spot and composed herself to come out of the starting gate again. Dellarobia grasped her strategy now, setting up the interview in different ways so it could be cut to ribbons later.

"Dr. Byron, you've studied the monarch butterfly for over twenty years, and you say you have never seen anything like this. It seems everyone has a different idea about what's going on here, but certainly we can agree these butterflies are a beautiful sight."

"I don't agree," he said. "I am very distressed."

Tina's teeth showed. "And why is that?"

"Why?" He ran one hand over his close-cropped head, a nervous habit Dellarobia had seen before, though rarely. "This is evidence of a disordered system," he said at last. "Obviously we're looking at damage. At the normal roosting sites in Mexico, in the spring range, all over the migratory pathways. To say the takeaway lesson here is beauty, my goodness. What is your name again?"

"Tina Ultner," she said, in a different, off-camera voice.

"Tina. To see only beauty here is very superficial. Certainly in terms of news coverage, I would say it's off message."

"You're saying there's a message here. And what is that?"

Ovid shot Dellarobia a vivid, trapped look. She felt sick. He was so good at explanations, he had all that education, he could handle little bony-nosed Tina, that's what she'd thought. She'd been out of her mind. After a long pause Tina tried again. "Dr. Byron, something new is happening here. Most of us are struck by the beauty of this phenomenon. But"—she cocked her head theatrically, as if burdened by keen insight—"do you think it might possibly be a sign of some deeper problem with the ecology?"

"Yes!" Ovid cried. "A problem with the environment, is what you're trying to say. Pervasive environmental damage. This is a biological system falling apart along its seams. Yes. Very good, Tina Ultner."

"And briefly, Dr. Byron, tell us the nature of the problem."

"Briefly? Unseasonable temperature shifts, droughts, a loss of synchronization between foragers and their host plants. Everything hinges on the climate."

She blinked a couple of times. "Are we talking about global warming?"

"Yes, we are."

Tina made a downward wave at Everett to stop the camera, and bizarrely her own animation clicked off too, her face slack as she walked across the lab, maybe starting to feel homesick for her average flaming interstate wreck. Tina checked something on the camera, then walked back to her interview spot and spoke in a subdued voice. "The station has gotten about five hundred e-mails about these butterflies, almost all favorable. Is this really where you want to go with this segment? Because I think you're going to lose your audience."

Ovid looked genuinely startled. "I am a scientist. Are you suggesting I change my answer to improve your ratings?"

"Not at all," Tina said frostily. Her composure was losing its smooth edge. She had an irritable way of sucking her front teeth and exhaling through her nose that gave Dellarobia to know this woman probably did have children, after all. After looking down at the floor for a moment, Tina signaled Everett and lifted her features to greet the camera. "Dr. Byron, let's talk about global warming. Scientists of course are in disagreement about whether this is happening, and whether humans have a role."

Ovid's eyebrows lifted in a familiar way, almost amused. "I'm afraid you have missed the boat, Tina. Even the most recalcitrant climate scientists agree now, the place is heating up. Pretty much every one of the lot. Unless some other outcome is written on the subject line of his paycheck."

She raised her jaw slightly, an edgier look, and started over once again. Her stamina for replays was unbelievable. "Dr. Byron, let's talk about global warming. Many environmentalists contend that burning fuel puts greenhouse gases into the atmosphere."

He pulled back his chin in such skeptical dismay he looked like a startled turtle. "They *contend* this? That burning carbon puts carbon in the air, this is a *contention*?" His voice notched up so severely it squeaked a little. "Tina, Tina. Think about what you are saying. All the coal that has ever been mined, that's carbon. All the oil wells, carbon, again! We have evaporated that into the air. What's in the world stays in the world, it does not go *poof* and disappear. It's called the conservation of matter. The question was settled well before the time of Sir Isaac Newton."

Tina blinked once, twice. "Scientists tell us they can't predict the exact effects of global warming."

"Correct. We tell you that, because we are more honest than other people. We know evidence will keep coming in. It does not mean we ignore the subject until further notice. We brush our teeth, for instance, even though we do not know exactly how many cavities we may be avoiding."

"Well, a lot of people are just not convinced. We're here to get information."

He rolled his eyes to the ceiling and showed his teeth in a grimace, the tip of his tongue just visible between his front teeth. When he finally looked at her again, this seemed to cause him actual pain. "If you were here to get information, Tina, you would not be standing in my laboratory telling me what scientists think."

She opened her mouth, but he cut her off. "What

scientists disagree on now, Tina, is how to express our shock. The glaciers that keep Asia's watersheds in business are going right away. Maybe one of your interns could Google that for you. The Arctic is genuinely collapsing. Scientists used to call these things the canary in the mine. What they say now is, The canary is dead. We are at the top of Niagara Falls, Tina, in a canoe. There is an image for your viewers. We got here by drifting, but we cannot turn around for a lazy paddle back when you finally stop pissing around. We have arrived at the point of an audible roar. Does it strike you as a good time to debate the existence of the falls?"

Tina sucked her teeth, eyes wide. The effect was not flattering. "If this were Niagara Falls, I'd have a decent background," she said. "I can't do anything with this without a visual."

Ovid's eyebrows pressed toward his hairline. "Intangible things are outside your range? Can't you people be a little imaginative?"

Tina did not reply.

"An election result!" he said, looking a little nuts. "A stock market! Those are intangibles. And yet you manage to cover them. Ad nauseam!"

Tina tossed her hair ever so slightly and used a voice she had probably honed as a teenager. "Because people *care*."

"You have a job to do, woman, and you are not doing it." Ovid's head dropped forward and his eyes narrowed, a posture that stunned Dellarobia. She'd never

507

figured him for a schoolyard fighter. He took a step forward, leveling his finger like a blade toward her chest, inciting in Tina an equal and opposite step backward. "Fire is an excellent visual, Tina. So are hurricanes, and floods. The whole damn melting Arctic." They edged into the part of the lab where the stuff was piled from the portion they'd cleaned up. "How will you feel ten years from now, when a serious lot of the farms in the world don't have a damn rainy season anymore? And you were party to that?" Ovid's long finger seemed to move everything, pulling him forward, backing Tina around the table.

Everett spoke up. "You're outside the shot."

"You keep out of this!" Ovid shouted. Everett looked slapped. "You think this will only happen to Africa or Asia," he told Tina. "Someplace that is not your assignment."

Tina suddenly held up one sideways hand as if she had a martial arts move up her sleeve. "Now you stop right there, buddy. I have two little boys adopted from Thailand."

Ovid did not seem impressed. "And so that's it, you've done your duty? Now you can chart your career on the path of least resistance?"

"You have no idea. Everybody thinks TV is so easy. This is *work*."

"Convince me, Tina. You are letting a public relations firm write your scripts for you. The same outfit that spent a decade manufacturing doubts for you about the smoking-and-cancer *contention*. Do you people never learn? It's the same damned company, Tina, the Advancement of Sound Science. Look it up, why don't you. They went off the Philip Morris payroll and into the Exxon pocket."

Tina's moment of anger turned out to be highly soluble in worry. She was backed up against the refrigerator now, eyeing an escape route. Ovid turned away from her abruptly and walked across the lab, unbuttoning his white coat. "You have no interest in real inquiry. You are doing a two-step with your sponsors." He began to pull off his lab coat before realizing he was wired up with the little microphone on the lapel and the gizmo in the pocket. He unclipped the lapel mike and looked around, possibly for a place to throw it. Finding no clear target, he faced Tina and held the clip to his mouth.

"Here is my full statement. What you are doing is unconscionable. You're allowing the public to be duped by a bunch of damned liars."

Tina raised both hands. "Like I could even use that word on TV."

Ovid clipped the mike back on his lapel and managed a fair reconstruction of his normal grin, the full revelation of eyeteeth.

"Sorry," he said. "You are allowing the public to be duped by a bunch of damned prevaricators."

"O-*kay*," Tina said. "That's a wrap."

Everett rolled up his cords in a flash. Tina already had her phone to her ear as they exited, her voice rising to a shrill pitch outside in the barn. The news Jeep was probably tearing up the highway before the stunned pall in the laboratory lifted. Preston and Cordie bore the wide-eyed, zipped-up expression children assume in the presence of unraveling adults. Dellarobia looked a bit like that herself, waiting for the return of some recognizable version of her boss. He was manically sorting through manila folders that had been shuffled in the fray, gathering things together.

"Well. A fine disaster," he said finally, without looking up.

"It wasn't so bad," Dellarobia said, feeling dumb as a cow.

"I could have tried to work with her. You are always telling me that, work with people. Show them we're not the enemy. I know this was important. And I threw it."

She realized he was looking around for his puffy green coat, which had fallen onto the floor near the refrigerator. Dellarobia fetched it up and handed it to him.

"But everything you said is true. Technically. You didn't do anything wrong."

"No," he agreed. "Except to make sure she will run over that cartridge with her vehicle. Repeatedly."

"But that's her nickel," Dellarobia said. "That's everybody's loss. I'm actually sorry nobody will ever get to see that."

"Yo, guys," Dovey said, holding up her phone. "Don't worry, I got it all. Posting it now. YouTube."

13

Mating Strategies

"March fourth," Dellarobia said.

"To where?" Preston asked.

She laughed. "Not forward march. It's the fourth of March. Friday. Your birthday is in one exact week."

Preston smiled broadly, though his spectacled gaze remained fixed on the road. They stood facing east, the direction from which the bus would come, along with the light of morning in its own good time.

"I have such a big surprise for you, you won't believe it," she added, causing his smile to broaden and compress, as if containing a significant internal pressure. They watched the sun break over one of the stippled backs of the wooded hills that swam along the horizon. First it was a shapeless fire blazing through bare trees, quickly gaining the yolk of its sphere, and then they could not look at it directly.

"Today smells like the time when the lambs get born," he said.

"It does. Like spring." She closed her eyes and inhaled. "What is that, dirt?"

They stood together drawing in the day through their noses. At length Preston said, "I think it's worms. And baby grass."

"Yeah, you're right. So. Do you want to see the lambs getting born this year, when they come?"

Preston nodded firmly.

"You could help other ways, you know. You wouldn't have to be there right when they're coming out."

"I want to see them get born," he said.

She was not afraid for him to see the writhing, fluid-soaked arrival of life, but also knew he might see death instead. That was the risk. "You might have to stay home from school," she warned. "When a ewe starts going into her labors, you have to stay with her. We'll call Miss Rose. She'll let you be excused."

"We're allowed to know about it," Preston said.

"About what?"

"Babies getting born from their mothers."

"Is that right?"

"Yeah. Isaac Frye's big sister did a baby on the toilet."

"Oh gosh, Preston. How did that come up?"

He shrugged. "It's okay. He made some of the girls cry, but Miss Rose made him stop it, and then she talked to us. About the family life."

Once again Dellarobia had to salute the spirited Miss Rose. "And you're okay with all that, for the time being?" she asked

He shrugged again. "Yeah."

It was hard not to press the question of Isaac Frye's sister, whose misery Dellarobia could imagine all too well, unfortunately. Another pregnant teenager sliding the loose broken latch on a bathroom stall, trying to stave off the unyielding future. She wondered if it was really born in the bathroom. And if it lived. Preston would never imagine his own family was forged through events hardly more graceful than these.

They watched the sun paint pink light across the belly of every cloud in the eastern sky. Preston suddenly pointed up into the middle distance. "Look."

A pair of monarchs fluttered together above the road. A surprising sight so early in the day, and not ordinary flight, but a persistent buffeting of one against the other. The pair moved up and down as if trapped in a vertical column of air. Eventually they locked together and dropped on the road, flapping. Soon they disconnected and rose again, returning to their aerial tango.

"Are they fighting?" Preston asked. "Or is that family life?"

A question for the ages. "I'm not sure," she said.

In a moment she added, "Wow. You know what?"

"What?"

"They might be coming out of their long winter's nap. Dr. Byron's been telling me to watch for this. If they wake up and start trying to mate, that's really good news for the monarchs. And you spotted it, Preston. You were the first one."

They watched the spiraling duo move up their path as if drawn along by invisible threads. *If* this was a pair, *if* they mated, *if* the female lifted her sights and went

513

out to the vernal hills to secure the right unfurling leaf. If, then.

"Dr. Byron says the males go a little bit crazy," she confided. "They'll start going after anything that moves, trying to grab hold."

"How come?" Preston asked.

"You know. Girlfriend stuff. Smooching!" She grabbed Preston and planted kisses all over his head, against his roaring grunts. Then let him go.

Both the butterflies fell into the road again, very close to where they stood, and for a moment the two insects lay stunned, open-winged. Then the one crawled slowly atop the other and they flopped around a bit. Preston and Dellarobia crept close enough to see the underneath partner, female presumably, stretch out her long black abdomen in a taut, expectant way. She's the one with the stiffy, Dellarobia thought, keeping that one to herself. The guy on top was using his abdomen more like an elephant's trunk, probing the tip around, feeling for its target. The search seemed to take a long time, and was weirdly erotic. Enough for Dellarobia to have reservations about crouching in the road watching an act of copulation with her kindergartner. Who was riveted.

"Gaa," he said quietly when the clasp connected. There was no mistaking the plug in the socket, both members stiffened with a visible energy. For a moment they all froze, mother and son, butterfly and mate. The male began to flap, still linked, trying for liftoff. His helpful wife folded her wings and consented to be dragged as he pulled their weight a wobbly few feet above the road, then dropped. Then lifted again.

"Mom!" Preston howled. The bus had appeared over the hill. She sent him out of the road and prepared to flag down the bus if necessary. But the butterfly lovers achieved liftoff, taking their business up into the big maple. She retreated to the shoulder.

"Okay, buddy." She stood a few paces from her son, giving him his dignity. "Make sure you learn stuff today."

"I will," he vowed, awaiting the driver's signal before he charged across the road to climb aboard. Dellarobia always found the blaze of alternate-flashing school-bus lights a little surreal, coming and going through the veil of morning darkness. The hiss of released brakes gave way to the throaty diesel grumble, and her son was off to the world once more, leaving her dumbly bereft, unsettled by the morning's several surprises.

She shoved her hands in her coat pockets and tried to move her mind into the day. If this was the end of diapause for the monarchs, that was huge. Ovid would be keen to do dissections, or if more sacrifice was unbearable, to palpate live females for the sperm packets that proved they were mating. She felt impatient with news she could not share. He was gone today. She didn't have a phone number, except the one from which he'd first called her back in December, presumably from his house in New Mexico. No way could she call there.

Very early this morning she'd heard his vehicle pull out, for parts unknown. He'd only said he would be gone all day. Some kind of interview seemed likely, given the way the Ovid-and-Tina video had gone viral. On Thursday Dovey had texted hourly updates on the number of views: hundreds, thousands, hundreds of thousands. Whatever qualms people had about scientists, they were thrilled to watch one rip into an ice-queen newscaster of some repute. Ovid was chagrined when he finally watched it himself, and Dellarobia felt for him; she knew that awful exposure. But he at least had put his turn at fame to good use. He'd been truthful. The first of his words Dovey had captured were "This is what science looks like," and that's what she tagged the post. She said it came up ninth on the list now, when you Googled "science."

Dellarobia reentered her house feeling guilty without cause as she met Cub's skeptical gaze. Not an unusual feeling. "Going to work in your pajama pants?" he asked.

"Nope. Dr. Byron's gone someplace today." He had urged her to take the day off too, she had put in many an extra hour. But the prospect of a workless morning didn't excite her. She hung up her coat in the hallway and came into the kitchen. Cub had just unsnapped Cordelia's terry-cloth bib and was wiping the oatmeal off her face.

"Cordie's not going to Lupe's, then?" The plane of his brow lifted in surprise.

Dellarobia filled and refilled her coffee mug a few times with hot water from the tap, and shook it out. It wasted hot water, but her mug always got so chilled by the bus wait, it would spoil a second cup if she didn't warm it up. "Sorry I didn't mention that. I was debating whether I should go in anyway. There's still stuff to do in the lab, without him around."

Cub made a game of dabbing Cordelia's cheeks and nose while she tried to smack his hand. Eventually they called a truce, and he lifted her out of the high chair. "Well, I'm going over to Mother's," he said, rolling down the sleeves of his flannel shirt and brushing oatmeal off the front. "She's got a load of stuff she wants me to haul over to the church for the town ministry."

Dellarobia took a gratifying swallow of scalding coffee and leaned back against the counter. "You know what? I've got a bunch of Preston's outgrown pants I could give them." The town ministry was a free food pantry for Feathertown's needy, now expanding to offer clothing and winter coats, child sizes needed especially. For those who found themselves even below the Second Time Around bracket. "What's Hester giving away?" she asked.

Cub shrugged, a gesture identical to the one his son had offered her ten minutes earlier. "Some of her canned goods, I guess. But she wants me to take my truck to haul over that old chifforobe upstairs. They're needing places to hang up all the coats."

Dellarobia was still trying on the prospect of being a

517

donor. She always took the kids' clothes back for the minuscule trade-in discount. Now that she thought about it, she couldn't recall having given anything away, ever. Not for charity, per se. "You mean that giant wardrobe in your old room?" she asked. "That thing's a beast."

"Well, Mother decided it needs to go to the ministry," Cub said.

"How about I go with you to help," Dellarobia offered unexpectedly. She and Cub had things to talk about.

Cub laughed. "A lot of help you'll be, moving a chifforobe."

"Brains instead of brawn, okay? I'll open doors and stuff. We can leave Cordie with Hester for a couple of hours, they'll both live. Just give me a sec to gather up those clothes." Dellarobia got dressed and efficiently culled the kids' drawers, where the outgrown items seemed to outnumber those that fit by a margin of two to one. Within thirty minutes they had packed up five grocery bags of donations and descended on Hester without warning, Cordelia and her toy bag in tow. Hester was in her living room with the niddy-noddy out and yarn all over everywhere, engrossed in winding skeins and measuring yardage. Cordie was going to be no help with this endeavor, it was plain to see, but Hester resigned herself, sending the parents upstairs to size up the chifforobe and carry down the boxes she'd packed. Dellarobia followed Cub's slow climb up to the

518

room that had contained his boyhood and, for its first few months, their marriage.

The room was unchanged, which hardly surprised Dellarobia. Nothing about it was ever altered even to accommodate the large life events she'd brought into it. She quaked at the barren familiarity of the 4H ribbons tacked along the crown molding, the ancient comic book collection, the two unopened bottles of Coca-Cola that were some special commemorative of something. Cub's football trophies ran along the bookshelf, a string of small golden men all frozen in the same sprint, helmeted jaw thrust forward, left foot off the ground. She knew their look was deceptive; the little athletes were not really bronze but some kind of weightless plastic.

"I wonder if Hester's even changed the sheets since we moved out," she said. The bedspread was the same white chenille, extremely thin and to Dellarobia's mind ungenerous, considering all the quilts that were folded away elsewhere in the house. But it was what they got. That was the weirdest part of living here as a married person, just accepting: this bedspread, this room, supper at seven. Cub's parents in the adjacent room. She fell onto the bed, face up, arms flung out. "Oh, man. Remember this bed?"

"I ought to," Cub said. He went to the wardrobe and pulled the metal cube of a tape measure from his pocket. The piece was massive, with twin oak doors and an inlaid cornice on top. Probably worth something. Dellarobia wondered what had possessed Hester suddenly to give it away. Anything to impress Bobby Ogle.

"I never really felt like a wife in this room, you know? Much less a newlywed."

"Well, what did you feel like?" Cub asked.

"I don't know. Like a kid. I know this sounds weird, but more like a sister." She laughed. "A really pregnant one."

"Dang it," Cub said. "Four inches too long for the truck bed."

Dellarobia viewed the ceiling. Old houses were supposed to give a warm vibe, but this one was bleak. The large, uncurtained window didn't help. North facing; maybe that was it. There used to be curtains in here, she was sure. She remembered the print, NFL team logos on a blue ground. Hester must have run across that bolt of fabric when Cub was just little, a Tom Thumb linebacker with big dreams. Strange, that those curtains came down.

"Dad says this thing comes apart," Cub said, sounding vexed. He ran his hand along the seam between the top of the doors and the cornice. "The base and the top are supposed to be separate pieces. That would sure make this easier to get in the truck."

Dellarobia rolled off the bed and went to get the desk chair, which she knew to have been the least used piece of furniture in this room. Her early married life had involved nagging her spouse to sit and do his homework. She carried the chair over to the wardrobe and stood on it to examine the cornice, peering between the back of it and the wall. "Get me a Phillips-head," she commanded lightly. "There's a long brace up the back that holds it together. We'll have to pull it out from the wall a little to get at it, so ask Hester for some throw rugs too, so we won't scratch the floor."

Cub hitched up his jeans and trudged off, thankful for clear instructions.

~

Heavy clouds scooted across the sky with disconcerting speed. After Cub and his father loaded the wardrobe in the truck they'd tied a tarp over it, and sure enough, a spittle of freezing rain began hitting the windshield before they got to Mountain Fellowship. On Highway 7 they sat waiting to make the left turn as a long line of cars with their lights on crawled toward them. A funeral, maybe, or just the weather. The turn signal clicked its untiring intentions.

"We shouldn't have let Bear carry that thing," Dellarobia said. "I thought he was going to have a heart attack when you all were halfway down the stairs."

"Nah, he's tough," Cub said, resting his forearms on the wheel.

"So you think," Dellarobia said. She'd seen the man's face. Straining, neck veins and ligaments bulging. He looked like a tied-up horse in a barn fire.

At length they reached the fellowship hall and drove

521

around back, as per Hester's instructions, to find Blanchie Bise and two other women inside, sorting donated clothes. They had layette sets arrayed all over the long, steel-legged folding tables, bringing to mind the shower these church matrons had thrown for Dellarobia, way back when. A sort of baby-wedding-come-to-Jesus package, not well attended. Evidently this strategy of welcoming pregnant sinners worked well for the likes of Crystal, but it had soured Dellarobia for life on this fellowship hall, which never failed to stir the same post-traumatic stew of panic and rejection. She stood in the doorway now trying to put those thoughts in their place, after this many years, good grief, while Cub had an overly long discussion with Blanchie down at the other end of the hall. This was one of those days when Dellarobia's past was tagging her around like a hungry cur. Finally Cub started back toward her, shaking his head. "They want us to take it downtown, to the mission. We can unload the boxes here for sorting, but they don't want to have to haul that chifforobe twice."

"Makes sense," Dellarobia said. "Is there somebody there to help us unload it?"

Cub turned on his heel and headed back to Blanchie, having neglected to ask. Unfortunately, they learned, Beulah Rasberry was down at the storefront running things by herself today. Beulah was no furniture mover, at eighty, with her string-bean arms. Blanchie called her son at Cleary Compressors to drive over on his lunch break to meet them in Feathertown and help unload the cabinet. He could be there in an hour.

"We can just wait here," Cub said, heading for his truck. Dellarobia slid in on the passenger side in time to watch him relax, letting his head fall back to its angle of repose. The man could not hold on to tension with a baseball glove. Dellarobia flipped open the glove compartment, which was tightly packed with tools, work gloves, napkins, and one squashed paper cup with a straw-impaled plastic lid. Extra pressure was required to get the door to close again and latch. Cub's breathing slowed to an oceanic hiss. She was envious of her husband's on-off switch. The prospect of sitting in here for an hour with nothing whatsoever to occupy her, not even a bad magazine, confronted Dellarobia as purely impossible. She checked her phone and found she'd missed a text, probably while they were at Hester's. It was one of Dovey's church-sign sightings, she must have sent it on her way to work: FORBIDDEN FRUITS PRODUCE A LOT OF JAMS.

Right, Dellarobia thought. Such as my entire adult life.

She closed her phone and punched Cub. "Let's go to the Dairy Prince."

He sat up straight, looking startled. "Really?"

"I'm not suggesting we rob a bank. Just Dairy Prince. We haven't gone out to eat in over two years."

"Really?" he asked again.

"Well. *I* haven't." She rolled her eyes toward the

glove box. "Let's go get a milk shake or something. I'll buy. Come on, take a shot. Your wife's gone wild."

Obediently he turned over the engine and slung the truck into gear. On the way to town they passed Dovey's white duplex, its grounds fully claimed by her brothers' automotive collection, and drove the length of Feathertown's mostly dead main street. The Fellowship Mission had had its pick of empty storefronts from which to operate its charities. Dellarobia tried to remember what used to be in the other buildings. A drugstore, a hardware, the diner where she'd worked. The fabric shop, her mother's mainstay. A little grocery run by a man with one arm who doled out hard candies to kids, probably to make them less afraid of him. Mr. Squire. People went to Walmart now, for all of the above. Even the Dairy Prince looked bombed out, with a square of brown cardboard like an eye patch covering one of the two walk-up windows in front. Cub went to place their order, which was valiant. The freezing rain was picking up. He came back with her milkshake and a burger and fries for himself. Their seductive fatty fragrance filled the cab, making her wish she'd gone a little more crazy here. She swiped his fries one at a time while they watched the windshield pale from blurry to opaque. Rain slammed the roof, isolating them from the world in their metal capsule.

"Here we are on a date," she said. "Right back where we started from."

"Not really," he murmured, having just taken a big

bite. She waited while he chewed and swallowed, curious to know what he felt had changed.

"Truck's got a different engine," he finally observed.

She swallowed too much of the icy milkshake and an ache seized her throat. "That's it?" she asked, when the pain passed. "Eleven years of marriage, and that's what we've got, a rebuilt engine?"

He retreated into his lunch. She stole some more fries and stared out through the blur. Like a cataract. Rushing water, a blindness. Her father hadn't lived long enough to be old, but he'd had cataracts, brought on by some trauma she'd never quite understood.

"So," she said. "Are we just never going to talk about the other stuff?"

"What other stuff?"

"Any of it. Why we did this. That poor little baby."

"What for? It's gone."

"It is not *gone*. Not like something that never existed. It *was*, Cub."

"But then it *wasn't*. Anyway, we had more kids. Just let bygones be bygones."

A change in the density of the rain now gave a vague visibility to certain shapes: the red rectangle of the Dairy Prince sign, a dark green Dumpster. She considered what her father must have endured with that kind of diminished vision. Seeing without seeing.

"They're not bygone," she said. "Everything changed, and that's still here."

"What do you mean?"

"Great day in the morning, Cub. We should have used a condom, and we didn't. No going back. Look at what's in your life. A house, a wife, Preston and Cordie. All because we accidentally got me pregnant in high school."

Cub looked hurt. "You're acting like we wouldn't have got married."

She blinked her eyes. "Cub, seriously? Were you, like, thinking of popping the question? Before that happened?"

He looked away from her, toward the shapes that came and went with the waves of rain. Dellarobia could imagine the inner structure of her husband's world, in which events confirmed themselves. Their marriage must be good, because marriages were. It had come to pass.

"I appreciate you for manning up. I do," she said. "I had no family, and then all of a sudden I had your family. But you were there too, Cub. You know what I'm saying. We were headed in different directions. You can't tell me we weren't."

Cub pressed his thumbs against the inside corners of his eyes, and his breathing grew ragged, and she felt terrible and cruel, as if she were prodding him with a stick. She should just let him be. It's what she had always done, let him be. "I honestly thought I was going to college," she said in a low, flat voice. "You'd find some nice girl and settle down. How come we can't say what's true?"

"We love each other now," he said. "That's what matters."

"I know. People say that. We do. You can make yourself love a person, we've done a fair job of that. But there's other stuff, Cub."

"Like what?"

"I don't know. Respect? You can't manufacture that. You can't demand it at gunpoint. Whatever. You earn it. Like a salary or something."

"I respect you," he said.

"I know. And you're sweet to me. It's just never quite—I don't know how to put this—" She pressed her lips together and shook her head. "It's like I'm standing by the mailbox waiting all the time for a letter. Every day you come along and put something else in there. A socket wrench, or a milkshake. It's not bad stuff. Just the wrong things for *me*."

Cub now sat forward with his arms and head on the steering wheel, mute with grief, his shoulders shaking. Dellarobia felt stunned. His reaction made this real. She could easily have stayed home and skipped this conversation. She leaned over to give him an awkward hug. "I'm sorry," she said. "I'm thankful for our children. But I'm not what you need."

He spoke without lifting his head. "You're different, Dellarobia. It's because of all that business up the mountain. I wish they'd never lit down here."

"That's not true. It started way before that. I never told you. But I went up there by myself one day before

527

anybody else knew about the butterflies, and I saw them." She felt breathless, as if falling through air. "I was running off."

He sat up and gave her a wary glance before reaching across to flip open the glove box. She helped him get a handful of the fast food napkins that were crammed in there. She took some herself, and they blew their noses in a companionable, married way.

"I knew about that," he finally said.

"What? *What* did you know?"

Cub looked at her directly, though it seemed to take more effort than he could sustain. "Mother found out some way. She said you meant to do away with yourself."

Dellarobia's heart thrummed in her ears. "Hester told you this? When?"

"I don't know," he said. "A while back. She's fretted over it."

The world in Dellarobia's mind took a tumble, and nothing in it felt true at all. Hester's strange confessions, Cub's attentiveness. She felt like a blind person grappling for the doorway. "That's not it," was all she could say. She sat quiet for a moment, considering the threshold where she found herself. "I wasn't going to kill myself. They put that on the news, but it's a lie. I was going to run out on our marriage in a stupid way. I'm sorry. I ended up not doing it. I ran into that . . . whatever it was, the butterflies, on my way up there. And it knocked me on my butt. It was like I had to come back and do the right thing."

528

"Which is what?" Cub asked, sounding more dismayed than angry.

"Which is I don't know what," she said. "I'm still trying to figure that out. To do something for the right reasons? Instead of another mistake that can't be turned back. That's my whole life, Cub. Just flying from one darn thing to the next."

"You're in love with him." Cub stated it, rather than asking, which relieved her of the burden of answering. Now he did look angry, heavy-browed. He scowled at the windshield. She wished this rain would stop. It felt like the end of the world.

"People make mistakes," she said finally.

"According to you, that's all you and I ever did."

She nodded. "Mistakes wreck your life. But they make what you have. It's kind of all one." She felt a humorless ripple move through her chest. "You know what Hester told me when we were working the sheep one time? She said it's no good to complain about your flock, because it's the put-together of all your past choices."

Cub nodded slowly, understanding this. He set his hands on the wheel. Soon he would start the engine, and they would go. "I can't help it," he said. "I still wish they'd never lit down here. Those butterflies."

You and the butterflies both, she thought. We wish.

℮

Dellarobia lay in the darkness trying not to begrudge her husband's profound and tranquil sleep. It could not be as easy as it looked, to be Cub Turnbow. After their conversation in the truck they'd said no more, and slipped back into a day that seemed bizarrely untouched. Furniture delivered, Cordie picked up, Cub congenial throughout. The sorrow she'd laid bare for him did not disperse. It would hang around as the long-toothed phantom it had always been, haunting even the commonest transactions of her household, haunting her skin, everywhere. While Cub failed to see it.

But something did follow them into the house, unsettling them both during supper with the children, making the air in their bedroom cold. He'd said good night as if they were friends parting ways, then rolled to his side and slept the sleep of a mountain range while she stared at the black air, dividing the river of her desperation into rivulets until some of them seemed navigable. At moments she felt light and untethered, the same glimpse of release she'd had many times before. The thrill of throwing a good life away, she remembered thinking once: one part rapture. Outweighed by the immense and measurable parameters of a family's life. She refused to be the first to act. If Cub saw fit to walk through eleven more years of marriage, after the blunt truths she'd told him, she could do the same. Maybe she didn't want Hester to be right about her character. For one thing. And maybe she was more like Cub than not, simply believing in what had come to pass. Marriage had its own heft, and that had to be respected. She watched lines of light grow slowly along the window blind as a day began to fill the void. The one impulse that transfixed her, that she understood to be of no real use, was to go to the window and look out. To see if his camper had returned.

He hadn't said how long he would be gone. Probably she would have time to turn over every conversation with Ovid she could recall, as she always did. That enterprise had a way of becoming furtive and miserable, like handling gritty coins at the bottom of a purse. Finding all the regrettable notes, her badly spoken self, her brashness, led on by Dovey, in forcing notoriety on him this week. It hadn't been wrong for her to bring Tina to the lab to interview him, but she could have protected him from the rest. Instead she'd claimed that video as an act of Ovid's courage. It proved his integrity, she'd told him many times, allowing him no other option. She avoided thinking about the selfish undertones of her enthusiasm: that the video redeemed Dellarobia, striking down all the falsehoods committed in her name, and with her image. There was no beautiful miracle, no small-town drama starring herself as the Butterfly Venus, she was no party to that lie. The butterflies were a symptom of vast biological malignancies, and all nicer bets were off. Ovid needed to set the record straight, whether or not he was ready to do that. This was the weight Dellarobia laid down like a sandbag at her center: that he did need her.

She waited until the clock's red numbers squared off at 7:00 before getting up, and she did not look out from the bedroom. In the kitchen, after making coffee, she allowed herself to lift the shade and see nothing. The barren rectangle of his absence. After she had poured bowls of cereal for the kids and listened awhile to their morning chatter, Preston in his robot pajamas, Cordie eating with a blanket over her head and bowl, Dellarobia allowed herself to get up and go look again. Each time, bereavement slammed her. An empty socket, an amputation. He must be angry with her.

After breakfast Preston stood on tiptoe and nearly pressed his glasses against the kitchen window to count the monarch pairs circling above the back pasture, committing themselves to family life above the placid pregnant flock. His thrill was electric. They were waking up. She tried to tap into that current but failed, standing beside her son at the window, waiting stupidly. She got out the roasting pan for the lamb shoulder roast Hester had sent home with them yesterday. She would slow-cook it all afternoon and they'd have leftovers for a week. On a different day she would have felt the joy of that too, the relief of plenty. She opened the curtains in the living room, stunned by her wooden spirit, gaining no purchase on the bright sky. She felt sealed inside her airtight house, a feeling so entirely familiar, wondering how long before they breathed up all the oxygen. With mechanical hands she vacuumed the kids' bedroom, then the living room. Cordie climbed onto the sofa and stood looking over its back, out at the road, having inferred that on this day windows held the key.

After a time she pointed. "Mama look. Lady."

The lady wore a short winter coat over a long skirt and strode slowly along the roadside, bearing her magnificent large head. Dellarobia shut off the vacuum and went to kneel next to Cordie on the sofa. It was moving toward them. Or *she* was, certainly a she, lean and graceful like a slow-motion shot of a fashion model striding down the runway of this landscape. Maybe from one of those project shows where people fashioned fantastical outfits out of silk handkerchiefs and dandelion fluff. The oversize head was an illusion, stout locks of hair emerging from a blue headscarf elaborately wound and tucked. A gift-wrapped head. The blue print skirt with its manifold tiny pleats rippled like curtains in front of a window fan. In the gravel margin between road and weedy ditch she came along at a dreamy pace, her head tilted back on the long recurved stem of her neck, with time stopped around her, it seemed. No cars passed, the cattle did not look up. Her skin was the brown color of winter pasture, her face a mysterious clause between the commas of long gold earrings: a completely impossible person to see out the window. Dellarobia and both the kids watched wide-eyed as she turned up their driveway and proceeded without hesitation alongside the house toward their back field. They all charged to the bedroom where Cub still slept, crowding close together to peer through the blinds. The camper was there. While Dellarobia was vacuuming, it had materialized. The lady moved unhurriedly toward the vehicle. The lady went to the metal door and disappeared inside.

In minutes, they both stood at the kitchen door. She was nearly as tall as Ovid, cut from the same sinuous cloth, one shade darker, but her accent was not like his. Her voice was a deep, honeyed song overlaid with precision, consonants so clear the touch of tongue to teeth was audible. Her name, of course, Dellarobia knew.

Juliet. Emerson. "I know, right?" Juliet said with a musical laugh. "Ovid and Juliet, Emerson Byron. People say we sound like an AP English exam."

Whatever that test might entail, it was not the source of Dellarobia's dismay. Ovid suddenly was talkative. He had gone to meet her plane yesterday in Knoxville, but everything went wrong. Dellarobia was at a loss to follow the train of mishaps. An equipment failure, a missed connection, he'd ended up driving all the way to Atlanta to meet her, and driving back after dark. They'd stopped somewhere in north Georgia to spend the night in a Walmart parking lot. Preston and Cordie stood close to their mother and stared at this new Ovid with his arm around the lady.

"Juliet is not crazy about long drives in the camper," Ovid said.

"It's okay, I just took a little walk to stretch my legs," she said, obviously not unhappy and surely, Dellarobia thought, long-legged enough. She had a way of slowly

534

lowering her eyes when she spoke that was not coy but generous, as if she hoped to send attention elsewhere. An unlikely expectation, looking as she did. Even her closed eyes were beautiful and enormous, like bronze tulip bulbs. The headscarf was printed with peacock feathers and twined in some inscrutable way with her vigorous hair.

"Have you seen our part of the country before?" Dellarobia thought to ask.

"No. I grew up in the South, but *flat* south. Mississippi. Ovid didn't tell me it was so beautiful here."

"Well," Dellarobia said. "Welcome."

They wanted a recommendation for where they could dine out that night. "My wife has found me out," Ovid said. "My trash bin is filled with pork-and-bean tins, and from this she deduces I have gone completely feral."

"Not fe-ral," Juliet said, lightly imitating his accent. "Just reverting to bachelorhood in the wilds, as always."

The accused stood with his arm around his wife's waist as if he did not mean to let go. They looked like two willow trees, struck by lightning and fused. Dellarobia told them dining out in Feathertown occurred at the Dairy Prince, and confessed that anything else was beyond her sphere. She did the only thing ordinary kindness allowed, not to mention the Scriptures, gesturing at the large joint of meat in the roasting pan on her counter: more than enough to entertain strangers.

For thereby some have entertained angels unawares, though angels, she knew, traveled with baggage.

e

Ovid and Juliet had met in Mexico City at a conference on monarchs. He was there as a representative of science, and she of art. She was not an artist herself, she was quick to explain in her demurring way, the smooth angular wrist flicking away attention, its bangles riveting the eye. A folklorist, she said, a word Dellarobia somehow linked with those painted wooden bracelets. They resembled toys you'd find in an attic, relics from the pre-plastic era. Juliet studied art made by other people who did not think they were artists, first in Mississippi and then Africa and eventually Mexico for her doctoral research. She'd made a study of decorative objects made by people who lived near the monarch roosts, down through the ages.

"You'd be amazed what the monarchs represent for them," Juliet said. "Even now. Some people believe they're the souls of dead children."

Dellarobia felt astonished by connections unforeseen. "One of Preston's little friends told me that. Her family used to live there."

Dellarobia's brain felt like a pot boiling over on the stove. There was way too much going on in there. Four adults and two kids at her kitchen table left no room for anything else, so she carved the roast on the counter and filled the plates, arranging the potatoes and carrots on each, spooning the gravy and delivering them fast so it wouldn't all go cold. In other times Cub would have announced, "My wife used to be a hasher," not in a teasing way but with the reverence of an ox in the presence of flight. His wife could handle three plates at once. The wide and bottomless emptiness she would feel, being admired for such a thing as that. But tonight Cub hardly spoke. She could see in his eyes that he had gained some drift of her expansive unhappiness. Although from her labored attempts to explain things yesterday, he'd probably picked up only one narrow band of the spectrum: that he disappointed her. He'd spent the day building lambing jugs, expressing himself with a hammer in an empty barn.

Juliet had walked through the back door this evening in slim jeans and tall shoes and a dazzling loose tunic, orange and yellow and black, and a yellow headscarf wrapped differently from the earlier one, allowing a greater overspilling of her hair. Dellarobia's eye kept going back to the innumerable glossy braids the same way she admired a gorgeous jacket lining, for the work involved. Ovid and Juliet handed her something in a twisted, candle-like paper bag they called a Riesling, which turned out to be wine. They apologized that it didn't really go with lamb, Dellarobia apologized for not really having a way to open it, and Ovid went to fetch a corkscrew from his home in the yard. Cub did not partake of the Riesling, though Dellarobia did, just a little. Their best glasses were heavy blue plastic. Preston asked for a taste and, denied that, wanted to smell it. He took a long, hearty whiff and howled, "Pew!"

"You probably think we're cave people," Dellarobia said, though she did not feel as if she were in a cave. That she'd stepped off a cliff was more like it, yesterday in the cab of Cub's truck, and was falling still. Every known feeling belonged to someone else, some previous occupant. This house was what it was, Ovid had seen it, and honestly there was no knowing what might please or offend Juliet. Apparently she collected paintings made by old men on discarded saw blades, which sounded like something Hester might buy at a yard sale. Juliet had six or seven years on Dellarobia, plus an education and fashion sense and many things Dellarobia suspected she was not equipped to detect. Juliet's face, alone, deserved its own audience. Her mouth was broad and expressive, somehow muscular, in the way her lips curled outward when she spoke. She smiled with her chin forward like someone singing in a choir. Cub had come late to the table with his hair still wet from the shower and his mind unprepared to be blown by the likes of Juliet. He scrutinized her with an attention span that was probably inappropriate, and definitely atypical. Tonight he did not channel-surf. He stayed with the Juliet channel.

Dellarobia sat down with the last plate and gestured for everyone to dig in. They both made appreciative groans, genuinely pleased, she could tell. It was hard to fake that kind of enthusiasm for a meal. She remembered his offhand remark about his wife's cooking that she'd taken for disloyalty, and now saw that Juliet probably would have agreed and laughed about it, had she been there. Juliet had bigger fish to fry. Suddenly Dellarobia thought of the knitters.

"You know what? There are people up here on the mountain doing what you're talking about. Making representations of the butterflies."

Juliet kindly spared her the embarrassment of going too far with this. She knew all about the knitters already, had followed their blog and communicated with them directly. She wanted to photograph their work and do interviews, but had had to wait until her break in classes to fly out for this visit.

"Juliet's teaching load is oppressive," Ovid said. "She is the departmental mule."

"Associate professor," Juliet said, with an unmulish smile. "Not a luminary like this one."

"She has a sabbatical coming up," Ovid said.

"I do," she agreed. "Our first whole winter together in seven years of marriage."

"I'm not sure how she will tolerate me," Ovid said, and Juliet smiled again with her amazing glossy mouth. Plainly, she would tolerate him.

Juliet knew things about monarchs her husband did not. Dellarobia asked about the name King Billies, and she knew it. From colonial times, she said. Protestant settlers noticed this butterfly wore the royal colors of their prince, William of Orange, who got around eventually to being the king of England. The name *monarch* came from the same old king.

"You never told me that," Ovid said to his wife.

Juliet's eyes blinked in their slow-motion way. "You never asked."

"You see my strategy, Dellarobia. I keep myself surrounded with smart women."

Ovid wore a loose, bright shirt similar to Juliet's with the same embroidered front placket instead of buttons. Dellarobia would not have dreamed he owned a shirt like that. Like the day he'd worn a tie for the kindergartners; here was a whole different Ovid she knew nothing about. He too had a father who'd died young, Alcidus Byron. Juliet never got to meet him but was great friends with Ovid's mother, Raquida, a forceful woman who supervised all postal affairs on the island of St. Thomas. Ovid's most comforting pastime as a boy had been to float in the sea and watch the sea turtles grazing in the sea-grass beds. Juliet was the one who described this. He'd taken her snorkeling many times, beginning with their honeymoon. "You can't be anything but happy when you watch them. Their little turtle mouths are always smiling." She demonstrated, moving her head slowly from side to side as if she were chewing sea grass instead of potatoes.

"When I look at your sheep, I am often thinking of turtles," Ovid confessed. "I will miss those sheep.

Especially the naughty brown fellows that stay up on the hill."

Dellarobia was floored. She didn't think Ovid paid one bit of attention to the sheep. "This is Reggie we're eating, by the way. One of the naughty brown ones. Maybe that's not an introduction for polite company."

"To Reggie," Juliet said, raising her plastic glass. Preston clinked with his cup and made Cordie lift her juice box. They were all hungry, and for several minutes everyone ate quietly, even Cordelia, giving Dellarobia the unaccustomed pleasure of hearing the clicks of forks against plates and tasting the melting texture of the slow-cooked roast. All the pasture and sunny days that had been Reggie.

"We get to name the lambs this year," Preston said. "Because we're the ones getting them born."

"What will you name them?" Juliet asked.

"Mama says one will be Tina Ultner."

"Oops," Dellarobia said. "Maybe don't mention that at school, Preston."

Ovid seemed appreciative. "You think she will be safe for consumption?"

"We'll probably just shear her," Dellarobia said.

"That post is brilliant, by the way," Juliet said. "Did you make the video?"

Dellarobia was surprised. "My friend Dovey. You heard about that?"

"Are you kidding? I saw it before he called me. A friend of ours in Canada forwarded the link. My Ovid

541

is a *star*." She reached her arm around his shoulders and hugged him like a little boy. He grinned like a boy. "Honestly? I think it's the best presentation he's given in years. I've probably told him that fifty times since Thursday."

Dellarobia's surprise gained a new dimension.

"He's so *reticent*. He hides his light under a bushel." Juliet playfully cuffed him under the chin. "The climate science community will probably give him a medal now."

"The purple heart," Ovid said.

"You're still in one piece," said his wife. They toasted to Tina Ultner.

Dellarobia wondered what Ovid had told her about his first evening at this table. All that lame-brained prattle, her monarch-fact parade, the testicle balloon above the table. The emergency-room fever of that evening's embarrassment seemed fairly tame now, given the litany of embarrassing delusions that were still to come, regarding Ovid and herself. Her vision of Juliet as an interloper now struck Dellarobia as bizarre. It was hard to feel the remotest sympathy for any of the different fools she had been. As opposed to the fool she was probably being now. People hang on for dear life to that one, she thought: the fool they are right now.

The climate subject left them a little subdued. Ovid confessed they didn't know where they would spend their sabbatical winter, with the monarch system disintegrating under the pressures of fires and floods. His life was now at the whim of a livid ecosystem. Dellarobia watched as Cub meticulously cleaned his plate, avoiding eye contact, not out of step with the present company but staring through it. If he'd said one word this whole evening she could not remember it. She thought it unlikely that he had any real issue with Ovid and Juliet, Cub was not one to put a lot of energy into tact; he was just brooding, as he had been all day. It was so public and implicating, his sulk, like a forehead bruise on one of the kids that customarily made her blurt explanations to casual strangers at the grocery. Yet here she sat, detached, as if this gigantic miserable husband were not her fault. Just being the fools we are right now, she thought: a condition that inevitably changed, often for the worse. In one transcendent moment buoyed by about two ounces of Riesling she saw the pointlessness of clinging to that life raft, that hooray-we-are-saved conviction of having already come through the stupid parts, to arrive at the current enlightenment. The hard part is letting go, she could see that. There is no life raft; you're just freaking swimming all the time.

Ovid was explaining something to Juliet that he called the theory of the territorial divide. With some confusion Dellarobia understood this was *her* theory, he was attributing it to her, though the terms he used were unfamiliar: climate-change denial functioned like folk art for some people, he said, a way of defining survival in their own terms. But it's not indigenous, Juliet argued. It's like a cargo cult. Introduced from the outside, corporate motives via conservative media. But now it's become fully identified with the icons of local culture, so it's no longer up for discussion.

"The key thing is," Juliet said, resting her elbow on the table, that beautiful wrist bending under the weight of its wooden rings, "once you're talking identity, you can't just lecture that out of people. The condescension of outsiders won't diminish it. That just galvanizes it."

Dellarobia felt abruptly conscious of her husband and her linoleum. "Christ on the cross," she said without enthusiasm. "The rebel flag on mudflaps, science illiteracy. That would be us."

"I am troubled by this theory, Dellarobia," Ovid said, "but I can't say you are wrong. I've read a lot of scholarly articles on the topic, but you make more sense."

"Well, *yeah*," Juliet said, "that's kind of the point, that outsiders won't get it." She looked at Dellarobia, moving her head slightly from side to side in some secret girl signal, as if they were in league. Dellarobia felt herself resisting the invitation. Juliet went to yard sales for entertainment. She'd seen the coral reefs. Which according to Ovid were bleaching out and dying fast, all over the world. Preston would never get to see one. Dellarobia felt like taking a tire iron to something, ideally not now, ideally not herself. She got up to clear the plates.

Cordie had been good through most of supper, if lifting her shirt and playing with her navel counted as being good. And squeezing boiled potatoes in her fists, watching white potato mush squirt out between her fingers. "Good" was a euphemism for quiet. But the internal weather of Cordelia always turned quickly, and now suddenly she was fussy, ready for a bath and bed. Cub lifted her by the armpits and retreated, barely nodding good night. Preston meanwhile was getting cranked up. His science buzz, Dellarobia called this. He remembered to ask Dr. Byron about the Perfect Females, the question he'd been nursing for weeks and weeks. Ovid explained they were females that had their full complement of parts.

Preston crossed his arms on the table and rested his chin there, scrutinizing Ovid for sincerity. "You mean like heads and legs?"

"Those, and more," Ovid said. "All the inside parts too. So they don't need helpers or auxiliaries to function, the way worker bees do, or soldier ants. A perfect female is the lady that can go out and start a new colony by herself."

Preston accepted this and moved on. "Just a sec," he commanded, dashing from the room.

"Excuse me please!" Dellarobia called after him.

"May-I-please-be-excused!" he yelled from the end of the house, and reappeared in a flash, sliding to a halt in his sock feet. He plopped a yellow book on the table: *Encyclopedia of Animals*, volume 15. "This says monarchs go to Florida in the winter."

"Florida and the Gulf," Dellarobia corroborated.

She'd read him the monarch entry so often the sight of the page depressed her. It was a deeply unsatisfactory account.

Ovid took the book and found the publication date, nodding. "This was the definitive version of the story in 1952. The monarchs were already a subject of scientific curiosity then. No one knew yet where they went in winter."

"Not true!" Juliet said. "Woodcutters in Michoacán knew."

"Outside of a mountain range in Michoacán," Ovid corrected, "no one knew where. And inside that range, no one knew where they summered."

"That's true," Juliet agreed. "They thought they came there to die."

"With my wife's permission, I will put it this way. At the time your book was written, the full story of the monarch migration was unknown to humanity."

"When did they find it out?" Preston asked.

The answer, to Dellarobia's astonishment, was within Ovid's lifetime. He had been just a bit older than Preston when the discovery was announced in the *National Geographic*, in 1976. A Canadian scientist chased the mystery his whole life, devising a tag that would stick to butterfly wings, recruiting volunteers to help track them, losing the trail many times. And then one winter's day, as an old man on shaky legs, he climbed a mountain in Michoacán to see what must have looked like his dream of heaven. Dellarobia listened to all this while she finished scraping the roast pan and crammed the leftovers into plastic boxes wedged into the refrigerator. Ovid could still quote passages of the article from memory: *They carpeted the ground in their tremulous legions.* He said he remembered exactly where he was when he read that article, and how he felt. She left the dishes in the sink and sat back down.

"Where were you?"

"Outside the post office, sitting on a lobster crate. I spent a lot of Saturdays there. My mother let me read the magazines before they went to their subscribers. I was so excited by the photos in that article, I ran all the way down Crown Street, all the way to West End and out a sandy road called Fortuna to the sea. I must have picked up a stick somewhere, because I remember jumping up and whacking every branch I passed, leaving a trail of flying leaves. When I got to the sea I didn't know what to do, so I threw the stick in Perseverance Bay and ran back. It was the happiest day of my life."

Dellarobia wanted, of course, to know why.

"Why," he repeated, thinking about it. "I was just like any schoolboy. I thought everything in the world was already discovered. Already in my books. A lot of dead stuff that put me to sleep. That was the day I understood the world is still living."

Juliet reached across the table to pour an inch of Riesling in everyone's glass. Ovid tapped the yellow volume with his thumb. "The books get rewritten every year, Preston. Someone has to do that."

"The monarchs are coming out of diapause," Dellarobia thought to announce.

"We saw them having their family life," Preston said. "In the *road*."

"Really," Ovid said, with convincing enthusiasm. But Juliet revealed that he already knew, he'd noticed it first thing when they drove in this morning. She claimed he was more excited about the butterflies than about seeing his wife.

It was so easy for her to say a thing like that, with full enthusiasm for the eccentric coordinates of her man. At some point in the evening Dellarobia had stopped being amazed that Ovid had turned into someone new, and understood he had become himself, in the presence of his wife. With the sense of a great weight settling, she recognized marriage. Not the precarious risk she'd balanced for years against forbidden fruits, something easily lost in a brittle moment by flying away or jumping a train to ride off on someone else's steam. She was not about to lose it. She'd never had it.

᭒

First Bear, then Hester, then Cub and Dellarobia: the four of them, it struck her, were arranged on this pew exactly as they were to be laid in the cemetery, according to a burial plan they'd paid money down on eleven years ago. Bear sitting in the sanctuary with his wife, rather than smoking it out in Men's Fellowship, was no ordinary event, probably part of the family negotiation Hester had mentioned a while ago. Right after this service, in Bobby Ogle's office, they would settle the question of the logging contract. Once she remembered this agenda, Dellarobia saw hints of it everywhere. The choir sang, *"Oh this earth is a garden, the garden of my Lord, and He walks in His garden in the cool of the day."* Maybe it was coincidence. But it also seemed possible that Bear was being set up.

Cub sat holding both Dellarobia's hands, not in the casual way he normally laid claim to her, but imploringly, his big fingers threaded tightly through all of hers. It felt like having both hands jammed through a wrought-iron gate. She abided captivity, for the complicated chain of trespasses that had gotten her stuck this way. Her detachment from Cub the previous evening seemed this morning to explode the minute the shades came up. The sight of his eyes in the mirror as he brushed his teeth, this immense sad man in his boxers, wrenched her stomach and made her turn from the light. This morning she was doomed to nurse Cub like a hangover.

"My Lord He said unto me, do you like my garden so fair?" the choir members sang earnestly, their many possible differences disguised beneath the words of a song. *"You may live in this garden if you keep the grasses green, and I'll return in the cool of the day."* In his sermon

Bobby warned against losing gratitude for the miracle of life. If God is in everything, he asked, how could we tear Him down? A love for our Creator means we love His creation. "What part of *love*," he paused, searching his audience, "do we not understand? The Bible says God owns these hills. It tells us arrogance is a sin. How is it not arrogance to see the flesh of creation as mere wealth, to be scraped bare for our use?" Dellarobia recognized a possible opening round aimed at Bear, though it might also be a metaphor for credit card debt. Living within your means was a major theme of Bobby's.

She was surprised to see Bobby had sprouted a beard since last Sunday, or the outline of one: no mustache, just a dark fringe that encircled his face like a basket handle, emphasizing its roundness. He looked to be aiming for millennial-generation today, wearing jeans and a long-tailed maroon shirt and plain black sneakers, the cheap kind she bought for her kids. Their white soles blinked as he paced around on the darkened stage.

"He'll speak to us if we let him. Little old raggedy us. We all know what it's like to come up short. We are southerners. We understand that macaroni and cheese is a vegetable." Bobby chuckled at the assent that came back to him from the darkened room. "And we are Americans." Assent came again. Bobby often spoke with his cupped hands, scooping the air toward him to emphasize his points. "We want the things we want, and we want them now. But that is not a reason to rob Peter to pay Paul."

Okay, credit card debt, Dellarobia thought, but in his closing prayer, Bobby requested of the Lord that they experience the blessing of His creation and share that with others. "May we look to these mountains that are Your home and see You are in everything. The earth is the Lord in the fullness thereof." So it could go either way.

The rest of her family headed for Bobby's office afterward, in the slow-moving way of animals maneuvering through a herd, but Dellarobia detoured through the Sunday-school building to make sure someone would still be there to watch the kids. She steered clear of Brenda's scary mother but got waylaid by Preston, who wanted her to admire the Lego enterprise he had going with Chad or Jad, an older boy she didn't recognize. This boy snarked his nose in a constant, repeating sniffle, and bore the marks of an encounter with a bag of Cheetos. The orange crumbs glowed on his hands and clothing and every Lego he'd touched, like fingerprint dust. Dellarobia made a mental note to scrub Preston before he touched food, and scooted to Bobby's office, where the rest of the family was already seated. Still in cemetery order, she noted, realizing she had no idea where the baby would fit in, even though it was the only one of them already buried. She stood a moment in the doorway, wowed by the tall windows rising behind Bobby's desk. They showed a whole lot more of God's mountains than she ever got to see from her house.

When she slid into the empty chair facing Bobby's

deep oak desk, she registered with surprise that it was Cub speaking. "There's the well water," he said, counting off points on his fingers, "and there's mudslides. That is a fact, Dad, about mudslides. I can show you where they logged over by the Food King and it brought the whole mountain down. In all this rain. What if we have another wet year again?"

"We won't," Bear said, sounding utterly sure of this.

"Well, they say it could," Cub said quietly.

Dellarobia understood she had missed something significant. Cub was already up to four fingers, and Bear looked wary and mad, as if he'd been gut-punched. Certainly he would not have expected this from his son's corner.

"That right there is all he needs to do," Hester said to Bobby with some finality, leaning forward to hand a stack of papers across the desk. The logging contract possibly, though some of those pages had come out of Hester's printer; Dellarobia recognized the weird black-to-blue fading ink color. She always waited too long to put in a new cartridge. Bobby turned slowly through the pages, giving careful attention to each, while Bear intermittently erupted in a legal-sounding phrase. "In perpetuity not to be breached," or words of that nature. Bear's black suit jacket pulled in horizontal creases across his shoulders and his white shirt collar bit into the meat of his neck. He looked like a pit bull on a short chain.

Cub examined his fingernails. Hester kept glancing

at the framed photo on Bobby's desk, probably wishing her own family had turned out that well. It was a dated picture, Winnie Ogle wore a ponytail in a scrunchy, and the twins were just toddlers. Dellarobia had lately seen those girls helping out in the nursery, preteens now, both a bit burdened by the look of too much metal around the face: braces, glasses, loopy earrings. But sweet girls, responsible kids. Dellarobia's eyes wandered around the office. It was no-fuss, like Bobby, with a simple cross on the wall and one of those colossal Bibles on a stand, the type that would break bones if dropped. He had a less menacing New American translation on his desk, she noted, pressed between a pair of weird, crudely made ceramic bookends that looked like fists. As if some superhero were trying to squeeze scripture juice out of that thing. A congregant must have made the bookends. This in fact she observed to be a theme of Bobby's decor: the Kleenex box wore a brown and pink crocheted cozy, and three hand-carved wooden wise men marched alongside his open desk calendar, carrying paper clips, Sharpies, and a yellow cube of Post-it notes. Dellarobia couldn't decide if that was tacky or astute. If born to the present day, what would the Savior find handier than Post-its?

At length Bobby laid the pages down on his desk and folded his hands together. "There's nothing in that contract to hurt you," he said, looking Bear directly in the eye. "Hester is right. You return that earnest money, and you're clear. She's got it worked out on the spreadsheet there, with the balloon paid off by your extra income this winter and the rest of the loan refinanced. I'd consider your son's advice about selling off some of that equipment, too, to keep your machine shop going. There are folks in this congregation who'd be happy to send work your way. Contractors and so on."

Dellarobia could see this rankled Bear, who would not want his working life in any way the concern of this flock. Bobby apparently saw this too, and subtly shifted gears. "Your financial concerns can be met. I think that's clear. That land has value to your family the way it is."

She was impressed with Bobby's acuity in negotiating these rocky shoals. But he still sounded a lot like a guy at the bank turning you down for a loan: overly benevolent, in a manner intrinsically related to the fact that he's about to sock you. Bear sat on the front of his chair with his big-knuckled hands on his knees and his elbows out, essentially in a crouch, ready to stand at any moment, if not lunge. Everything about Bobby Ogle must infuriate him right now. The new beard, the bank-manager demeanor, the undeviating spell cast over Hester.

"Well, sir," Bear said, "I'm not aiming to return that money. Not when there's trees standing that could be trees laying down. All due respect, Bobby, that's money in the bank and it's my call."

Bobby nodded, leaned back, folded his hands behind

his head. "What I hear you saying is you want to log that mountain because it's yours, and because you can. And my job here I think is to warn you about the sin of pride."

Cub's head came up suddenly as if someone had grabbed him by the chin. "That's true, Dad. When a man is greedy and gets too big for his britches, he pays for that. You've seen that."

"You pay with your health and your peace of mind," Hester agreed. "You heard Cub about the well water. If you can't live by the laws the Lord God made for this world, they'll go into effect regardless."

"My name's on the deed of that land too, Dad. My family's house."

"That land was bestowed on us for a purpose," Hester said. "And I don't think it was to end up looking like a pile of trash."

For a moment Bobby's and Dellarobia's eyes met, as bystanders to the family arbitration. To all appearances, they could just as well have fought it out in their own living room, but Bobby probably did this all the time. Witnesses changed the stakes. Not just the pastor but this setting, those mountains in the window, the mondo Bible containing thirty pounds of higher laws. And Bear in his Sunday suit, this was no small part of it either. He was an older and smaller man here than at home in his work clothes, without access to his ordinary tools of contempt. It crossed Dellarobia's mind that he would be buried in that suit. Bobby now advised him that strength did not come from laying down his own law on the land. Strength came from elsewhere. Bear, apparently at the end of his argument rope, responded by calling Bobby a tree hugger.

Bobby looked amused. "Well now, what are you, Burley, a tree puncher? What have you got against the Lord's trees?"

In a sense the meeting went like the faked wrestling matches on TV, Dellarobia thought, where the winner is called abruptly for no discernible reason. Suddenly Bear was defeated and Bobby was beaming, congratulatory, leading the family in prayer. Hester seemed swollen with admiration, the nearest thing to maternity she'd ever seen in her mother-in-law. Too bad it was not her son but Bobby in those high beams, and too bad Bobby didn't notice. His eyes were already sneaking toward the big open calendar on his desk, where the squares of his days were jammed with little handwritten notes in various inks. Maybe Dellarobia was mistaken about his distraction. But she did not imagine the condescending way he patted Hester's shoulder when they left. Doing his best, she knew. Bobby's flock was needy and his duties large.

Dellarobia went to collect the kids and brought them out to the empty parking lot, where her station wagon and Bear's red pickup sat together like family dogs. Bear had one hand on the roof of his truck and was slicing the air with the other as he spoke to Cub, regaling him with the specs on some piece of equipment. A wood splitter. Cub and his father had been selling firewood, spoils of all the downed timber after the winter's floods. Bear now explained that this fellow he knew was selling the splitter for next to nothing because it needed a little work, one of those fools who'd throw out something rather than fix it. Bear's voice had a pit-bull growl underneath the dimensions of this bargain, and his blood pressure was still measurable in his face. Dellarobia knew they probably had not seen the last of his arguments about the logging. She watched the three of them: accusatory father, contrite son, mother standing ten feet away ignoring the grandkids, absorbed in untwisting the strap of her yellow purse. As if everything that had just happened to this family had not happened. What was *with* these people?

It was decided somehow that they needed to go look at the kindling splitter right now, Bear and Cub together, in case he bought it and needed to load it. The place was out toward Cleary, in the opposite direction from their farm. It made no sense for them to take their wives home and come back.

"I'll take Hester," Dellarobia told Cub. "You go on with your Dad."

"You think?" Cub asked. "He still seems pretty pissed off."

"Just wear something bulletproof," she advised. This was a fairly recent habit, talking this way in plain sight of Bear. The old man's hearing was shot. All those years of power tools and a disdain for ear protection.

"Why don't I take Preston?" Cub asked. "To keep things rated PG."

"Sure, go for it, Preston. Man stuff!" she urged, pretending for the sake of others present that her son was that kind of kid. "Don't you want to go with Dad and Pappaw to check out the wood splitter?"

Preston behaved as if she'd suggested he go watch a public hanging. He moved slowly toward the man-stuff truck, dragging his feet so dramatically they turned upside down, scraping the tops of his toes on the pavement.

"You'll be fine," Dellarobia told him, while his writhing sister wrestled against submission to her car seat. Hester required similar help getting into the passenger seat, seeming vaguely to disapprove of the shoulder belt, as if it were different from any other one. If baby- and in-law wrangling was woman stuff, somebody else could take a shift, Dellarobia thought, sighing as she turned the wheel hard, angling her station wagon out onto Highway 7. "That was something today," she said to Hester. "That meeting. You must be proud of Cub. I know I am."

Cordie fell asleep in her car seat almost instantly, as Dellarobia had known she would. The fit she'd just pitched was standard, the storm before the calm. Hester looked narrow-eyed and dreamy, like the sandman might be hitting on her too.

"You've got a job on your hands now, I guess," Dellarobia proposed. "Looking after things up on that mountain. Turning it into an enterprise."

Hester remained inscrutable, but that was Hester. The appearance of happiness to be avoided at all costs. Dellarobia remembered she had a different bone to pick, and had better pick it now before Cordie regained consciousness. Sensitive material. "So Cub says you saw me on the news a while back," she said.

"Everybody and his dog saw you on the news a while back," Hester replied.

"Right. Well, he said you saw something about me wanting to take my life."

Hester looked awake now.

"Don't worry," Dellarobia hurried to say. "I just want to let you know that's not true at all. I've had a lot of things going on these last couple months, there's no doubt. But that wasn't one of them. You can't believe everything they put on TV."

"It was you saying it," Hester parried. "They showed you talking."

"I know. The interviewer tricked me. They did stuff with the film, editing I guess. Okay? I'm just telling you."

With a doubtful countenance, Hester said nothing.

"So you're arguing? Wouldn't I kind of be the *expert*?" Dellarobia started to raise her voice but checked it, glancing at Cordie in the rearview mirror. "Wouldn't I be the expert," she asked quietly, "on whether I intended to kill myself?"

"Maybe you wouldn't," Hester said, infuriating Dellarobia. The woman had issues with authority.

559

After a silence Hester added, "I'm not just talking about the last couple months."

"What in the heck is that supposed to mean?"

In silence they drove through outer residential Feathertown, where cement birdbaths had been emptied and overturned and tipped against their stands for the winter. Forlorn dogs lay gazing at their chains in small front yards. Dellarobia envisioned swerving into a tree, just to get a rise out of her mother-in-law. "Wouldn't you just accept me as family," she finally said, "after ten years? I mean, what would have convinced you I was going to stick around?"

"Wasn't my business to be convinced."

"Cub and I weren't a match made in heaven, I'll grant you. But people make do."

"Wouldn't I know it."

Dellarobia chuckled. "You and Bear? You guys nursing a lot of regrets?"

Hester narrowed her eyes strangely. "You don't know anything."

"Okay, I don't," Dellarobia said, chastened. "Tell me something, and then I will."

Hester did not oblige. They were now on Main Street, stuck waiting for a line of pedestrian Baptists a mile long to move out of the crosswalk in front of the church. Where were all those saved souls headed? There must have been an auxiliary parking lot.

"Well, I know this much. You and Bear didn't get married for the same reason we did. You all celebrated your thirtieth a while back, and Cub's not thirty. So you were sure-enough married before he came along." Dellarobia only knew of their anniversary because it was in the bulletin at church, the full extent of their celebration.

"So we were," Hester said. "So you were. Before Preston."

"Yeah, but—" She saw a break in the Baptists coming up, but stole a quick glance at Hester's face. "What, you're saying you lost one too? Before Cub?"

They cleared the crosswalk at last, but then had to wait through Feathertown's one stoplight. They were out near the Dairy Prince before Hester answered. "Didn't lose one. Gave one up."

"Whoah. You had a baby you gave up for adoption? Why in the world?"

"I had my reasons."

"Well, gosh, Hester. Can I ask what they were?"

"Bear was away in the service."

"That would have been hard. But still. Bear was coming back." She tried to imagine a young Hester left on her own, waiting. Dellarobia put the dates together, and again they didn't add up. "You all weren't married yet, when Bear was in 'Nam."

They drove past the house that famously kept its elaborate blaze of Christmas lights up all year. And then, conveniently located next door to it, the volunteer fire department.

"I was still debating about marrying him when he

561

went off to the service. My folks said I'd better go on. He had the farm and the house. You know. He was all set up. I just didn't . . ."

Dellarobia said, "Just didn't love him." She nodded with each word, her full sympathy stretched across that sentence.

"Well," Hester said, "I didn't know if I did. We'd hardly said words, he was so standoffish. I didn't know if I would love him or if I wouldn't."

Dellarobia laughed a little. "Sounds like you'd had more than words. If you were cooking a little bun in the oven while he was away."

"No."

"No, you weren't pregnant?"

"No, we hadn't been together."

"So how does *that* happen, exactly?"

Over the next mile or so of silence, Dellarobia replayed the words, studied them out, and wished she could eat those last ones. "I'm sorry," she said. "You're saying you were pregnant, and the baby wasn't Bear's."

Another mile came and went, with Dellarobia feeling very strange at the helm of this woman-stuff car, as if the road might abruptly lift them into some other plane. Maybe she should have gone to look at the wood splitter. She was not sure she was ready to hear about Hester's wild side, Hester's other life. She must have been a pistol, with that flair of hers, those handmade fashion statements and whirlwind energy. Bear must have been smitten. A bright-eyed girl from a dilapidated trailer on the back side of a mountain. A man with a house and a farm. What Dellarobia was not ready for, she realized then, was Hester's legitimate claim on her sympathies. Just going on the basics, a person would think she and Hester had lived the same story line.

"Did you ever find out who adopted it or anything?" she brought herself to ask quietly. "This baby, was it a boy or girl?"

"A boy."

"Does Bear know?"

"Just that it happened. He said we'd marry if there was nary a word said of it. So that's how it is. The ones that adopted him never knew who I was, I don't think. If they did, they took it to their grave."

"All this time. Gosh. He'd be, what, like in his thirties now?"

"There was a home for unwed girls in Knoxville."

"You went there?"

"I should have. Mommy said I ought to go away, but I was pigheaded and stayed with my cousin Mary in Henshaw and gave the baby up to some church folks over there. I was thinking of myself. Staying near friends and Mommy and all."

"And some fellow, whoever he was. The father."

"He's long gone. Dead."

"I'm sorry. So you gave up the baby in Henshaw."

"See, I wasn't thinking. A city would have been the thing. Hereabouts you never know how something will keep turning up."

563

"Isn't that the truth. I've seen suits of clothes my mother made twenty years ago hanging on the rack at Second Time Around. I always feel kind of proud, you know? That they're that well made." She glanced at Hester and shut off her babble. The woman was miserable.

"Hester, are you okay?" she asked after a minute. "Have you *seen* him? I mean, is he around? Does he know who you are?"

She shook her head deliberately. "He doesn't, nor Bear. They can't any of them know. And I can't do a thing in this wide world but live with it."

Dellarobia glanced in the rearview again. Cordie was still asleep. A ten-mile nap, and out poured this. When they rounded the bend and Hester's mailbox came into view, Dellarobia exhaled a deep relief. They were finished. End of story.

"A person could think about doing away with herself," Hester said. "I'd not tell you any of this, except I fear for you. You make your bed, but you can't always keep lying in it. Getting older is no help, Dellarobia. You might forget whether you took your pressure pill ten minutes ago. But there's your regrets of thirty year ago, still just sitting there. A-looking you in the eye."

"I don't even know what you're telling me, Hester. It's a lot to take in. You had a son. You did your best. I'm sure he's had a good life somewhere."

She turned into the driveway, bypassing the mailbox and the dreadful swan planter, a remembrance of

564

unkindnesses past. The ties that bind, Dellarobia thought, and follow us to the sweet by and by. But there stood Roy and Charlie waiting in the yard, the winter-killed flower beds, the house with its empty upstairs windows, work to be done, disagreements settled. Not such a terrible bed for Hester to lie in, surely. And then it hit, with such unexpected clarity she slammed the brakes.

"Oh, dear God, Hester. It's Bobby."

14

Perfect Female

At some unmeasured moment the temperature fell through the floor and the rain turned crystalline, descending noiselessly in the dark and stunning Dellarobia the following morning when she let Roy out the front door. *Snow*. Roy bounded wolfishly through the white deep, nosing into drifts, leaving a tangled line of tracks as he hurried to put his small yellow tags on all of the yard's most notable points. The dog version of Post-its.

The cedars in the Cooks' front yard were flocked with white, and their holly tree was enveloped in ice, giving the effect of a commemorative Christmas plate. The big maple on the property line was less enchanting as it dropped limbs onto the driveway at steady intervals, crash, crash, like an angry drunk. Needless to say, school was canceled. Dovey called around eight to report she hadn't even gotten halfway to Cash Club before she had to turn around. The way she described the cars sliding around on Highway 7 sounded like a slow-motion automotive ballet.

"This is so wack!" Dovey said. "Who ever heard of a winter like this?"

"Nobody," Dellarobia replied.

She couldn't stay away from the front window. Everything looked so clean and transformed, so fresh-start. All ramshackle aspects of the neighborhood's houses and barns had disappeared under white roofs against white fields. The mailbox sported a white toupee. Icicles fringed their entire roofline, the massive one down at the end unfortunately suggesting a backed-up gutter. It was three feet long and curved slightly outward like a movie villain's sword, just dangling. The icicle of Damocles. "Don't you walk under that thing," she warned Preston.

From the couch Preston shot back a look that said, *No chance.* He and Cordie were snuggled under blankets in their pajamas, watching cartoons. They'd waited all winter for this. A snow day was not to be wasted.

Dellarobia moved to the kitchen windows to stare out in a new direction while she made hot chocolate for the kids. Despite the biological treachery of this snow, its beauty moved her. Even a field of mud and sheep droppings could be rewritten as a clean slate. She admired the white-edged bristle of the hedgerows along the pasture, and the way the trunks of the big trees were visibly cut off from the ground, so they appeared to be standing on top of the snow like elephant's feet rather than rooted beneath it. The distant mountains had the fuzzy, off-white color of a plush toy that's been around a while. For the whole of the morning she wondered if any butterfly could survive this. Now she also wondered, in a different manner from days past, with uncomplicated sadness, if Ovid was already climbing the mountain to find out. She had come to terms with the idea of Ovid and Juliet, not that she had a choice, given that they were having their marriage here on her back forty. Certain ramshackle aspects of Dellarobia had also gone undercover, it seemed, just like the snow-covered barns. Some defects lurked, but for now her way seemed clear. She'd made plans.

She stood watching the sheep, which seemed undismayed by the dazzling ground, maybe forearmed with ancestral memories of Iceland. Cub had made a brief early trudge to the barn to feed hay, and now they wandered out over the white land to chew their cuds. Their pointed feet broke through the crust, and they lurched along dragging broad, pregnant bellies, leaving the oddest imprint on the snow, like the trail of a dragged sandbag punctuated with holes. Their wool colors stood out sharply, the blacks and moorits especially. But even the white sheep against the blazing snow looked yellowish, the color of actual rather than commercial teeth. Most of the sheep were standing, she discerned, though their legs were invisible. But a few had knelt down into little snow-bowls to rest placidly in the glare of a new kind of day. Very high up on the hill, one coal-black ewe was lying down oddly, with her nose up. Like a seal balancing a ball: that color and that posture, her nose sticking straight up in the air.

"Cub!" Dellarobia called. "Come here a minute."

Cub padded into the room in his socks, agreeable

and in no hurry. He was watching cartoons with the kids. "What?"

"Take a look at that ewe up near the fence. That black one that keeps arching her neck. You see her?"

After a moment Cub did.

"I think she's in labor."

"It's too early," Cub said.

"I know it is. But she's acting weird." As they watched, she struggled to her feet and shook the snow off her wool, an impressive muscular shudder even from a distance. She turned several times in a small circle like a dog preparing to lie down, and then lay down. Once again her nose lifted in a great, arcing sweep like a circus seal. Like an exercise video for livestock. An unconventional move, by any standard.

"It's too early," Cub repeated. "And it's colder than heck out there."

Dellarobia blew out air through her lips. "I'm not asking if this is *convenient*." She turned off the burner under the pan of milk, which had scalded while she wasn't looking. "Fix the kids some hot chocolate and give them breakfast. I'm going up there."

She rushed to pull on warm layers and waterproof layers and lace up her boots, noting that Cub had ignored instructions and gone back to watching *The Backyardigans* with a blanket pulled around everything but his face, just like the kids. Dellarobia stomped out the back door and was amazed once again by the made-over world. It was abnormally quiet outside, as if sound

569

itself had been blanketed and extinguished. Some sound-absorbing property of the snow, she gathered. Under her boots it made a squeaky crunch. She took the hill at an angle because straight up was out of the question, she discovered, after slipping several times onto her knees. She set her feet perpendicular to the grade and made broad switchbacks up the pasture.

The black ewe, when Dellarobia attained her altitude, was lying in the same spot. From the looks of the wallow she'd made in the snow, she had been at this project for a while, whatever it might be. She looked glassy-eyed and bored, staring ahead, only mildly perturbed by Dellarobia's sudden arrival.

"So what's up, lady?"

The dark lady turned her nose away, checking out Dellarobia through the horizontal pupil of one pale amber eye. Her breath clouded the air in quick, visible puffs.

"You're not making my day here, you know that?"

After two or three minutes Dellarobia felt ridiculous. The ewe uttered a low, productive belch and began to chew her second-time-around breakfast in the most normal fashion known to sheep. Dellarobia backed off ten paces down the hill, then ten more, in case the ewe was faking her out. She should have called Hester first, for a consult. The cold caught up to Dellarobia when she stood still, racking her with hard shivers that rattled her teeth. "You couldn't do this in the barn, could you?" she asked.

The sheep did nothing helpful. She even stopped chewing. Dellarobia's eyes wandered up the mountain to the flocked forest, the hummocks of branches and glittery, ice-enclosed twigs like glass straws. This was no country for insects. The real grief of this day came to her in waves, like dry heaves, throbbing against her initial good spirits. It couldn't even be called a freak storm. Probably there was no such thing, in a freak new world of weather. Three days ago it had been fifty degrees. The springtime smell of mud was a clear memory. She'd been so sure this winter was over and they'd made it. Even Ovid thought so, with the end of diapause. Now, from her vantage point in the snowy field, she saw a trail of tracks leading from Ovid's trailer up to the gate. So he was up there already, maybe both of them. His wife supporting him in grief. The High Road was now a shadowy lane, narrowed to a tunnel by snowy overhanging boughs.

Dellarobia also noticed the crisscrossed paths of animal tracks faintly traced over the hillside: deer, rabbit. Strange to think what a small fraction of the comings and goings out here they'd ever know about. The ewe called her attention back with a strange, high grunt and pointed her nose again. She was on the small side, this ewe, maybe a first-timer. Probably clueless and going into panic mode, just because it seemed a truck might have parked on her stomach and bladder. Dellarobia remembered the feeling. The ewe stood up, shuddered, took a couple of steps forward, and out dropped something from her backside. A dark liquid puddle, really it had poured out. Fluid or blood. Dellarobia felt a restriction of vessels in her chest as she scuttled back up the hill, scrambling to recall words from the vet book she and Preston had lately neglected. Amniotic sac, placenta. She dropped to her knees in the snow and bellowed to see a lamb. Black, strangely flat against the snow, unmoving inside its translucent sac: a tiny sheep child. The ewe walked away from it and nosed into the snow, looking for graze.

Yelling for Cub, Dellarobia ran and slid down the hill in a direct path for the back door. Amazingly, he appeared there. She sat on her cold bottom, panting, still fifty feet or more from the house. "Get up here!" she yelped. "Get that bucket in the barn, the emergency stuff. No, bring towels and hot water. Bring that hot milk on the stove."

"What's going on?" he asked.

"Damn it, Cub, just do it." She rolled onto her knees and clambered back up the slick path she'd just compressed, a perfect sledding route. Without ever fully gaining her feet she made it back to the puddle of lamb, swearing at the mother that stood blandly chewing now, some distance away from this thing that had definitely not happened to her. Dellarobia flung off her gloves and touched the dark creature. Its heat shocked her, the warmth of the place it slid out of one minute ago. She unwound her wool scarf and scrubbed the lamb out of the milky caul, then cleared its eyes and nostrils, but it was not breathing. It was limp as a rag when she lifted it, legs dangling. Dellarobia shut her eyes tightly so tears wouldn't freeze in them. It looked like a toy, with big Yoda ears, the legs and tender hooves perfectly formed, the body covered with glossy black curls.

She'd never known Cub could move so fast. Huffing loudly he came, with kitchen towels slung over his shoulder, hustling sideways up the hill carrying her Revere Ware pot by its handle, the milk. By some miracle he stayed upright with that. She ran the last few paces to meet him and grab the pan and towels. The milk was still very warm. What other man, ever again, would just do as she commanded, no questions asked? She felt overwhelmed with love and loss and nostalgia for this bond that was not even yet in her past, while she sopped a towel in the warm milk and watched Cub see the lamb. Watched his face fall open like a glove compartment, helplessness and sorrow jammed inside. She could lose her nerve again. She always did.

"I don't know, Cub, I don't know," she kept repeating. Hester had predicted she would fail at this. She rubbed the little ringlet-covered body, scrubbing hard, like shining up the kids after their baths, warming this corpse with the soaked towel and then with her own breath. She blew into its tiny damp nose, then compressed the small belly, feeling for life, but felt nothing and nothing. The small head lolled, no hint of resistance. The body was already starting to go cold.

"Don't you *dare* die on me. Damn it!" She wound a dry towel around the hind legs for a grip, it was so very slippery, and staggered to her feet. "Okay," she said to Cub. "Okay, watch out, stand back." She stomped out a tiny arena in the snow and spread her boots wide and began to turn, gaining traction as she could, swinging the lamb in a circle. By the third revolution it flung out like a girl's ponytail on the merry-go-round, she felt liftoff. Its small weight pulled as she turned and kept turning, mindless of her own voice as she thrummed out a pulse of curses: *Breathe, damn it, damn it, damn it, come on, breathe!*

When she fell on the ground, the world kiltered on its axis. The boughs of the forest behind her lurched, blackish and mossy looking. The sun creeping up behind them was a crystalline brightness popping and shimmying through the glass branches.

"Dellarobia, what in the hell?" Cub asked finally. Or she finally understood what he was asking. He was beside her on his knees. She sat up.

"Here, put it against your skin. To warm it up."

Cub unzipped his jacket and thrust the lamb under his sweatshirt, wincing only slightly at its slimy chill. He held it there.

"Oh, my God, Cub. Where are the kids?"

"They're fine. The stove's off. They're watching TV."

"Did you tell them not to get off the couch? Was Cordie eating anything?"

"They're fine," he repeated.

Dellarobia fell back against the snow. A snow angel, waiting for the crazy world to give her an all-clear for landing. Shortly she sat up again.

"Let me see it," she said. He extracted the limp thing, and she held it close to her face, watching. "Cub. Its heart is beating, I swear to God." Faint and fast, a pulse fluttered through the damp curved belly against her cold hand. No muscle tone, no flicker of eyelids, no sign of life, but that pulse. She stuck her index finger down its throat and scooped at a viscous phlegm that completely filled the narrow, serrated shaft of the little gullet. She felt the sandpaper texture of its tongue. Faintly it pulled against her finger, suckling. Dellarobia exhaled a loud cry that could have passed either for pain or laughter. She rewrapped the hind legs in the towel and got up to swing it again.

This time they both shouted, Cub begging her to stop. But she didn't, even though this flinging felt murderous to a mother who'd cradled feeble infant necks and sheltered soft fontanelles. Dellarobia felt reckless, turning and turning, swinging that child until she lost her feet again. She lay panting. Cub looked both outraged and deeply anxious, basically positive that she'd lost her mind.

"Go call Hester," she said. "Ask her what to do if a lamb's born not breathing."

"Jesus, Dellarobia. What are you doing?"

"I don't *know* what I'm doing. Just go!" she screamed.

575

Cub fled. Dellarobia massaged the little body again, noticing it was a female, then tucked it under her shirt and lay back down until the worst of her dizziness passed. It seemed fully possible she might kill something here. She sat up and cradled it in both hands, watching. Faintly it moved, *moved*, the narrow head lifting at an angle, tilting the outsize ears. She listened to its belly and could faintly hear breathing, not wheezy like a croup but stuffy, like a head cold. She blew into the nostrils and pressed the belly again, again, compelled by the near sensation of breath. She rubbed and massaged and warmed it until Cub returned and collapsed beside her.

"Mother says if there's no sign of life when it comes out, it's dead."

"You came back up here to tell me that."

"That's what she said. She says lay it in the straw with the mother in the barn. If you let it be dead with the ewe awhile, that helps them some way."

Dellarobia glared. "Helps *who*?"

"I don't know. I'm sorry." Cub retreated to the familiar grounds of remorse and insufficiency, the terms of his existence, ratified by marriage. He could construct defeat from any available material and live inside it, but for once Dellarobia didn't go there with him. She was going ahead. She found she could not abandon the effort. Accepting death, she'd done that, but here was another story: bringing life in. Not good-bye but hello, screaming it, *please*. She massaged the dark curly hide

576

until her own knuckles glowed red against it, and when she paused, the lamb tried to lift its head again. It opened its eyes and looked out. Life arrived. Dellarobia began to cry, yelping sobs.

"What do we do?" Cub kept asking.

Get it warm, get it to nurse, make the mother accept it. She told Cub to go get grain and lead the mother into the barn while she warmed up the lamb in the house. They would milk that stupid ewe right now, because the colostrum was crucial. The newborn intestine only stays open a few hours to receive the mother's antibodies. They had a bottle somewhere. But instead of jumping to her feet, Dellarobia found herself curled like a fist around the lamb with Cub's arms around her so tightly she could hardly draw breath. The sobs in his great chest racked them both like the bucking of a terrified animal. She sobbed too, for nothing, it seemed. It was all impermanent, the square white corners of house and home, everything. This one little life signified nothing in the long run; it would get eaten.

"It wasn't all a waste," she told him over and over, holding on. Some things they got right, she was sure of that. The children. And for all the rest they wept, a merged keening that felt bottomless. For the years and years of things that didn't exist, fantasies of flight where there was no flight. Nothing, really, but walking away on your own two feet. She felt tears frozen on her face.

"How can you know?" he kept asking her. She told him she was never really sure how she knew. Reading, filing stuff away, or just guessing, if that was the only choice. She and Preston had read about swinging around a newborn lamb. But never in a million years did she think she'd actually do that. Things look impossible when you've not done them.

She pulled away in order to look her husband in the eye. "This is all going to scare us to death," she said. "You and me. But we're still going to have to do it."

"Maybe," he said.

"Not maybe, Cub. For real."

They found their feet and edged down the precarious slope to their separate tasks. With the lamb cradled inside her coat Dellarobia followed the fence line, for something to hang on to. She thought of the times she'd walked this fence with Cub, tearing out honeysuckle and briars to mend it. But the weeds were still here, it was plain to see, encircling the whole pasture, threaded through wire and post and skeletal trees. With their glassy stems encased in ice the weeds looked more substantial than the fence itself, the seasons of secret growth revealed in a sudden disclosure of terrible, cold beauty.

℮

She felt Preston's hand slip into hers while she stood at the stove making pancakes. She'd decided to tell him today, before the bus, and not tomorrow on his birthday. In her mind he was still in bed, so the cool hand startled her and the eyes rising solemnly to hers made her heart seize. "What's wrong, honey?"

He tugged on her hand. She turned off the range and followed him to his bedroom, where Cordie breathed in her crib, asleep. She knelt with Preston on his unmade bed and looked out the window and saw what he saw, a bud colony on the neighbors' dead peach orchard.

She knew what it was, despite the absence of any expectation. Ovid had apprised her to be on the lookout for something like this, in the unlikely event, but not to look *there*, on these puny saplings whose tops now drooped over like Charlie Brown's Christmas tree. Whose limbs were copiously flocked with vivid orange. "Oh my gosh, Preston," she said, bouncing on her knees, looking at him openmouthed, bounding off the bed. "Look how many. Put on your boots and coat. Let's go see."

The resurrection and the life, she kept thinking over and over, a natural hazard with words like those, as she bundled wool onto Preston and they crunched out over the yard. Those little trees looked alive again, resurrected. Enveloped with the souls of dead children. It was no easy trek across the field. Preston had to hang on to her hand as they stomped through thick layers of melting, collapsing snow. Sometimes they broke all the way through to the dark, soaked ground that stood as wet pools in the bottoms of their footprints. It was hard to see where all this could possibly go when it melted.

But the deep snow remained, the white of it dazzling them all over again, even now at dawn.

More dazzling still were the monarchs. Down here in the open without the camouflage of forest, with their cover utterly blown, it looked as if some other world had touched this one and bled orange. She could not guess the number of individuals in these clusters, maybe a few thousand. She was still no good at estimating. It wasn't a million, that much she knew, and if these were the sole survivors, it wasn't enough. It would take a bigger gene pool to get them through. And mortality was still dogging them, she saw; dark flecks of bodies were sprinkled over the snowy ground here like pepper on mashed potatoes. Maybe those were males that had already mated, their DNA packaged to go. Ovid had shown her pictures of bud colonies in Mexico where the butterflies descended from their roosts in March to cluster in the valleys, staged for liftoff, blanketing roofs and hedges and fields of dry cornstalks. Theoretically this meant they were ready to launch out. In the known world, anyway, it meant that.

Preston had brought his sit-upon from the kindergarten field trip so they could sit on the snow in the dead peach orchard and look at the butterflies. Dellarobia brought a raincoat to sit on. They chose a spot at the base of a little tree high on the hill so they could look up at butterflies, and down at butterflies. She had never allowed herself to picture this. After the storm on Tuesday Ovid had told her they were still on the trees up there, a few million butterflies frozen onto the branches beneath a covering of snow. Probably they would slough off with the thaw like so much dead skin. In the last two days he'd packed up the lab with the mood of closing a house after a death in the family. Deciding what to keep, what to give away. Survival wasn't possible, he said, given the mortality under that snow. It would take a crowd of variations and mistakes and resilience, at least a million individuals, he thought, to add up to survival of a species. So what about the animals two-by-two on Noah's ark, she'd asked, and he replied that they would have marched off that boat to die out in a couple of malformed generations, thanks to inbreeding. His bitterness was understandable. As they broke his laboratory down to its bones, Dellarobia watched the void of this man where once there had been wonder, and she despaired of her future. In such a short time he had relieved her of a lifetime of illusions, and already she missed them. Noah's Ark and better days ahead. She found herself still rooting for this sliver of a generation that had made its way down the precarious mountain to rest on a blighted orchard.

They were so beautiful, that was the thing. The hardest work of all was to resist taking comfort. She and Preston gazed up together at their spindly butterfly tree. The wings were mostly still, but a few slowly opened as the sun arrived. A week ago she'd seen the sun come up at seven, and today it was well ahead of that. Dellarobia felt her heart slide, everything moving fast. Today was the day. Every day was the day.

"Mom," Preston said, sounding anxious. "What if we miss the bus?"

"If we miss it, we miss it. I'll drive you. Miss Rose won't care if you're late this once. It's your birthday tomorrow!"

Preston seemed profoundly unconvinced. Dellarobia despaired to see her worldly powers already trumped by those of Miss Rose. She persisted.

"We'll just sit here and yell at those kids when it goes by. *So long, suckers!*" she yelled aloud, to no one, nonetheless embarrassing her son. She tickled him and he tensed and then relaxed, finally, laughing.

More of the butterflies opened their vanes, drinking light. They looked more purplish here than in the woods, a richer brown, more red. Changeable in the light. She noticed they had covered the trees disproportionately on their eastern sides, where the first sunlight fell, though the butterflies must have landed here in the evening. For the souls of dead children, they were good at planning ahead. She thought of Josefina's small hands fluttering out from her chest. And the little black lamb blinking its eyes open, drawing its breath, taking hers away. They'd gotten the mother to accept it eventually, after Dellarobia had done the hard part. Preston was still giving it a few bottles a day for good measure. He knew they weren't out of the woods.

"So. I've got something to tell you."

His happy eagerness looked so complete, she felt

something inside her splitting. Like a flowerpot left outside to freeze, some stupid wasted thing like that. Belatedly she identified it as *hope*, just as the word itself drifted out of reach. She stared downhill at all the snowy little hummocks with meltwater flowing through them, a miniature river in a forest of white, conical, snow-covered weeds that looked like tiny fir trees. A small world, melting.

"I've got several somethings to tell you," she said. "Actually. One's kind of sad, so we'll just get it over with. The second one is awesome, that's your present, a day early. And the third one is, I don't know what. Kind of a shocker. You ready?"

He nodded earnestly, bobbing the red pom-pom on his stocking cap. His bangs had gotten long, spilling out the front of his cap.

"Your remember what Josefina said about the monarchs, that when a baby dies, it turns into a butterfly?"

He frowned. "Is that real?"

"No. It's just a story people tell, to feel better. What I want to tell you is, one of those is ours. We had a baby that died."

He gave her an acute look. "Where is it?"

That was so Preston, wanting the GPS coordinates. "In the cemetery," she said. "There's a grave, no stone. But see, Preston, that was your brother. He came first, a long time before you. So you should know about him."

Down on the road, cars began to pass. People going to work, restarting their lives. Preston looked sober but

583

not really sad, probably maintaining appropriate sentiments for her sake, she realized. This grief was not his.

"You know how every year I tell the story of the day
you were born? Going to the hospital and the whole
deal. And sometimes I back up and tell you one more
thing, right? Like how I was vacuuming under the bed
and kind of got stuck under there and had to yell for
Daddy because my water broke?"

He nodded.

"We'll do all those stories tomorrow. We'll have a
cake and everything with Dad and Cordie, after you
come home from school. But I've been wanting to tell
you about the other baby that came first. Because if that
one hadn't come and gone, there'd be no Preston. He
cleared the way, with Dad and me. So later on I would
get to carry you around in my tummy until you were
born on your birthday. Make sense?"

"Not really," he said.

"Yeah, I know. Stuff doesn't always. You don't have
to be sad about this. I'm just telling you the whole story.
There's tons of people that aren't alive anymore, like
my Mom and Dad and that little baby, that all helped
get you here. The other baby gave us a present, which
was you."

Preston avoided looking at her.

"Ta-daa! Preston gets to exist!" She coaxed out the
smallest of smiles. "Okay, now for the totally awesome
surprise, your big present from me. This is a snap decision, to give it to you a day early. I didn't wrap it yet. I

just happen to have it in my coat pocket. Reach in."

She held open her pocket. He gave her a skeptical look and moved his gloved hand slowly into her coat's interior, as if something rabid might be in there.

"Whoa! A pod-thing!" he yelled, cradling the smooth little tablet close to his face. He pulled off a glove with his teeth and immediately revealed a knowledge of things Dovey had spent half an hour teaching Dellarobia: how to turn it on, touch the tiny icons on its face, brush the screen to move the pictures around. How to reach into the river of all knowledge and pull out your own darn fish.

"It has a little keyboard," she said. "So you can type in your search." He already knew that too. She could not imagine kids in his school actually had these. The monthly payment was going to be her biggest expense, after rent.

"Is it mine?" he asked.

"Here's the deal. I'll hang on to it when you're at school, and when you're home it's yours. Your own computer. You can go on the Internet, whatever you want. Within reason. But when it rings, you have to give it to me, because it's my new phone."

"What's wrong with your old one?" he asked. Ninety seconds in possession, and already miserly. She laughed.

"Here, give me that, you stinker. I've been saving up for three months to get you online, but we have to share." He surrendered the phone with a good-natured grin, the type of kid who already knew very well, there was no free lunch.

"Surprise number three," she said. "I need a new phone because we're moving."

"Moving! Gaa, Mom, no way."

"Yes way. We're getting an apartment in Cleary with Aunt Dovey. We already checked it out, there's a bedroom for her, and one for Cordie and me, and a kind of a sunporch thing that will be all yours. You get a special bed that's a couch in the daytime and a bed at night. And get ready for the shock of your life. Ready?"

He nodded doubtfully.

"I'm going to college. We'll both be in school this fall. In Cleary. We can do our homework together."

"In the same school?"

"No. Different ones. You'll see. Dr. Byron did this totally amazing nice thing and talked to professors over at CCC. He's like a superhero. They set me up with a job and stuff. I went over there one day when you were at school."

"What will you be?"

"I'll work in a lab, like now. Except not in a barn. It's work-study, they pay you and you go to college. It's not very much, so I'll probably be something else too, like a waitress. We'll see. We'll be eating beans and rice, let me tell you."

"Like at Josefina's?" he asked, interested.

"Yeah," she said, a little surprised, unsure she had meant it literally. But he obviously had a taste for the

586

fare. Here she went, one more step down the Mr. Akins lifestyle pledge into the "Not Applicable" basement. If that list was the wave of the future, as he'd declared it, her kids were way out ahead of the game. Thriftiness skills: check.

"But what will you *be*?" Preston asked.

"You mean, like, when I grow up? I don't even know. There's too many choices. Maybe a vet. So people would pay sixty dollars to see me get out of a truck."

Preston eyed her, his tongue under his lower lip, wary of her spoofing. Which was fair, given the full complement of unbelievables she'd just laid on him.

"Okay, seriously?" she asked. "Some kind of scientist, I think. Like you, Preston. We're peas in a pod."

"But will you still be my mom?"

"Well, *yeah*. You don't get to fire me."

Preston's voice dropped to a different level, registering something new. "Where will Dad sleep in the apartment?"

"Oh. No. Dad stays here. You and Cordie will visit him."

Preston looked at her as if she had gone insane.

"Not visit. I don't mean that. You'll live here too, this will still be your home part of the time. Like on weekends, or after school. And you'll see Mammaw and Pappaw. And the lambs. All the time."

"And it will be your home too?"

"No. I'm the apartment. You get to go here and go there, you'll migrate. Like the monarchs. Alternation is supposed to make you sturdy. You and Cordie will grow up ready for anything." This was probably beyond him, she realized. But then again, he was Preston. And he wasn't liking it. He still had one glove off, and now began rubbing his thumb sideways across the grain of his brown corduroys, making a tiny zipping noise.

"Why do you have to go have an apartment?" he said. "Daddy will *kill* you."

"Preston, what a thing to say. Your dad wouldn't hurt a fly. He knows about all this. He thinks it's an okay idea."

"Why does he?" Preston insisted, not looking at her. Over and over he ripped his thumb across his corduroy knee, making that sound, like strumming an instrument. Her powerful inclination was to make up a better-days-ahead story. Nobody ever thought kids wanted the truth. And right on from there it went: the never-ending story.

"Well, I'll tell you," she said. "Daddy and I got married kind of accidentally."

Preston's brow took an angular dive, anxiety tinged with improbable remorse. With that expression and the hair flopped in front of his glasses, he was the very image of his father. That's what killed her. The laws of biology. She would never escape that particular face. It occurred to her that this was not an ideal choice of words, either: *accident*. He would be picturing car wrecks, or first-graders wetting their pants.

"It wasn't the end of the world, that's the thing,

588

honey. Dad and I made you and Cordie. On purpose, we wanted to. So that part was totally good."

"And the dead one."

"Yes," she said, surprised he already thought to claim this sibling, the dead one. Her mind ran onto forbidden ground: the kind and influential uncle, the sweet twin cousins. She'd finally dismantled one secret on the cusp of another rising. Dellarobia doubted she could sit on all those Ogles as long as Hester had, but they would have to play it by ear. Her children had people, and that was important. Kinship systems.

"Why did you and Dad get married by accident?" he asked.

"People do wrong things all the time, Preston. Grown-ups. You're going to find that out. You will be amazed. There's some kind of juice in our brains that makes us only care about what's in front of us right this minute. Even if we know something different will happen later and we should think about that too. Our brains trick us. They say: Fight this thing right now, or run away from it. Tomorrow doesn't matter, dude."

He stopped strumming his knee, and appeared to think this over.

"If I could teach you one thing, Preston, that's it. Think about what's coming at you later on. But see, all parents say that to all kids. We don't follow our own advice."

He sat perfectly still, staring at snow.

"You know what else? Grown-ups will *never* admit

what I just told you. They'll basically poop their own beds without saying they made a mistake. Even the ones that think they are A-number-one good citizens. They'll lie there saying, 'Hey, I didn't make this mess, somebody else pooped this bed.' "

The tiniest of smiles pulled his mouth out of line, like a snag in a stocking.

"You and Cordie are going to grow up in some deep crap, let me tell you. You won't even get a choice. You'll have to be different."

At that moment the glazed yellow cartridge of the school bus appeared on the road down below. It paused in front of the house, in case Preston should by chance emerge, but he and his mother laid low in their spot in the snowy field. They did not wave or call attention to their truancy, and eventually the bus went on its charted way. Despite everything, the end of the world impending, Dellarobia had a glimpse of strange fortune. The sun was well up now and the sky clear, suggesting some huge shift was under way. Scraps of snow were falling from the trees along the road, silently letting go, drifting down like shredded tissues from the big maple by the driveway. In the woods behind them she heard a quiet steady prickling sound of falling ice needles. A whole melting world surrounded them. She noticed Preston's eyes wandering back to their house, and could read his thoughts like a book: Mom, Dad, apartment, etcetera, all starting to sink in. The loss or rearrangement of everything he'd ever known and trusted.

Bravely he did not cry, though his mouth turned down at the sides and his eyes pinched.

"What if I want everything to stay how it is?" he asked.

"Oh, man. That's the bite. Grown-ups want that too. Honestly? That's what makes them crap the bed and stay in it. I'm not even kidding."

His eyes scooted away from hers, avoiding the verdict.

"It won't ever go back to how it was, Preston. You have to say that right now, okay? Just say it, and I'll give you a pod-thing."

He glanced at her, making sure, and said it. "It won't ever go back how it was."

"Okay." She handed it over. "You're the man."

❧

On Friday she expected both the children home at noon, Preston from school, Cordelia and her father from Hester's, where they'd gone while she prepared for her son's birthday. But well before that hour she was pulled outdoors by the flood. She left a cake in the oven and many things undone to walk out the kitchen door in a state of inflated edginess, as if she had become suddenly too large in her skin. The radio had churned all morning with strange accounts, regardless of station. Flood and weather warnings, disasters. Something beyond terrible in Japan, fire and flood.

Outdoors she was startled by watery brightness. The ground was spongy with snowmelt and sank strangely under her feet. The hill on the other side of the road remained fully snow-covered in its own bluish shadow, north facing, but on this side the sun had leveled its light and the whole mountain of snow was melting in a torrent. Every channel gouged in this slope by a long wet winter was now filled to overflowing, and the run-off swelled out into sheet flow across the full breadth of the pasture. Ovid's vehicle was gone for the weekend, nearly gone for good, and the sheep had retreated into the barn, alarmed by the running hillside and unaccustomed roar. She was alone out here. Water poured over the tops of her boots, as clear and cold as the ice it had recently been, and numbed her feet and pressed down the grass all around, the sodden pelt of a drowned earth. Tall weed stalks intermittently rose at angles above the water and were slammed down again, waving like skeletal arms.

Her feet sank deeper as the water reached her knees and the current pulled in a way she understood to be dangerous. This was where she lived. The phone was in her sweatshirt pocket, but she knew of no one to call in the event of something like this. She aimed for higher ground, slogging toward a spot where she could stand on a hummock in the high pasture, close to the spot where she'd rescued the lamb. That sheep must have had a nose for the terrain. It was the pasture's summit, and now that she had climbed onto it, a tiny island nation of one. She was completely surrounded here by moving water. She turned to face south and the whole field lifted to her eyes as a single reflected sheet of brightness. An ocean, stippled and roiling in waves over submerged rock and rill, rising as she watched. She felt the reckless thrill of being at sea. Like Columbus on his ship, maybe, after he'd spent his life begging himself into debt, getting cornered. In no other way could a person strike out for probable disaster at the edge of the known world. Insofar as a person could understand that, she did.

On the hill behind her crows flew one by one into the bare trees, arranging their dark blots in the scrim of branches and adding their warnings to the drear sounds of this day. Gone, gone, they rasped. Here was a dead world learning to speak in dissonant, unbearable sounds. The topsoil, the slim profit margin of this farm, the ground itself, rushed away from her, and when water spilled over her boots again she backed slowly into the violent current to find a better place. A chill of fear evacuated all her thoughts beyond simple locomotion. A slip could be the end of things. She wondered about the sheep in the barn, but concentrated on her own two feet, inching slowly uphill to avoid her demise. When she felt the fence behind her she rejoiced to meet that cold safety net of wire. She turned around to grip the mesh with both hands and pull herself along the fence line. At the upper gate she tucked in her toes and climbed over to the higher side, gaining dry ground again, at the foot of the forest this time. She sized up a stand of medium-young trees, any of which would hold her, she thought, if it came to that. Then looked back downhill.

She was stunned to see the water had now risen level with the porch and doorsills of her house. Its foundation and cement steps were no longer visible and the yard had eerily vanished, its embankment dissolved into the road, all memories of her home's particular geography erased. All morning she'd listened to water pouring through the huge metal culvert under the road, echoing its thunderous threats of inundation over those that came in on the radio. Now that roar was engulfed, the culvert had been overwhelmed and the road was a broad, muddy river. Something floated there, a ragged V-shaped assembly of lumber that moved slowly past from the west. A portion of a roof she guessed, inverted. It moved with such ponderous, unhurried purpose it seemed to be yielding to a migratory urge. She noted that her station wagon was also following the call, relocating itself gently without a driver in an eastward direction.

She comprehended the terms of what she saw, but couldn't turn away from it. Her children were elsewhere, at Hester's and at school, facing this by other means, as she understood they would have to do. For the moment her fascination transcended ordinary fear and safety. It struck her that she had stood here months ago with her heels newly unearthed and her mind aflame, unexpectedly turned back to the place she'd fled. She remembered scrutinizing the dark roof and white corners of her home for signs of change or surrender, invisible then. Now they were plain. One corner of the house appeared to tilt as she watched, shifting the structure a scant but perceptible few inches on its foundation. This time she had to see. Soon the whole thing would drift away from its anchored steps and cement-block foundation, departing as gently as an ocean liner. Then it would not be a home, but a rigid, rectangular balloon with siding and shingles and weather-stripped doors, improbably serene, floating on the buoyant command of the air sealed carefully inside. Its windows would hold their vacant gaze on the wheeling view as the whole construction slowly turned in the current.

And even now, little dark birds gathered on the few high spots that shouldered above the flood. They poked in the mud for drowned earthworms, sustaining a far-fetched and implausible appetite for staying alive. Starlings, they must be. The day was absurdly temperate and bright. Last week she'd seen the pointy-nosed buds of daffodils coming up, and Preston had found hyacinths in their yard. The inundated, the gone, the somewhere-else-now yard. She'd forgotten she ever planted those. Their snub green leaf bundles had looked to her like the beaks of turtles rising from an underworld.

Some of the starlings let out a collective metal cry and flew off at low angles across the field. Man is born unto trouble as the sparks fly upward, she thought, words from the book of Job, made for a world unraveling into fire and flood. Among the dark birds were wavering flints of light, the same fire that had unsettled her so drastically on first sight. Now it was irresistible. She'd come out here to see the butterflies. Since yesterday she had watched them leave their clusters in the dead peach orchard and scatter downhill into cedars and tangled brush along the roadsides. Now they dotted every small muddy rise that was not yet swamped. Wherever she looked she saw their aggregations on the dwindling emergent places: forming bristling lines along tree branches and the topmost wire of the fence, clustered on driftwood, speckling even the distant, gleaming roof of her car. Orange clouds of the undecided hovered in the air space above them. The vivid blur of their reflections glowed on the rumpled surface of the water, not clearly defined as individual butterflies but as masses of pooled, streaky color, like the sheen of floating oil, only brighter, like a lava flow. That many.

She was wary of taking her eyes very far from her footing, but now she did that, lifted her sights straight up to watch them passing overhead. Not just a few, but throngs, an airborne zootic force flying out in formation, as if to war. In the middling distance and higher up they all flowed in the same direction, down-mountain, like the flood itself occurring on other levels. The highest ones were faint trails of specks, ellipses.

Their numbers astonished her. Maybe a million. The shards of a wrecked generation had rested alive like a heartbeat in trees, snow-covered, charged with resistance. Now the sun blinked open on a long impossible time, and here was the exodus. They would gather on other fields and risk other odds, probably no better or worse than hers.

The sky was too bright and the ground so unreliable, she couldn't look up for very long. Instead her eyes held steady on the fire bursts of wings reflected across water, a merging of flame and flood. Above the lake of the world, flanked by white mountains, they flew out to a new earth.

Author's Note

In February 2010, an unprecedented rainfall brought down mudslides and catastrophic flooding on the Mexican mountain town of Angangueo. Thirty people were killed and thousands lost their homes and livelihoods. To outsiders, the town was mainly known as the entry point for visitors to the spectacular colonies of monarch butterflies that overwinter nearby. The town is rebuilding, and the entire migratory population of North American monarchs still returns every autumn to the same mountaintops in central Mexico. The sudden relocation of these overwintering colonies to southern Appalachia is a fictional event that has occurred only in the pages of this novel.

The rest of the biological story, like the flood of Angangueo, is unfortunately true. The biotic consequences of climate change tax the descriptive powers, not to mention the courage, of those who know most about it. I've looked to many expert sources for guidance in constructing a fictional story within a plausible biological framework. My greatest debt is to Lincoln P. Brower and Linda Fink for graciously opening their home, laboratories, research records, and most impressively, their imaginations. Their enthusiastic indulgence of a novelist's speculations was so generous, as is their scientific dedication to the world and its life. Any errors that persisted beyond the careful tutelage of Drs. Brower and Fink are purely mine.

I also thank Bill McKibben and his 350.org colleagues for the most important work in the world, and the most unending. His book *Eaarth* gave me important insights, as did Sue Halpern's *Four Wings and a Prayer*, and Clive Hamilton's *Requiem for a Species*. Lamb rescue notes by Carol Ekarius in *Storey's Guide to Raising Sheep* have proven crucial in both art and life. *The Illustrated Encyclopedia of Animal Life*, edited by Frederick Drimmer (1952), was a fortuitous find. I'm grateful to Rob Kingsolver and Robert Michael Pyle for early encouragement, and for the published work of many other entomologists including Sonia Altizer, Karen Oberhauser, William Calvert, and Chip Taylor, founder of Monarch Watch. Francisco Marín was an intrepid companion through the unspeakable in Angangueo and the unearthly at Cerro Pelón. Dr. Preston Adams was the first person ever to tell me I was a scientist. I've not forgotten.

For thoughtful comments on the manuscript and invaluable support I thank Terry Karten, Sam Stoloff, Frances Goldin, Steven Hopp, Lily Kingsolver, Ann Kingsolver, Virginia Kingsolver, Camille Kingsolver, Jim Malusa, and most of all, from beginning to end, Judy Carmichael. Steven and Lily climbed the mountains and plumbed the depths. Margarita Boyd provided spiritual insights, and Rachel Denham opened doors. Walter Ovid Kinsolving wrote the engaging genealogy that gave me virtually all the first and last names that appear in this novel (remixed), picked from my own family tree. For the spirit in which they rise to every occasion, from shearing day to publication day, I thank my family. Part and parcel, I am yours.